Robert MacSpoon

in

LAND OF THE PIRATES

I.R. YOUNG

Typeset in Baskerville Old Face

Editing, design, typesetting and publishing by UK Book Publishing

www.ukbookpublishing.com

ISBN: 978-1-913179-24-3

Robert MacSpoon

in

LAND OF
THE PIRATES

1. Robert Says Goodbye

William Robert MacSpoon lived in the heart of Edinburgh, Scotland. Although William was his first name everybody knew him by his middle name Robert, as when he was small, even before he could talk, he would stubbornly never respond to William but only to Robert, and so it stayed.

Robert had no brothers nor sisters, just his lively mum and a grumpy dad. He'd never had a dog nor a cat. In fact, he'd never had a pet of any kind whatsoever, a continual bone of contention in the MacSpoon household.

Robert's home was an old three storey house in which he'd lived his entire life. He was a very lucky child as the whole of the house's top floor was devoted to his bedroom and how it was a paradise. Toys and games lay everywhere, while countless books, knickknacks and trophies lined the walls. On the playroom's floor a humongously sized train set lay permanently in place, forever ready to play with, as it frequently was.

The trophies were a result of Robert's most favourite sport of all, fencing. He was, in fact, interested and capable in many sports but it was in fencing that he greatly excelled. He couldn't really explain his attraction to it but when an exhibition had come to his school a few years back he became so mesmerized by the sport that he instantly enrolled in classes and quickly became one of the area's finest. He enjoyed immensely the thrill of pitting his wits against a much larger opponent and defeating them.

Robert's best friend was not a boy, as is usual for boys of his age, but a girl called Margaret. She lived but a stone's throw away, just around the corner. Although a girl, everybody treated her like a boy. She looked like a boy, behaved like a boy, and so in Robert's eyes she was as good as any boy. She was the perfect best friend.

Not surprisingly, Robert loved his life very much. But things were about to change. He and his family were leaving Edinburgh behind and moving to Rum, an isolated island on the west coast of Scotland. The entire island was a nature reserve and his mother, a landscape gardener, had recently accepted employment there. She would be tending the vast gardens of the island's solitary castle.

Robert's dad was a policeman and as luck would have it, or unluck in Robert's eyes, a position of chief of the island's police force had come up at exactly the same time. Robert only found out later that the police force consisted of just one policeman, his dad!

Alas, today was the day of the big move. Their house had been sold and a new one purchased on the island. Robert's room now lay almost empty. Everything which hadn't already been removed was packed tightly in neatly stacked boxes, to be collected the following day, the final final day. Robert, however, wouldn't be around to see it, as he and his mum would already be in their new home on Rum, tonight. A long drive, followed by a few hours on a ferry – his first time ever on a boat – would take him to his new life and he was thoroughly miserable.

'Robert!' shouted his mum from outside his bedroom door.

Robert didn't reply. He hadn't replied for the last hour, ever since he had awakened.

Suddenly, Mrs MacSpoon shook the door handle. The door was locked.

'Don't be silly,' she said, agitated. 'You'll have to come out sooner or later. Come on! Your chocolate milk's already developed a skin on it and you know how much you hate that. And your cornflakes look more like porridge than a breakfast cereal.'

Robert was unimpressed and he changed position on his bed, now leaning on his left elbow. The pins and needles, which had just started in his right hand, began to disappear.

'Anyway, there's nothing we can do now,' continued his mum, with little hint of remorse in her voice. She hated town life with all its hurly-burly and endless cars. 'The house is sold, and that's that.'

For Robert this was like a red rag to a bull and he exploded. 'Then you shouldn't have sold it! Should you!' he shouted, before clenching his teeth, something he always did whenever he was angry.

'It's too late now,' said his mum. 'We're going and that's final. You'll make new friends. It'll be fun. You'll see!'

'New friends!' cried Robert. 'How can I make new friends if there aren't any other children on the stupid island?'

Joan MacSpoon ran her fingers through her long dark hair and adjusted her glasses. It was practically the truth what her son had just said, and she knew it. The only other children on the island had just started primary school. There were no children within a country mile of Robert's age.

'So!' cried Robert, noticing the pause. 'I'm not going and you can't make me!'

'Don't be like that, your great grandfather Bob MacSpoon was from the island. He'll be turning in his grave if he heard you now.'

'Whoopee-woo!' cried Robert.

'And what do you intend doing?'

'I can stay with Nana and Grandad.'

'They're too old and besides they don't have the room. You're being problematic and I've had enough. One hour, young man and we're going. Together! Like it or lump it!'

With these words Mrs MacSpoon turned and headed back down the stairs. A tall, headstrong woman, she was used to getting her way.

Once more there was total silence in Robert's bedroom. He disliked arguing with his mum but sometimes she left him with little option. He didn't want to go to the dumb island and if he couldn't stay with his grandparents then he was left with little choice. He would run away.

Tap! Tap! Tap! Robert jumped. Someone was knocking on the door.

'It's me,' came a pleasant voice.

It was Margaret, his best friend, and her amiable voice soothed him.

Robert sprang up from his bed and raced to the door. Then he stopped, his fingers poised on the large rusting key. 'Are you alone?'

'Of course,' replied Margaret.

Robert turned the key, opened the door, grabbed Margaret by her school jumper and yanked her in. Then quickly, he shut and locked the door.

'How's things?' Margret asked cheerfully, wrinkling her nose.

Margaret was always cheerful and therefore liked by everyone. And when she wrinkled her nose, as she had just done, any person's bad mood would invariably disappear.

'Not good,' said Robert, trying to ignore her twitching nose. 'The house is still sold and I'm still going to that stupid island.'

'There's nothing you can do, you know,' said she, sitting down on Robert's bed and observing the stacked boxes. Her short, dark hair was possibly even shorter than his. 'Adults always get their own way. It's just the way it is.'

'Not if I can help it,' said Robert, with a steely determination, and then lowering his voice added, 'I'm going to run away.'

Quickly, he dropped down onto all fours and began pulling out a rucksack from underneath his bed. Margaret immediately bent over and ruffled his hair. She was familiar with the result.

'Get off!' he shouted.

He had hated people ruffling his hair ever since he was small. Everybody used to do it to him, with one auntie in particular the biggest culprit.

'So where are you going?' asked Margaret, maintaining a straight face. She knew Robert inside out and was well aware of his delicate pride.

'Your house!'

'And what? Don't you think my mum and dad would somehow notice?'

'It wouldn't be for long.' And he sat down beside Margaret holding the dark blue rucksack in a tight embrace. It was stuffed to bursting.

'So what's in the bag?'

'Oh, just some clothes, carton of juice, a packet of biscuits, a bottle of vitamins...'

'You know what you are, don't you?' shot out Margaret, cutting him off. 'You're a valetudinarian, my mum always calls my dad it.'

Robert gave his best friend a puzzled look. She was always coming up with big complicated words picked up from her mum. She certainly wasn't more intelligent than him, she just used bigger words.

'So what's that?' he asked, grudgingly.

'It's not a compliment,' said Margaret, while looking at her watch. 'I need to go or else I'll be late for school.' And she jumped up and made for the door.

4

It was the last day of term before the summer holidays and Margaret always enjoyed it. Some children wouldn't bother with the final day of term but that didn't apply to the super conscientious Margaret.

'If you stay up here then we won't say a proper goodbye,' she added, and with those final words she turned the key and was off, leaving the door wide open.

Alone for a second, Robert swiftly made up his mind and meekly followed. How his mother would gloat.

On descending the first flight of steps and hearing nothing below, Robert literally bounded down the second flight, suddenly afraid that Margaret would indeed leave without a final farewell.

But his apprehensions were unfounded, as standing at the bottom of the stairs were Margaret and his mum both smiling up at him. A ruse perhaps. He couldn't be sure.

'Ah, the jailbird breaks out!' said Mrs MacSpoon, with a friendly arm around Margaret. She too would miss this feisty young lady.

'So how about a goodbye hug for your bestest friend,' said Margaret, looking straight into Robert's eyes. Her chirpiness had all but disappeared.

Robert descended the last few steps and could see his friend had a build-up of tears in her eyes. Unconsciously, she looked down. He stuck out his hand and took hold of hers.

'Bye Margaret,' he said, neither shaking nor releasing the girl's hand. He was a boy and he wouldn't allow himself to cry like her, but he too dropped his eyes to the floor, just in case. An uncomfortable few moments then passed between the two pals.

'I'll need to be going,' said Margaret, breaking free from them both. She hadn't expected him to comply. Speedily she brushed her cheeks with the back of her hand. Her grey school jumper had started to develop spots.

Mrs MacSpoon reached for the door handle and opened the door wide. 'We'll see you at Christmas,' she said, squeezing Margaret's arm one last time and stepping aside. 'Bye Margaret!'

'Bye, Mrs MacSpoon,' said Margaret tearfully, walking towards the garden gate. 'Bye Robert!'

'Goodbye Margaret,' said a dejected Robert, as his best friend passed through the small metal gate and turned round for one last look. He couldn't stop himself now and a tear sprang up and started to roll down his face. 'I hate Rum,' he muttered to himself, and he repeated it over and over again.

2. Rum And The Captain

The journey to Rum was somewhat of a disaster for Robert and his mum. Firstly, before they had even reached the port where the ferry was docked, the car broke down in the middle of nowhere and they had had to call out a mechanic from a far-off village. Secondly, both Robert and his mum had been violently sick on the boat. The sea had been rough and the voyage had taken much longer than expected. It had been a miserable two souls which had entered their cold and desolate cottage late that evening.

Things though weren't to improve, as for the next two days solid it rained, only varying in intensity from heavy to very heavy and back again. Mum and son were virtual prisoners in their new home.

Mrs MacSpoon, shortly due to begin her new employment, was getting increasingly worried at the sight of Robert continuously moping around. He was barely coming out of his room. And with Mr MacSpoon still not having arrived from the mainland, she was becoming obsessed with checking the weather forecast, pinning her hopes on a break in the weather and some much-needed sunshine to snap Robert out of his depression.

Fortunately, their third morning on the island gave Mrs MacSpoon exactly what she had been waiting for. There wasn't a cloud in the sky and the temperature was positively tropical.

Joan MacSpoon's mood was buoyant as she tossed the morning pancakes with gusto. She had already been to the island's solitary grocery and brought back some much-needed fresh supplies.

'Robert!' she shouted, with an air of optimism in her voice. 'Come on! Rise and shine. I've got pancakes and strawberries and fresh cream to go on top. Hurry up! It's a beautiful day.'

The cottage wasn't as big as the house they had left behind in Edinburgh and being only on one level, Robert could clearly hear his mum's voice ringing round the rooms. He quickly pulled the quilt up to cover his nose. It was how he liked it. It used to give him a feeling of protection against any monsters in the room, but now of course he didn't believe in them. Today though it felt rather stuffy. Perhaps his mum was telling the truth and it was a nice day.

Robert jumped out of bed and pulled back the thick, darkly coloured curtains, and felt the warmth flood in. His bedroom faced west so there was no morning sun but the sky was a deep blue, contrasting sharply with the luscious green grass of the garden. It had certainly been well watered. A crumbling stone wall, full of large gaps, separated the blue top from the green bottom.

'Yahoo!' he shouted. Today he would explore, but first there was pancakes.

The kitchen was unsurprisingly smaller than the one in Edinburgh, but still a good size. It had two smallish windows, two doors, one of which led directly into the back garden, and a dark wooden floor. The centre of the room was dominated by a gigantic wooden table, a gift from the previous owner to Mr MacSpoon when he had purchased the house. It was unlikely, however, that the table could have been removed without breaking it into bits, such was its immense size.

Robert lapped up the pancakes at an astonishing rate and his mum was delighted when he asked for second helpings.

'A healthy appetite fuels a healthy mind,' she beamed. 'You're looking so much cheerier.' And she poured the last of the cream over a further plate of pancakes and strawberries. Then, as always, she popped a brightly coloured vitamin tablet beside it.

Robert's mum was a firm believer in potions and cures and remedies, and therefore vitamins too. She insisted he take one vitamin tablet each and every morning after breakfast. He never objected as he had been taking them for as long as he could remember and he was a child that was very rarely ill, a result they both attributed to his daily dose of vitamins.

'Can I go exploring today, Mum?'

'Of course,' said Mrs MacSpoon. 'There's nothing to stop you. Just be careful near the water, and watch out for the island's wolves.'

Robert's jaw dropped. He didn't know there were any wolves left in Scotland.

'It's a joke. You should have seen your face!'

He breathed a sigh of relief. Wolves indeed!

'But I'm not joking about the water!' said Mrs MacSpoon. 'It's deep and it's dangerous. Do not go near it!'

Shortly after, Robert stepped out of the creaking front door, and came face to face with two large woolly white sheep. Their front garden had no wall nor fence; where the grass ended the one track road began. The two sheep had clearly eyed the succulent uncut grass around their cottage and invited themselves over for breakfast.

Robert looked at them warily, unsure what to do. The biggest farm animal he'd ever come across was a hen. Then, the larger of the two animals stared back and started to head straight towards him. He quickly retreated until he was backed up against the closed front door.

'It's a sheep, Robert, not a lion!' shouted his mum, throwing open a window. She was grinning from ear to ear.

'I know!' said Robert feebly. 'I didn't want to frighten it.'

'A likely story.' She smiled, and shooed Robert forwards.

Bravely ignoring the gawping sheep while stepping over their black mounds of droppings, Robert walked down the short garden path and onto the narrow road.

Formed from a once active volcano, a long, long, time ago, Rum was an island of hills with the ground covered mainly by grasses and heathers. The large forests of rowan, holly and birch had long gone, and few trees now remained.

Robert stopped and observed the unfamiliar scenery. He found the sea particularly captivating. Although brought up in Edinburgh, which stands on the mouth of a river, he had little experience of the sea. His mum's words of warning momentarily echoed in his head. He immediately decided what to do. He would investigate the harbour.

Robert knew where the harbour was and covered ground quickly, glad to be out of the claustrophobic cottage and into the open air. He compared the narrow winding road to a large path in Edinburgh. On the way he passed only a few homes, some more inquisitive sheep and a lone brown, extremely hairy cow with curved horns, which also observed him closely. Again, however, he noticed that there were no birds in the sky above nor close to the ground. He'd noticed this peculiarity over the last three days while stuck in the house, forlornly looking out of the window. He had always loved to watch the birds from his bedroom window in Edinburgh. Magpies were his favourite, with their distinctive black and white plumage, and their crafty ways.

The harbour was not at the end of the road but on a bend, and the tarmac continued on past it for as far as the eye could see. Robert couldn't remember what it looked like from the day of his arrival, he had been so sick. He now saw that it was u-shaped, much lower down than the surrounding land and there were only two approaches. The first way was by large concrete steps where he now found himself, and the second was by road farther along on the bend. Steep cliffs rose from the sea on the road side. The ferry had docked on this side and there was a small new building.

The concrete steps led to his side where there was a mixture of gravel and cut grass. This was clearly the fishing side as there were a number of weather-beaten sheds, two upturned small fishing boats, a couple of wooden benches and a bundle of creels. A lone man was visible, painting the bottom of one of the upturned boats. Robert headed in his direction.

As he approached he could see the man wasn't young, possibly a pensioner. He had dark blue dungarees and a flat cap on, the type of hat Robert's own grandad would often wear.

'Good morning,' said Robert politely.

'Morning,' replied the man, scarcely raising his capped head.

'Are you painting your boat?' Robert asked, longing for a conversation after three whole days indoors with only his mum to talk to.

'Aye,' the man replied.

'Are you a fisherman?'

'Aye,' replied the man, moving away to tackle an unpainted part of the boat.

Robert decided to give up: if this man couldn't be bothered talking then neither could he. He would head for the other side of the harbour.

The water was visibly deeper here but Robert couldn't stop himself from walking along the raised edge. There was a steep grassy bank directly in front of him now, with the soaring cliffs farther off to the right.

Passing the ferry building he noticed a lone shed, and on getting closer he could see an old man sitting behind a small plastic garden table. This man was probably older than the grumpy man painting the boat, and he was stooping considerably. A cup and spoon lay on the faded green table. Robert hoped this man would be more talkative than the first.

As he got closer the old man looked up with weary eyes, but surprisingly spoke first.

'Haven't seen you here before, sonny,' he said.

'No, we've just moved to the island,' Robert replied. 'Three days ago. I couldn't get out because of the rain.'

'You're not made of sugar, are you?' grinned the man. 'Now where would you be from with an accent like that?'

'Edinburgh,' said Robert, delighted at the old man's interest and friendliness.

'Well, I've been there but I won't tell you how long ago. You wouldn't believe me.'

The old man's face was a weather-beaten brown and heavily wrinkled, and the exposed hair at the back and sides of his head was pure white. His face was friendly but there was a hint of mischief in his eyes. He wore a tartan shirt with rolled up sleeves and he too had a flat cap perched on top of his head.

'You look like my grandad,' Robert suddenly said. 'Only older!'

'Oh,' said the old man, slightly taken aback by the insult.

'My grandad doesn't stoop as much as you though.'

'You're a friendly fellow, aren't you,' said the old man, beckoning Robert forward.

Robert advanced but chose not to sit on the large oily chopping block the old man was gesturing to.

'Are any of the boats yours?' Robert asked, pointing towards the small number of boats on the opposite side of the harbour.

'No, none are mine, sonny,' replied the old man solemnly. 'My body's finished with the sea. This old seadog's lowered his sails for good.'

Robert observed the man closer. His hands were thick, brown and strong, yet his fingers were twisted and bent.

The old man noticed Robert's interested gaze. 'Rheumatics! Too much time pulling on wet ropes.'

'My nana has it too,' said Robert. 'My mum says you can't catch it, it's genetic,' he added with a boastful knowledge.

'That may be so,' said the old man. 'But few seamen escape it. I'm the Captain by the way,' and he proffered his thick hand.

Robert gripped the hand and shook, completely forgetting to introduce himself. 'So, you used to have a boat then?'

'Aye, I did that. A big boat and a big crew to sail her. I had plenty smaller ones, mind you, but none like The Lightning. She was the apple of many an eye.'

Robert turned and observed a total of five boats in the harbour, only three of which were actually in the water. The other two were upturned on the grass, one of which the untalkative man had been working on, but he had now gone. None of the boats would require a crew anything like the size the Captain was describing and he kind of felt that the old man was exaggerating. Robert decided to change the subject.

'Why are there no birds on the island? I've been here three days and haven't seen one. Not one!'

The Captain's face immediately lit up and his body stiffened like a poker, wiping off at least ten years from his age.

'Well then,' he said mysteriously, when he did eventually speak. 'That would be because of the pirates, and Blackbird's curse.'

Robert's ears pricked up at the very mention of pirates. Perhaps this old man had some interesting and exciting stories to tell. 'Did there used to be pirates on Rum?'

'There sure did,' replied the Captain, motioning for Robert to take a seat on the chopping block. Robert duly obliged. 'Their leader was a Captain Blackbird and along with his crew they used the island as a hideout. You see that gap in the cliff face over there?' He turned and pointed to a dark hollow area on the soaring cliff front.

Robert screwed up his eyes due to the brightness of the sun's reflection on the water, and tried to see what the Captain was pointing at. There seemed to be a small gap in the rock face.

'Em, sort of,' he said, somewhat unconvincingly.

'Well, that was the entrance to a deep water cave completely invisible from the sea. Mind you there was the fog. Of course, it's all collapsed now and pretty dangerous, but it once led to a hidden quay.'

'What's a quay?' Robert quickly asked.

11

'Aye, you're a landlubber if ever I've seen one. A quay is where you berth a ship. Tie it up!'

'Oh,' said Robert, but now he didn't understand landlubber, but guessed it was somebody who always stayed on the land.

'Anyways,' continued the Captain. 'What with the hidden quay and the ever-present fog, the island was perfect for a pirate's hideout. Blackbird and his men would plunder the seas all over the world and come back here to Rum to safety.'

Now Robert was an intelligent boy and there was again something about the Captain's story which didn't ring true. To use Rum as a base for piracy all over the world just didn't make sense. It was far too far away from the Caribbean or Asia where he knew piracy was practised all those years ago. The Captain may not be mad but he was certainly strange, and like all children, Robert wasn't sure how much he liked strange. He did, however, find the tale interesting and listened on.

'Then, one night there was an almighty argument between some of Blackbird's crew and the island's innkeeper. The innkeeper said they hadn't settled their last bill.'

'Now normally when on the island, Blackbird would throw his money around and that would be the end of it. But he must have had a bee in his bonnet about something that day, because in a flash he had the point of a dirk at the innkeeper's throat.' The Captain placed two fingers to his neck.

'But what happened next was the most amazing thing of all. The innkeeper, with the sharp end of a knife pressing against his neck, ordered the lot of them out. Well then, you might think that a foolhardy thing to do, ordering around a bunch of bloodthirsty pirates, but the innkeeper was no fool. He knew Blackbird and his men needed Rum just as much as Rum needed them.

'And he was right. Blackbird had a change of heart, lowered his dagger and ordered his men out. Not a drop of blood was spilled. But then the innkeeper made a big mistake, for as the last pirate was leaving he muttered his intention to free the island, and turn every last one of them into the authorities. Piracy of course was punishable by death in those days.'

The Captain stopped his narrative and took a large gulp from his cup. Robert had no intention of interrupting, by now his imagination was going wild and his eyes were as big as saucers.

The Captain continued. 'Anyways, later that night the inn burnt down, killing the innkeeper. And that very same night, Blackbird's ship was gone.

'The next day the islanders held a meeting and all agreed to rid themselves of Blackbird for good. They knew where his ship had likely gone, to Glasgow, and so two islanders followed. There, they identified him to the government soldiers as the notorious pirate Captain Blackbird, as he sat drinking in one of the town's taverns.

'Two days later he was hanged in the town's square, and on his execution he put a curse on an island nobody had ever heard of. He said his birds would never fly there again. The two islanders witnessed everything and took his body back with them to the island. While Blackbird's men were never seen again.

'He's buried here now in the old cemetery on the south side of the island. Some say he should be dug up and reburied at sea, to try and remove the curse. Others say leave him be, as he was wronged by the islanders and they must accept their punishment.'

Robert adjusted himself on his increasingly uncomfortable seat. 'How was he wronged?' he asked, enthralled by the Captain's tale.

'Well, first I'll go and get my pipe and then I'll tell you how it all began.'

With that, the Captain disappeared into his shed and Robert was left to contemplate all the pirates that had once walked this very harbour. He stared at the gap in the cliff, imagining a pirate's ship nosing herself slowly out. Of course he knew all boats were ladies.

After returning with a large crooked pipe, the Captain restarted his story.

'Well now, Blackbird was born on the island. His real name was John MacSpoon.'

Robert couldn't believe it, his eyes were ablaze with excitement. His dad was called John MacSpoon too. Maybe his dad was related to Blackbird, maybe he was too. He couldn't wait to tell his mum! The Captain amazingly didn't notice Robert's jaw dropping and just continued.

'One day when he was a young lad, a young lass saw him whistling to some birds, blackbirds they were. The birds were dancing all around him like magic, she said. And so he earned the name Blackbird. Anyways, he became a fisherman like most on the island, until one day his fishing boat disappeared, right off the face of the earth.

'Then, some years later, straight out of the blue, he came back. Now though, he didn't have a small fishing boat, he had his own ship with a crew, and plenty of money to go with it. Of course, he wasn't a fisherman now. He was a pirate! And the longer he stayed, the thicker the fog got.'

Robert glanced at his watch; it was getting near lunchtime. A little bit longer and he would have to go. The Captain again didn't notice him.

'Now for the interesting bit,' said the Captain, finally acknowledging that he wasn't alone. 'One of his crew was a man called Crabb, Cut-throat Crabb, they called him, because of his penchant for blood. A sleekit man who nobody cared for, but a top-notch sailor. He too was from the island and on that fishing boat.

'Anyways, after a time, this Crabb fellow gained his own ship. But the two captains never saw eye to eye, and bad blood between them simmered. Over a lassie they said.'

'But that doesn't mean Blackbird didn't burn down the inn,' said Robert.

'Hold yer horses a second, laddie. Some years later, one of Crabb's men got to drinking too much and boasted that it was him and Crabb burnt down the inn, knowing full well Blackbird would shoulder the blame.'

Robert looked at his watch for the final time; he would really have to go. His mum would start to worry as she always did in such circumstances. He rose from his low position, his muscles tense from lack of movement. The heat too was getting unbearable, with the sun now directly overhead. His face was positively baking.

'I'm sorry but I need to go,' he said, starting to move away.

'Now tell me,' said the Captain mysteriously. 'Your name wouldn't be Robert MacSpoon, would it?'

Robert was surprised and it must have shown because the Captain grinned with such a peculiarity that Robert developed goose bumps all over his body. He hadn't said his name, he knew that for sure. The Captain must have heard some news about the new family coming to the island and put two and two together.

'Yes,' said Robert, still edging away.

'Well then,' said the Captain, his eyes dancing. 'You know what that means. The pirates are coming, lad! And soon. And they're coming for you!'

Robert didn't answer and finally walked away, the pebbles crunching underneath his feet. Did the Captain really say the pirates were coming for him? He hurried back home.

While running up the garden path, Robert noticed a bicycle on the driveway, propped up against the end of the house. Good, he thought to himself, Mum would be much less likely to complain about his being late if there was a guest present. He entered the front way, knowing he would shortly be told to only use the back door. His nose was immediately met with the unmistakable smell of moth balls. The guest was obviously elderly.

'Robert!' cried his mum, poking her head around the kitchen door. 'Come here a second please.'

Robert did as he was told and found the source of the revolting aroma. A lady in her sixties was sitting at the great kitchen table. Her hair was totally grey but neatly packed into a bun. She had a round reddish face and he guessed she was quite small.

'This, Robert,' said Mrs MacSpoon, turning to the woman and smiling politely, 'is Mrs Crabb, one of our neighbours and the lady who runs the island's shop.'

Mrs Crabb, however, was not at all smiling, indeed her face was positively disagreeable. Her black peering eyes were only barely visible beneath the furrows in her brow. Robert couldn't stop himself from staring. She looked quite mad.

'I thought you said the boy's name was William?' she said bluntly.

Robert gave his mum an angry look.

'Well, yes it is,' said Robert's mum, rather uncomfortably. 'He just prefers to use his middle name, Robert.'

'Ah,' sighed Mrs Crabb. Her face now the polar opposite of what it had been. 'My ears are not what they used to be you see and I don't like mishearing people. My husband's always telling me to see Dr Stewart, and I thought just then, maybe he's right after all.'

Mrs MacSpoon relaxed too, and laughed at the explanation. She understood the labours of a complaining husband.

Robert, however, didn't know what to make of this rather changeable woman. She too was strange, just like the Captain, and he wondered if everyone on the island was, well, strange!

'I take it you've met my husband then?' Mrs Crabb said, smiling at him.

15

Robert stared back with a vacant expression on his face. He was not at all sure what she was talking about.

'He was painting his boat down at the harbour,' she added. 'He said he'd seen a young lad fitting your description poking about.'

'Ah, yes,' said Robert, recalling the scant conversation he'd had with Mr Crabb.

'Of course I told him not to go anywhere near the water,' said Mrs MacSpoon wryly.

'Boys will be boys, Joan,' said Mrs Crabb. 'And did you see the ever so strange Captain on your travels? You know he really is quite mad.'

'I'm not sure,' said Robert. He found the Captain strange certainly, but he didn't wish to agree that he was mad. A bit like the pot calling the kettle black, he thought.

'He thinks he was a pirate, you know, and he point blank refuses to answer you unless you address him as Captain. The man is nuttier than a fruit cake. My husband says he sits on that stool for hours on end, just staring into the sea. Keep well clear I say,' and with that she took an almighty slurp of tea.

Robert nearly burst out laughing at this odd guest.

'Mrs Crabb has a surprise for you,' Mrs MacSpoon said, smiling triumphantly. 'Just what you've always wanted.'

Robert's eyes widened and his heart began to beat more rapidly. He'd always wanted a dog of course but he didn't want to be too optimistic.

'I can't guess,' he said, shaking his head.

'A dog!' cried Mrs Crabb. 'My Lucy had two puppies a few months back and your mum said you'd love to have one of them.'

'It's in your bedroom now,' said Mrs MacSpoon grinning. 'Fast asleep in a cardboard box.'

Robert needed no more information and rushed to his bedroom. Sure enough, there was a small white bundle tucked up in the corner of a giant cardboard box. It was gently snoring.

'It's Sparky!' he cried joyfully, bending over and gingerly stroking the bundle of fluff.

The two ladies were thoroughly pleased with themselves as they watched from outside Robert's bedroom door.

'You're lucky it's a boy then,' said Mrs Crabb. 'And it's a West Highland Terrier.'

'I know,' said Robert. He knew about dogs, but in truth all dogs were the same to him. They all had a head, four legs and a wagging tail.

'Oh, and I forgot to tell you,' said Mrs MacSpoon. 'Your dad will be arriving in a couple of hours.'

Robert was oblivious to this last piece of information. He now had his very own dog. He'd pleaded, begged and promised to be good for all those years, and finally he had a pet to call his own.

'Thanks, Mum. Thank you, Mrs Crabb,' he said, grinning from ear to ear. 'So when can I take him for a walk?'

3. The Pirates Are Coming

For the first time since he'd been on the island, Robert set his alarm clock. He'd set it for seven, with the intention of going down early to the harbour. After turning things over in his mind the whole evening, he'd decided he wanted an explanation for what the Captain had said. Robert had intended going after lunch the previous day, but with the introduction of Sparky and his dad's belated arrival, things had gotten a bit busy.

Setting an alarm clock and getting up are, however, two very different things and Robert slept straight through, not even recalling stretching out his arm and silencing the offending sound. He also didn't notice the patter of tiny feet towards and out of the slightly ajar bedroom door. Sparky, unlike his master, was an early riser.

'Robert!' shouted his dad, suddenly banging on the bedroom door.

Robert wakened with a start. It was unusual to hear his dad's gruff voice after what seemed ages with his mother's more amiable tones.

'It's nearly nine. Are you going to sleep all day?' Mr MacSpoon continued.

John MacSpoon was a large, well muscled man, not fat nor thin. He had a full head of dark hair with only a smattering of grey poking through. With piercing blue eyes and shovels for hands, coupled with his athletic build, he was an imposing character. Robert, however, feared the ire of his mother far more, as although a formidable sight, his dad was generally slow to anger whereas his mum was most definitely not.

'I'm up!' Robert cried. 'Keep your hair on, Spooner!'

That was what his mum would call his dad when she was annoyed with him. Robert had quickly cottoned on to its effects, much to his father's annoyance.

'You're a Spooner the same as me,' his dad fired back, and returned to the kitchen.

After a long, late breakfast, a refreshed Robert set out for the harbour. He had wanted to take Sparky but was told it was too hot. His dad had been left in charge as his mum had already gone to the castle to prepare for her first day at work the following morning.

It was already late morning and the heat was like an oven. Robert couldn't recall ever having such a hot day in Edinburgh. The air was actually shimmering in the near midday sun.

As he approached the harbour a strong feeling of déjà vu suddenly swept over him. Mr Crabb, whom he now knew the name of, was still painting his boat and everything else was deathly still. A shiver ran down his spine. He wasn't sure why.

After the previous day's encounter, Robert had decided that he didn't really like Mr Crabb. He also disliked being accused of poking around. Whether it was Mr Crabb's words or his wife's made no difference, it wasn't their harbour and Robert had as much right to be there as them. He was, however, in a bit of a dilemma, as they had generously gifted him Sparky, his new best friend.

'Good morning,' said Robert.

Mr Crabb looked up and then checked his watch. 'It's not morning. It's afternoon, lad.' Then he ducked his head back down and continued with his painting. A pot of bright red paint was precariously perched on the boat's upturned hull.

Robert wanted to say thank you for Sparky, but changed his mind and quickly moved on. This man was not the most friendly person he had ever come across.

Robert found the Captain in exactly the same spot he'd found him on the previous day, sitting in front of his ramshackle shed, nursing a cup of something. As he approached, the Captain's face lit up and he pushed the cup away from him as if to somehow generate more room for his welcome visitor.

'Take a seat,' said the Captain, patting the chopping block. 'I thought you might have come sooner!'

19

'Why?' replied Robert, sitting down.

'Because of what I said yesterday of course, about the pirates coming.'

Robert looked at the Captain but with his head lowered.

A perceptive individual, the Captain recognised the signs. 'They've said something. Haven't they? Am I mad?'

Robert didn't reply.

'I'm right, amn't I? Who's been telling tales? No matter. They don't know. Nobody knows! Only us!'

Robert hadn't a clue what to say. It was very unusual for him. He was a boy who innately always had something to say, no matter the situation. Now, however, he was dumbstruck, and suddenly wished that Margaret was there to help him. Her brain was lightning fast and her mouth unstoppable.

'I'm sorry,' said the Captain, seeing Robert's discomfort. 'I'm making no sense. First of all, I must tell you my name. My name is Robert MacSpoon, just like you.'

Robert didn't move but the wheels were certainly turning in his head.

'Don't you see!' exclaimed the Captain. 'You're the same as me. You're a pirate too!'

'But my name isn't Robert MacSpoon, not really,' said Robert. 'My real name is William MacSpoon.' How he hated saying that. He wasn't sure how the Captain would respond but was surprised at what happened next.

'But what do you feel?' asked the Captain. 'In there!' And he gently prodded Robert's torso with one of his bent fingers.

Robert was taken aback by the question. It wasn't possible the Captain knew he disliked the name William so much that he had only ever answered to Robert. Could the Captain read minds?

'You feel a Robert because you are a Robert,' continued the Captain. 'Your parents just got it wrong. You're Robert MacSpoon, just like me, and just like me you're a pirate. And your enemy, our enemy, is Captain Blackjack. It's your destiny, Robert, just like it was mine all those years ago.'

'Captain Blackjack?' smirked Robert. 'Does every pirate have to be called Black something? Maybe Captain Blackboard or Captain Black Pudding!'

'Don't be so pedantic, Robert,' said the Captain, shaking his head. 'Come. I'll show you. Follow me.'

The Captain headed towards the steep banking which eventually led to the sheer cliff face. For a man undoubtedly in his eighties, he was surprisingly quick on his feet. Robert only managed to finally catch up when the old man eventually stopped. What was it all about?

'You see that hole there,' said the Captain, pointing to an area where the rough grass ended and the cliff face dramatically began.

'No!' said Robert. 'I don't.'

The Captain started to kick at the mud and long grass, and after a few minutes a small hole began to appear in the side of the dark rock.

'It's been filled in by somebody,' he said. 'But you can clearly see it's the entrance to a tunnel. A tunnel which takes you along to the hidden harbour. This is the tunnel that the pirates used all those years ago and which I also used when I was a lad the same age as yerself. Sure some of it's blocked now and maybe it's a bit precarious, but when the pirates land don't worry it'll open up for you good and proper, just like it did for me when I was a lad.'

Robert bent over the tunnel entrance, if indeed that's what it really was. 'So when will the pirates come?' he asked half-heartedly.

'You'll know, don't worry,' said the Captain, nodding his head. 'The sky will turn the colour of blood. A blood red sky will tell you they've arrived. You've heard of the old proverb, a red sky at night, shepherd's delight.'

'And a red sky in the morning, shepherd's warning,' Robert added.

'Yes, well now you know. When the sky turns a powerful red in the morning. They're here!'

The Captain turned and made for his shed. 'I've got something for you. Hurry, there's little time.' Again, there was a spring in his steps that truly belied his advanced years.

After arriving, the Captain promptly disappeared inside. The door was left ajar but Robert preferred to stay on the outside. Noises started to emanate from within, scraping, grating sounds, as if things were being moved and stuff searched.

Robert peeped through the small gap but quickly retreated, critical of himself. If he didn't have the courage to go inside then he shouldn't be sneaking a look. Instead, he turned to view the sea. It was so calm, and what with the sun so strong and the stuffy atmosphere, and everything else so absolutely still, deathly still, his mind started to wander and then invariably to daydream. He didn't wish to stop himself it was so pleasant and magical. Nor could he.

21

Men were appearing in rowing boats, coming towards the shore. As they neared, Robert could clearly see they were pirates, scores of them. Some were already disembarking, shiny cutlasses dangling by their sides and pistols stuffed into their belts. And still they kept coming, more and more, filling up the harbour with their bodies as well as their laughing, shouting and arguing. Now they were so close he could even smell their foul odour.

'Here!' suddenly said the Captain, touching Robert's shoulder. Robert jumped. 'So they're getting closer! Can you see them?'

Robert eventually turned, but didn't reply.

'You know what premonitions are, don't you?' said the Captain.

Robert slowly nodded.

'Well you're seeing yours. I don't know how much time we've got left. Maybe two days at most.'

Robert was confused.

'The pirates are coming for you, Robert. Some are your friends, most are your enemies. Here take this,' and he handed Robert a circular object with a piece of string running through it.

'What is it?' asked Robert, taking the item and examining it.

It was creamy coloured, hard and perfectly round with a hole drilled through for the string to be attached. In the centre was a straight line, with numerous marks of varying sizes engraved above and below it.

'It's a bone necklace,' said the Captain. 'Wear it around your neck. Never take it off, ever. It's very, very important. Do you hear me?'

'I won't wear a dead animal around my neck,' Robert stated firmly, offering it back. 'My mum doesn't even wear leather shoes, she's a vegetarian.'

'Is she now?' mused the Captain, cocking his unshaven face.

'You probably think it's silly.'

'Now why would I think that?' said the Captain deliberately. 'I think it's most admirable that a person has such goodness inside them that they don't wish to harm another living creature. But you shouldn't worry, this animal likely died of natural causes and was long dead before it became of any use. Now, will you wear it?'

'No, I can't. Sorry!'

'Please Robert,' said the Captain. 'Wear it for one week, that's all I ask, and then you can give it back if you want to.' His voice was quite serious.

Robert kicked the dry earth with his foot, deciding what to do. Eventually he relented, and put the string around his neck.

The Captain emitted a sigh of relief.

'So what is it?' asked Robert.

'It's a sort of map, I'll explain later. There's so much I need to tell you about. I'm not sure where to start.'

'Can I ask you something first?' said Robert, sensing an opportunity to tackle one of the Captain's mistruths from yesterday.

'Fire away,' said the Captain.

'I know for sure that piracy, years and years ago I mean, took place in the Caribbean and maybe Asia. How then could the pirates use Rum as a base. It's far too far away. It would take weeks, even months to travel back and forth. It's not possible.'

'Good! I'm pleased you've asked,' grinned the Captain. 'It means you're thinking,' and he bent forwards. 'They used the fog of course. They would enter a patch of fog in one place and come out in another place, anywhere they pleased. They could travel great distances in no time, crossing seas and oceans in the blink of an eye. But only a chosen few can use the fog, and even fewer summon it when needed. And you're one of those ones.'

'I don't want to be one of them,' said Robert.

'I'm sorry you feel like that and I don't mean to frighten you, but you don't choose it, it chooses you. Your crew is waiting for you, whether you go or not, well that's up to you. But consider, without their captain, yerself, they will ultimately perish.'

Robert hated being pressurised and although still not overly convinced about everything, he definitely felt a weight had somehow settled onto his shoulders.

'I need to go and take my dog out,' he said, and turned to go.

But the Captain, sensing that time was slipping away and fearing that he had frightened Robert off, wanted to hang onto the conversation.

'I had a dog when I was your age, a real lively thing it was. Called it Sparky I did!'

Robert jumped. A coincidence or a lie. He wasn't sure.

'Will you come back in the afternoon?' the Captain continued. 'At least show me your dog!'

'Yeah sure,' said Robert. There was little else to do anyway, and strange or not, the Captain was anything but boring.

23

'Promise?' said the Captain, a grin appearing and softening his whole face.

'I promise.'

When Robert arrived home his mum had returned. Her bicycle was not alone, however; a second bicycle was placed alongside. He already recognised Mrs Crabb's old fashioned contraption, totally black except for a brown wicker basket on the handle bars and a bright red seat.

'Shoes off!' said his mum crisply.

'Taking my shoes off!'

He didn't have to be told. Mum was probably only doing it to show off to Mrs Crabb. More like crab apple! He entered the kitchen.

'Ah, my Robert,' said Mrs Crabb, as Mrs MacSpoon stood pouring a kettle.

On finishing, Mrs MacSpoon turned round, and immediately noticed the pendant around Robert's neck.

'What's that?' she asked, peering as best she could from her position behind the oversized table.

'It's nothing,' he replied, quickly turning away. He'd totally forgotten about it.

'Looks suspiciously like a bone necklace to me,' said Mrs Crabb, leaning forwards and making her stool wobble.

Mrs MacSpoon's mood immediately darkened on hearing this precise description. She had been a vegetarian ever since she was twelve years old and had always encouraged Robert to share her compassion for other living things, and indeed he willingly did. So why was he deliberately flouting her now?

Robert was anxious to leave. Mrs Crabb was most definitely a crab apple!

'Take it off please and go and wash your hands,' said Mrs MacSpoon.

'They're not that dirty,' said Robert, looking at them, but he did remove the pendant and turned to go.

'Leave it on the table please.'

'I can't,' said Robert, recalling the Captain's words. 'I mean, I don't want to.' Then he had an idea, and opening a drawer he tucked the pendant inside, right underneath a dishcloth.

What Robert hadn't noticed on his arrival was that his dad was also home, only in the garage. It was a large garage, made of corrugated metal sheets, with a peaked roof and creosoted front wooden door. John MacSpoon wasn't alone, however; Mr Crabb was also present, and they were excitedly discussing tools.

After washing his hands, Robert checked his bedroom for Sparky. He was sound asleep and snoring gently. Mr MacSpoon had been playing with him the whole time Robert had been away and the young dog was utterly exhausted.

Robert scanned the room, then looked out of the window. His mum and Mrs Crabb were walking to the far off end. Now was his chance! He returned to the kitchen to retrieve the pendant.

'Hello,' said a voice, and Robert nearly jumped out of his skin.

It was Mr Crabb and he was alone. And he was smiling. On seeing Robert, he had quickly pushed shut a cupboard door with his knee.

'I'm looking for a torch, your dad said it would be here someplace. How's Sparky? He's a wee cracker, isn't he?'

It was the most amount of words Mr Crabb had ever spoken to Robert and it was mightily suspicious. A man who normally couldn't string two words together suddenly becoming talkative, undoubtedly had something to hide.

'It's there,' said Robert, pointing to a large silver torch on the shelf above the sink. He could even remember him and his dad buying it last year. It had been the biggest in the shop.

'I'm blind!' exclaimed Mr Crabb, and was about to pull the torch down when all of a sudden everybody else arrived at the back door.

'It's gotten ever so cloudy,' said Mrs Crabb. While at the exact same time Mr MacSpoon said, 'No need, John, I got it off.' Possibly referring to a problem which had somehow required the use of a torch.

'Come on, we're going home,' continued Mrs Crabb, looking at her husband. 'It's going to rain for sure.' But she could see her husband wasn't paying attention. 'Are you listening to me, John?'

Instantly, both John MacSpoon and John Crabb turned to look at her.

'Oops! I am sorry,' she immediately said to Robert's dad. 'I didn't realize you were also a John!'

Mrs MacSpoon smiled at the thought of her husband heading home with Mrs Crabb and everybody else joined in. All except for Robert that is, who left the kitchen deep in thought.

During lunch it did indeed start to rain, just as Mrs Crabb had predicted, and after lunch it was coming down in sheets. That feeling of déjà vu was returning.

Robert donned his jacket, and Sparky, appearing from nowhere, started to dance around, delighted to be going out again.

'Forget it! No way!' declared Mrs MacSpoon, catching Robert in the hallway. 'Besides, you've got far too much to do. Your dad's got boxes which need unpacking and Mrs Crabb said the rain is on for the day.'

'It's not that heavy,' argued Robert, but the noise of rain lashing against the kitchen window did little for his argument. Grudgingly, he removed his jacket, and Sparky skulked away.

That night, after everyone was tucked up in bed, Robert silently retrieved the necklace.

4. A Blood Red Sky

For the second day running, Robert set his alarm clock, and this time he got up! Sparky was again nowhere to be seen. His large cardboard box was empty, with only a small damp circle on the newspaper inside, evidence of his earlier presence. The bedroom was hot and stuffy. Yesterday's rain had further increased the humidity.

Looking at the room's tired walls as he put on his slippers, Robert recalled what his dad had said the night before. The bedroom needed painting and he was to be the painter, and no amount of protestations had worked. It would take him days, if not weeks, to complete such a job.

Robert raised himself and tugged open the curtains. He gasped at what he saw. The sky on the bottom was typically blue not surprisingly, but the rest of it was red, the colour of a tomato, or an apple, or blood.

'A blood red sky!' Robert cried, and he swallowed so deeply he nearly choked.

For a few moments he stared disbelievingly, waiting in case his eyes were deceiving him. But nothing changed. He even took the skin on his forearm and pinched himself strongly.

'Ouch!' he cried. He was definitely awake. This was no dream.

Robert's dad was alone in the kitchen and had been up for some time. He was a bit of an insomniac, and struggled to sleep at the best of times, and so a different house only made matters worse. Robert's mum was already at work.

'You're up early,' said Mr MacSpoon, as Robert entered the kitchen. Sparky instantly leapt around, his little feet scratching and scraping the wooden floor.

'Have you seen the sky, Dad?' said Robert. 'It's really, really, strange.'

'I've never seen anything like it. I expect a big storm's brewing,' said Mr MacSpoon, as he continued to replace what he had just taken out of the kitchen cupboards.

Mr MacSpoon was a stickler for order, and the cans of peas and beans were now perfectly lined up.

Robert paid him no attention. 'Red sky at night, shepherd's delight. Red sky in the morning, shepherd's warning,' he mumbled to himself.

'Are you speaking to yourself, son?' said Mr MacSpoon, peering over a tower of tinned soups.

'No!' said Robert, and continued with his breakfast.

'You shouldn't worry,' said Mr MacSpoon cheerfully. 'All the best people talk to themselves. Isn't that right, John? Sure is! You look great today, John! Thanks very much.'

But the joke was lost on Robert. He was miles away. There were more important things on his mind, like had the pirates really landed.

Outside, the heat was again oppressive, even more so than yesterday. Fortunately, Mr MacSpoon had relented today and Robert was accompanied by Sparky, his thin lead tugging in his master's hand.

'No chance of you ever chasing birds,' Robert said, as boy and dog walked side by side. 'There aren't any!'

Sparky looked up at his master, and then quickly to one side where a tabby cat lay on the windowsill of one of the few houses they were passing. The little dog immediately strained on the lead. The cat looked on inquisitively, but showed no sign of any fear, instead it yawned provocatively. Sparky barked playfully but Robert tugged on the lead and pressed on towards the harbour. He was desperate to see the Captain. The bone necklace hidden under his t-shirt glued to his chest.

As he approached the harbour and descended the crumbling concrete steps, Robert yet again saw Mr Crabb working on his boat. However, instead of going over, Robert simply raised his hand to say hello. Mr Crabb stared back indignantly and did not respond.

The ground was damp after the previous day's rain and a number of small gullies had appeared. As usual the ferry building was locked up tight.

Only on the days the ferry operated did it open, and then only for a short time. All the other days it remained totally deserted.

Around the corner from this building was the Captain's solitary shed, a fairly large structure in comparison to the others at the harbour. Big prickly gorse bushes surrounded three sides. The Captain was apparently not at home. His usual chair lay empty and a large piece of wood was leaning up against the shed's front door. Robert considered what to do.

The sky was by now nearly all red and becoming increasingly menacing in nature by the second. Robert pulled on Sparky, who had been happily sniffing around the Captain's table and chair, and headed back the way he had just come, to see Mr Crabb.

'Good morning,' said Robert politely. The words, however, stuck in his throat, as he recalled yesterday's events.

'Ah, I thought the cat got your tongue,' Mr Crabb said sourly, his wispy hair catching in the gentle breeze. Surprisingly, he had no hat on.

'Have you seen the Captain?' Robert asked, ignoring the old man's barbed comment.

'I certainly have. Last week, last month, and oh yes, let me think, last year too!'

'I meant today,' said Robert.

'Then you should be more specific, young man. But in answer to your generalised question, no I haven't seen him today. I haven't seen him for quite a few days for that matter.'

'Didn't you see him yesterday?' asked Robert, a little surprised.

'No! Can't say that I did.'

Robert looked at the old man wide eyed and opened mouthed. He was lying, but nothing could be gained from pressing the point.

'It's a very strange sky, isn't it?' said Robert.

'It is that. A very strange sky indeed. You'd better get back home with yourself fast, the water's ebbing, a big storm's coming.'

'Okay, I'll let Sparky off the lead a little and then I'll head back home.'

'Don't take too long, for the storm's coming fast,' pressed Mr Crabb.

Robert headed back to the other side of the harbour. One more look around the Captain's shed and then he would return home.

The shed was situated right back against the sharply sloping hill, with the solitary window to the rear of the structure. Along with the surrounding gorse bushes there was a considerable multitude of weeds, nettles mostly, but also one or two thistles. Only the front area had been tended to.

Robert quickly decided what to do, and lifting up the leg of the Captain's table, placed the handle of Sparky's lead underneath. Without Sparky hindering him, he could have a closer look around. He also secretly peeked sideways, back towards Mr Crabb, but he'd gone. The wind had now gotten decidedly stronger and was coming in gusts.

Robert skirted round the shed and after seeing nothing out of the ordinary, viewed the rear window. It was half hidden by one almighty greyish coloured thistle, brimming with lavender flowers and spiny leaves. It was an excellent burglar deterrent.

While paying close attention to the thistles, Robert neglected the accompanying nettles and brushed against them. 'Ouch, that hurt!' he cried, as the stinging hairs touched his hand and forearm. Sparky immediately barked. 'It's okay, I'm okay. I'll just be a second.' Small red bumps began appearing on his skin.

Accepting the warning, Robert gingerly approached the window, doing his best to avoid the thistle's formidable armour. A grubby screen covered the bottom half, but on tiptoes and with one hand to the glass he could see inside. The interior was an absolute shambles. Loads of things lay strewn on the floor, along with the drawers from an upturned chest of drawers. There was no sign of the Captain. An impatient Sparky started to whine.

When Robert went round to release Sparky's lead he was aware that it had become very, very dark. He gazed awestruck at the heavy sky, no longer blood red but fearfully black. Then a drop of rain spattered on his nose. Suddenly, a powerful flash of light shot across the sky directly overhead.

On hearing such a frightful noise, Sparky panicked and bolted. It was his first experience of lightning and running felt like the best thing to do.

A loud peal of thunder quickly followed and then came driving rain, but that didn't matter to Robert now, as he feverishly pursued Sparky who was heading directly towards the cliffs.

'Sparky!' he shouted in vain. 'Sparky!'

The ground had become instantly slippy and Robert lost his footing, tumbling to the sodden grass in a heap. When he got up Sparky was nowhere to be seen. Soaking and covered in mud, Robert made for the cliff face, hoping the terrified puppy was hiding in the adjacent long grass.

'Sparky! Sparky!' he shouted.

It was now nearly as dark as night-time and with the rain coming down in sheets, Robert was struggling to see. He blindly kicked at the long wet grass, becoming fearful that Sparky might have fallen into the water. Lightning again flashed overhead and he glimpsed the ferocious waves crashing against the harbour wall. Sparky would never survive that.

'Sparky! Sparky!'

Then a noise came from behind him, a whining sound. Then it stopped. It must be Sparky crying for help. Immediately, Robert got down on all fours and grabbed frantically at the long wet grass.

'Sparky!' he cried, feeling the dog wasn't far away now.

Again another whine came, just to his right, closer to the start of the cliff face, exactly where the Captain had been kicking open the old pirates' tunnel the previous day.

Sparky had not, in fact, gone into the old pirates' tunnel; instead he had lodged himself in an old rabbit's burrow not very far away. His whining and whimpering for his master's help had become distorted by the wind and rain, and had not revealed his true location. Oblivious to this, Robert crawled towards the tunnel. The driving rain had somehow opened up the hole from yesterday. And so in he crawled.

The tunnel entrance was tight, but once inside, the sides quickly widened and the ceiling rose. Robert was entirely unaware of his surroundings as it was so dark. It was, however, totally dry, from both above and below.

'Sparky,' said Robert in a hushed voice. It was deathly quiet inside the tunnel, in stark contrast to the battering wind and rain, and the crashes of thunder and lightning he had left outside. He inched on a little farther and tried to stand up.

'Sparky, I'm here,' he whispered.

It was so unbelievably calm inside the tunnel, the only thing he could hear was his feet scuffing the stony ground. Just then, he saw light through the darkness, nothing major but certainly less dark. He moved forwards, arms outstretched, as the less dark patch became lighter and lighter.

It surely had stopped raining but he couldn't explain where he now was. It could only be another entrance as he hadn't backtracked one solitary step, even in this darkness.

31

Thereupon, the tunnel turned sharply and it became light. Now he knew where he was, he was in the secret harbour. The pirates' secret harbour. And it wasn't empty.

Robert stared at the conglomeration of things. There were barrels, different sizes of wooden boxes, coils of rope, a broken wheel, crates, stained canvas sheets, sacks filled to bursting, even a small cannon standing on its end. And some piles were so high he couldn't see over them.

Robert ducked down on all fours and slowly sneaked forwards in amongst the items. Suddenly he halted, and looked with open mouth. Right before him stood one almighty ancient ship nestling against the water's edge. It was nearly within touching distance.

The ship had three tall wooden masts, the middle one being as high as a tree. The ship was also significantly lower in the middle, while being raised at the front and back, with loads of mainly round windows absolutely everywhere. Canvas sails and ropes were hanging and dangling all over, but all stood perfectly still as there was barely a breath of wind. The stench of wood and tar and salt was overpowering. Had this whole place lain untouched for over three hundred years?

Robert scanned the cave excitedly. It was very large, with an expansive walking area all around a central water basin where the ship was moored by a number of ropes as thick as a man's arm. The cave's roof was much higher than the topmost part of the ship yet only a touch of sky was visible towards the mouth of the cave. There was no sound of water sloshing around, indicating the sheltered nature of this hidden quay.

Even although the whole place was quite clearly deserted, Robert continued to wait. Minutes passed, and then some more minutes, as he scanned the entire area. It wasn't perfectly light, but he could confidently see everything. It was so deathly quiet.

Robert gradually raised himself, properly straightening his body for the first time since entering the tunnel. He stared at the boat and observed some thick planks of wood connecting the roughly hewn stone of the quayside to the stationary ship, evidently a gangway. He looked at the open invitation presented before him but did not budge. Then some more minutes passed but still he checked himself, listening and watching intently. Nothing happened. He adjusted his position, edging ever so slightly closer to the gangway.

Robert had now totally forgotten about the real reason he was there: to find Sparky. Instead, he was captivated by this huge muscling ship. Again he surveyed it, up and down, side to side. How so very tall and mysterious it was.

Suddenly he lunged forwards, and heart pounding raced towards the planks of wood. In a split second they were traversed and he was on board. Here too there were stacks of goods everyplace and scurrying behind a fat wooden barrel, he held his breath. Silence surrounded him, except for the wooden planks creaking ever so slightly beneath his feet. The barrel emanated a sweet, tantalising smell, but did little to dispel the corrosive and overpowering smell of salt.

The ship seemed smaller now that he was on board. The bow of the ship was to his left, where a fair-sized cabin, partially obscured by the foremast and rigging, rose up from and spanned the deck. Straight ahead was the massive main mast, with a third smaller mast on his other side. Sails and ropes seemed to hang everywhere, while a large blackened hatch and other strange contraptions, which Robert had never seen before, occupied the deck. To his right was the back of the ship, where another cabin was sited with twin stairs on either side, a balcony and accompanying balustrade. There was a door in the cabin and tantalisingly it was open.

Bursting with excitement, Robert lifted himself up and tiptoed to the rear of the ship, and slipped through the door.

The room was medium sized and fairly bright due to the presence of four square windows and the open door. Numerous items hung from the walls, including lanterns and a black and gold ornamental wheel. Directly ahead was another door, which was closed, and on the floor was a hatchway, which was smallish, had a protruding handrail, and was open.

Robert tried the door; it was locked. He turned and approached the hole in the floor, and holding onto the handrail peered inside. A damp stuffy smell rose up, but no sounds came to his ears. He stalled for a few moments and then tentatively lowered himself down the first few rungs of a creaky ladder. What an adventure this was! His heart was racing fit to burst. Then he heard something.

'Achoo!' And then again. 'Achoo!' Somebody was sneezing.

Robert held his breath, but the sneezes were not those from an adult, but without doubt those of a child. They were high pitched, squeaky even.

He was certainly not scared of a sneezing child and so he continued his descent.

This lower deck was darker, with only a few holes in the ship's side permitting light to enter. The smell of salt was weaker now, but the distinctive aroma of wood much stronger. Massive black cannons were arranged on either side in perfect lines for as far as the eye could see in the semi darkness, and with numerous stretched out hammocks also hindering the view. Another hatch lay at his feet. His choice was simple: explore this deck with all the cannons or descend further into the belly of the ship to find out who was sneezing.

Robert climbed down the second hatchway and now it was considerably darker. Immediately, he changed his mind and turned to go back up when he caught the glimpse of a small light just beyond the many crates and barrels that were surrounding the bottom of the hatchway ladder. Easing himself forwards, he followed the light through an open door and was astounded at what he saw. A small boy was sitting lifelessly on an upturned bucket in the back part of a room, and shockingly, he was behind bars. A lighted lantern hung outside his prison cell. On seeing Robert, the boy instantly jumped up.

'Hey Captain!' he exclaimed. 'Yer alive!' And the scrawny boy stared with open mouth.

The lantern showed up his thin face and tousled hair. His clothes were little more than rags and he had no shoes on. He was not the healthiest looking boy Robert had ever come across.

'Who are you?' asked Robert. 'And why are you calling me Captain?'

'Titch is my name and ye look the spitting likeness of our captain. He is alive, isn't he?'

'Of course. But how did you get in there?'

'Pirates, Cap'n! Don't ye know?'

Robert was unsure. Pirates, really! There wasn't another soul in the place. He shook the metal door vigorously. It hardly budged.

Robert looked around and noticed a row of keys on a wooden rail. 'Maybe one of these will open the lock,' he said, grabbing a few.

'No, Cap'n. None will open it.'

Robert wasn't listening and he tried a key: too big. It didn't even go into the hole. He tried another.

'Cap'n,' said Titch. 'None will fit.'

But Robert had found a key that fitted perfectly. Alas, it did not turn the lock. He did, however, slip it into his pocket. 'I'll come back,' he said, defiantly.

'Are ye sure, Cap'n?'

'Yes,' said Robert, and was already beating a hasty retreat. He raced straight up the two ladders, through the cabin and into the outside air. He paused momentarily. Yet still, there wasn't a soul in sight. Then, he hunched himself up and hared back over the gangway, through the packed quayside and into the tunnel. Inside was still pitch black but he knew where he was going.

'Wow! That was exciting,' he said out loud. So there were other children on the island!

With arms outstretched and edging slowly forwards, Robert found the tunnel entrance. He crawled out on all fours and into the rain, the long wet grass grabbing at his clothes.

'Sparky!' he cried, as the little dog bounded towards him.

The clever dog had managed to free himself from the rabbit's burrow, and sniffing out his master, had waited beside the tunnel entrance. This, however, had only taken a few minutes from start to finish, but Robert felt that he had been away for ages.

On the way home Robert felt the key inside his pocket. He had an idea!

'You should have sheltered someplace,' his dad said, greeting him at the front door.

'I did,' said Robert, but stopped himself short.

Sparky meanwhile bounded into the house, with Mr MacSpoon giving chase after the sodden dog.

'Dad?' said Robert, after he had gotten out of his wet clothes.

'Yes,' answered Mr MacSpoon suspiciously, as he towel-dried a very uncooperative Sparky. Using the hairdryer had lasted a mere two seconds.

'Do you still have those keys which can open any door?'

'If you mean skeleton keys, then yes I do,' replied Mr MacSpoon. He finished drying Sparky and got up. 'Why?'

'Oh, no reason,' said Robert, and disappeared into his bedroom with a fluffed up Sparky at his heels.

When Robert's mum arrived home a little later, his dad left the house. Mrs MacSpoon immediately set about preparing lunch. Robert seized his chance and hurriedly went to the garage. Sparky stayed with the food.

It had stopped raining by now but the sky was still dark with a reddish tinge. He opened the side door to the large double garage and went inside. He daren't put the light on, although it wasn't very light inside. Now, where were those keys?

Mr MacSpoon was a very neat and tidy man, and everything in the garage had its place. He had only been on the island for barely three days, but Robert was amazed to see the organization that had taken place in such a short period of time. There were metal filing cabinets with labelled drawers, metal shelves with hundreds of tools neatly placed on them, coat hooks, hat rails, a work bench, and that was only on one side. The other side was filled to overflowing with gardening utensils. He sighed at the enormity of his task as a drip of water fell onto his head. The garage roof had sprung a leak.

Robert opened the drawer marked K in the filing cabinets, but it contained only folders. He hurriedly closed it. Then he proceeded to open and close every single drawer in the cabinets - unfortunately nothing but colourful folders stared back at him.

'This is a waste of time!' he moaned out loud.

He continued to pull out every other drawer he could see, and lots of different things appeared before him, but no keys. He checked the cupboards too, but nothing. He paused, thought a little, and returned to the drawer in the filing cabinet marked K. After reopening it, he proceeded to remove the heavy folders, dumping them onto the worktops.

'Bingo!' he shouted on removing the last folder. A big metal tin was hidden underneath.

Robert opened the tin to reveal numerous keys of all different sizes, and after taking out his key he started to compare. Four keys were of a comparable size and shape. He popped the five keys into the pocket of his long shorts and zipped it up. They were surprisingly heavy.

Suddenly the door was flung open and Robert nearly jumped out of his skin. His mum was standing with a curious look on her face, while Sparky ran to greet his master.

'What are you doing, Robert?' she asked coolly.

Robert stared back with a guilty look on his face. He had good reason. Filing cabinet drawers lay wide open, umpteen folders were dumped in a mess on the table, doors weren't properly closed and no lights had been switched on.

Mrs MacSpoon asked again. 'Robert, what are you doing?'

'Tidying up,' he blurted out. 'Can't you see the mess? Dad said I could help him and put away the stuff on the table. I didn't know where anything went so I've been opening the drawers. I'm not lying!' This was all said in one long breath.

'But I didn't say you were lying. Anyway, why aren't there any lights on?'

'I didn't want to waste electricity. You shouldn't put lights on during the day, especially in the summertime.'

'Yes, okay,' replied Mrs MacSpoon somewhat doubtfully. 'I'm just surprised that your father allowed you anywhere near his things. Anyway, lunch is ready. Come on, Sparky.' And Sparky followed her out.

Robert breathed a sigh of relief and quickly started to tidy up.

After a double helping of fish fingers and beans, during which his mum repeatedly told him to slow down, Robert went to his bedroom to prepare. He scooped out the keys and placed them on the quilt cover of his bed, and immediately set about searching for something to wrap them in. A sock would do just fine he thought. Now they wouldn't clink together. He placed the tight bundle into his large side pocket and zipped it up.

Then, he waited impatiently for his mum to leave the kitchen. Soon enough she needed to visit the bathroom. Like lightning he raced to the kitchen and started searching the cupboards for food. Titch looked hungry. Robert wouldn't be able to take much but a packet of biscuits would certainly do, and he burst open a packet of wafers, pocketing four in total. Then, for some inexplicable reason he removed a brown bottle of vitamins from the shelf and zipped them up in his bulging pockets. He was ready.

While heading towards the harbour for the second time that day, Robert experienced pangs of conscience. His mum had no idea that he had gone, and probably assumed he was still playing in his bedroom. He also hadn't given Sparky, who had been curled up sound asleep on the couch in the living room, a goodbye clap. The little dog was exhausted from the morning's exertions.

Moving swiftly, Robert neared the harbour. He really hoped to find the Captain there, in his usual place, but something inside him told him otherwise. And sure enough, on crossing the harbour front, there was no Captain to behold, nor anyone else for that matter.

The sky was now much lighter and the redness had all but disappeared, with only a thin rusty line on the horizon remaining. The ground was already beginning to dry as Robert hurried along. After checking all around for possible onlookers, he approached the tunnel entrance. Ducking down, he squeezed into the gap in the dark wet rock, and again the saturated long grass soaked his clothes.

Immediately he was annoyed with himself: he'd forgotten a torch. In his haste to steer clear of his mum it had gone straight out of his mind. But it was too late to turn back now.

Everything was as it had been before, nothing was moved, nothing was different, even the ever so slight breeze was identical. He stopped to look and listen, using the exact same hiding spot as before. Satisfied, he boarded the ship and descended the two flights of wooden steps back into the heart of the floating beast.

Titch was even more surprised to see Robert than last time, and his eyes lit up in the rays emitted from the oil lantern.

'Cap'n!' said the small boy. 'You're back.'

'There's no point in saying and not doing,' said Robert, and he immediately unzipped the pocket containing the five keys.

Titch looked on, intrigued by the fat zip and pocket on the side of Robert's long shorts. He had never seen such funny trousers.

'I've brought some keys to try,' said Robert, tugging out key number one from the sock and inserting it into the square mounted lock. It was a touch too big.

The second key was slightly too small and rattled in the lock. The third key fitted perfectly but failed to turn. The fourth key was the original from the ship itself, leaving a fifth and final key to try. It entered smoothly and gripped the insides perfectly, but alas it did not turn one hair's breadth. Robert grabbed the metal bars and shook them in the hope of changing something. They were thick, cold and rough to the touch.

'How many more keys do you have, Cap'n?' asked Titch.

'None,' groaned Robert. 'That was the last one. Whereabouts do you live on the island, Titch?'

'What island, Cap'n?'

'This island of course.'

'Are we berthed in Rum then, Cap'n?'

Robert was confused.

Suddenly, Titch felt his left leg drop ever so slightly lower, then it was the turn of his right leg, then back to his left again. He recognised the feeling.

'Cap'n!' he said. 'We've set sail.'

Robert instantly turned and stared at the door aghast. It was shut!

In horror he ran over and tugged it. It didn't budge. But there was no lock. It was surely bolted from the outside. He continued to tug and push the door, as the ship started to sway from side to side.

'We've rightly put to sea, Cap'n,' said Titch.

'But this can't be happening,' said Robert. 'This isn't real.'

5. Captain Blackjack

The Thunder left Rum harbour and headed southwest. This was the name of Captain Blackjack's ship. His previous ship had been The Lightning, but he'd lost that one.

Blackjack stared out to sea as The Thunder displayed full sails. His plan had worked and he was relatively content as he stroked his spiky beard.

Down in the ship's belly Robert and Titch stood staring at each other as the fluctuations under their feet grew ever stronger.

'Ye should hide, Cap'n,' said Titch. 'There's loads of nooks and crannies ye could squeeze into.'

'From who?' asked Robert.

'Them, Cap'n. The pirates.'

Robert was puzzled and it was making him uneasy. He looked around him. The room, if indeed that's what it was, was fair sized and positively jam packed with the exact same goods and equipment that had been on the quayside and upper deck. Above, the ceiling was not much higher than his head with wooden beams crisscrossing everywhere. The ship's curved side meant that there was much less floor than ceiling, and Titch's prison cell was taking up a large chunk of this floor space. Wooden posts were dotted everyplace, rising up from the deck and pushing on through the ceiling on their journey upwards.

'I'll tell them we want to go home,' said Robert eventually. 'They must know I'm here.'

'What makes ye so sure Cap'n?' asked Titch, the swinging lantern producing dancing shadows behind him.

'They closed the door, didn't they?'

'They're always shutting and opening it, Cap'n. I think ye should hide. They're bound to check on me soon.'

Thereupon, the timber above creaked heavily and then came the unmistakable sound of footsteps. Robert instantly dived for cover and was just in time before the wooden door was flung open.

A moment of silence elapsed as Robert huddled down into the expanses of ropes and cloths which were dumped higgledy-piggledy at the side of the prison cell. He was fully covered. Holding his breath he waited, as his heart tried to burst through his t-shirt. Surely they could hear it?

Suddenly a voice boomed, 'Come out! Come out! Wherever you are!'

Robert's heart jumped full speed into the back of his throat and he struggled to breathe properly. Was the man really speaking to him? Instinctively, he pulled his body in even tighter forming the shape of a ball. Silence returned to the room. Total silence.

'Come out now, boy!' snapped the man. 'Or so help me I'll run ye through with ma cutlass.'

Robert was now in no doubt whatsoever, the man was indeed speaking directly to him. Reluctantly, he eased himself out of his hiding spot.

'Well hoist ma main sail. What have we here, lads?' said the man. 'A stowaway! On my ship.'

Grunts of ridicule filled the room as Robert stared at the terrifying bunch, who were all squeezed in and around the doorway.

The man doing all the talking was of course Blackjack, a strong looking fellow with a big mop of dark hair and a full beard. His jacket was blue maybe purple, with two belts slung across each shoulder and baggy trousers below. A dagger and two pistols were stuffed into yet another belt on his waist, and a cutlass swung by his side.

'So the laggard's turned up, lads!' Blackjack said. 'Like a bad penny.'

'Aye,' cried the bunch.

Robert didn't understand what Blackjack was saying. But a disagreeable smell had now appeared.

'Who are you?' Robert asked. But he already knew the answer.

'Are ye playing a game, lad? Am partial to a game, assuming the victory is mine. Captain Hack Blackjack, at yer service,' and he held out a large hand.

Robert didn't budge, he did not wish to go anywhere near this foul man.

'Shake the hand, lad or I'll slice you from top t'toe,' barked Blackjack.

Robert edged forwards and quickly touched the hand. It was thick and calloused.

'Now then,' said Blackjack. 'Seeing as we're friends, so to speak. Where's The Book of Maps, lad?'

Robert stared back blankly.

'Don't take me for a fool, boy,' said Blackjack irritably. 'I'll cut yer belly open the same as any grown man I've ever cut open.'

His crew were growing impatient and there were grumblings. One fellow in particular was irked, and what a fellow he was. He was simply huge and was clearly struggling to remain upright in such confined quarters. The man was as black as coal, with a head as big as a bull. He looked on with a massive pair of eyes, above a broad mouth and nose; surprisingly, though, his ears were tiny. He had no neck to speak of, just a giant head on gigantic shoulders.

'I reckon he's more fearful of Giant,' said Blackjack.

'I'm not scared of any of you,' said Robert, gutsily. 'Can you let us go, please?'

'Well ye should be fearful, lad,' said Blackjack, looking Robert up and down. 'Ye appear somewhat smaller than I remember ye. But ye healed well, lad. I'll give ye that. I swear I thought I'd killed ye.'

Robert remained confused. Who were these people? And why were they being so mean?

'Now we trade,' said Blackjack, his black eyes glaring. 'I set ye free as a bird and you give me The Book of Maps. Can't say fairer than that.'

'I don't have it,' said Robert in earnest. 'I don't even know what it is.'

'My men would torment ye right now, if they had their way. But there's time aplenty for that recourse. Lock'em up, Mr Weasel.'

'Aye, aye, Captain!' said Mr Weasel.

He was a smallish thin man, with a long pointed nose that ended in a sharp bony bit. His head was little and round with thin ginger hair combed over a balding top. Buck teeth of an unsightly colouration made this man repulsive to look at in every way. Like Giant, he was aptly named.

Thereon, Blackjack pulled out a key from a small pocket in his jacket and flipped it in the air.

Weasel seized it and opened the cell door. Then, reaching over, he grabbed Robert by his top and manhandled him inside.

Robert was shaken.

'Shall I discipline him, Captain?' sneered Weasel. 'He's got disrespect in his eyes. It's plain.'

'Get back, ye scurvy dog!' cried Blackjack, and a disappointed Mr Weasel quickly locked the barred door.

Blackjack took the key and hung it on the wooden rail that Robert had earlier removed a key from. Then, turning sharply the pirate said, 'I want what's mine, MacSpoon, and I aims to have it! Or this lot can have ye.'

Again the crew grunted.

'Catch yer sea legs, lad. There's time enough till we get to the Americas.'

Robert gulped in horror. Americas! He had to get back home, his mum would be worried sick. 'But you can't keep us here!'

'Harken to his lordship, men,' scoffed Blackjack. 'I can do anything that pleases me, lad. The lamp, Mr Weasel.'

'Can you leave the lamp?' Robert quickly asked, as Mr Weasel began to unhook the lantern from a metal peg in the roof.

'Does darkness bring ye fear, lad?'

'No, but evil spirits will start to appear,' said Robert. He sort of knew people in the olden days believed in evil spirits and were scared of them.

'Leave it, Mr Weasel,' said Blackjack.

The door was again latched from the outside and the two unfortunate boys were left to themselves.

6. The Book of Maps

'Is it true, Cap'n?' asked Titch immediately. 'About evil spirits visiting us.'

'No, Titch,' said Robert. 'It's just pretend.'

Titch wasn't overly convinced.

'Titch, what's The Book of Maps?' asked Robert. He wanted to know what he didn't have.

'The Book of Maps,' Titch began, 'is a whole bunch of treasure maps from dead pirates. But that's not all. Some say it holds magic. Do you believe in sorcery, Cap'n?'

'No,' said Robert. 'It's just pretend again.'

'But you're here, Cap'n,' said Titch, his searching eyes looking back at Robert. 'Isn't that sort of magic?'

'Maybe you're right, Titch and maybe I'm wrong. But I don't even know where here is. Where am I, Titch?'

'Yer aboard Blackjack's ship Cap'n, heading for the Americas, in the year seventeen hundred and .... that I don't rightly know.'

'Seventeen hundreds!' exclaimed Robert. 'It can't be.' And he slumped to the deck. 'It's all true then. Everything was true.'

'I reckon so, Cap'n,' said Titch, but he wasn't exactly sure what he was agreeing to.

'And why would I have this Book of Maps?'

'Cos you stole it, Cap'n, from Blackjack. Well the past captain did. But yer such alike, like two peas in a pod they say. Blackjack couldn't even tell ye apart!'

'And where did Blackjack get it from?'

'He stole it, Cap'n!'

'From who?'

'Don't know, Cap'n,' said Titch, shrugging his slight shoulders.

Robert felt as if he was getting nowhere and pulled out one of the shiny wrapped biscuits from his pocket. 'Want a biscuit?'

'Aye,' replied a mesmerized Titch. And after turning it over a few times, he accidentally unwrapped it.

'Blimey! That's tasty,' he said, wolfing down the crispy chocolate wafer.

Robert didn't have the heart to have one himself and so Titch proceeded to scoff all four biscuits one after the other.

'Wow!' said Titch, licking his lips. 'They were about as scrummy as bee's honey. Ye know I tasted honey once, it melted all over ma tongue and right down the back of ma throat. Have ye ever tasted honey, Cap'n?'

'Yes,' said Robert, but not wishing to sound boastful he decided to tell a white lie. 'But only once.'

'Maybe when we find the treasure we can buy some more, Cap'n. The real stuff, mind you, not the pretend stuff. And then we'll both have had it twice.'

'Seems a good idea,' said Robert, but he was not thinking of honey at this moment. His mind was in a whirl, he needed answers.

'Titch, how could I take The Book of Maps from a bunch of pirates?'

'It's not the only thing ye took from them, Cap'n.'

'I took other stuff?'

'The Lightning of course, Cap'n. Our ship. It was theirs.'

'No!' said Robert. 'I stole The Book of Maps and stole their ship. How? When?'

'The Lightning ye took in Edinburgh, and ye took The Book of Maps in Africa. On an island it was. Ever so green.'

'An island in Africa?' said Robert. 'Was it very big?'

'It went on forever it did. A proper country it was.'

'Madagascar!' cried Robert, delving into his geography knowledge. 'That's where it was.' The old Captain was unbelievable.

'Things is looking tricksy, Cap'n?' said Titch, but then he livened up. 'How beautiful that big island was, Cap'n. It was like paradise, Fraser said. Plants with flowers that were more wonderful than a rose, every colour of the rainbow they were, and the smell from them was like the finest

45

perfume. I've never smelled perfume before, so Fraser told me that bit. And the animals, birds so handsome ye couldn't take yer eyes off them, and monkeys which weren't monkeys, with long thick tails longer than themselves.'

'Who's Fraser?' asked Robert, when Titch stopped for breath.

'He's the helmsman, Cap'n. He's the most intelligent of all the crew. Ye know he can read and write. He's even made a library in one of the cabins on The Lightning. Nobody uses it, though, cos we all can't read.'

Robert was shocked that only this Fraser could read and write. Everybody could read and write in his class in Edinburgh, even Dozy Dougal.

'What does a helmsman do?'

'Why, he steers the ship, Cap'n,' said Titch. 'Nobody better in the whole world. What's that?' he asked, pointing at Robert's wrist.

'It's a watch,' Robert answered, unsure whether watches had been invented yet. 'It tells the time. Look!' and he held out his wrist to show Titch.

'I've seen a pocket watch before, but never one on somebody's arm. How small it is, and it's got so many pointers,' marvelled Titch, and he gently touched it.

'They're called hands,' explained Robert. 'One for the hours, one for the minutes and one for the seconds.'

'Wow, the pocket watch I saw only had one pointer for the hours. It's a strange kind of metal, Cap'n. It's not even shiny.'

'It's not metal, it's plastic.' And Robert now knew the next question, but then he noticed something wasn't right. 'That's funny, it doesn't seem to be working,' and he shook his wrist feverishly. The hands didn't budge and the watch remained stuck at ten minutes past twelve - unbeknown to Robert, the exact moment in time he had entered the pirate's tunnel.

'Ye need to wind it up, Cap'n. Have ye got yer winding key?'

Robert was just about to explain what batteries were, when suddenly the ship went up and down violently, and both boys were thrown onto the rough wooden floor.

'We must be getting farther out to sea, Cap'n,' said Titch, clutching the metal bars. 'The waves are getting more powerful.'

Thereupon, running and shouting could be heard as the crew commenced preparations for a storm. In a matter of minutes, the ship began to creak noisily as it was shifted one way then the other.

Captain Blackjack viewed the worsening weather from the poop deck, hoping for a possible solution - fog, and plenty of it. With it, he could avoid the advancing storm and make quick passage to his destination, the Caribbean, at the same time taking Robert as far away from home as he'd ever been in his entire life. But unlike his captive below decks, Blackjack was powerless to call the fog, and was resigned to lady luck.

In their dingy prison cell the two boys huddled together for stability. Robert was amazed that the unpleasant feeling of seasickness hadn't reappeared. His second time ever on a boat was clearly agreeing with him far more than his first.

But Robert still had so many questions. 'How many crew are on The Lightning, Titch?'

'Don't know Cap'n. Can't count.'

'But are there more than a hundred or less?'

'More I reckon.'

'Are there any adults?'

'None, Cap'n. Only children. Small children, tall children, fat children, although there's only one of them, thin children, there's plenty of them, but all children, every last one of us.'

'But where did you all come from?' Robert asked, finding it difficult to believe that a ship could be run entirely by children.

'You found us, Cap'n! Well, the last Cap'n, but ye look more alike than two kegs of pork.'

'But where?'

'Em, not sure, Cap'n,' said Titch, rather unconvincingly and shrugging his thin shoulders. 'It feels a long time ago.'

'But where are your mothers and fathers?'

'I don't reckon we have any. Maybe some do. Fraser says we were the children nobody wanted, that was until you came. Boy, things changed then.'

Robert scratched his head in puzzlement; nothing made any sense, absolutely nothing.

'How old are you, Titch?' he asked, guessing he was the older.

'Don't rightly know, Cap'n,' said Titch, pursing his lips while deep in thought.

'You don't know how old you are? When's your birthday?'

'Don't have a birthday. Nobody on board does. It's a pity I'm not a tree!' Titch said thoughtfully.

'Why?'

'Cos Fraser says ye can tell how old a tree is by cutting it in half. Mind you, I would be a dead tree then!'

Robert chuckled. He would like to meet this Fraser.

Just then, the outside bolt on the door was ground open and in stepped the vile Mr Weasel. In his hands he was balancing a bashed metal tankard and a wooden plate with biscuits on it. He now sported a red scarf tied tightly over his head and knotted at the back.

'Hallo, me lads!' he said. 'I've brought yous some water and grub,' and he kicked a small wooden stool with three legs into the middle of the floor, and plopped himself down with an exaggerated sigh.

'Now, ye young scamps, you'll be needing some refreshments,' and he placed the tankard with the broad base onto the floor, while balancing the plate on his lap. 'I do love ship's biscuits, more so when they're nice and fresh and there's no any weevils in them.' Then he ate a biscuit.

Robert and Titch stared on. Robert wasn't particularly hungry, although his belly had started to rumble a short time ago. He was, however, pretty thirsty, what with the heat.

One after the other, Mr Weasel maliciously ate the entire plate of biscuits.

'Yum, yum,' he said, patting his belly, while never taking his eyes off the two boys. 'Now then, what shall we do with the water?' And he got up and approached the cell bars. 'Behold. It doesn't go through the gaps.' And he proceeded to knock the tankard against the solid bars as the water sloshed around inside.

Robert was raging at this heartless man, but he tried to contain his anger.

'You can open the door,' he said. 'The keys are only hanging there.'

'Not allowed,' said Mr Weasel. 'I'd feel ten lashes on my back for doing such a forward thing. No, I'll need to leave it here,' and he placed the large metal cup with its prominent handle on the floor.

Robert breathed a silent sigh of relief, he was sure he could raise the tankard to his mouth through the bars, but Mr Weasel had other ideas.

'Too easy?' he asked, and swiftly pulled out a piece of thick twine from within his filthy jacket, and began tying the large cup to the base of the bars. Knot after knot was expertly and superbly fastened, until the tankard and bars were one. After a final tug on the thin rope he smiled and said, 'Drink up, laddies,' and left.

The two boys looked at one another. They had a puzzle to solve!

'We can untie it, Cap'n,' said Titch. 'And then lift it up to our mouths.'

So both boys dropped down and started to untangle the knots. Alas, nothing budged. The cords had been thoroughly tightened.

'I've got an idea,' said Robert, and unzipped his pocket containing the bottle of vitamins. 'If I empty these into my pocket, then we've got a bottle to fill up.'

Titch's eyes flashed. What strangely coloured buttons, like nothing he'd ever seen.

Robert felt that his friend was more in need of a drink than himself, and so he handed over the small brown bottle. Titch reached out and dipped it into the tankard. He, however, drank less greedily than Robert had expected.

'Thank ye kindly, Cap'n,' said Titch. 'There's more than half left.'

There was indeed enough water for both boys to quench their thirsts, and with Titch's small dexterous hands most of it was successfully removed. The water was not, however, to Robert's taste, and had he not been so thirsty he would certainly have given it a wide berth. It smelt funny too.

'What were those buttons in the bottle, Cap'n?' asked Titch.

'Vitamins,' said Robert, and after unzipping his pocket he removed two tablets. One he put into his mouth, and with the remaining drips, swallowed. The other he put into Titch's hand, who quickly copied. Only then did the small boy seek an explanation.

'What are they for, Cap'n?' he asked, as Robert dried the inside of the bottle with his t-shirt.

'Ah,' said Robert. He knew full well what vitamins were, but explaining it would be complicated. Would Titch be capable of understanding?

Titch patiently waited as Robert searched for the correct words.

'Humans eat food,' Robert began. 'And inside food is stuff which your body needs to grow. Some of this stuff is called vitamins, but they're only in some foods and only in teeny weeny amounts, and some foods don't have any at all.'

Titch looked on thoughtfully.

'Anyway,' continued Robert. 'These wee buttons are called tablets and inside them are all the different types of vitamins which we should be eating in our food, but might not be.' He stopped and waited for a response. Titch continued to look thoughtful.

'Here, they're yours now,' said Robert, and handed Titch the replenished bottle of vitamins. 'One a day, every day, and you'll be as strong as a lion.'

Titch took the bottle, somewhat apprehensively, and then jammed it deep down into his scruffy trouser pocket.

'Thanks, Cap'n, maybe I'll get stronger than Bennett.'

Robert wondered who Bennett was and would he ever find out.

'Will you give them The Book of Maps, Cap'n?'

'Can I tell you a secret, Titch?'

'Sure, Cap'n, on my honour. I'm as honest as the day's long.'

'I don't have The Book of Maps and I don't know where it is.' Robert immediately felt a great pang of conscience when he saw Titch's shocked face.

'Then they're definitely gonna kill us, Cap'n,' said Titch. 'Both of us. And that's as sure as the moon follows the sun.'

'Nothing's going to happen to us, Titch. I promise you.'

'But how can ye be so sure, Cap'n?'

'Because I'm here to help you. That's why.'

Just then, the flame inside the lantern flickered and died, and the room fell into darkness. Although the two boys were still side by side they might as well have been a million miles apart such was the intensity of the blackness now surrounding them.

'We should sleep,' said Robert. 'I think tomorrow's going to be a fun day.'

'I knew ye would come back, Cap'n,' said Titch.

'A captain never abandons his men!' said Robert. So now he was a captain!

Up on deck, Captain Blackjack grinned with mounting satisfaction. A cry from the crow's nest high above had informed him that a blanket of fog had been spotted in the distance. The Thunder was now veering hard to starboard, directly in its path. The storm had petered out so the fog's principal task was now in transporting The Thunder thousands of miles across the Atlantic to the Caribbean. Robert was within a whisker of being a very, very long way away from home.

The two boys slept surprisingly soundly as the evening passed into night-time. Although, Robert did have one brief unpleasant dream where Blackjack was asking about the whereabouts of The Book of Maps.

7. The Thunder Attacked

'Stir yerself Cap'n! Stir yerself!' cried Titch. 'Something's happening.' Robert awoke with a start and felt totally disorientated. The lantern which had burnt itself out the previous night had surprisingly been replenished, and was burning even more brightly than before. Then reality started to come back to him. He checked his watch: it was still stuck at ten past twelve. Everything was not, however, normal.

'Listen to that!' said Titch, standing straight up and cocking his head this way and that like a dog to his master.

Prior to the storm that had never materialized, shouts and sounds had reverberated throughout the ship. Now, however, the shouts were screams and the sounds were deafening. Thunderous explosions were regularly rocking the ship and screeching sounds peppered the cacophony. For a moment there would be a relative lull before it started up all over again.

Robert couldn't believe he hadn't woken up on his own account.

'We're under attack, and The Thunder's replying,' said Titch excitedly. 'Those are the cannons making the most noise.'

'How long has this been for?'

'Not long, Cap'n.'

Suddenly, the boat turned sharply and the two boys were thrown against the hull. The noise abated with the same rapidity and they both wondered what was happening.

'Something's strange,' said Robert. 'There must be more than one ship attacking. Why are we firing and turning at the same time? We need to get out of here. Can I have your belt please, Titch?'

'Aye Cap'n,' said Titch, and tugged out his long brown belt with accompanying buckle.

Robert undid and removed his own, and in a couple of ticks he had them joined together.

'What are you going to do, Cap'n?' asked Titch.

'I'm going to knock that key off and see if I can drag it along the floor to us.' Thus, holding one end of the connected belts, Robert flicked the buckled end at the hanging key. No luck! He tried again. No luck. And again. The key was well hooked on.

'May I try, Cap'n?' asked Titch.

'Sure, but hold onto the end tightly. Otherwise we could lose it.'

'Aye Cap'n,' said Titch, and promptly flicked the dangling key right off on his first attempt. It dropped onto the planked floor with a clonk.

'Wow!' said Robert, impressed.

'We play something similar on The Lightning, Cap'n. And I can lick anybody.'

Titch seemed a modest fellow by nature, but this new boastful version was also agreeable to Robert.

It didn't take the boys long to nudge the key near enough to snatch it through the bars. They were free!

'What now, Cap'n?' asked Titch. 'Should we try and open the door?'

'Not yet,' said Robert, thinking.

'What then, Cap'n?'

Suddenly, there was a horrendous crash and everything in the room became fuzzy for a few seconds. Instinctively, Robert and Titch threw themselves onto the floor and covered their heads as splinters of wood and other debris flew around, while a cloud of dust puffed out from the opposite end of the room. The lantern flickered but had not been extinguished by the jolt.

'What was that?' cried Robert. 'We must've been hit by a cannon ball!'

Titch, raising himself first, checked the other end of the room. 'Not a cannon ball, Cap'n, probably from a saker, the impact was too small. A forty two pounder would have taken the whole room out. Now that they know our distance though, I reckon the forty two pounder is next up.'

'Then Blackjack's in big trouble,' said Robert, standing up. 'And so are we!'

'Damage report!' yelled a voice, not far away. 'Damage report!' And quick heavy footsteps thudded back and forth, but no replies were forthcoming.

The two boys viewed the aftermath. Broken bits of wood seemed the main damage, but it was difficult to estimate what had been done as there had been little order in the room in the first place. A constant stream of fruity smelling liquid leaked from a couple of chunky casks and had given the place an appealing smell, but a somewhat sticky floor.

The cloud of dust which had followed the explosion cleared quickly and Robert saw why. There was a gaping hole in the side of the ship. Its perimeter covered in jagged pieces of wood. Debris lay everywhere. If this was an example of the damage a small cannon ball could inflict, what would a forty two pounder do!

Robert had guessed their prison cell was right on the waterline but on approaching the hole he could now clearly see that they were thankfully a little above this. A short bit of dark brown boat was all that was between them and the relatively calm water below. Then, on looking up, he saw what all the fuss was about. A ship, with enormous white sails, was well below the horizon and heading this way. It was likely the one that had fired the shot.

'Blimey!' exclaimed Titch. 'Check the size of her!'

'I know. It doesn't look good for Blackjack,' said Robert. 'Here, help me push this over.' And he positioned his arms around a large wooden barrel.

'What are ye going to do, Cap'n?' asked Titch, placing his shoulder against the barrel.

Robert wasn't listening, so wrapped up in his new plan was he.

The barrel dropped onto its side with a thud, and the boys congratulated each other.

'What are ye gonna do, Cap'n?' asked Titch for a second time, while wiping his nose on his sleeve.

'If my mum saw you doing that,' said Robert quickly, 'she'd go ballistic!'

'Go what?'

'Go ballistic. Go mad. She hates it when I wipe my nose on my sleeve.'

Titch just stared back with a blank expression on his face, unsure whether he'd done something wrong or not.

'What we'll do is roll the barrel over to the hole and drop it into the water,' said Robert. 'Then we'll jump out and use it to hold on to. That ship's bound to see us and help. We'll tell them we were taken prisoners, which is the truth.' He was pleased with his plan.

Titch, however, looked troubled on hearing the proposal.

'What's wrong?' asked Robert.

'Two problems, Cap'n. That other ship, even if it does stop and doesn't just run on over the top of us, will reckon we're pirates too, fish us out, and hang us. No questions.'

'Oh. And the other problem?'

'I can't swim, Cap'n. None of us can.'

Robert was speechless. Living a life on the sea and being unable to swim! What happened if they fell in? They just drowned!

'It's easy,' he said, realizing they had to get a move on. 'You just move your arms forwards and backwards while kicking your legs like mad. Have you never tried it before?'

'Aye, once, Cap'n. We were anchored in a bay someplace really hot, and I jumped overboard. Reno said that's the best way to learn.'

'And what happened?'

'I nearly drowned. Bennett had to jump in and save me. He's the only one that can swim. I forgot about him.'

Robert stared at Titch, imagining him struggling and panicking in the calm bay. Now it would be the open sea, with big waves. Robert was a good swimmer, but he couldn't support Titch as well.

'I reckon yer right, Cap'n. Maybe I learned from the first time. How difficult can it be?'

But before Robert had thought any further, the door was thrown open and in hurried Mr Weasel.

'Eh! What skulduggery is going on here?' he cried, pulling out a dagger from his belt. 'I'll jab yous in the back. See if I don't!'

Robert was literally hanging out of the jagged hole at this point and it wouldn't have taken much to drop right out, but without the barrel for help and having to leave Titch behind, he knew it was hopeless. He raised his hands into the air.

'Come closer!' demanded Mr Weasel. 'How did ye get out?'

'The door blew open,' said Robert.

'Ugh,' grunted Mr Weasel. 'The Cap'n wants ye up top.'

Robert's mind started to race. What did Blackjack want him for? He couldn't very well ask Mr Weasel. The least spoken to him the better.

'Move!' ordered Mr Weasel, replacing his dagger.

As Robert passed by, the pirate cuffed him around the head. Robert stumbled.

'Move!' repeated Mr Weasel.

Climbing through the deck above, the pungent smell of used gunpowder was everywhere, with clouds of white smoke from the discharged guns struggling to clear. The boys' eyes immediately started to sting and they were both mighty grateful to get out into the open air of the top deck.

Nothing was as Robert had expected though. He had anticipated a somewhat frantic scene, men shouting and running, guns firing, smoke billowing, noise, blood, everything that happens in the movies. Instead, they were greeted by an idle Blackjack.

'Ah, the scallywags have joined us,' he said.

Blackjack was different now, though, sweat was trickling down either side of his face and his clothes were covered in a fine dust and bits of debris.

The two boys looked around themselves and quickly grasped the severity of the situation. On the starboard side was the warship they had seen through the cannon hole, except that now it was even closer, and on the port side was, as Robert had suspected, a second ship.

'Now ye see my problem, MacSpoon,' said Blackjack, while producing a colourful handkerchief to mop his wet brow. 'If ye could do us a little turn and call the fog then we'd be mighty grateful.'

There were grunts of agreement, and the boys subsequently noticed that they were right in the middle of Blackjack's well armed crew.

What the boys couldn't see was a white flag of surrender fluttering high up on the main mast.

'Call the fog, lad and look sharp about it,' said Blackjack.

'Oh,' said Robert. 'I don't know.'

The crew were not best pleased at this reply. 'Let Giant whip the skin off his back,' said one. 'Kill the little 'un,' said another.

'Three quarters of a mile, Captain!' hollered a voice from the crow's nest high above in the sails. 'Still closing fast!'

'They'll hang ye, lad!' said Blackjack, his eyes fiery.

Robert's head throbbed. He couldn't do it, even if he wanted to.

'Call it!' snapped Blackjack. 'Or I'll let ma men have ye.'

Robert was frozen to the spot.

'I'll kill ye myself!' roared Blackjack, drawing his dagger.

Robert had to think fast. 'I'll do it,' he said. 'Give us a boat and I'll call the fog.'

'You'll get yer boat,' nodded Blackjack. 'Any man have any objections to giving the rascals a boat?'

None spoke.

'Half mile, Captain!'

Robert momentarily caught the eye of a small dumpy man with a set of biceps to match a wrestler's and a face to match an angel's.

'What ye looking at!' snarled the man. Nugget was his name. 'Got something to say?'

'Nothing,' stuttered Robert. Everybody was so aggressive.

'You'll get yer boat,' said Blackjack. 'Now where's my fog!'

'Boat first, then fog,' said Robert. He was not about to put his trust in Blackjack.

'Quarter mile, Captain!'

'Make ready the skiff!' ordered Blackjack. 'And look lively!'

A rowing boat was hastily unfastened and lowered as the two huge warships drew endlessly closer, their protruding cannons now clearly visible and individual sails no longer merged into one but easily definable. The crew were clearly jittery in the presence of such raw power, but they went about their task with the utmost efficiency. In no time Robert and Titch were ushered to the starboard side of the ship where a rowing boat was bobbing up and down in the moderate swell.

'Can we get some food and water?' asked Robert, as he and Titch gripped the side of the ship and peered down into the small rowing boat. A rope ladder dangled above it and ropes at either end prevented it from drifting away.

'Give it to them,' ordered Blackjack. 'Don't double cross me, MacSpoon, cos I'll blow ye out of the water.'

Mr Weasel immediately flung a small sack and a swollen bag into the boat.

'I won't double cross you,' said Robert. But he was going to. He couldn't call the fog.

Titch climbed down into the little rowing boat and Robert quickly followed. He'd never used a rope ladder before and it was far trickier than it looked, each rung tilting perilously with every step.

'Don't be a fool, MacSpoon,' said Blackjack. 'Them on those there ships will hang ye, laddie. And I want ma Book of Maps, so get yourselves out of here.'

Mr Weasel bent over the ship's side to watch, his face seething. A more spiteful and evil man Robert had never set eyes on.

'Cast off!' shouted Blackjack, and the two holding ropes were untied while the rope ladder was hauled up. A tall thin pirate with a long pole prodded them away.

The two vessels eased apart as the pirates watched on.

'Take yer drink!' hollered Mr Weasel.

These were the last words the boys heard from The Thunder as the gap swiftly grew.

'The warships are nearly upon us, Cap'n,' said Titch nervously. It was the first time he had spoken since they had left the lower deck.

'I know,' said Robert, but he was racked with worry. He couldn't call the fog. One blast from Blackjack's cannon and that would be it. Everything over. On the other hand, the British Navy could hang them both.

Shouts and movements from the starboard warship were now clearly audible and the ship's immense size was alarming. Hundreds of soldiers were lining the side of the ship, muskets raised, while rows upon rows of black cannons poked through their hatches. The sight was terrifying for Robert.

'I don't know what to do,' he blurted out. 'I've never done it before.'

'Close yer eyes, Cap'n,' said Titch. 'That's what the last captain did.'

Robert closed his eyes tightly, rather hoping that any second he'd open them and be back home.

Titch too had his eyes firmly shut, while his hands covered his ears.

Forthwith, the cries and sounds from the warship and The Thunder disappeared, and a wetness and coldness enveloped the small rowing boat. Robert instantly opened his eyes, and was overwhelmed by what he saw, or rather what he couldn't see. Nothing was visible in front of him, Titch could have been a million miles away, such was the thickness of the fog blanket. Robert touched his nose to be sure. Now he was certain he wasn't dead.

Titch too felt the wetness and chill on his body, and opened his eyes with a violent shiver. 'You did it, Cap'n!'

'Shh!' whispered Robert, wary of the fact that they might alert someone, and he bent forward and clapped what he thought was Titch's knee. 'I guess I did,' he said softly, as relief flooded through his chilled body, and he too shivered.

They were free. But this time, they were totally free.

8. Prisoners Again

The small rowing boat drifted aimlessly for what seemed an eternity to the pair of bedraggled boys. In truth, the time passed was of no great significance. The fog was simply playing tricks on their minds. With nothing to focus on in front or all around except for a cloud of greyish white, time was impossible to judge and therefore seemingly stagnant.

Neither boy took up the oars; with every other direction alike, it would have been pointless. Robert had also discovered, after tracing the contents of the boat with his hands, that one of the oars was split - a few strokes would have likely broken it in two.

'Do ye reckon we're safe now, Cap'n?'

'I think so. There doesn't seem to be any sounds. But this fog could be blocking them. For all we know, we could still be right in the middle of the lion's den.'

'I'm cold,' said Titch, and his teeth started to chatter. His bony body was not best designed for the cold.

'Come over here. I'll put my arm around you,' said Robert, sympathetically.

Although the water was fairly calm, the boat was clearly being taken by a current. The fog, however, showed no such movements and clung around them in a most oppressive fashion. Their prison of bars had been replaced by a prison of fog.

'We should eat something,' said Robert, after his belly gave one almighty rumble. He hadn't eaten for ages, and now that the adrenaline had faded away, it was only presently that he was conscious of the fact.

'Biscuits!' said Titch, after rummaging in the small fibrous sack they had been given.

Robert blindly accepted a biscuit and took a bite. It was dry, hard and salty. But his hunger overcame the taste, and the two famished boys scoffed them greedily.

'I need a drink,' said Robert, as the moistureless biscuits began to suck away the saliva from inside his mouth.

Titch fumbled for the swollen bag of water and nudged it to Robert.

'No, you go first,' said Robert.

'No I can't, Cap'n,' said Titch. 'I'm not really allowed. The captain should always go first. If the others found out, they wouldn't like it. I shouldn't have gone first before.'

'But there's only us two here. How are they going to find out?'

Titch didn't reply. And not wishing to upset the apple cart, Robert reluctantly accepted. He uncorked the top and just as he was about to take his first gulp, had second thoughts. Instead, he poured a little of the liquid into his hand. Unable to see what was there, he sniffed it. It smelt fine.

Robert took a swig. 'Phooey!' he cried, spitting it out. 'It's sea water!'

'Weasel!' said Titch.

Robert continued to spit.

Right then, the fog completely vanished and there were blue skies all around. An intense heat instantly hit them and the brightness dazzled their unaccustomed eyes.

'Water, water, everywhere, but not a drop to drink!' said Robert, as he poured out the seawater into the clear turquoise sea. He had never seen such a beautiful colour of sea.

'What was that, Cap'n?'

'It's a saying. Everyplace is water, but you can't drink any of it.'

'Yer sure to like Fraser. He has a saying for everything.'

Robert smiled.

'Yer teeth are ever so pearly white, Cap'n,' said Titch.

'I just clean them normally,' said Robert.

'So how many times a month, Cap'n? Fraser uses his finger, I've seen him.'

'A month!' exclaimed Robert. 'Every day. Twice a day. Morning and night, my mum says.'

Titch went momentarily silent at the mention of Robert's mum. Then eventually said, 'Maybe we should row, Cap'n.'

'I don't think so,' said Robert, licking his cracked lips. His mouth too was bone dry. He knew they wouldn't last very long under these conditions but he was wary of trying to call the fog again. Not being able to control their destination was a huge problem. They couldn't just continuously jump around the seas, that might be even more dangerous. Now the water was at least calm. Deep down, he hoped for a passing ship, a friendly one, perhaps even one homewards bound.

'Ship ahoy!' cried the wiry barrelman high up in the crow's nest on the warship HMS Dumbarton. 'Five miles! Straight ahead! Port side!'

'Friend or foe!' queried Captain Donald Lighthouse, peering up at the crow's nest sited on top of the main mast, his dimpled chin pointing skywards. Poor eyesight prohibited him from seeing the aloft man, but he had good reason to keep up the pretence. He was growing old, and his time remaining as captain was dwindling fast. His hair, although plentiful, was now entirely grey. His joints ached ceaselessly and he was continuously fatigued. He was a spent force, but still he had no wish to retire. Being a widower with no children, the navy was his family, his life; without it he had nothing except a pathetic pension and death to look forward to. A somewhat pernickety fellow, he was nonetheless a decidedly noble man.

'Can't say yet, Captain!' bellowed the barrelman high above with a spyglass pressed to one eye. 'Small vessel! Rowing boat, Captain! Straight ahead!'

Captain Lighthouse pulled a brass spyglass from his pocket and after extending it, pretended to view the distant object. 'Yes! Yes! I see it! How many on board!'

'Two, maybe three, Captain!' shouted the man immediately.

'Pirates likely, from our skirmish,' said Officer Campbell, his hooked nose protruding from his mahogany face. 'Shall I give the orders to run them down, Captain?'

'No we shall not, Officer Campbell!' said Captain Lighthouse, curtly. 'There'll be no barbarism on this ship. They shall be retrieved, trialled, and hanged as pirates. We are the ones with morality and righteousness on our side.'

Campbell was furious.

Officer Campbell was a below average sized man with an above average sized ego. He hated being subordinate to anybody, let alone to a decrepit old man such as Lighthouse, and he yearned for the day that this cripple retired. With dark beady eyes and thin stretched lips, it was his nose that dominated his face and left a lasting impression on anyone that met him, that and his brutal heartlessness.

'Aye, Captain,' he said sourly.

'I'll be going to my quarters now,' said Captain Lighthouse. 'I've some matters to attend to. I do not wish to be disturbed.'

'Aye, Captain,' repeated Campbell, well aware that his captain was going for a lie down.

When Captain Lighthouse had gone, Officer Campbell gave a sigh of relief. Now he had full control, not that bumbling buffoon. 'Full speed ahead!' he ordered. 'Run them over!'

'But the Captain said to pick them up?' questioned Bert Brown, the man at the helm.

'Two persons on the boat!' hollered the barrelman. 'Youngsters, both of them!'

'Captain's been laid low. I'm in charge now!' snapped Campbell. 'I've given you an order, Quartermaster Brown. Are you disobeying me?'

'No, Officer Campbell,' replied Bert Brown. He had no desire to cause the needless death of two children, pirates or otherwise, but he had no choice but to obey the order. Otherwise, the consequences would be severe.

Robert and Titch did not notice the warship making haste directly towards them. They had no telescope and the dazzling sun on the water made scanning the sea painful on their eyes. They had agreed that there was nothing they could do for the time being except let the current take them wherever it was going. Robert had still not settled on whether to again summon the fog, but with no water and in this heat, he felt he was only delaying the inevitable.

'I'm so thirsty,' said Titch, touching his dried lips.

But Robert didn't respond. He had his eyes fixed on a dark speck far off behind Titch's left shoulder. He stared transfixed, then shielded his eyes best he could against the sun's vicious glare with both hands.

Titch turned, unsettled by Robert's actions. 'It's a ship, Cap'n.'

'Yes,' said Robert. 'What else can it be?'

'Do ye reckon she's seen us?'

'For sure.'

'But how can ye be so sure, Cap'n?'

'Cos it doesn't move. It only gets bigger. It's like a tornado. If it's not moving then it's coming towards you. I've seen loads of them on TV.'

'What's TV, Cap'n?' asked Titch immediately.

'Ah! Mm. It's complicated. I'll explain it some other time.' But Robert wasn't sure he exactly knew where to start. I mean, how do you explain what a television is? And then there was electricity, that definitely hadn't been discovered yet, or had it?

'Do ye reckon they're friendly, Cap'n?'

'I hope so. I think we should take a chance and wait for them.'

They now waited as the ship got bigger and bigger and its sails fuller and fuller. Robert still wasn't sure whether he'd made the right decision, and hadn't just escaped one lion's den and jumped smack bang into another. They desperately needed something to drink, though. Shortly they would find out, as the ship was gaining on them at a good rate of knots. Actually, at an alarming rate of knots.

'Captain!' said Titch, in a concerned voice. 'It's one of those warships and she's not slowing down. Her sails are still full. Why isn't she reefing any canvas?'

'It looks like she's speeding up!' said Robert. 'Why would she do that?'

'I think she's gonna ram us!' cried Titch.

'They're gonna try and kill us!' shouted Robert. 'We need to get out of here.' And immediately, he grabbed one of the oars and jammed it into the rowlocks.

'We must do it together, Cap'n. Otherwise we'll just go round in circles,' said Titch, gathering up the second oar and placing it in the rowlocks. 'Ready, Cap'n!'

The two boys pulled on the oars with all their might. One stroke. Two strokes. Three strokes. Snap! Titch's oar came apart.

'I forgot about that,' groaned Robert. 'Try paddling with it! We need to get out of their path.'

Titch tried his hardest and the rowing boat started to move, ever so slightly, at right angles to the path of the oncoming ship. But time was running out. The boys were now frantic with fear. Robert had to call the fog.

On the warship HMS Dumbarton, Officer Campbell lowered his spyglass and retracted it. He was now nearly upon his quarry and wished to enjoy the moment with the naked eye. Soon, he would relish the snapping and splintering of wood as the warship, his warship, crushed the tiny rowing boat in the blink of an eye, ridding the seas of two more loathsome pirates. He had become quite excited with anticipation, nervously licking his lips dried by the sun and hot salty air. He imagined himself as the captain. How his crew would cower before him! The crew, too, were anticipating the spectacle

'Why are we not slowing down?' exclaimed Captain Lighthouse, suddenly arriving on deck, his arms flailing. 'Why have you disobeyed my orders?' And he glared at Bert Brown the helmsman.

'Officer Campbell changed those orders, Captain,' said Bert Brown firmly.

'Hogwash!' cried Captain Lighthouse. 'Stop this ship at once!'

'Aye, aye, Captain!' voiced Bert Brown, and he breathed a sigh of relief. There would be no senseless killings on his conscience.

'Officer Campbell! What is the meaning of this? Insubordination will not be tolerated.'

'They're pirates, Captain,' retaliated Officer Campbell, his nose in the air. 'This whole area is a haven for pirates. I was merely bringing them to justice, as is our mandate.'

'I don't believe that falls within your ambit, Officer Campbell,' snapped Captain Lighthouse, sensing the officer's lack of respect. 'What you were about to do was be judge, jury and executioner. Do I make myself clear, Officer Campbell?'

'Aye ... Captain,' said Officer Campbell.

The massive warship quickly slowed down in the crew's accomplished hands, while Officer Campbell looked on bitterly. He couldn't stand having to obey this softhearted invalid.

'Boat alongside, Captain!' declared a member of the crew, a shortish man with a pronounced lisp.

Immediately, another man stuck out a long wooden pole with a hook on the end of it, and snagged the small rowing boat. The boys looked at each other sombrely as they became prisoners yet again. At least they're not pirates, thought Robert.

'They won't shoot us, will they, Cap'n?' asked Titch under his breath, as the two vessels bumped gently together. 'I don't want to get shot.'

Robert twisted his neck to view the scores of soldiers lining the bulwarks. 'No they won't,' he whispered. 'They would have done it already. Just don't make any sudden movements.'

The end of a rope ladder was dropped into their rowing boat and Officer Campbell peered over the side of the gigantic warship, a frightful scowl on his face.

'Climb up!' he barked. 'Do you hide any weapons?'

Robert and Titch shook their heads obediently.

'Answer! Or you'll face the cat-o'-nine for impertinence!'

'No!' shouted Robert and Titch as one. They were already fearful of this rancorous individual.

'No, sir! Repeat!'

'No, sir,' said Robert and Titch together.

'Then what are you waiting for, you couple of filthy sea rats!'

Titch climbed up first, with exquisite nimbleness. A much more cumbersome Robert followed, and as he boarded, he received a sharp clout round the ear hole from Officer Campbell.

'That'll teach you to make the Captain wait!'

Captain Lighthouse stepped forwards and introduced himself gracefully, his mainly dark blue attire impeccably turned out.

'My name is Captain Donald Lighthouse, and I am captain of the warship HMS Dumbarton.'

Robert immediately grinned at the funny name. His name was also amusing to those unaccustomed to it, and it was of some relief to learn that others too had entertaining names.

Straightaway, Campbell rapped Robert on the legs with a short black stick similar to a policeman's truncheon.

'Ouch! That really hurt!' cried Robert, pain shooting up through his entire body. There would certainly be a bruise by nightfall.

'One more show of insolence, boy and you'll get a lot more than that,' barked Officer Campbell.

'Enough, Officer Campbell,' said Captain Lighthouse, adjusting his hat needlessly. 'What are your names, boys? Speak up. Time waits for no man.'

'My name is ... ' said Robert deliberately, but he didn't have time to complete the sentence.

'Duncan Stewart,' said Titch. 'And I'm his brother, Jim Stewart.'

Robert glanced at Titch discreetly. Why had Titch lied? Was the name Robert MacSpoon so dangerous?

'Don't slouch, boys. Stand up straight,' ordered Captain Lighthouse, who was a stickler for details. 'Come on, shoulders back, chests out.'

The two boys immediately straightened their backs and withdrew their shoulders.

'Are you pirates?' asked Officer Campbell, impatient at the slow nature of the interrogation. 'Were you the ones abandoning that pirate ship we were firing at?' And he swiftly prodded Titch in the belly with the truncheon. 'Let him speak.' And he nodded at Robert.

'Eh, no and yes,' replied Robert, but his answer only served to irritate Officer Campbell, who immediately raised his truncheon to strike again.

'Enough!' said Captain Lighthouse. 'The boy has answered. You state you are not pirates, but yet you say you were aboard that pirate ship. How can that be?'

'We were their prisoners,' said Robert. He paused momentarily to think. 'But they let us go.'

'And why would they do that?'

This was getting difficult, thought Robert. Telling the truth was definitely not an option. 'It was some sort of trap. But they didn't tell us what they were doing. They only said we were to get into the boat. And that we would probably die.'

'Likely story, Captain,' grunted Officer Campbell. 'It's crystal clear they're pirates. If it hadn't've been for that blasted fog we would have purged their comrades too.'

'Where are you from, boy?' asked Captain Lighthouse, addressing Robert.

Campbell held the truncheon across Titch's stomach, a sign to keep quiet.

Robert hesitated, but couldn't think fast enough. 'Rum,' he said. 'The Isle of Rum.'

Laughter erupted from all, except for Titch and Captain Lighthouse.

'I think he's been drinking some of the stuff,' said a second officer who had been speechless until then. He was clearly an officer as he was dressed identically to Officer Campbell, a dark blue uniform, pointed hat, flashy buttons, everything that set him apart from the ordinary seaman. A fair skinned, tall individual, he was the exact opposite of Campbell.

'And that would be beside the Isle of Whisky?' queried Officer Campbell, and a second bout of laughter ensued. But Captain Lighthouse immediately showed his displeasure and the crew hurriedly returned to their tasks.

'The lad's a spinner of yarns, Captain,' said the tall officer, whose name was Officer Bright.

'There is no such island,' said Captain Lighthouse, viewing Robert with a heavy frown on his face. 'Insubordination will be severely dealt with, my boy.'

'Shall I shackle them to the main mast, Captain?' asked Officer Campbell. He had torment on his mind.

'A second if you please, Officer Campbell,' said Captain Lighthouse, and he again turned to face Robert. 'Why do you lie to me, boy?'

'I don't,' said Robert, unsure as to what was happening. Surely this so-called captain had heard of Rum!

'And where lies your Isle of Rum?' Captain Lighthouse asked, irritation creeping into his voice.

'Why, off the coast of Scotland,' said Robert, assuredly.

'Well, boy, I've sailed around the whole of Europe and indeed most of the known world, yet I've never come across an Isle of Rum. Perhaps you are of the opinion that I am blind, boy?'

'The lad's a liar and a scoundrel, Captain!' cried Officer Bright. 'We should hang him high this very instant. Both of them! A good strong rope around their necks. It would set a good example to the men.'

'Aye!' agreed Officer Campbell. 'You've heard their lies, Captain. Now let me teach them a lesson they'll take to their grave.'

'For the last time, Officer Campbell. There'll be no lynching on my ship. These boys will be given a fair trial in Port Jamaica and then hanged as pirates. We are not the barbarians. They are!'

'But I'm not lying!' said Robert. 'I'm telling the truth.'

'You will come with me, boy,' said Captain Lighthouse, addressing Robert.

'And the other one, Captain?' asked Officer Campbell, as Titch gulped nervously at the thought of being left alone with such a brutish character.

'Take him below. And leave him be, Officer Campbell! That's an order!'

'Aye, Captain,' replied Officer Campbell coldly. 'And their vessel, Captain. What's to be done?'

'Target practice. Shoot it out of the water!'

The boys briefly glanced at each other before they were separated. Robert did as he was told and followed Captain Lighthouse towards the stern of the ship, while Titch was marched in the opposite direction.

Captain Lighthouse walked briskly and Robert hurried after him, unsure where he was being taken and why they had been separated. He was, however, relieved that he hadn't been tied to the main mast.

Captain Lighthouse stopped at the door of a large cabin in the stern of the ship. Robert couldn't help but be intrigued. Why was he getting a personal audience?

'In you go, boy,' said Captain Lighthouse.

The captain's cabin was predictably big inside, and extremely well lit from sloping windows on the sides, composed of numerous individual squares, and a large skylight in the ceiling. A dark wooden table, with umpteen papers and charts scattered on it, sat in the middle of the floor. With dark, reddish brown mahogany panels lining the walls and six hardwood chairs upholstered in red leather pushed up against them, the cabin looked impressive. As the skylight and windows were all closed, the room was hot and stuffy.

Captain Lighthouse immediately went over to a chair and sat down. 'Now boy,' he said, in a hushed voice. 'Do you stand by your tale or have you come to your senses?'

'Yes,' said Robert. 'I mean no,' he swiftly added, again confused at the wording of the question. Could they not ask a question and then wait for an answer before asking another question! They were worse than his mum!

'No need to fret, lad, I understand.' Captain Lighthouse then rose from his chair and went over to a second smaller table in the corner of the room, where a little metal box, some books, and an ornate lamp lay. Opening the tin, he removed a sweet and popped it into his mouth.

'Now then,' he said, striding over to the stern wall. 'Point out your Isle of Rum, boy,' and he pulled a cord which unrolled a gigantic map of Europe. Then he proceeded to draw miniature curtains in front of each and every window. The skylight, however, still amply lit the room.

Robert hadn't moved from the spot he had been standing on since entering.

'Well, you won't see it from there, boy,' said Captain Lighthouse, and he beckoned Robert closer with a wiry finger.

Robert obeyed and viewed the map. However, everything was so poorly drawn. The countries were there pretty much, but the detail was severely lacking. The scale was also too large to make out an island the size of Rum.

'The scale is too big. Do you have anything more accurate?'

'Of course,' said Captain Lighthouse, and pulled down a second map directly over the first. This one was of the British Isles.

Robert peered at the map, but the islands around Scotland were poorly defined and many weren't even named. And there was definitely no Rum. Meantime, he licked his dry lips. How he yearned for a glass of cold water. He would never again complain about having to drink tasteless water!

Captain Lighthouse then moved sideways and extended yet another rolled up map. This one was smaller than the two previous ones and contained only Scotland with its many islands.

Robert turned to examine this third map. He went up close and raising a finger pointed to where Rum lay, except for the fact that there was nothing to point at.

'That's funny,' he said. 'It should be there. This map is probably too old!'

'No, my boy. This map is brand new,' said Captain Lighthouse coolly. 'It hails from the finest Dutch cartographers. Your island does not exist.' And he began clucking his tongue noisily.

Robert stared at the map, completely flummoxed. He wasn't sure he could take any more strangeness.

'Are you frightened, boy?' asked Captain Lighthouse, after a few moments.

'No,' said Robert, and he truly wasn't.

'Mm, perhaps you're not fully aware of the situation you find yourself in.'

Suddenly, there was a loud knock on the cabin door.

'Go away!' ordered Captain Lighthouse. 'Now, tell me, boy. What do you know of The Book of Maps?'

Robert jumped, but continued to stare at the map on the wall. He didn't know much about The Book of Maps himself, and it was probably this that saved him.

'Tell me what you know,' whispered Captain Lighthouse.

'Book? What book?' said Robert.

'Mm,' said Captain Lighthouse, pacing around the warm, airless cabin. And then, all of a sudden, he grabbed a chair and dragged it over to the large central table. Next, he collected the sweetie tin and placed it on top of the table. 'Do you like sweets, boy?'

'Yes, sir,' replied Robert. Who didn't? But he would have much preferred a glass of cool water, dripping down his throat and hydrating his gluey saliva. Mmm.

'Well help yourself, boy. Here, take a seat.' And Captain Lighthouse pushed the mahogany chair forwards for Robert to sit on.

Robert sat down and delved into the silvery metal box. The sweets were not hard but not soft either, and were covered in a white sugary powder. They tasted simply delicious, and he consumed them greedily having barely eaten anything in what seemed a lifetime.

Beside the main door lay a third table, small but tall, and on it were two fair sized glasses and a jug of water. Robert had been too preoccupied in the beginning to notice it, but on hearing the tinkling of water being poured, his ears pricked up and his appetite quite disappeared. He licked his parched lips hopefully.

'Would you like a drink of water, Robert?'

Robert was within a hair's breadth of answering, but he recovered. 'That's not my name, sir. But yes I would like a drink of water. Thank you, sir.'

'Then take it,' Lighthouse grumbled, clanking the filled glass down. He knew it had been a shot in the dark, but the boy had referred to a mysterious island. The whole affair did seem somewhat far-fetched, however, having Robert MacSpoon clutching The Book of Maps fall straight into his lap. Did the boy even exist? Did the book? I mean, it was all from some condemned fellow who would have said anything to keep himself alive. 'Guard!' he shouted. 'Guard!'

Robert gulped down the warm water. It felt delightful, but he knew he only had seconds.

'Take him below,' ordered Captain Lighthouse, when a soldier with very few teeth appeared.

When he was alone, and after opening the curtains, Captain Lighthouse sat down on the same seat Robert had been using. The elderly captain mused while rubbing his chin with his thumb and forefinger. Eventually he picked out one of the few remaining sweets and popped it into his mouth. His desire for sugary treats had oddly increased with age, as had his gullibility it seems. Isle of Rum indeed! What he wanted more than anything right then, was a refreshing nap.

The stairs to the decks below were narrow and steep. The first deck Robert arrived on was full of cannons, of immense size, and men, the majority of whom were sitting or lying on strung out hammocks. The mood was surprisingly relaxed and the atmosphere light and airy due to most of the gun ports being wide open. Nobody gave him a second glance.

He was marched downwards two more flights of tight wooden steps, firstly into the heart and then into the bottom of the ship. The lower they went the darker it got. The soldier eventually stopped over a generously sized trapdoor, raised it, and prodded Robert downwards.

'Hey, Cap'n,' said Titch, when the trapdoor had been bolted shut.

'Hi Titch,' said Robert, inhaling the damp musty air, his eyes hurriedly adjusting to the lack of light. 'Are you alright?'

'Aye, Cap'n. They let me be.'

Robert could now make out his friend, sitting on the stinking wooden floor, his hands wrapped around his skinny knees.

'Thanks for the new name,' whispered Robert.

'Yer welcome, Cap'n,' said Titch. 'It's always best to give nothing away. Did the captain beat ye, Cap'n?'

'No, he only asked about The Book of Maps. But I don't know anything.'

'The last captain is who ye should speak to, Cap'n,' said Titch, then he paused. 'We're in the Caribbean, Cap'n. We dock tomorrow morning.'

'Oh,' said Robert. 'Well, I like the sunshine. And I've never seen a real life coconut tree before.'

But it was going to be another unpleasant night, in their dank, dark surroundings.

9. In A Real Prison

Port Jamaica was one of the largest and busiest ports in the Americas. Scores of ships and boats of every shape and size under the sun lined up to be loaded or unloaded, whilst others anchored themselves a little farther out, patiently waiting their turn to dock or simply to avoid docking fees. The quayside was literally, and continuously, humming with life, everybody having their own particular job to carry out.

The houses were small and cramped, mostly one or two storey, and invariably covered with grey black moulds encouraged by the ever present warm wet air. Streets were narrow and side streets were narrower still. The main ones were generally cobbled but the rest were composed of compact mud, squashed down by the endless movement of people and things to and fro.

The town was deceptively pretty and picturesque when viewed from offshore, with its beautiful mountains behind and golden sands in front. The reality was somewhat different though. It was dirty and decaying. It was also dangerous, very dangerous, being a magnet for pirates and privateers, and altogether bad characters. Such persons were tolerated to varying degrees in the town and surrounding areas, very much depending on the particular governor in charge. The current governor was the recently appointed William Haggish, a strict disciplinarian, and determined to clean up the town.

Governor Haggish resided in a modest mansion adjacent to the soldiers' barracks and the town's jailhouse. Since good ground was at a premium, his home was the only place in town with a meaningfully sized garden. A high wall provided seclusion, and although not perfect, it did offer some degree of security.

The Governor was married and had one child, a girl called Annabel, who was nearly in her teens. He was also guardian to his niece, the child of his brother whom, along with his wife, had died when the girl was a mere toddler. Her name was Rebecca.

The warship HMS Dumbarton docked at daybreak as Robert and Titch slept in her belly. Their sleep was surprisingly pleasant considering the conditions and circumstances. Titch had, however, stated the night before that he was so tired he could sleep on the edge of a knife. Robert had agreed, so perhaps their productive slumber was not so wholly unexpected.

As the HMS Dumbarton was a warship and not a cargo ship, there would be very little transfer of items to and from the quayside. The main movement of goods would take place at a later date when the ship was being resupplied prior to setting sail again. For now, the ship, like the crew, was in need of a break. The sails were furled, and the soldiers and sailors were busily disembarking. Soon, only a skeleton crew would remain.

'We've definitely stopped, Cap'n,' said Titch sleepily.

Just then, the bolt on the trapdoor above was dragged sideways and the hatch was yanked open.

'Prisoners out!' ordered a soldier in a gruff voice.

Robert wasn't sure what to expect when he stepped out into the bright sunshine after ascending the decks, but everything still took him by surprise. There were ships and boats, schooners and sloops, big vessels and little vessels, all for as far as the eye could see. And the quayside was simply teaming with people, animals and wares from every place under the sun. As the people talked and shouted, the animals bleated and clucked. The noise was intense and merged into one almighty din.

'Have you been here before?' whispered Robert, as the two boys stood by the main mast awaiting their fate.

'No, never,' said Titch, without moving his lips.

Captain Lighthouse approached from the stern, accompanied by Officer Campbell. 'Well, boys,' he said. 'I shall see you both tomorrow morning.' And with that he promptly departed the ship.

Campbell, alas, remained. His eyes gleaming with malice. 'Do you know why he'll see you both tomorrow morning?'

'For breakfast?' said Robert. It just shot out.

In a flash, Campbell flicked up his truncheon and jabbed it right into Robert's belly. Robert doubled up breathless. 'Not so amusing now, eh,' said the officer. 'But tomorrow is when you'll get yer real comeuppance, lad. Both of ye. The gallows is where you're going. We'll see if yer so jocular then. Take them away!'

The boys were escorted off the ship via the gangway by two overly enthusiastic soldiers, who kept prodding them in the back.

'Blast! Where is that idiot jailer with the wagon,' grumped one of the soldiers. 'I'm not walking all the way up to the jailhouse in this heat.' And he wiped his brow with his sleeve.

'Stop moaning, man! At least we're off that ship,' said the second soldier. 'I always get bothered with seasickness. My old woman said I should have been a farmer.'

'Oh, give it up. You sound like my old lady,' returned the first soldier, who had a clearly defined squint.

'And what are you two looking at?' snapped the soldier with the squint. 'Have you heard about the entertainment tomorrow? You're it!'

'Leave them be,' said the second soldier. 'They're only bairns.'

'Pirates! That's what they are, and they'll swing for it! Couple of sea urchins.'

'Not if we escape first,' said Robert, looking at the soldier with the squint. Although Robert wasn't a hundred percent sure if his gaze was being reciprocated.

'Ha ha!' the soldier exclaimed. 'If only I could wager on that.'

'Wagering is like throwing yer money down a wishing well,' said the second soldier.

They were interrupted when a rickety old wagon with a man upfront drew up.

'Yer late!' grumped the soldier with the squint.

The driver didn't respond, instead he turned his raddled face away from the sun and patiently waited, his long greasy hair hiding every last bit of his large head. Meantime, the two boys were ordered onto the cart, the soldiers quickly followed, and after all had settled down, the driver, still not having uttered one word, flicked a short whip and they set forth.

The ground at the quayside was very uneven and the ride was extremely bumpy. Robert observed the multitude of faces and goods, staring longingly at the piles of pineapples, mangoes, and coconuts that were stacked up on numerous trestles lining the streets. How he longed to bite into one. Titch too had noticed them, and the boys exchanged hungry glances.

The cart was being pulled by a single grey mule which had certainly seen better days, and what with the excess weight and mugginess, it began to really struggle up the gradient, panting and snorting noisily. Robert noticed the poor animal's suffering and wanted to say something, busily preparing himself, but their journey was to end before he had the chance.

They had come through a narrow iron gate, which was guarded by two soldiers with muskets who barely looked up. A high wall now surrounded them. They were in the prison yard. A massive pile of muck was piled up high against one of the side walls and hundreds of flies were buzzing around it feverishly. Old bits of wooden crates had been placed on top of the pile to reduce the stink, but it had not been overly successful.

Robert whacked a fat juicy fly which had landed on his arm and watched it drop onto the dirty floor of the cart. He wondered what was about to happen to them. He knew they were going to be locked up. But when was the trial? Tonight? Titch smiled at him nervously.

'I could have crawled quicker!' moaned the soldier with the squint, as he sprang out of the wagon. 'Time you bought yersel a new mule, driver.'

The driver ignored the unpleasant comment and sat motionless as the party jumped off.

The prison was built on two levels, with the ground floor having small square windows with vertical bars covering them, and the top floor having tiny windows, again with vertical bars protecting them. It was constructed of red brick with patches of weather beaten whitewashing, and had a tiled pointed roof. On the whole, like everything on the island, it was not in very good shape.

The soldier with the squint led the way, with the second soldier bringing up the rear. After crossing the yard the boys were escorted through the main door, and instantly the stench that hit them was overwhelming.

'Yuck!' said Robert. 'I think you need some fresh air in here!'

'If ye think this is bad, wait till ye get upstairs,' laughed the soldier with the squint.

Sure enough, after passing a bored looking guard who was picking his fingernails with a knife, and after climbing more than two dozen stone steps, the stench actually got worse.

The stairs opened out into a room that was large, dirty and shadowy. A young thin man, sitting on a stool whittling a piece of wood with a small knife, watched them coming in. He was right next to a strong wooden door which had a rectangular barred window at the top.

'Get up, lad! Show some respect!' snapped the soldier with the squint.

The young man duly jumped up and straightened himself out, giving an awkward half salute in the process. He longed to be a soldier one day himself, or maybe even a sailor. If only his father would give his consent.

'Where's the usual fat one?' asked the soldier with the squint.

'Err, well, I'm not really sure,' said the young man. 'I think he's gone to the privy,' he added, rather unconvincingly.

'Pathetic story! Likely had a skinful and sleeping it off somewhere. Dereliction of duty, that's what it is. I've a mind to report it. Anyway, we've got two prisoners to house. Have you got the space?'

'Lots,' said the young man. 'Everybody's been hanged. We've only got four prisoners left in the whole place. Came in last night they did. Drunken rabble.'

After glancing around nervously, the young man took hold of a large key which was already in the door's lock, and turned it noiselessly. Port Jamaica clearly had a master locksmith in its midst.

'Eh, I'll need to search them first,' the young man said, after plucking up enough courage, and he turned his head and looked gingerly at the two soldiers, awaiting their permission.

'Officer Campbell already searched us,' said Robert quickly. 'He probably didn't do it well though.'

'No, no,' said the young man. He knew of Officer Campbell's reputation. And then he recovered himself, annoyed at a prisoner, particularly one younger than himself, being so outspoken. 'I'll search ye if I want to search ye!'

'No need,' growled the soldier with the squint, keen to speed things up.

Just as the thick wooden door was being opened, a large fat man bustled into the room. 'Everything's under control!' he cried. 'Had a bit of a predicament.'

'Run out of rum, did you?' said the soldier with the squint.

'No need for accusations. I don't say anything against you.'

He was a man of over fifty, little hair, an enormous red nose which matched the rest of his crimson face and possessed heavy jowls. He was sweating profusely.

'We don't have many in,' he continued, pushing through the open door first. 'They've all been hanged by that new governor.'

The air inside was boiling and stale as well as the ever present stench, and Robert found it difficult to inhale. With few windows, it was also not at all light.

'I'll house them at the end of the corridor,' continued the fat jailer. 'Away from these other fellows. And what have you been up to, ye young scamps?' he added, turning to Robert and Titch who were deliberately walking slowly behind.

'Pirates!' said the soldier with the squint. 'To be hanged first thing tomorrow morning. You'll no earn much from these ones.'

'Won't we be having a trial first?' asked Robert, shocked at what he'd just heard.

'Shouldn't think so. The last ones never did,' grinned the soldier with the squint.

Robert gasped. 'But we haven't told our side of the story. It's not fair. It's illegal!'

'Listen to him, a pirate gabbing about legal stuff! Life isn't fair, boy. If it was, I'd be a captain by now.'

'Maybe yer just not able enough,' said the second soldier.

'What do ye mean by that? I can read.'

'Well, if ye were any good you'd have made promotion by now.'

As the two soldiers verbally jousted with each other, Robert felt a pair of eyes boring into the side of his head. The argument had stopped them a short distance from the end of the corridor, and someone was definitely observing him from within one of the darkened prison cells. Then a pair of hands gripped the rusting bars and a face emerged from the darkness, a recognizable face. It was Blackjack, and seeing that he had been recognized, he grinned.

'Do ye know this man?' asked the fat jailer, staring at Robert inquisitively.

'No,' said Robert. 'Should I?'

79

The two soldiers immediately stopped their petty squabble and the soldier with the squint assumed control. 'Do ye know these lads?' he asked, turning to face Blackjack directly.

Blackjack pushed his face even closer to the bars, and ignoring the soldier's question, stared straight at Robert.

'No,' Blackjack eventually replied. 'I'm just a poor honest fisherman who likes his rum and sometimes sups a bit too much when he's with his mates. I know no pirates.'

'And how, pray tell, do ye know they're pirates?'

'I have ears,' replied Blackjack curtly. 'I heard ye telling the fat man.' And everybody automatically turned to the fat jailer, who looked around himself uncomfortably.

'I hope yer not referring to me?' he said, jabbing a finger at Blackjack.

'None other,' said Blackjack. 'And be wary of who yer pointing a finger at, matey!'

'You're probably just big-boned,' said Robert immediately. 'My mum says some people have bigger bones than others.'

'Thanks, young man. It's a pity you won't be with us after tomorrow morning,' and the fat jailer patted Robert on the head affectionately.

'Get them inside a cell,' snapped the soldier with the squint. 'We need to be off.'

'I'll put them in one of the middle ones,' pondered the fat jailer. 'Away from these ... fishermen, and seeing as they're to be executed first thing tomorrow morning.'

Robert winced. They didn't have to keep repeating it.

The fat jailer quickly backtracked and opened a heavy barred door; Robert and Titch reluctantly stepped inside.

'We're off then!' said the soldier with the squint, departing with his comrade.

The door was locked without a further word being spoken and the two boys were now inside their third prison cell in a very short period of time.

'Ye did search them? Didn't ye, lad?' said the fat jailer to the young man who was again seated on his wooden stool, whittling away.

'Yes, Father,' replied the young man, but he kept his head down.

'Good! Well I've got some really important chores to attend to, so I'll take my leave.' And with that, he wheeled his portly body around and left.

The young man sighed heavily, resigned to his task, and continued with his carving.

Robert and Titch sat down together on an extremely uncomfortable bench which was positioned hard up against the brick wall of the cell. A tiny window with two tiny vertical bars down its centre provided only the merest of light, and meant little fresh air percolated through. Across from them was a second identical wooden bench.

'I reckon these are our beds for tonight, Cap'n,' said Titch.

'Yep,' said Robert, but his mind was elsewhere. The wheels in his head were beginning to turn.

'Do ye really think they'll hang us, Cap'n?'

'They won't get the chance,' said Robert softly. 'Remember the keys? I've still got them and I just know one of them will fit.'

Just then, a heavy wagon trundled into the courtyard outside and the sound of hefty wheels on uneven cobbles echoed around the prison.

'I hope it's not more prisoners,' said Robert, ears pricked up. 'The less prisoners the better.'

'Should we try the keys now, Cap'n?' whispered Titch, and then he paused. 'But what about the prison guard, and all the soldiers we passed, and the other doors.' And rapidly his enthusiasm drained away.

'My mum always says, one step at a time,' said Robert. 'And I think that's what we should do. Let's wait for dark and see if we get something to eat or drink first.'

'Aye, Cap'n. Wonder what they'll do with Blackjack?'

'Something's fishy there,' said Robert quietly. 'I don't think they know who he is. But when they do, he's not going to like it. Some fishermen!'

Then, Robert took a deep breath and shouted. 'Where's our food and water? Captain Lighthouse and Officer Campbell and Officer Bright of the warship HMS Dumbarton told us we'd get food and water. And they'd find out if we didn't!' He just knew the young man was back on his own again.

10. Escape

Robert's outburst soon paid dividends. They were hurriedly given biscuits to eat and water to drink. The jailer's son had been quick on his toes. The water was surprisingly sweet, being from one of the many streams originating in the island's mountains.

Blackjack and his three comrades had also gotten their share. Indeed, on receiving theirs they had even jeered the jailer's son emboldened in the knowledge that the young man was quite alone.

The boys waited patiently, as late morning turned into afternoon and then into early evening. As the evening wore on the sun started to set, remarkably quickly as it does in the tropics, and darkness rapidly began to envelop the town. Port Jamaica at night was even more terrifying than Port Jamaica during the day!

Robert traced the five keys in his pocket. He was itching to try them out, but had so far managed to restrain himself. In the darkness noises seemed different, usually more scary, and he was hoping the jailer's son would be much less likely to investigate if he heard something untoward.

'We'll try the keys soon,' he whispered. 'A few more minutes should do it.'

'But what about Blackjack and his men, Cap'n?' asked Titch.

'We'll be really quiet.'

'And what about the other locked door and that guy on the stool, Cap'n?'

'Don't worry so much, I've got a plan,' said Robert confidently. 'We unlock this door. Sneak up to the other door. It's solid so he can't see us.

We wait until he goes to the toilet or something ... Did you see that the key was left in the lock?'

Titch nodded, not sure why this was relevant.

'I'll take off my shirt and flick it under the door. There's a bit of a gap I noticed. And then we'll knock out the key from our side. It lands on the shirt and we pull it through. Hey presto! We're free!'

Titch was so pleased he clapped his hands.

'Shush!' whispered Robert loudly. 'We need to be quiet. But first we wait till it gets totally dark. That way nobody will see us.'

'It's a fair plan, Cap'n,' said Titch quietly.

Robert nervously felt the keys in his pocket for a second time. He couldn't imagine what they would do if none of them opened the door.

Suddenly, there came a shout from Blackjack's cell, but it wasn't Blackjack. 'More water, lad! My mouth's as dry as the Arabian desert in here! That is, unless you've got some rum lurking about! I'll pay ye handsome, mind!'

'Oh great,' said Robert. 'That's all we need.'

But no reply or response of any kind came, even after the shout had been repeated, almost word for word.

'Nobody's there,' whispered Robert into Titch's ear. 'As soon as Blackjack's lot quieten down, we're going.'

They waited, but not for long, as Blackjack's companion had come to the same conclusion.

Robert hurriedly unzipped his pocket, pulled out a key and tried it. It didn't fit. A second key was too big. Immediately he selected the smallest one, and unbelievably in it slid, turning effortlessly and soundlessly. He breathed a huge sigh of relief. They had taken a big first step towards freedom. And a key had actually worked!

The two children looked at each other in the near total darkness. They had the broadest grins on their faces.

The heavy door opened noiselessly and out they tiptoed, gently closing it behind them. Now in the corridor, it was minutely lighter, due to a more normal sized window at the end of it, which clearly showed complete darkness had all but arrived in Port Jamaica. Everything was incredibly spooky for two young boys out all on their own.

'Achoo.' Titch let out a muffled sneeze. It was barely audible. The boys froze. Silence returned and they continued.

'Psst!'

Robert and Titch stopped dead in their tracks. They had both heard it, so it hadn't been their imagination playing tricks on them in the twilight.

'Psst!' came a second time, louder and deeper.

They both turned with sinking hearts to see a hand waving at them. Titch looked at Robert, but Robert was already heading towards the hand.

'Well, if it isn't my old shipmate,' whispered Blackjack, when their eyes met. 'No need to look so guilty, lads, it's not as if you've been caught scrumping.'

Robert showed a blank expression on his face but even in the darksome corridor Blackjack noticed.

'Thieving apples, lad,' he said in a whisper. Then he shook his head. 'Yer not bailing out on us, are ye, lads? I mean, with us being mates an all.'

'Why should we help you?' said Robert, his eyes straining to see who else was inside Blackjack's cell.

'Now let me think,' replied Blackjack, rubbing his beard. 'And let us agree we don't have much time. I'll give ye reasons, and mighty big reasons they are too. I'll get ye out of here. I know where to go. You'll only get caught if ye go the front way, but there's another way, into the backyard and over the wall.' He paused momentarily. 'And then there's Rum, I'll get ye back. None else can.'

Robert's heart skipped a beat. 'How can we trust you?'

'There's honesty in all fellows, MacSpoon,' said Blackjack, deliberately. 'And what does yer mate say? He looks a canny sort.'

'What do you think?' whispered Robert into Titch's ear.

'We need to hurry,' mumbled Titch. 'Maybe it's a fair deal.'

Still gripping the same key which had opened his door, Robert freely unlocked Blackjack's door.

'A key, behold,' said Blackjack. 'That I reckoned.'

But Robert wasn't listening. He had his eyes fixed on a creature who had just stepped out from the darkness.

'MacSpoon, lad,' said Weasel. 'We'll be mates now.'

Robert and Titch swiftly turned to go.

'Get that other door opened!' growled Blackjack. 'We'll be right behind ye.'

The corridor was fairly long, with many empty cells on either side. The boys kept low but with the only light coming from behind the locked door in front of them, there was little chance they could be seen. They reached the thick wooden door without a sound, and straightaway Titch lay down on his belly, eyes fixed to the gap under the door. Robert held his breath.

'All clear,' whispered Titch.

Robert instantly pulled off his shirt and flicked it out underneath the door, directly below the installed key. Then, after removing one of his own keys, he started to push out the door key. Plop! It dropped onto his shirt and he reeled it in. The key was slotted home and the heavy door opened. Immediately, he turned to gesture to Blackjack, but he was too late. The four pirates were directly behind him and he hadn't heard as much as a whisper. A cold shiver ran down his spine.

Just then, a cough followed by a sharp sniff echoed in the stairwell. Blackjack instantly motioned for everyone to line up against the wall. All obeyed. A second later the jailer's son scuffled through the archway, whereupon Blackjack dropped his muscular arm onto the neck of the slender youth, who crumpled unceremoniously to the floor.

'Get him out of sight!' ordered Blackjack. 'And no killing, mind.'

Sure enough, Weasel was the one to carry out his bidding. The jailer's son was partially stripped and his own clothing used to tie and gag him. He was then dragged away to a cell by the bowlegged pirate.

Light from a burning torch now showed up the other crew members. The first was a man of medium height and build, bald on top with his remaining hair greased back into a pigtail. His most defining feature, though, was the deep cut running down the left side of his face, straight through his eye, and consequently he had no left eye, just a semi-closed gap. The result was one of the scariest individuals a person could ever hope to meet. His name was One Eye.

The final crew member making up the quartet, was a young man not yet scarred by a life of piracy and good looking in all respects, but for round shoulders and an obvious hump on his back. His name was Hunch. Robert felt that this man was probably the only one of the motley bunch with an ounce of decency inside him.

'Now look sharp, ye laggards,' growled Blackjack. 'Time's a running and that fat oaf could be back any moment.' Then, in the blink of an eye he was gone.

Everybody immediately followed. They were led through the adjacent room and down the stairs which the jailer's son had just come up, but instead of descending to the ground floor, Blackjack guided them off to the side about two thirds of the way down. The odd flaming torch offered just enough light to navigate.

'Hush yersels!' snapped Blackjack, as everybody bunched up together.

They were before an open door and a clear stretch of corridor lay ahead, but to the right underneath a series of shadowy archways, sat a soldier. Thankfully, his back was towards them.

'One at a time,' whispered Blackjack, raising his index finger to emphasize the point. Whereupon, he decamped, and as quiet as a church mouse traversed the open quarter.

One Eye went next, followed by Weasel, and time most definitely stood still for those left behind.

When Hunch took his turn, Titch whispered to Robert. 'Do ye trust Blackjack, Cap'n?'

'About as far as I could throw him,' replied Robert softly. 'And I don't think I could throw him very far!' Then he viewed the disappearing pirates in front of him. 'But I don't think we have much choice.'

Hunch had made it across by now, and the soldier was still seated, musket on lap.

'You go,' whispered Robert, and Titch was off.

The small thin boy tiptoed effortlessly across the sizeable corridor until he had reached about halfway, when suddenly the soldier stood up, musket in hand. Titch froze, his foot still in midair. Delicately he placed it down. Robert held his breath, but along with Titch he was the only one, as Blackjack and his men were already gone. The soldier stood motionless, scratched his rear, and plopped himself back down. Robert breathed again, and immediately set off after his friend.

On reaching the other side, Titch turned round and was surprised to find Robert nearly beside him. They didn't speak, however, they simply had to catch up with Blackjack and his men.

It was now quite dark where they walked, the light from the solitary lantern beside the soldier having finally dissipated. It was eerily quiet too as they moved hurriedly forwards, more in hope than expectation. They had no real plan and time was surely running out.

'I reckon we've lost them, Cap'n,' said Titch.

Robert pointlessly nodded in the darkness. Then, he stopped dead in his tracks and inhaled slowly and deliberately. 'This way,' he said, tugging Titch's arm, and turned into a narrow passageway.

Robert now confidently led the way, right to the end, where a tiny square window ever so slightly lit up a coarse door on their right side. 'They're in there!'

'How do ye know, Cap'n?'

'I can smell them,' said Robert.

Tentatively, Robert opened the door and was just in time to catch a shadowy glimpse of a head disappearing out of a hatchway near the floor.

The two boys quickly followed, down through the hatch and into the warm yet refreshing night air. A short wooden ladder propped up against the wall allowed them to descend, and in no time they were down and out of the prison building. They were still, however, trapped inside the prison yard.

Suddenly a voice came from behind them. 'Nice of ye to join us, lads.' It was Blackjack.

The backyard was not as dark as inside the prison building, and everything was quite visible, albeit to varying degrees. There was even a slight breeze which was quite remarkable considering the height of the surrounding walls.

'You left us behind,' said Robert.

Blackjack ignored him and instead sped off, immediately followed by One Eye, Weasel and finally Hunch. The boys quickly tagged on. The pirate captain kept in tight against the massive wall, aiming for the corner of the yard where an enormous pile of wood stood. Then, after skirting around the pile, he proceeded to follow the line of the adjacent wall. All three members of his crew mirrored his every move, as did Robert and Titch who were somewhat confused with what was happening.

The wall was simply immense. It was made of brick and consisted of two distinct sections. The bottom section was thick, tapering ever so slightly inwards as it gained height. This part was poorly maintained with numerous broken bits and soft furry masses of moss and other larger plants having set up home. In contrast, the top part of the wall was significantly thinner and in better condition. It had obviously been added on as an afterthought, resulting in a clearly defined ledge approximately two thirds of the way up the wall as a whole.

Suddenly, Blackjack stopped, setting off a chain reaction right the way up to Robert, the last in line. After all movement had ceased, Blackjack popped two fingers into his mouth and emitted a short sharp whistle. All were quiet, waiting with bated breaths for something to happen, but nothing did. He repeated the whistle, a tension now evident. Again nothing happened. After a short pause, where nobody uttered a single sound, the whistle was once more replicated. Yet again, nothing happened.

'Damnation!' cried Blackjack. 'Where are they?'

'Avast there!' came a deep voice from the other side of the wall, and the end of a rope dropped right beside them.

'One Eye, you're first,' ordered Blackjack. 'And no shilly-shallying.'

'Aye, Cap'n,' said One Eye, and he tugged on the heavy rope with both hands to ensure its strength. Then, in the blink of an eye he was up and over the wall as Blackjack held the rope firmly and readied himself.

Such a climb would not be so easy for the sturdy captain. And so it proved, an enthusiastic start soon stalled and his ascent became much laboured. Indeed, a couple of times the pirate captain even lost his footing, sending pieces of broken brick hurtling downwards. Eventually though, he succeeded and disappeared over the summit.

Mr Weasel went next, leaving the boys alone with Hunch. Mr Weasel moved like lightning as Hunch readied himself, hand on rope.

Then unexpectedly, Hunch whispered, 'Follow me fast, lads.'

Robert stared at Titch in amazement as the last pirate started to climb.

'You go,' said Robert quickly. 'You'll be faster.'

'Aye, Cap'n,' said Titch, and after spitting on his hands he set off after Hunch who was already nearing the top.

When Hunch dropped out of sight, Robert decided to heed the pirate's warning and after giving one fleeting glance upwards, gasped in horror. Someone was hanging over the top and it was clearly visible against the night sky what they were doing.

'Titch!' cried Robert. 'They're cutting the rope. Hang on!'

The small boy was right at the dividing ledge of the wall and managed to drop onto it as the severed rope fell to the ground with a thud.

All of a sudden, a commotion erupted from inside the prison building, and it got noticeably lighter as lanterns and torches were moved, raised and ignited.

'Climb!' shouted Robert, grabbing at the wall himself.

'Ye want me to leave ye, Cap'n?' exclaimed Titch.

'Yeah! You must!' declared Robert, slowly lifting himself upwards. 'Can you make it?'

'Easy, Cap'n. There's more grips than ye think, and I'm topnotch at shinnying up things.'

'Then go! I'll see you sometime.'

Sure enough, Titch climbed effortlessly and promptly disappeared over the top.

Robert surprised himself at how well he was tackling the wall, and he started to gain some height. Then came the thing he'd been dreading.

'Prisoner in the yard!'

Robert clawed at the wall frantically, desperately trying to pull himself up. 'This is like a nightmare!' he groaned. But he had managed to get his fingertips onto the ledge, when he heard the first CRACK! Then another, CRACK! He was being shot at!

All at once, he dropped like a sack of potatoes, crumpling onto the compacted ground below. Instantly, he felt a sharp pain in his leg, just above the knee. Had he been shot? He wasn't sure. He touched his leg gingerly, uncertain what a gunshot wound should feel like. It definitely felt sore. Then his fingers found a raggedy hole in his long shorts, and something was wet. Blood! His blood!

Panic immediately engulfed Robert and he couldn't move. He was in a trance, like a rabbit caught in the headlights. His state was only broken by the further shouts of soldiers. He jumped up, his leg surprisingly capable with only a slight discomfort. If the wall was too high then he simply had to find another way out. The massive pile of wood in the corner of the yard offered the best hiding spot and he threw himself behind it. It was pretty dark here and he felt relatively safe. But for how long? They weren't stupid! If he hadn't managed to climb over the wall, then the pile of wood was the obvious hiding place. He had to keep moving.

Robert raised himself, and keeping tight in against the yard wall, just as he had done half an hour or so ago when he and Titch had followed Blackjack, returned to the side of the prison building. They had escaped from midway along the building and cut out this first corner, but now he hoped it offered an escape route. It was darker here and he stuck out his hands to guide himself. He could feel some large leathery leaves right in front of him, and after pushing through them, his hands touched a wall.

Suddenly, there were more shouts. This time from the yard itself.

'They've scarpered,' exclaimed a gruff voice.

'I'm telling ye, I shot one of them,' declared another. 'He fell like a ton of bricks. I saw it with these very eyes!'

'Then you need spectacles, man, cos there's nobody here, and we're in a whole heap of trouble.'

'He's hiding! I can feel it in ma bones.'

Robert gulped on hearing this, as he groped around in the darkness. He could easily see the two soldiers as they talked and approached the perimeter wall. Each held a lantern which they swung in all directions. Soon they would check the pile of wood and then after finding nothing, the remaining areas. He felt thankful for how poor the lanterns did their job, a couple of decent electric torches and he would already have been spotted.

Shortly, his hands came to a narrow gap in the wall and then onto a barred metal gate. Maybe he could climb it and slip over the top? They would hear the clanking a mile off! He put his hand through the gap, then his arm, then his shoulder, but his head got stuck and no matter how much he tried to push it, it just wouldn't go. Quickly, he dropped to the ground and tested for any differences in gap size, remembering how squint their gate was in Edinburgh. He was in luck, right at the base the gap was indeed bigger, either the post or the wall had shifted, but who cared. He'd found a possible way out.

'Over there! Let's try over there in the corner,' bawled the soldier with the gruff voice, pointing to the exact same spot where Robert lay.

The lanterns swiftly moved closer, but Robert was gone. He'd managed to squeeze and crawl through the gap at the bottom, and on his hands and knees had slipped into the front yard, right behind a bunch of wispy bushes. They were scant camouflage.

A lone soldier stood guard at the main gate with two good sized lanterns hanging either side of him. Typically, the lights were attracting insects, which were clearly pestering him as his hands were continuously flapping about. Good, thought Robert, the soldier's attention will be diverted by the beasties. Then there was the stink from the pile of muck stacked up high against the wall, now unfortunately right beside Robert. Along with this fetid heap there was only a sprinkling of bushes and weeds, otherwise the front yard was quite empty, and but for the darkness he would have stuck out like a sore thumb. Anxious, he pulled himself in tighter against the wall, a hair's breadth from the wonky gate.

The two soldiers arrived forthwith and were now standing exactly where Robert had been a mere ten seconds ago. He could hear them breathing.

'So much for ye shooting one of 'em! So where is he?' sneered the soldier with the gruff voice.

'Maybe he squeezed through the gate,' offered the second soldier. 'I'm sure it was one of the kids. Maybe he wriggled through this gap.' And he rattled the gap with his musket, from top to bottom. The noise reverberated throughout both sides of the yard.

'Ye couldn't get a cat through there,' said the soldier with the gruff voice. 'Nope, they all escaped over the wall. Just like I said!'

'Hey, Lenny!' shouted the second soldier, and he held up his feeble lantern against the fastened gate. 'Ye haven't seen one of those kids have ye? I think I shot him.'

Lenny, the solitary soldier at the main gate, collected his larger lantern and took a few giant strides towards his comrades. 'No chance!' he shouted. 'I've got eyes and ears like a bloodhound. Nothing's come or gone in this here yard. If I could just get rid of these pesky beasties ... ' And promptly he started beating his ears. 'I'd be over the moon.'

'Alright, Lenny, you'd better get back to yer post, or you'll be up on a charge.'

Lenny made an about turn and resumed his position at the main gate, much to the delight of the resident beasties.

'What did ye ask him for?' muttered the soldier with the gruff voice. 'He's as dumb as there is. Did ye hear him? Eyes and ears like a bloodhound. It's nose like a bloodhound! The fool. Only last week he was saying the moon is made of silver. Can ye believe it?' And he guffawed at his own remark.

'Yeah, but nobody really knows, Lex. Not for sure,' returned the second soldier. 'I mean, it's not like anybody will ever walk on it.'

'Larry, Larry, Larry. Are you for real? The moon's not made of silver. The same as the earth's not flat.'

Just then, Robert recognized their voices. They were surely the two soldiers who had escorted him and Titch from the ship to the prison.

Which meant the one with the squint was called Lex. Eventually though, they moved off out of earshot, taking their inadequate lanterns with them.

Tentatively, Robert lifted his head out from the pile of muck he'd been hiding in, and breathed some proper air again. It was the worst smell he'd ever smelt in his whole life, plus it was all soft and gooey. He immediately blew a lump of something mushy from his lips. At least he hadn't been caught! He was now so close and yet still so very far.

Robert considered his options while keeping his head clear of the hairy mound, and concluded that he didn't have many. All of a sudden, Lenny, the guard at the main gate, stopped dancing about like a madman and stood up straight, musket by his side. Robert quickly sucked his head back into the sweating heap, but left a tiny hole to watch the proceedings. He'd always had excellent night vision.

Straightaway, a considerable number of clattering soldiers came into view. One was smaller than the rest and Robert instantly recognized him. Officer Campbell! Robert could even make out the silhouette of the officer's head and nose from a lantern's rays.

'Why are ye standing there, soldier?' barked Campbell, ignoring Lenny's ungainly salute.

'In case any prisoners escape, sir.'

'In case ye hadn't noticed, ye imbecile. They've already escaped!' barked Officer Campbell, sweat cascading down his forehead. 'And what were you doing at the time? Asleep!'

'No sir. Nobody passed me, sir. I've got the eyes and ears of a bloodhound.'

'Well give them back, soldier. Cos they're no doing you any flaming good!'

Lenny didn't understand the insult and stood in silence as everyone roared with laughter.

'Enough!' cried Campbell. 'Everybody inside! We'll need a plan of action to get these prisoners back before I'm the laughing stock of the whole Caribbean.'

More than a dozen soldiers quickly marched into the prison building, but Lenny stood stock-still, his musket still at his side.

'Do ye need permission from yer mother, soldier?' yelled Campbell. 'I said everybody!'

'Shouldn't I stay, sir, just in case they're hiding somewhere,' stammered Lenny.

'Has the backyard been searched?'

'Yes, sir.'

'Has the building been searched?'

'Yes, sir.'

'Well then, I reckon that covers it,' snarled Campbell. 'Unless of course one of them is hiding in that there pile of muck! And fetch that stupid mutt of yours. It's got work to do!'

Robert immediately pulled his head in tightly and couldn't hear the rest of the conversation. When he eventually raised it, everyone was gone. And for a moment, he couldn't believe his luck. Officer Campbell had actually helped him. It was now or never!

What with the muggy weather and being covered for so long, Robert had really started to perspire, and everything that could glue to him, did. Consequently, when he extracted himself from the stinking, squishy, squelchy heap he was a terrible sight and felt two stones heavier.

There was no one about. His exit was clear. The gate was wide open. And he ran. Straight as an arrow he sped, right up until he slipped and theatrically landed on his bottom. But worst of all, he emitted a cry. His beaten up yet brand new trainers, with their untouchable traction had failed him.

'Prisoner! Prisoner escaping! Prisoner in the yard!' shouted a soldier on hearing Robert's cry.

Robert righted himself unconsciously, and ran as fast as his legs would carry him, right out of the front prison yard and into the night town. His injured leg was forgotten.

A major commotion now ensued inside the prison building, quickly spilling out into the yard as Officer Campbell barked out orders. 'You lot go west! You go east!' he cried. 'Johnstone, you take the rear if he's stupid enough to go that way. And we'll go straight ahead,' he continued, gesticulating to four soldiers beside him. 'And remember! The time for hanging is over. Kill him! I want that pirate dead!'

Robert ran like he'd never run before, even counting his old school's sports day. He sped straight across the cobbled street and immediately turned into an unlit side alley. The street wasn't long and abruptly ended giving him two options, left or right. He chose right. His heart pounded as he gasped for breath in the hot humid night air. Onwards he flew, not knowing where he was heading, just trying to put as much distance between himself and his pursuers as possible.

He stopped. His legs felt wobbly and leaden. He listened. Shouts immediately reverberated around the tight streets, but laughs quickly followed, and he sighed with relief. Probably just revellers from the town. Suddenly, a light went on in the house right beside him and a face appeared at a window. A face with a bushy beard and staring eyes, cut into four by the quartered window pane. Robert jumped and ran for his life.

On and on he raced in the virtual total darkness, his feet continuously slipping on patches of damp mud, but still somehow managing to keep upright. He needed to rest though. It wasn't possible to just go on and on. He sprang into an even narrower side alley and ducked down, gasping for air. He was thirsty, hungry, tired, and being pursued by people who probably wanted to kill him. Could things get any worse?

After regaining his strength, Robert sat in the crouching position and listened to the eerie silence. What should he do? He had to find Titch. But where? Just then, voices appeared from along the street where he had just come from. Tentatively he peeped out, straining his eyes, until a lantern came into view, followed by several soldiers with muskets and accompanying bayonets. Instantly Robert backed up and started to race along the tight alleyway, his tiredness gone, replaced by the need to escape. The fight or flight response had been won by flight. But the alley was a dead end, and in the blackness he crashed into a brick wall directly in his path. Desperately he pounded the hard immovable object. Was this the end? He had to climb.

The wall was the back of a large dwelling and offered little hope. However, adjacent to this the buildings were smaller and constructed partially of wood and partially of brick, making them much more climbable. Robert chose a side and started to climb, the irregular shaped frontage giving him something to hold on to. Although he couldn't see it, he could feel the years of dirt and grime under his fingers.

Suddenly, the whole alley from beginning to end lit up. The soldiers found their quarry.

'Prisoner!' cried two soldiers in unison, and their footsteps thudded forwards on the ground.

CRACK! CRACK! Two rounds of gunshot ricocheted off something hard. But Robert was already gone.

The poor boy slipped and slid over the tiled roof, thankful that the sky was cloudy and there was no moon or stars to expose him. Onwards he ran, over the roofs of adjoining houses, a little higher, a little lower, but altogether passable. Gradually, the shouts from the soldiers got quieter. But then a crashing sound from behind and above told him that at least one of their number was tailing him. Now, he had to get off these rooftops. He was on a raft and the sharks were circling!

Then he brushed against some leaves, again large leathery ones, and straightaway decided to use them as cover to climb down. In two ticks he was on his bottom with his legs hanging over the roof edge. Then he jumped, easily catching one of the tree's slender branches, and dropping through the foliage to the ground.

Hidden by the large bushy vegetation, Robert peeped out. He was on one of the main roads. To his left, not too far off, was a street lamp with a bunch of people hanging around it. Their exuberant voices carried in the night air. Straight in front was more thick vegetation interspersed with a number of tall trees. To his right he was certain led back to the prison. After speedily looking left and right, and then left again, he zipped across the cobbled street and straight into another bushy tree. He paused for a second and turned to check if he was still being followed. He was! The soldier was just about to start his descent. But things didn't go too smoothly and he tumbled to the ground.

Robert ran! He was now fleeing down a side street with big walls on either side and a sprinkling of trees pushed up against them. This didn't look good! If this was another dead end, it would probably be the end of him.

'I need to get over one of these walls,' he said to himself.

In the darkness and with little time, he couldn't be choosy. He picked the nearest tree and climbed. Fortunately, it sloped towards the wall and in a second he was slithering over the coping. He dangled for a moment, unsure whether he was doing the right thing. Then he dropped to the ground on the other side, right into the middle of a massive flowery bush. The fragrance of which nearly took his breath away. It was like a thousand roses stuffed under his nose. An oasis within an inhospitable desert.

Robert paused to catch his breath. He was certain he hadn't been seen. All of a sudden, however, shouting flared up nearby, and then it got closer and closer.

'He definitely came this way!' declared a soldier from the other side of the wall, as little as an arm's length away from Robert.

'Did ye see him climb over?' asked another soldier, with apparent scorn.

'No, but he couldn't have climbed that,' said the first soldier, pointing to the much higher wall running parallel to the wall Robert had just scaled. 'And straight ahead's a dead end. So he's gone there, over that. He must be in the governor's garden. Or else they're having tea together!' and he chuckled to himself.

'Well you can go and tell him,' said the other soldier. 'I heard he's a right old windbag and sour as a crab apple. A lot worse than the last one!'

'Why should I go? You go!'

'Shh! Hold yer tongue. Lenny's coming with that stupid mutt.'

Lenny approached, lantern in one hand and dog in the other. The dog was a bloodhound and its name was Bouncer.

'I heard that,' Lenny said indignantly. 'He's not stupid. He's still only a puppy really.'

'Kinda big for a puppy,' said the other soldier, whose gruff voice was returning after his exertions. Robert now realized it was Lex.

Just then, Bouncer flipped himself up and plopped his giant paws onto Lex.

'I think he likes you!' said Lenny. 'They say a dog can always tell if a person's good or not. Although I don't know why he's jumped up on you then!'

'Get off! Daft mutt!' grumped Lex, taking a step backwards. 'Anyways, we think the escaped prisoner's gone into the governor's place. So you'll need to go in and tell him.'

'Who, the prisoner?'

'No, the governor, dumbo!'

'Why me?' complained Lenny.

'Cos you've got the dog,' explained Lex.

'I can't see how that makes a difference,' grumbled Lenny. 'Come on, Bouncer boy, we've got work to do.' And dog and master retreated back towards the mansion's front gates.

'Don't worry,' shouted Lex. 'We're right behind ye!' But Larry and Lex didn't move an inch.

Robert had heard everything. Now they were taking in the dogs. He couldn't stay here. Maybe he could try and hide in the big house. Otherwise, he would have to go back over the wall when the soldiers left. If they left. But he simply had to get out of this garden.

Unfortunately, as he was making up his mind, it was already too late. There was a clanking of the mansion's front gates and a knot of soldiers quickly filed in, lighting up the garden in variable patches with their lanterns and torches. Spooky shadows danced in and around the many trees and bushes. Robert held his breath. He was shaking.

'Where's the dog!' shouted a soldier. 'Everybody spread out and keep yer eyes peeled. Where's that darned dog!'

'Coming, sir!' hollered Lenny, somewhat relieved that others had now turned up. Bouncer bounced joyfully beside him. 'Find boy!' ordered the soldier. 'Find boy! He'll bark if he finds something.'

Bouncer immediately dropped his big wet nose to the ground, and like an arrow from a bow, the large gangly dog headed straight for Robert.

'No,' whispered Robert. 'Go away. Shoo! Shoo!' But the wrinkly animal just came closer.

Bouncer went right up to the massive flowery bush and dug his head, with the enormous floppy ears, right in. Sniff, sniff, sniffing the whole time. Then, as Robert feared the worst and pulled himself into a tight ball, the dog's fat juicy nose touched his forearm. Was this the end? The animal gave a snort. It didn't bark. It didn't growl. It didn't howl. It just snorted. And then disappeared momentarily, before bounding into the centre of the garden and rolling onto its back on a patch of grass.

'That dog's flaming useless,' shouted Officer Campbell, who had just arrived and witnessed Bouncer's pantomime. The officer was accompanied by yet more soldiers. 'Fix bayonets, men! I want me some fresh pirate meat! I just know he's in here.'

Robert gulped and automatically sped off towards the large forbidding house. He was well hidden by the abundant vegetation which thankfully grew particularly around the perimeter. The previous governor had been an avid gardener, until his unexplained disappearance. A sudden outburst of chirping crickets drowned out any sounds the fleeing boy made.

11. In Annabel And Rebecca's House

The governor's mansion was the largest house on the island by a country mile; however, as mansions go, it was merely average sized. Still, it had twelve bedrooms, consisted of three levels, not including the basement, and had umpteen other rooms each with their own specific purpose. The roof of the building was on many different levels, quite unique in many respects, and there were a great many balconies, mainly on the first floor. There was also a sizeable garden all around, which was decidedly overgrown, with many varieties of trees and bushes.

On approaching the house, Robert quickly decided that the front and sides were not his best options, and he continued on past the building, to the rear. He guessed the ground floor was likely to be the most used and thus the most dangerous, so he set his sights on hiding on the roof or better still sneaking into an empty room until the danger had passed.

The back of the big house was totally unlit, and in the darkness Robert gripped onto something protruding from a wall. Then, carefully but quickly, he raised his weary body off the ground. He'd never climbed so much in his whole life, and once more wasn't going to faze him, until something jagged touched the gunshot wound on his leg.

'Ouch!' he cried, before he remembered where he was and instantly held his breath. He recovered and wriggled up onto the lowest part of the roof.

'Did you hear something?' suddenly said a soldier from nowhere.

Robert felt a quiver of anxiety run through him. He hadn't realized anybody was so close.

'Maybe we should check the roof,' said another soldier. 'I mean, let's face it, if he isn't in the garden then he's either sneaked inside the house or he's on the roof somewhere.'

'Good reckoning. I'll say it to Campbell. Come on! Before anybody else gets the same thoughts.' And they headed off to put their suggestion to Officer Campbell.

As soon as they were gone Robert scrambled up the warm roof; now he simply had to somehow get into the house to hide. He moved swiftly, aware that time was of the essence. With tired limbs he crawled along the inclining slate roof, right up to where it finished and joined the next part of the house. Directly above him appeared a sizeable balcony. If only he could get into it. There would surely be a window open in these temperatures.

Robert stood bolt upright with his hands raised high; alas, even on tiptoes his fingers were some way off the balcony base. The brick façade, however, was not perfectly flush and he could feel the irregularities in the darkness. After a second in thought, he edged over a touch and started to climb up the façade. In two shakes of a lamb's tail he had gained access to the corner of the balcony and was up and over the side.

The glass windows which Robert had expected were absent, and in their place were substantial wooden shutters, each one all the way to the floor. He felt the slats with his fingertips. The paint covering them was blistered by the incessant sun and they were rough and flaky to the touch. With mounting trepidation, he put his whole hand on one and eased it open. The shutter creaked gently and momentarily he halted, but on hearing nothing, he continued and entered the room.

It was nearly pitch black inside but for a weak sliver of light underneath a door straight ahead. Gradually though, he could make out a large four-poster bed on one side, and numerous wardrobes and giant chests. The room seemed to expand as his eyes adjusted to the further lack of light, and he saw another door off to the adjacent side. A twinge of fear followed, but quickly passed, and for a moment he was lost in his own curiosity.

Suddenly, the main door handle moved and Robert's heart jumped. He still managed to dive head first underneath the bed, the shiny floor aiding his disappearing act. Again the door handle moved, more vigorously now, but the door didn't open.

'What's in there?' barked a voice with obvious authority.

'You can't go in there. That's my room!' came a sharp reply.

'We should check all rooms, sir. We are talking about a desperate pirate here.'

'Shh! My daughter could be overhearing. Besides, I thought it was only a child you were searching for.'

'A pirate's a pirate, sir,' came the scornful reply. It was Officer Campbell, and Robert easily recognized him.

'And the room next door has been searched?'

'All checked, sir. Clean as a whistle! Now, if you can step aside and furnish me with the key, sir.'

Robert's ears pricked up - if he could get into that room, then he would be safe. They wouldn't search the same room twice.

'I don't think I like your tone of voice, Officer Campbell!' said William Haggish, and the governor moved from leg to leg nervously. He was not used to being spoken to so discourteously.

'That may be so, sir. But if ye don't open this here door I'll get one of my men to break it down.'

'You'll do no such thing, Officer Campbell!' declared Governor Haggish, his face visibly turning more and more red under the rays of a nearby lamp. 'Do you know who I am?'

Campbell stared at the portly, balding governor arrogantly, and considered what to say. 'The last governor fell off the cliffs. So the rumour goes.'

'I've heard the rumours, Officer Campbell. What relevance do they have to me?'

Then, straight out of the blue, Officer Campbell changed tack and even attempted a smile. Next, in a hushed voice, and double checking that no one was within earshot, he said, 'Do ye want to be rich, sir?'

Robert was hearing everything, but the last sentence was barely audible, and so after rolling gently from underneath the bed and a little farther, he righted himself on his haunches closer to the door. Now he was perfectly positioned to overhear the remaining discussion of the two schemers.

'Who doesn't?' replied Governor Haggish smarmily, flicking his eyes all around so as to make sure they weren't being observed. How he would love to be rich. How his wife would fete him. How they all would.

'Well, I can make ye rich. Richer than you've ever dreamed of.'

'But how?'

'Now I can't say. All I need is for you to not hinder me in anything I do on this island. And when the time comes I'll tell everything and we'll share the bounty.'

Governor Haggish grinned, and again looked all around. 'Here!' he said. 'Take the key!'

Quickly, Campbell opened the door and a lamp was held up. The two men entered and the room became illuminated. Immediately, Officer Campbell checked under the bed. But Robert had come to his senses and had already taken flight. The wardrobes were next to be inspected, while Governor Haggish entered the side door. This room he would check alone.

'All clear!' said Campbell, somewhat displeased.

'All clear in here too,' said Governor Haggish, stepping back into the main room. 'But, shouldn't we shake hands on our agreement. I mean, if we're to be partners.'

'Certainly,' said Campbell, striding towards the governor.

The two men shook, their clammy hands momentarily sticking together.

'Now we're partners for sure,' declared Governor Haggish.

'Remember, sir. It's our secret,' said Campbell, turning to face the French windows. And with that he approached them and walked out onto the balcony. Holding up his lamp, he checked all around, and on seeing nothing of note, re-entered the room. 'Best fasten those windows and shutters, sir. They're an open invitation to a thief or vagabond.'

William Haggish was not offended by the order, nor did he reply to it. Instead, he was already dreaming of his impending riches. Being a governor certainly had lots of perks, but hard cash was significantly more appealing.

Following his swift and ultimately fortuitous exit, Robert had faced an immediate dilemma. In which direction was the searched room they had spoken about? He chose in hope and after again successfully negotiating the uneven façade, had slithered into the adjacent balcony. Then, in the very nick of time, he crept through a set of shutters, just as Campbell had appeared on the other balcony.

Robert now found himself behind a large, thick, velvety curtain which went all the way down to the floor. The spacious room in front was well lighted which, although comforting, warned of danger. Would an empty unused room be lit up for no reason? In any case, it made no difference. He couldn't go back the way. Presently, his options had evaporated.

Suddenly, a door opened and in walked a youngish girl wearing a long flowing, fluffy dress. Instantly, she made a beeline straight for the window and tugged the curtain aside.

'Got you!' she cried triumphantly.

The two children stared at one another, each as surprised as the other.

'Don't be frightened,' stuttered Robert. His eyes wide open in amazement.

'Frightened? Why should I be frightened? I'm taller than you,' retorted the girl.

'No you're not!' said Robert, and he stood fully upright, straining every muscle and sinew in his body. He was now ever so slightly the taller of the two.

'Alright! So we're the same size,' said the girl, emitting a short sniff.

What a big fibber, thought Robert. But he was not in the best position to argue.

'So who are you?' asked the girl with the incredibly calm, friendly face. 'And what are you doing in my bedroom?'

'Ah!' mumbled Robert. 'My name's Robert.' And he stopped, disgusted with himself. He'd given his real name. Too late now. 'And I'm being chased by some soldiers who want to shoot me.'

'Oh! Why should they want to shoot you?'

Now Robert was in a predicament, and it reminded him of his old teacher Mr Gibson who was very fond of quotes, and one of his favourites was, 'Oh what a tangled web we weave, When first we practise to deceive'. Should Robert tell the truth? She might be angry or frightened if he said he was a pirate. Then again, was he a pirate! He didn't have an eye patch or a wooden leg or a hook or even a parrot.

'I stole some bread,' Robert began. 'Because I was so hungry, but the shopkeeper saw me and shouted, and then the soldiers started to chase me, and then they began to shoot, and I got hit. Look!' And he showed the ragged hole in his long shorts and the smear of blood which encircled it.

The girl's mood immediately changed, from jovial and slightly mocking to quite serious and sympathetic. 'And you're so dirty as well. Poor thing! Don't you have a mother or father?'

'No,' answered Robert, cringing.

'Well neither do I. My name's Rebecca by the way.'

'My name's Robert,' said Robert, raising his hand.

'Yes, you already said,' and she stuck out her pale hand to formalize the greeting. 'Pleased to make your acquaintance, Robert.'

Robert shook the pretty girl's hand keenly, and marvelled at her long golden hair cascading down onto her slim shoulders. Her eyes were blue and piercing, her complexion pale and flawless. He wondered if she ever went outside. But one thing was certain, he'd made a friend.

'Could you help me please?' he eventually asked, but he guessed her heart was already softened.

'Of course, I should love to. I shall be your guardian angel. My little Roberto.'

Robert flushed and was just about to complain when voices sounded from the other side of the door.

'No I won't!' came a girl's high pitched voice. 'I'm playing hide and seek with Rebecca.'

'Quick! You must hide!' said a startled Rebecca. 'It's my cousin Annabel. She might give you away.' And she promptly about turned and rushed into the centre of the room. 'Here, get in,' she said, lifting up the lid of an oaken chest which was situated at the foot of the bed. 'There's enough room. Quickly!'

'But dearest,' came a man's voice from outside the door.

'You know how ill I am, Father,' interrupted Annabel. 'You shouldn't be upsetting me. I shall tell Mother.'

As the confrontation continued, Robert hastened over to the dark panelled chest and got in. 'I might not be able to breathe,' he whispered, on settling down.

'Put your finger into the corner,' Rebecca whispered, and carefully dropped the top shut.

Just then, Annabel stormed into the room and slammed the door shut behind her. 'Why aren't you looking for me?' she demanded, in her usual brusque manner.

'Sorry,' replied Rebecca. 'I've a bit of a sore belly. Do you mind if we stop playing?'

'Mm. It didn't stop you scoffing loads at dinnertime,' retorted Annabel sourly. 'You must have devoured at least five jam scones.'

'Yes, I might have been a little too greedy. But whatever is happening outside?'

'Oh, apparently they're looking for an escaped prisoner and they think he's hiding somewhere in our house. They wanted to search our rooms. Can you believe it! Obviously, I said no. I mean, can you imagine those stupid oafs rummaging through our things. It gives me the shivers just thinking about it.'

'What does he look like?'

'How should I know? I only overheard a little bit.'

Robert's curiosity eventually got the better of him and he peeped out of the slight gap. Annabel was roughly the same height as Rebecca; however, she was not as slim, and had a more rounded, plump face. Her complexion was not as clear nor vibrant as her cousin's, but her eyes were also blue and with the same mischievous sparkle. With blonde hair, which was more of a strawberry blonde than golden, and a scowl which didn't seem to leave her, Annabel was on the whole not as pretty as her cousin.

'Well, what shall we do now?' Annabel continued, and began to move her eyes around the room in a show of displeasure.

Immediately, Rebecca edged over to the chest and covered most of it with her voluminous dress. The material rested on Robert's fingers and a warmth ran through his body. He admired her ingenuity. Although now, he couldn't see a thing.

'Rebecca?' said Annabel, while playing with a golden locket around her neck. 'Whatever are you trying to hide?' And she fixed a gaze upon her cousin.

A bashful Rebecca averted her eyes. 'Don't talk silly,' she said. 'What could I possibly wish to hide?'

'How about those two fingers sticking out from that chest!'

'Oh, please don't say anything, Annabel,' begged Rebecca immediately. 'He's smaller than us and he's so dirty and skinny, and he's been shot, in the leg.' And with that plea she raised the curved lid of the dark wooden chest, and Robert popped up like a regular Jack-in-the-box.

'Hello,' said Robert, gently waving a hand. 'Don't be scared. I won't hurt you.'

'I think you are mistaken,' retorted the girl sharply. 'You are the one who should be scared. All I need do is cry out, and ten soldiers would be in here before I finished my breath.'

'Please Annabel,' implored Rebecca. 'Can't you see he's in need of our assistance.'

Annabel stared at Robert coldly, and her eyes gleamed with malice. She would benefit from her compliance. Otherwise, she would blab. 'And what do you propose?' she said, as Robert extracted himself from his hidey hole.

'Well, we could tend to his wound, and maybe clean him up a bit, perhaps a change of clothes, and give him something to ... '

'I don't think you understand,' interrupted Annabel. 'What do I get for keeping my mouth shut?'

Quickly Robert glanced at Rebecca. His life lay in her hands. But what did she have to offer?

'Beatrice!' said Rebecca. 'I'll give you Beatrice.'

'Mm,' pondered Annabel. 'I'd like Georgina too.'

'Done! It's a deal. I'll go and get them.'

'Not so quick! I also want Elizabeth.'

'But I only have three dolls, and Elizabeth is my favourite.'

'Then don't help the little urchin, and I'll go get Father.'

Robert had had enough of this horrible little girl and he couldn't restrain himself any longer. 'You're being really mean to your cousin!' And he moved closer to her.

Instantly, Annabel turned to face him. 'When I want your opinion, urchin, I shall ask for it. And keep away from me. You smell like a pile of poo!'

Robert did indeed look and smell like something the cat had dragged in, in stark contrast to the pristinely turned out girls. He'd never felt so filthy and underdressed in his whole life, and this obnoxious young lady was only rubbing salt into the wounds.

'I beg of you, Annabel,' said Rebecca. 'Have mercy. He's been shot, look at the blood on his leg.'

'Oh, do stop swooning over him,' mocked Annabel. 'Come on then, urchin, let's see the hole in your leg.' And she turned back to face Robert.

Robert immediately sat down on the side of the bed, not giving a second thought to his filthy state, which was unfortunate as the bedspread, which was a mixture of light blues and white, was also immaculate in every way.

'Get off! You beast! You can't sit there,' cried Annabel like a shot.

'It's my bed. It doesn't bother me,' said Rebecca soothingly. 'It's only a bit of dirt for goodness sake. Please, stay just where you are and show us your injury.'

Robert carefully lifted up his holed trouser leg, as Annabel, while pinching her nose, went over to examine the wound.

'Why it's only a scratch!' she laughed. 'I acquire bigger cuts while sewing.'

Robert hated the sight of blood. Indeed, one time he had even come over all giddy. And so it was with a measure of trepidation that he bent forwards and checked out the damage for himself. Then the embarrassment arrived, for his gunshot wound was a mere scratch, just as Annabel had so ruthlessly put it.

'Does it really matter how big the injury is?' said Rebecca. 'He's been shot, Annabel. The hole is evident. He's a wounded bird, surely this can be his aviary.'

'Oh do stop charming him. It's making me sick, along with the stink. So are you giving me the dolls or not?'

'Yes of course,' said a delighted Rebecca. 'I'll go and get them.' And she went over to a large dark coloured wardrobe situated in the corner of the room, and buried her head inside.

They were alone. Robert looked at Annabel while she stared back at him. He couldn't bring himself to start a conversation with such a tyrant but she was of a different disposition.

'You're doubtless a chimney sweep. Am I right?' Annabel scornfully began. Robert opened his mouth to respond but was too slow. 'You know people like me, who are extremely important, don't need to work. Whereas, people like you have no choice. You've probably never received a formal education. Look at your hands, all brown and calloused. Those are the hands of a poor person who is wholly uneducated.'

'I'm probably more educated than you!' said Robert.

'Listen to the little urchin. Pray tell, do you speak Latin? It's a language.'

'No.'

'Then I rest my case. All educated people can read, write and speak Latin.'

'But why? It's a dead language. Name one country that speaks it.'

'Well, eh,' answered a flummoxed Annabel. 'Well no countries still speak it.'

'Then I rest my case,' said Robert.

'But,' retaliated Annabel, however she'd been outwitted and didn't take it lightly. 'You're a pauper, and no doubt you come from a long line of paupers!'

Robert had had enough. 'And you're a snob!'

'Take that back, whatever it is, otherwise tonight you'll be eating bread and water in the town's prison. And tomorrow morning you'll be swinging from a rope.'

Just in time, Rebecca appeared as peacemaker and presented the dolls. They were all made of wood and looked more like miniature ladies than the baby kind Robert was used to. Each one was slim with perfectly formed hands, and each had a long neck, dark hair and small black eyes. All were dressed exquisitely, just like their owners, and finished off with a frilly bonnet tied under the chin.

Robert could see that one of the three dolls had a particularly full head of long luxurious hair and was in better condition than the other two. He knew this one was Elizabeth and felt sorry for Rebecca. It was a big sacrifice.

'Oh, she's so pretty,' cried Annabel, on receiving Elizabeth. She placed the other two dolls onto the bed. 'Her hair is so beautiful.'

'And it's so realistic,' said Robert.

'Of course it's realistic, you fool,' retorted Annabel. 'It's real hair!' And she lovingly caressed the doll's abundant chestnut locks.

'You mean they killed somebody for it?' asked a stunned Robert. His nanas and grandads would always tell him about the good old days. They didn't sound very good!

'Don't be silly,' giggled Rebecca. 'I expect people sell their hair.'

'Yes, people like you,' laughed Annabel. 'Poor people! Anyway, I'm not sure I agree now. He called me a bad name. What was it? Snob!'

'What's a snob?' asked Rebecca, desperately trying to smooth things over. 'Is it so bad?'

'Em, not really,' said Robert, his mind working overtime. 'It really only means somebody who boasts about having lots of money.'

'Oh,' said Annabel. 'I am a snob then.'

Suddenly, there was a knock on the door and everybody jumped. Rebecca recovered and ushered Robert back into the chest, although he needed little persuasion. The lid was dropped shut.

'Annabel dearest, can you open the door please,' said William Haggish, but there was an edge to his voice. 'Otherwise, I shall just have to invite myself in.'

Annabel went over to the door and reluctantly opened it. Immediately, her father and Officer Campbell stepped inside. Campbell wore a frightful scowl on his face. On the other hand, Governor Haggish looked rather sheepish. He was not accustomed to snooping around the girls' rooms.

'And what now, Father? Are you going to search my stockings?' cried Annabel.

'Don't say that, dearest,' responded William Haggish. 'Officer Campbell, I think you can see that there's nobody but the girls in here. Shall we leave now!'

'And the adjacent room?' said Campbell. 'We haven't searched it.' And he started towards it.

Instantly, Annabel ran to the door joining her room to Rebecca's and planted herself firmly in front of it. 'I think I'm coming over all faint,' she cried melodramatically.

'Oh, just tell them the truth!' cried Campbell, irked by the whole situation. He was not used to a minor having so much influence on things. A child should be seen and not heard was his firm belief. 'The individual we're hunting is a pirate, who'd cut yer throat in the blink of an eye.'

Annabel gasped. 'And what if he should come during the night and murder me, Father?'

'Oh Annabel, you and your imagination. You mustn't worry. There'll be a soldier just down the corridor, two at the front door and more walking around the gardens. If he's here, we'll catch him!'

Rebecca couldn't work out if Annabel was being serious or not and she stared at her cousin searchingly. 'And when will the soldiers be leaving?' she asked.

'I can't see what that's got to do with you,' William Haggish retorted. And turning to Annabel he added, 'They will all be gone, along with the little villain, before you can lift your pretty little head from the pillow tomorrow morning.' Then subtly, he approached his daughter. 'At least allow me to have a little peek for my peace of mind.'

Annabel relented and moved ever so slightly to allow her father through, but she continued to block Officer Campbell. She would die before permitting a ruffian like him into her bedchamber.

'All clear!' announced William Haggish, after a brief inspection.

'Well, he's got to be somewhere!' growled Campbell, and promptly departed, followed close on his heels by Governor Haggish, who bade the girls a brief and uncomfortable farewell.

'So you're a pirate then!' said Annabel, on opening the lid of the chest and stepping back.

'No, I was kidnapped by pirates,' said Robert, getting out and stretching his squashed limbs.

'So, did you steal the bread or not?' asked Rebecca.

'Yes,' answered Robert, but lying was becoming more and more problematic and he feared he'd soon be tying himself in knots. 'I stole the bread after I'd escaped. They wanted to turn me into a pirate!'

'Mm, but if you had already escaped before you stole the bread,' pondered Annabel. 'Why would the soldiers think you're a pirate?'

'Because,' began Robert, and he really had to think fast. 'Because somebody shouted "That pirate's nicked my loaf!" when I started to run.'

'That's alright,' said Rebecca, totally reassured. But Annabel was not so convinced.

'They're just not very intelligent,' continued Robert.

'And who are you to call our soldiers stupid!' snapped Annabel.

'I'm only repeating what you said earlier,' said Robert.

Once again, Annabel was stumped. She loved to squabble and argue but it wasn't so enjoyable if someone retaliated so effectively. Again, she started to finger the golden locket on her neck. 'And what do you propose we do with the little villain?' she asked momentarily, turning to Rebecca. 'Keep him here like a bird in a cage and feed him breadcrumbs?'

'I thought we could hide him until the soldiers left,' replied Rebecca, smiling timidly. 'You won't tell, will you?'

'I'm not a sneak,' retorted Annabel, while giving Robert a somewhat steely look. 'Oh, it's so tedious with you two!' she suddenly blurted out. 'I'm going to play with my new dolls.' And the conceited little girl traipsed off to her own room.

Robert immediately wanted to criticize her, but decided against it. He needed to be friends with her, even if it meant being a bit two-faced. Instead, he looked at Rebecca.

Rebecca gazed back all starry eyed. She didn't have her very own friend. For sure she had Annabel, but she was her cousin, grumpy cousin most of the time. They were taught from home, so there was little opportunity to make other friends. She would be the best friend ever!

After realizing that nothing was happening, Robert said, 'Do you think I could have something to drink please, and maybe something to eat?'

'Why of course, how unpardonable of me,' cried Rebecca, and she blushed and turned away. 'I'll go to the kitchen at once and ask Cook for something tasty. But you'll have to hide again until I return.'

Robert stared with wide eyes. 'But I don't have to go back into that chest again, do I? I think I'm becoming claustrophobic.'

'No, no,' chuckled Rebecca. 'I'll make some room in a wardrobe.' And she immediately went over to a big fat one, opened it, shuffled some things around inside and held out her hand. 'Your chariot awaits!'

Robert made himself comfortable inside and the door creaked shut.

'I'll lock it and keep the key,' Rebecca explained. 'Just in case. I shan't be long.' And she departed.

The wardrobe was more spacious than the chest and being infinitely more comfortable, Robert soon fell asleep. And not long after, his mum's homemade apple pie started to keep him company.

Creak! The wardrobe door opened. Robert jumped. He'd nearly fallen asleep. He breathed a sigh of relief. It was only Rebecca.

'You can come out now, sleepyhead,' she smiled. 'Cook has done us proud!'

Robert tumbled out of the wardrobe, his exit not helped by a dose of pins and needles in his right foot. Instantly, his nostrils filled with the smell of roasted chicken. It was simply divine and his mouth watered like a tap. Cook had indeed done him proud, for on the dressing table lay a large silver tray on which sat two plates brimming with food. On one plate was a hunk of roasted chicken, some bread, cheese and a gravy boat filled up to the top, while the other had an entire fruit tart on it, with delicious looking crisscrosses of shiny pastry on top.

'Wow!' said Robert. His appetite was on overload.

Forthwith, Rebecca pulled over a chair, waved a hand, and after accepting the invitation, Robert sat down. Water was poured from a large porcelain jug, and the feast began.

In next to no time the chicken was practically devoured and Robert grabbed some bread and took a bite. Rebecca stared at him in astonishment.

'Is there something wrong?' he asked, with full mouth.

'It's just that ... ' began Rebecca. She was not a naturally critical individual. 'Uncle says to always break the bread with your fingers, and never to bite it. It's supposed to be a sign of good manners.'

'Oh! Does it bother you?' asked Robert, disbelieving that such a stupid rule could exist.

'I don't suppose it does.'

'Good. Where I come from, everybody dips bread into their soup.'

Rebecca looked sceptical and then asked, 'And where do you come from?'

'Edinburgh,' replied Robert, while taking a huge slug of water.

'Me too!' cried Rebecca, overwhelmed with excitement. 'Which part?'

'Beside the castle. You can see the castle from my bedroom window.'

'So, does that mean you have a mother and father then?' Rebecca quickly asked.

Robert was nearly caught out, but recovered sufficiently to answer. 'No, they died and I became an orphan. Then I got a job as a cabin boy, and then I got kidnapped when our ship was attacked by pirates.' How good was that story!

'Oh, you poor lamb, and I thought I'd had a difficult life,' Rebecca said. Robert immediately felt guilty. 'Have you had enough to eat?' she continued. 'Maybe you can't manage that tart. It's one of my favourites. It's apricot.'

'No, no, I think I'll squeeze it in. I love apricot tart too. My mum always makes it. Made it, sorry!'

Then, much to Rebecca's amazement, Robert scoffed the entire tart, and after licking up every last crumb, lolled back on his chair fully satisfied. It was then that he viewed himself in the mirrors of the dressing table. He was horrendous, and couldn't believe Rebecca had been so understanding.

'I look terrible,' Robert blurted out.

'I know, but I have a surprise for you,' and Rebecca beamed with delight. 'I've asked Maid for a bath. And she said as soon as the water heats up she'll call me.'

'Won't she be suspicious?'

'No, why should she be? I'm always having baths, unlike some I could mention, but won't. I also asked Maid to wash some clothes, your clothes.'

'But she's bound to notice something's not right,' said Robert, rolling his eyes. 'My clothes look nothing like yours.'

'Don't worry, we're always dressing up in funny clothes when we role-play. And sometimes they get really dirty, especially when we explore the attic or outhouses.'

Robert couldn't imagine one speck of dirt on Rebecca, let alone enough to make her dirty. 'So where's the bathroom?'

'You know, sometimes you act like you're from another world. Please don't think me rude, but even your clothes are somewhat strange. I've never seen writing on a shirt before, and how unusually brilliant the colours are.' Then, Rebecca smiled, just in case she'd been too harsh. 'The bath by the way is where it normally is, in the corner behind the screen.'

And then, as if on cue, there came a knock at the door.

'Quick! Back into the wardrobe!' cried Rebecca, all a fluster. 'Coming!'

'I thought I heard voices, Miss,' said the maid on entering.

'Quite possibly,' replied Rebecca confidently. 'Annabel's just disappeared.'

'Shall I bring the hot water up now, Miss?'

'Yes please, that would be super.'

'I'm surprised you're having another bath so soon, Miss. You only had one yesterday. You'll be getting ill if you continue on like this!' And without waiting for a reply, the maid left to begin the process of fetching hot water to fill up the bathtub.

For what seemed an eternity, Robert sat crouched in the wardrobe listening to the comings and goings in Rebecca's bedroom, with only the redolent smell of the oak cupboard to keep him company. Eventually though, the all-clear was given and for a second time he crawled out of his wooden hidey hole. A shiver ran down his back. It was like emerging from an oversized coffin.

Rebecca smiled at him but seemed flustered and was all flushed up. 'Everything's ready,' she said modestly.

'Why would having baths make you ill?' Robert asked, while following Rebecca to the screen.

'Because baths are supposed to open the pores on the skin allowing infections to enter the body, but I don't believe it. I think it's just an excuse for being dirty. Why cover yourself in perfume when bathing is so much more effective!'

Robert looked at Rebecca. She had her hair tied back now, in a kind of bun. It didn't suit her, but it didn't detract one iota from her youthful beauty. Initially, he had thought that she was not very bright, but now he was of a different mind. She was intelligent, as well as beautiful.

'Do you wish to say something?' asked Rebecca.

It was then that Robert realized that he'd been staring. 'No, no, it's just that ... I've never seen such a large bathtub before.'

In truth, the metal bathtub was of no great size, except for perhaps in height. But Rebecca accepted the explanation cheerfully.

'I think, what should happen now,' she began, 'is for you to bathe while I go and see what Annabel is up to. And if you can put your dirty clothes to the side, I shall give them to be washed. But don't worry, I shan't be looking! Firstly though, I'll need to find you something to put on while your clothes are drying.' And she promptly left to begin her search.

Robert viewed the narrow metal bathtub with curiosity. He knew for a fact his dad, with his big broad shoulders, wouldn't have managed to submerge much above his belly button. Plus, there was hardly any water in it, and absolutely no sign of bubbles. A couple of squirts of his mum's lavender and rose bubble bath would have really made a difference. Still, he was unbelievably grateful for the kindness being shown to him.

'Here we are,' said Rebecca, placing a bundle of clothes onto a side chair. 'The soap's just there on the table,' and she pointed with her pale slender finger. 'I think that's everything. I'll fasten the door just in case, but auntie and uncle are playing cards so nobody should bother you.'

After Rebecca had departed, Robert gathered up the soap and hurriedly undressed. Back home, his mum would frequently have to order him to have a bath, but now he could hardly wait. Hurriedly he placed his dirty bundle of clothes on the opposite side of the screen and plopped himself into the inviting water. He couldn't imagine a greater bliss in the whole world. In no time, layers of grime and dirt, accumulated over the past few days, started to slide off.

What happened next, however, was exactly what his mum always warned him about. He fell asleep in the bath. At least the water wasn't deep, otherwise he might have drowned.

'Is everything alright?' asked Rebecca, after hearing nothing but silence on her second and then third visit to the bedroom. The first visit had been to collect the dirty clothes.

Robert jumped and opened his eyes. 'Yes, nearly finished, another few minutes,' he said, and immediately grabbed the bar of soap, which had become a bar of mush.

'I'll come back in five minutes or so then,' said Rebecca, and again left.

Robert quickly finished bathing, and after drying himself in a brick hard towel, picked up his temporary clothes. There was an extra long pair of unelasticated socks, a pair of linen shorts, which he guessed were instead of pants, a linen shirt with long sleeves, a pair of dark trousers cut just below the knee, and a funny looking waistcoat thing. After dressing, he checked himself out in the dressing table mirrors. He looked like somebody from an old painting, but was more than satisfied. He'd even managed to wash his hair.

At that moment the side door opened, but it was only Rebecca. 'Oh, I am pleased everything fits so well,' she said, on coming closer.

'Yeah, it's cool, I can't thank you enough,' Robert said, and did a twirl like a model. 'When will my own clothes be ready?'

'Tomorrow morning. They've already been washed, I watched Maid doing them. They only have to dry now. But is it really so chilly in here?'

Robert didn't understand. The place was like an oven. Then suddenly, he went pure white. The keys! He'd totally forgotten about them.

Rebecca somehow understood and pulled out the sock and keys from underneath her apron. 'I think these belong to you. I wasn't being nosy. Your pockets were ever so lumpy. I had to empty them before washing.'

'I don't know how I'll ever thank you.'

'You shouldn't worry about it. That's what friends are for. But you could tell me what the keys are for.'

Robert felt another lie coming on. In for a penny, in for a pound! 'The keys are from my old house, before they stole it from me.' It sounded quite believable.

Predictably, Rebecca took it all to heart, and Robert again felt terrible.

'You wouldn't have a toothbrush would you?' he asked, keen to change the subject. 'My teeth feel like they haven't been cleaned for a year.'

'Oh my, you use them too?' said Rebecca, somewhat surprised. 'How knowledgeable you are. They're such a fantastic invention. Don't you think? I couldn't do without one. Uncle acquired them all the way from Asia, and I most definitely have a spare one.' And she delved into a drawer in the dressing table. 'Here we are, and some fresh toothpowder to go with it.'

Robert had never heard of toothpowder before, but he had other much more important things on his mind. 'Rebecca, what am I going to do?'

'Oh, you shouldn't worry about that now. What you need is a good night's rest. Annabel's already in bed and that's where I'm going.'

'Going?' asked Robert.

'Yes, I shall sleep with Annabel tonight, and you can have my bed. It's very comfortable, I always sleep like a baby.'

'But won't it look suspicious?'

'No, no, I'm always sleeping with Annabel. I think she's frightened of the dark, but would rather die than admit to it.'

'And what about tomorrow?' asked Robert, unsure whether Rebecca fully understood the great peril he was in.

'Oh, tomorrow's another day. Anyways, I think I may have a proposition. Must hurry because Annabel's already grumping. Goodnight, Roberto.'

And before Robert had a chance to quiz her further or to complain about his new name, she beamed a handsome smile, about turned and skipped off.

'Be sure to turn out the lamps,' were her final final words.

After brushing his teeth with the harshest toothbrush he'd ever used in his entire life, along with the strangest and most disgusting substance he'd ever put into his mouth, Robert extinguished the two lamps and slipped into bed. His new lengthy shirt was the perfect pyjamas.

Rebecca's bed was large, soft, and immensely comfortable, and it didn't take Robert long to fall into a deep satisfying sleep. And then he started to dream.

12. A Betrayal And A Mouse

Robert had many dreams that night, a full belly just before bedtime was most accommodating in that respect. In one, he was a knight, rescuing Rebecca from the tower of a castle. In another he was running through a field of brightly coloured flowers with Titch and Sparky by his side. In yet another, Rebecca was beside him, nursing him as he lay in an enormous bed. She was gently rocking him backwards and forwards, while lullabying him. Then she spoke, urging him to get up because they were coming to get him. The rocking got stronger and stronger, until it was so forceful he really did wake up, opening his eyes to discover this last dream was in fact reality. Rebecca was indeed standing over him, frantically shaking him to waken up.

'Robert, thank goodness you're awake. You must flee quickly. Annabel has betrayed us!'

It was early morning as the room was neither dark nor light. Robert jumped out of bed all a panic, and promptly ended up on his bum.

'I don't understand,' he said, after righting himself and starting to dress. 'I thought she promised!'

'I know, but we must hurry. She sneaked out a few moments ago. Normally she never rises before me. I'm certain she's going to tell.'

Robert was now fully dressed and after fumbling with his laces, was all set. But for what?

'What am I going to do?' he asked. It was the exact same question he'd asked the previous evening.

'My plan, remember!' Rebecca said, eyes sparkling. 'Follow me and hurry.'

She immediately dashed to the door and noiselessly unlocked it. Robert was right behind. Tentatively, she stuck her head out of the small gap. In a flash, she opened the door and leapt across the corridor. Whereupon, she entered the door opposite.

'Quickly,' she mouthed. Robert obeyed, hastily shutting the door behind him.

Rebecca pulled him in, and after a brief glance either side, secured this second door.

The room they were now in was large, poorly lit, and clearly unused. There were dust sheets everywhere, covering the tops of wardrobes, lamps, tables, and other indiscernible items. Stacks of wooden boxes and other packings littered the floor. It would be perfect for hide and seek, Robert thought.

'We play hide and seek in here,' Rebecca said, hurrying over to a spot she was evidently familiar with. 'Nobody ever comes in here except for Annabel and myself. Everything belongs to the previous governor, before he mysteriously disappeared. Uncle doesn't know what to do with it all. Auntie wants to sell it.'

Robert was confused. Was she expecting him to hide in here for ever? It wouldn't take them more than a couple of minutes to fish him out.

'I can see you're a little bewildered,' said Rebecca, and she grinned from ear to ear. 'Watch!' and with that she reached down and did something to the bottom of the oak panelled wall. Within a second, part of the panel had shifted.

Robert was agog with excitement. Was a light really appearing at the end of a very dark tunnel?

'It's a secret passage,' Rebecca explained. 'And don't worry, only I know about it. I found it one day when I was exploring. I use it sometimes when I'm playing hide and seek with Annabel. And don't say it, I know it's cheating.'

Robert couldn't care less if Rebecca was cheating the loathsome Annabel. He needed an escape route, and this was it.

'Where does it go to?' asked Robert, peering into the small passageway.

'To the outhouses at the back of the garden. It can only be opened from inside the tunnel so nobody's discovered it yet. It's the perfect escape route, don't you think? If we can just get clear of the outhouses undetected, then I know where to climb over the wall.'

Suddenly, Robert stopped and stared at Rebecca. 'Why did you say we?'

'Because I'm coming with you!'

It was only then that Robert paid attention to what Rebecca was wearing, cut trousers, shirt, jacket, boots. She was dressed like him, even her hair was flattened and tied back. He was a hopeless detective!

'I've even got a cap to hide my hair,' she said triumphantly.

'It's impossible. You can't come with me,' declared Robert.

'Don't say that. I've got it all worked out,' beamed Rebecca. 'I've got money. We can pay for our passage back home to Edinburgh. Then, we can stay with my great auntie Margaret. I wanted to stay with her in the first place, but Uncle objected. I know she would welcome us, both of us, unless of course you have some relatives to stay with.'

'You can't come with me, Rebecca. It's too dangerous. Look at what's happened to me. Is it so bad with your auntie and uncle?'

'They don't love me, I don't think they even like me. They only want to control my inheritance. I shan't be any bother, I promise.'

'No, I'm sorry, you can't come,' repeated Robert. 'It's not safe for a boy, never mind a girl.'

It was like a red rag to a bull. Rebecca instantly got annoyed and her face flushed scarlet. 'Girls are as good as boys! I'm coming with you!'

'No you're not!'

'Yes I am! Give me one good reason why I can't!'

'Because I'm a pirate!' Robert blurted out. Now he'd opened a can of worms. 'I'm sorry. It's true. I am a pirate. But a good pirate.'

Rebecca was speechless and clearly upset. 'So you lied to me. And is Robert your real name, or just another grand fib?'

Robert felt ashamed. She'd shown him only kindness, and he'd repaid her with only lies. 'Robert is my real name.' And he paused in contemplation. Should he tell her that he's not an orphan? Best not. 'I'm sorry. Do you forgive me?'

Rebecca stared at him, her eyes searching for the truth. She'd broken a vase last week and pretended to know nothing about it. Was she a bad person? At least he had owned up and asked for forgiveness. She hadn't!

'I forgive you,' she said quickly, and she smiled in all sincerity from the bottom of her heart. 'You must have had a very good reason. We all lie sometimes.'

Robert breathed a sigh of relief. Their friendship had overcome its first hurdle.

Suddenly, the door handle shook violently. 'Is there somebody in there?' demanded a voice. The two children nearly jumped out of their skins.

'Quickly,' whispered Rebecca. 'You must flee. Please listen to me. It's totally dark in the tunnel, very narrow, and there are lots of steps. Be careful! The tunnel leads to a dead end; however, there are openings along the way. You must choose the third opening on the left. All the others lead nowhere.'

Robert tried desperately to absorb the information, while readying himself beside the small tunnel entrance.

'But what about you?' he asked nervously. 'Won't you be in an awful lot of trouble?'

'If the cause is good, then the sacrifice is worthwhile.'

A key sounded in the lock but it was of course blocked by their key.

'Go now,' she whispered. 'And don't dilly-dally. Oh, I nearly forgot, climb behind the Hibiscus bushes. It's lower.'

Robert turned to say a final farewell and Rebecca kissed him on the forehead.

'Goodbye Roberto! Until we meet again.'

'Goodbye Rebecca!' And he disappeared. He hadn't once objected to the silly name.

As their key plopped to the floor and the door opened, Rebecca slipped into the tunnel and silently closed the panel behind her.

Robert moved quickly along the low narrow passage, with the open entrance panel providing sufficient, if somewhat scant, light. It was very smelly but surprisingly cool inside. The thin corridor soon led to a flight of stairs, but halfway down all light ceased, and visibility dropped to zero. He knew Rebecca had sealed the panel. How much trouble was she now in?

Progress was slow now, and he took each step downwards like an elderly person. Then, he stopped. He'd totally forgotten about Rebecca's directions. What were they again? On the left. 'Second on the left,' he said aloud. He'd remembered.

Almost immediately, his left hand felt a gap in the wall. Exit number one, he said to himself. Then, the steps stopped and the corridor got tighter. He moved steadily, stretching one foot out first to check for steps, and then pulling forwards the other foot. The corridor was never-ending and he was becoming more and more sceptical. Thereupon, his hand glided over a vacant spot. Tunnel number two! He reassured himself by feeling the gap with both hands and carefully tracing the outline. Suddenly, he was confused. Which way was he facing? Which hand had touched the gap first? His mind was all mixed up and he was now totally disorientated.

'I'm going mad!' he shouted. 'Stop! I write with my right. The tunnel was on my right. Which is wrong! It has to be on my left. So I must leave with it on my right. Phew!' He was feeling composed again.

Soon enough, his foot once more found open air, and he prepared himself for further stairs. This time though the steps were narrower on one side, and he knew that he was descending a spiral staircase, unfortunately minus the handrail. As quickly as the stairs had started though, they stopped, and he geared himself up for yet another long corridor. But he was mistaken, for after only a few seconds his left hand detected tunnel number two.

Robert was wholly unaware but fortune had smiled upon him. For this tunnel was in fact the third opening on his left. He was oblivious to tunnel number one as he had already passed it before remembering about the directions. What was different about this current tunnel was its temperature, it was cold, and Robert shivered. The walls too were now wet and slimy. He was surely underground, and with a slope beneath his feet, going deeper.

Downwards he shuffled as the air got thicker and breathing became more unpleasant. And then his journey stopped! His toe stubbed against something hard and putting out his hands, he concluded the tunnel was indeed finished. What now? Was there a way out as Rebecca had described? Or had he taken the wrong tunnel? Would he have to retrace his steps? Could he?

He felt around in the pitch black, and his hand grabbed onto something, a ladder. With no other options, he climbed. At the top was a cubbyhole, and as he groped around he touched something cold and pitted. Metal! A metal wheel. Without a moment's hesitation, he turned it anticlockwise, for all things open anticlockwise, he recalled. A mild grating noise followed, and before his very eyes, a thin ray of light penetrated the darkness. He continued to turn the wheel and in no time light flooded into the tunnel as a large stone slab was displaced. He was free!

After slipping through the opening, Robert lay on his back, breathing in the fresh air and momentarily soaking up the mellow golden light of early morning. Then he considered, and after placing both feet onto the slab, returned it to its former position and kicked some earth over it. Now what? And what did a Hibiscus bush look like?

He was at the back of a series of higgledy-piggledy stone, brick and wooden buildings. There were tangles of thick roots everywhere, with numerous broad-leaved plants creating ample camouflage, but an unhealthy dampness. The perimeter wall was not far off and visible through the undergrowth. He could never imagine Rebecca here, crawling around in one of her immaculate white dresses.

Which way now? There were fewer buildings to the right, meaning a shorter way to the garden, therefore his selection was swift. And so, half walking, half crawling, he followed the backs of the outhouses, until they abruptly ended along with the overgrown vegetation. In front of him now lay the gardens of the mansion. But what drew Robert's overriding attention was a massive bush as high as the wall and displaying oodles of large brightly coloured red flowers. His mum would have given her eye teeth to see this Hibiscus bush. For he knew that's what he was now looking at.

Robert huddled down, scanning the surroundings with his keen eyesight. And then, on impulse, he was off, headfirst into the heart of the Hibiscus. The leaves caught onto his clothes but thankfully there were no thorns to contend with. As expected, Rebecca's information was spot on, and in the blink of an eye he was up and over the wall. Immediately, he sped off towards the water and the port. With so many ships, surely some opportunity would present itself to get off this island.

Although nervous, Robert's changed clothes helped him blend in, and no one gave him a second glance. He kept to the quieter streets, skirting the busier areas. And so, with head down he succeeded in avoiding any unwanted attention. He reflected on his good fortune at meeting Rebecca, and so his mood was one of melancholy at having had to say goodbye.

'Hey! Got ony spare coins?' came a young voice from out of nowhere. Robert jumped. He hadn't noticed anyone.

A small raggedy boy promptly appeared. 'Got ony spare coins?' he repeated cheekily.

Robert shook his head deliberately. 'No, sorry!' And he continued onwards.

'Are ye in a hurry?' asked the boy, who was now following closely behind.

Robert ignored him. The last thing he needed was some cheeky wee child dragging after him.

'Are ye hurrying up because of the black clouds?' persisted the boy. 'It'll be thunder and lightning for sure, mark my words.'

'Go away!' shouted Robert, twirling around abruptly to face the annoying little boy.

The boy was small and skinny, with a mop of dark hair, underneath an oversized cap. His eyes were big and brown. His face and clothes were dirty and threadbare, and he was barefoot. He observed Robert intensely with an expression bordering on rude.

'Some rum. That's what ye need,' continued the boy.

Robert was rapidly losing his patience and he could feel the anger building up inside of him. What did this obstinate little fellow want? Instinctively, he squared up to the boy. Robert wasn't one for picking on those smaller than himself, unlike some at his old school, but this boy was really winding him up.

'I'm not old enough to drink rum,' exclaimed Robert. 'And if you don't go away, I'll .... '

'Ye wouldn't hit somebody so small would ye? I'm just a titch!'

And then everything clicked. Thunder and lightning! Rum! Titch! 'Do you know me?' asked Robert immediately.

'I do now, Captain!' and the small boy instantly grabbed hold of Robert, and hugged him like a grandmother would hug a grandchild after time apart. 'I knew ye wouldn't abandon us, Cap'n. I said it to the others but nobody would believe me. I'm Mouse by the way. I did recognize ye, it's just that I had to be really really sure. There's loads of shifty characters hanging around, ye know.'

Then, after taking a step backwards, Mouse began staring up at Robert, with not a word passing from his lips.

'Is there something the matter, Mouse?' asked Robert, feeling slightly uncomfortable. He used to hate it when older relatives sat and stared at him. His mum would always tell him to be less sensitive but it still bothered him.

'No,' said Mouse, and then he paused. 'It's just that I thought ye would be, well, bigger!'

'You're not very big yourself, Mouse!'

'But I'm no the captain, Cap'n.'

Robert was stumped. Mouse might be small, but his attitude was way big. Robert changed the subject. 'How did you know where to find me?'

'I didn't. We've got lookouts all over.'

'But how did you know I'd escaped?'

'That's easy! Ye always come up with something, Cap'n.'

'And Titch made it too, to safety?' asked Robert, as Mouse slipped off his rather large cap.

'He sure did, Cap'n. Titch is as safe as a castle. And he told us everything. Here, take my cap, it'll help yer disguise.'

Robert willingly accepted the gracious offer, and as he was putting it on, Mouse pulled out a piece of chalk from his pocket and drew a hangman on a nearby wall.

Robert was intrigued. 'Why did you do that?'

'To tell the others I've found ye, Cap'n. When somebody else sees it, they'll know to head back to The Lightning. They'll draw a few themselves, and in no time everybody'll know. It was your idea, Cap'n.'

Robert was impressed. The previous Robert MacSpoon, aka The Captain, was proving to be a hard act to follow. Robert only hoped he lived up to everybody's expectations.

'If yer ready, Cap'n, we should be off,' said Mouse, right after he'd drawn a second hangman on the opposite wall.

'Where are we going?'

'To The Lightning of course, Cap'n. We've got two row boats moored on the other side of town. As soon as everyone else turns up we'll be off.'

The two boys walked briskly through the dirty streets. On a few occasions strange individuals cried out to them, but Mouse was sharp with his retorts.

'Shouldn't we keep to the quieter streets?' said Robert, just as Mouse was about to turn into one of the more livelier areas.

'Why, Cap'n?'

'So that nobody sees us.'

'But nobody knows us, Cap'n. Who knows what ye look like? A few soldiers. And you've no chance of coming across the hoity-toity ones again. Not here that's for sure. They're all at home, stuffing their faces with roasted chickens and fruit pies. And you've got my cap on, remember.'

Robert was pleasantly surprised, Mouse was spot on. Virtually nobody could identify him. There were no photographs or televisions or artist impressions like what they show after bank robberies. Nothing had been invented yet. It was like a massive weight had fallen from his shoulders.

'Are ye hungry, Cap'n?' asked Mouse, with a twinkle in his big brown eyes.

'Starving!' answered Robert, rubbing his rumbly tummy. He didn't say anything about last night's feast of roasted chicken and apricot tart.

Thereupon, they came across a fruit stall, with a plethora of fruits for sale. Mouse instantly halted. Immediately though, a bald headed shopkeeper appeared brandishing a stout club.

'Get off with ye!' he roared. 'Yer always thieving. Ye filthy scamps!'

'We're only eyeing,' retaliated Mouse. 'Keep yer hair on!'

In a flash, the shopkeeper raised his club and came storming towards them. The two boys bade a hasty retreat.

When the shopkeeper was far enough behind them, Mouse sprang into a side alley and beckoned Robert in after him. And then, like a magician pulling out a rabbit from a hat, Mouse produced a bunch of fat juicy bananas.

Robert was open-mouthed, and then annoyed. He had never stolen anything in his entire life, until now. It might not have been him directly, but he was without doubt an accomplice.

'We have to give them back!'

'But why, Cap'n?'

'Because it's stealing, that's why!'

'But we're pirates, Cap'n. That's what we do.'

'No, Mouse. We're not just any old pirates. We're good pirates. We only steal from those who are greedy or bad. I don't mean to be horrible, and I know you meant well, but it's best we give them back.'

After listening intently, Mouse smiled. 'Okay!' he said, with not the slightest sign of offence being taken. 'But I'm not sure we can, Cap'n. What happens if the shopkeeper calls the soldiers?'

'Ah,' said Robert. Why didn't he think of that? Then he eyed the inviting bananas. 'No point in wasting them, I suppose. But next time, no stealing. It's not right and it's dangerous.'

'Aye, aye, Cap'n,' Mouse earnestly replied, while ripping apart the bunch of colourful bananas and proffering Robert half.

The boys quickly gobbled up the fruit and set off again. Mouse continued to draw identical hangmen on prominent areas, as Robert considered what lay in store for him. What would The Lightning and its crew be like? Would the crew treat him the same as Mouse and Titch had done? Could he be a captain? Did he want to be?

The streets, people and animals of Port Jamaica were soon left behind, and Robert found himself following Mouse along a dirt track with the sea on one side and flourishing vegetation everywhere else. The sun was hot and getting hotter with its relentless ascendancy directly upwards. This was a novelty to Robert, being more used to the arcs of a more northerly latitude.

Suddenly, Robert started. What if this was all a trap? Mouse hadn't really recognized him, but Titch had. And Titch would never have stolen something. What if the hug was false? What if Robert was the hangman! He deliberately slowed down.

'Is everything alright, Cap'n?' asked Mouse, turning abruptly around. A knife flashed in his hand.

Robert gulped. His fight or flight response was in full swing. Should he tackle Mouse, who was significantly smaller but armed? Or should he run into the bushes? He was certain he was the faster.

'A nice dagger, wouldn't ye agree, Cap'n,' grinned Mouse. 'Don't worry, it won't take a second.'

Not if I can help it, thought Robert, and he grabbed a broken branch from the ground. He would fight!

'Ye won't need that, Cap'n,' said Mouse, in a deceptively friendly manner.

'Why not?' asked Robert. It was always best to keep the enemy talking. He knew this from watching numerous police programmes.

'Because we've already got oars, loads of them. Fraser always insists we carry spares. Do ye row well, Cap'n?'

'Row?' asked a puzzled Robert.

'Yeah, Fraser said whoever finds the Cap'n should come straight back to The Lightning. It would be the safest. He's the most intelligent out of all of us, you know. Anyways, I've found ye. So if ye row well, and ye agree, I'll cut the rope with my dagger and we should easy make it. I might be small but I'm really strong. Look!' and Mouse pulled up his tatty shirt sleeve and exposed his bicep.

Robert had seen a bigger spider's knee, but that was a side issue. He'd made a mistake. Mouse was genuine. At least Mouse hadn't noticed. How embarrassing would that have been?

'So should we go it alone, Cap'n?' repeated Mouse. 'Like Fraser said.'

'Yeah, I think Fraser's right,' nodded Robert. 'If you're sure we can make it, I think we should go.'

'Great! I'll just go and slice the rope and we'll be off. Bennett always ties the knots too tightly. He's as strong as an ox, ye know.'

Mouse promptly disappeared into the bushes. After a quick check all around, Robert hurriedly followed.

As Robert emerged from the particularly dense patch of bushes, he found himself in a small clearing with an inlet directly in front of him. At the water's edge sat, side by side, two smallish rowing boats neatly tied up. Both had branches placed on top of them for camouflage, but the effect was minimal. Mouse was already active in cutting through one of the mooring lines.

'Ye should get in Cap'n. Just in case the current takes her. We'd be in a pretty pickle then, all having to squeeze into the one.'

Robert removed the light branches and hopped in, and after Mouse had drawn one last hangman on the remaining boat, they pushed off.

'How did you remember where the boats were hidden?' asked Robert intrigued. 'Everything looked the same.'

Mouse grinned. 'That branch ye picked up was a marker, Cap'n.' He paused. 'Mind you, I thought ye were gonna hit me with it at first!'

Robert smiled. Mouse had indeed noticed.

With oars in hand and the wind in their favour, the two boys headed for deeper water and the whereabouts of The Lightning.

13. Robert's First Fight

When Robert observed The Lightning for the first time, he was awestruck, and instantly wonderful feelings welled up inside of him. He recalled the wow factor of The Thunder, but this creature was even better. It was simply beautiful, magnificent, breathtaking. The sails were a brilliant white contrasting spectacularly with the dark brown of the body and masts. Even the multitude of ropes looked bright, orderly and agreeable. This ship was clearly recent and in exquisite condition. Was he really her captain?

'Finest ship in the whole world! Don't ye agree, Cap'n?' said Mouse, between strokes.

'Yeah, I don't think anybody could disagree, Mouse.'

Robert's arms were tiring rapidly but he continued unfalteringly at the steady pace they had struck up. He had no intention of showing himself up as weak. He also wanted to get to The Lightning as quickly as possible. It was so tantalizingly close now. Their backs were towards it but Robert could feel its overpowering presence.

'I reckon we should stop now, Cap'n, otherwise we'll ram her,' said Mouse. 'The current will take us the last few yards.'

Robert followed Mouse's lead and stopped rowing. Then, both boys turned to face the seemingly expanding ship.

Instantly, Robert gulped as a sea of faces peered down on him, and a swathe of trepidation engulfed him. He had never been so nervous in all his life. What if they didn't like him? What if they laughed at him? It was horrible being the new kid. He recalled the anguish of new children joining his class at school. Now that was him!

As Mouse had predicted, the current completed their journey and the rowing boat glided gently up to The Lightning. Although the sea was bright blue with hardly a ripple of white, a current was evidently present as the rope to the ship's anchor was taut. Immediately, two grinning boys with long poles with hooks on the ends snagged their tiny boat, ropes were thrown, and a climbing net was dropped.

Alas, Robert's entrance was less than ceremonious. In his haste to match Mouse's speedy ascent, his foot got tangled in the ropes and he flopped over the gunwale like a fish on dry ground. The deck stank of tar and salt. Fortunately, nobody laughed, but a crowd of faces stared at him with burgeoning interest. Robert cringed and wished for the ground to swallow him up.

Suddenly, someone erupted in laughter, and a tall figure pushed through the gathering. The boy was bare chested and his body was tanned and muscular. His hair was of a light brown and his eyes were dark and moody. He had the swagger of self importance.

Robert hurriedly picked himself up and moved to confront the boy. But the tension was swiftly broken when a second boy stepped forwards.

'Hey, C-Captain. I'm F-Fraser,' said the boy. 'Welcome to The Lightning.' And he offered a hand, which Robert gratefully accepted. 'That's R-Reno,' he added, nodding to the tall, muscular boy.

'I don't need you to introduce me! Ye stuttering fool!' snapped Reno.

'He's no fool!' shouted Mouse, appearing from the crowd. He had been swallowed up by the ever decreasing circle as everyone vied for position.

'Shut it, Mouse! It's a pity you came back too,' snapped Reno.

'As well as who?' asked Fraser, who was getting visibly more nervous by the second.

'Him!' snarled Reno, jabbing a finger straight at Robert.

Robert was beginning to feel decidedly uncomfortable. Did they want him to be their captain or not? He had no intention of hanging around where he wasn't wanted. Although, where was he to go?

'But he's our C-Captain,' stammered Fraser.

'Not any longer!' announced Reno. It was obvious that he was speaking to the whole crew now. 'Yer last captain deserted ye and his replacement is worthless! Why, he can't even stand up!' Again he pointed at Robert provocatively. 'He should stand aside! I'm yer new captain!'

'Nobody voted ye!' shouted Mouse defiantly. There were a few mumbles but most were unwilling to pick sides.

'Nobody voted him!' snapped Reno.

'Then we v-vote,' said Fraser immediately.

'No!' said Reno. 'The Pirate Code says a captain can be voted out or fought out. And I intend to fight!'

Robert looked at the tall, muscular boy. If it came to fisticuffs he wasn't sure he fancied his chances. But then he had a solution. 'We can share the captaincy! There's probably loads to do!'

'I've heard of a wolf in sheep's clothing. But you're a sheep in sheep's clothing!' cried Reno, jabbing his finger again.

A meaty boy, of a similar height to Robert, was clearly enjoying the spectacle. He repeatedly smirked and nodded his large strong head. Robert guessed it was Reno's sidekick.

'I reckon Barrel here could lick ye,' continued Reno. 'What do ye say, Barrel, ye old sea dog, ye fancy taking ma place?'

'Easy,' said Barrel, stiffening himself up to appear taller.

'Alas, rules is rules! I'll have to kill ye myself!' and Reno eyeballed Robert. 'Unless ye choose to step aside yersel.'

Robert didn't like the way this was heading, and was about to say something, anything, when Fraser once more stepped in.

'C-Captain, can I speak with ye p-please?' he asked in a muted voice, as Reno looked on triumphantly.

'If you want to,' replied Robert, expecting Fraser to begin talking.

'In p-private, p-please.' And he looked at Robert with his large blue eyes.

'Alright,' said Robert. It was certainly a good time for a breather.

'Hurry back, lads! Yer captain awaits!' trumpeted Reno.

Fraser quickly led the way to the back of the ship, the curious crowd barely parting to let them through. After passing the mizzen mast they entered a cabin, whereupon Fraser shut the door.

There were many windows in the ample sized cabin, making it very light. It was, however, decidedly sticky inside, as none of them were open. Everything was in a terrible mess, as if a number of people had been sleeping there until just moments ago. Piles of dirty wooden plates were strewn haphazardly in the centre of the floor, and small side tables were piled high with debris.

Robert watched as the slim boy with the straggly fair hair latched each and every window. Whatever was to be said was to be said without interruption and in private.

Fraser turned abruptly. 'Ye will have to f-fight him, C-Captain.'

'Fight him? I don't think so!' said Robert, somewhat surprised.

'No, ye m-must! He challenges you, humiliates you. The c-crew d-don't know what to do.'

'So we can work something out. Compromise.'

'Unfortunately R-Reno doesn't do c-compromise. Ye must f-fight, C-Captain!' Fraser repeated.

Robert was rapidly becoming annoyed with this insistent boy. It was easy to push others into a fight. Maybe Fraser should step forward himself!

'No, I won't,' declared Robert firmly. 'I won't fight and that's that. If he wants to be captain so much, he can have it.'

'But R-Reno is no c-captain. We will surely p-perish with him in charge.'

'He got you here, didn't he?'

'No, C-Captain, you got us here. Not him. He just thinks he did, and now his head's grown to the size of a p-pumpkin. It's you that guides The Lightning. Without you, we're all f-finished.' Fraser paused. Then quickly he tried a different tack. 'What do ye think of the c-cabin, C-Captain?'

'It's like a pigsty.'

'It's your c-cabin, C-Captain. It still hides yer c-cutlass.' Fraser was calculating this would whet Robert's curiosity.

Robert became distracted. Would he appear two faced if he asked for a look? 'Can I see the cutlass?'

Fraser released a delicate smile, and after tapping open a piece of wood in the cabin wall, he pulled out a rounded sword and presented it to Robert.

Robert's eyes lit up like candles. 'It changes nothing,' he said, feeling the curved blade with his fingers. Boy was it sharp!

'B-But surely ... ' began Fraser.

But Robert interrupted. 'No! Here, take it.' And he handed back the shiny cutlass. Now he was curious though. 'How did you know where it was hidden?'

'Because the old you showed me, C-Captain. Ye t-trusted me. And I c-can tell ye, that what yer d-doing is wrong. You will b-beat him.'

Robert couldn't stop himself from disliking Fraser. The boy's nonstop pushy attitude was really getting under his skin. 'You're not my mother,' Robert grumbled. 'I'm going!'

On deck, a disgruntled Reno was becoming impatient. They had had long enough to talk! Thereupon, Robert exited the cabin followed by an awkwardly moving Fraser. Straightaway the chatter of the crew subsided.

'What is yer decision?' asked Reno directly.

'I say, we can share the captaincy. What do you say?'

Reno erupted in vicious laughter. His dark unforgiving eyes alive with sheer spite. 'No, my shipmate, you will fight or you shall yield!'

'I won't fight,' said Robert, and for a moment you could have heard a pin drop.

'Then, crew! I am yer new captain!' announced Reno, swishing his arms around melodramatically.

'Yer no captain of mine!' cried Mouse.

In a flash, Reno lunged at the small boy and thumped him square in the face. Poor Mouse was propelled backwards, landing heavily against the ship's side.

'You're nothing but a big bully, Reno!' shouted Robert, running to Mouse's aid.

Piteous Mouse had a bloody nose but was defiant to the end, glaring at Reno steadfastly.

'Yeah, but as we've seen there's nothing ye can do about it,' crowed Reno.

'Then I shall fight you, whether I win or lose,' declared Robert.

'With c-cutlasses!' said Fraser, forthwith.

Robert turned acutely, and he was wild. 'Why did you say that?' he shouted through clenched teeth. It was bad enough losing in a fist fight, but to lose in a sword fight could spell the end.

Fraser averted his eyes uncomfortably. He was playing a dangerous game and he knew it.

'Don't worry, I shan't kill ye,' said Reno, withdrawing his cutlass excitedly. 'I was only jesting before. We might still need ye.' Things were turning out better than he had expected. In a few moments they would all be eating out of the palm of his hand! 'Hurry up, someone give the challenger a cutlass!'

'B-But it's you who is the challenger,' said Fraser, and immediately pulled out Robert's cutlass from behind his back.

Robert's heart jumped into his mouth. He was about to fight. With real swords. No protection. No rules.

'I knew ye had that squirrelled away somewhere,' said Reno. 'And you, holding out on me, Fraser, lad!'

Robert held the heavy curved sword for a second time. It was totally different to a fencing sword. He swished it from side to side. Instinctively, the crowd backed up, with many clambering up the rigging for a better view. An arena was being formed.

'I shall wish the Captain good luck,' declared Mouse, going against the flow of bodies. The small boy's shirt was scarlet with blood, his eyes red from tears, but his defiance remained intact. 'Cap'n,' he whispered directly into Robert's ear. 'He always strikes straight on.'

'Now we fight!' said Reno, and with those words he swished his cutlass from side to side, and within a whisker of Robert's face.

Robert jumped back, raised his cutlass, and the fight was on.

Reno lunged forwards, not only confident of victory, but confident of a quick victory. Automatically, Robert parried the blow, but the attack was strong and he stumbled backwards.

'Yer weak!' cried Reno. 'Perhaps yer an imposter. Come here to spy on us.'

'I'm-no-spy,' countered Robert. The wind had been squeezed out of his lungs and gasping for breath, his words were weak.

Reno continued the onslaught, slicing from side to side, as Robert, struggling to defend himself, stumbled for a second time.

'After victory you'll kneel before me,' hissed Reno.

Robert didn't respond. Instead, he was trying to think what his fencing coach would have said. But it was difficult under these circumstances. Reno was like a madman. He wanted to hurt someone.

Again Robert stumbled. And then ping! He realized why. Of course, he was on a boat. It was constantly rocking. Consciously, he tried to adjust himself, moving with the undulations instead of fighting against them.

It worked! After yet another parry, Robert was on the attack, thrusting his cutlass at Reno's torso. The blood rushing through his veins. He was revitalized. He was fighting for his life. His opponent was backpedalling.

Then disaster struck! The ship bobbed. A crew member perched on the rigging lost his grip. A dangling rope with a large knot on it went swinging. Reno dodged it. Robert got it, right on the side of the head. Dazed, he fell backwards, crashing forcefully against the bulwarks, but cutlass still in hand. Like a cat, Reno seized his opportunity and pounced. With cutlass primed the victory was his.

Is this the end? thought Robert. After all he'd been through, to be skewered by a member of his own crew. In a flash though, two things ran through his mind. Firstly, Reno needed him. He'd said so himself. Secondly, Mouse's advice. Unmoving, Robert stared at his victor. Waiting. But nothing happened.

Suddenly, a wildness appeared in Reno's dark eyes, and his right one started to twitch ever so slightly.

'Hey!' shouted Mouse. 'It's over!'

But it was too late. Reno jabbed his cutlass forward. Except Robert, anticipating what was about to happen, had already begun his defence. The two cutlasses clinked together, the cutting edge of Robert's striking the blade of Reno's. The tall boy's sword tumbled to the ground. Instantly, Robert flipped himself up and pressed the sharp tip of his cutlass against Reno's naked belly.

'Do you give up?' demanded Robert. But there was no malice in his voice, only relief that he wasn't dead.

'Aye,' mumbled Reno, sweat pouring from his brow. He was clearly stunned. Defeat was something he had not contemplated.

Robert slowly withdrew his cutlass and Reno's relief was palpable, as was that of the crew. All the previous tension disappeared and excited chatter took its place. Ripples of laughter even flowed through the advancing throng.

Reno turned and left with his tail firmly between his legs.

Forthwith, an exultant Mouse sprang forwards and hugged Robert jubilantly. 'Ye beat him, Cap'n! I knew it. I just knew it.'

'Only just,' said Robert, as dozens of children suddenly pressed inwards.

'Hey Cap'n, I'm Boxer,' said one, with a blue-grey neck scarf on.

'I'm Leo, Cap'n,' said another.

'Ignore them, Cap'n. I'm Cooper,' said another.

The rest of the morning was taken up by introductions - Robert gave up counting after being introduced to the same boy for a third time - and a guided tour of The Lightning. The latter was carried out by Mouse. Fraser was conspicuous by his absence.

An ultimately pleasant morning became an even more pleasant afternoon when the remaining crew returned from the island.

'Ship Ahoy!' came the cry from the crow's nest. Immediately, all hands lined the ship's perimeter.

'Cap'n!' said Titch, on boarding the ship. 'Ye made it. I thought I heard shots.'

'You did,' said Robert. 'I even got hit.' Instantly he felt guilty. Now he was showing off. Even so, how good it felt.

The crew were agog in unison, jockeying for position, awaiting the next part of his adventure. But a tall boy was having none of it.

'Back to work!' he ordered. 'This isn't a holiday ship. There are jobs to be done!'

At once, the disappointed crew dissolved into the ship and only four boys remained. Although many eyes and ears were trained in their direction.

'I'm Bennett,' said the tall boy. 'Captain,' he added hurriedly.

Bennett was big, bigger than everybody else on the ship, including Reno. Along with thick arms and a thick neck, he was a substantial individual. But his size belied his years. His face was childish, with an abundance of small freckles and something akin to puppy fat. Lank brown hair only added to his youthful appearance.

'Pleased to meet you,' returned Robert. But this wasn't just one more name to remember. He could tell that this strapping fellow was an integral part of everything aboard The Lightning.

'There was a fight,' said Mouse, matter-of-factly.

'Reno and the Captain?' said Bennett, half asking, half stating.

Robert nodded but he had no desire to enter into any details.

'He's a fool,' said Bennett. 'I reckoned he was up to something. But I didn't think he'd be so wooden-headed. I hope nobody was injured!'

'Only Reno's pride,' said Mouse.

'Well hopefully he's learned his lesson. Only together do we stand a chance,' said Bennett.

'Come on, I've still got things to show ye, Cap'n,' said Mouse, champing at the bit.

'Patience is what you need,' said Titch.

'My lack of patience comes from being taller than thee,' returned Mouse at once.

'But yer not taller than me!'

'Yes I am. A blind man could see it. Bennett, will ye do the honours please.'

The two small boys immediately backed up against each other, straining every last sinew to gain extra height.

'Identical!' announced Bennett.

'Ye always say that,' moaned Mouse.

'We should weigh anchor, Captain,' said Bennett, looking towards the shore uneasily. 'We're all back now and the open sea will be a lot safer.'

'I agree,' said Robert. He'd been thinking something similar.

'Weigh anchor!' roared Bennett, and the ship really sprang to life.

Dinner was served on the open sea. And never again would Robert complain about his mum's soups. What was dished up masquerading as soup was simply revolting, and he made a mental note to approach the problem.

As ever on the equator, night fell rapidly, and in minutes the once bustling vessel became a ghost ship as everyone took to their hammocks. They rose when the sun rose, therefore they went to bed when it fell, and to do otherwise would be a stark waste of lighting opined Bennett. Robert also retired, after a brief tidy up of his newly acquired cabin, but unlike his new friends he couldn't sleep. His mind was racing about what to do next and the confrontation with Reno. Also, something was gnawing in the back of his head that he might be due Fraser an apology. After everything that had happened, he was feeling somewhat lonely.

Robert flipped his feet out from his bunk. A near full moon gave sufficient light to don his trainers. He wondered who was still awake. The wooden floor creaked, as did the door when he opened it. Directly in front of him was the ship's wheel, but much to his surprise it was unattended, with only a rope holding it in the desired position. Ahead, the mizzen and main masts were reasonably distinguishable. He wasn't scared but he was hardly at ease.

Just then, a gentle cough sounded in the darkness. It was coming from behind him, on the raised platform that was the poop deck. Silently, he climbed the steps. A figure was leaning against the balustrade, his back towards Robert. It was Fraser, and instantly he turned.

'Ah, C-Captain,' he said. 'It's a nice night.' He owed an apology, but he didn't know how to begin. 'Do ye know what r-rigging is, C-Captain?'

'I think so,' replied Robert, rather puzzled. 'Why do you ask?'

'No r-reason, C-Captain,' answered Fraser uncomfortably. He simply had to get things off his chest, but he was unsure of the reaction.

Robert wanted to apologize too, but he hated apologizing. His mum would always tell him that it takes a man to say you're sorry.

'I'm sorry, C-Captain,' blurted out Fraser.

'No, I'm sorry,' said Robert, almost simultaneously.

'No, C-Captain. I should not have p-pushed ye to f-fight. I was wrong. He could have k-killed ye.'

'He nearly did!' exclaimed Robert. 'He really wanted to. If it wasn't for Mouse's advice I wouldn't be standing here.'

'I know what it m-might've looked like, C-Captain, b-but he wouldn't have h-hurt ye. I don't believe it. He m-merely wanted to f-frighten ye.'

Robert couldn't agree and shook his head.

'I should have explained things b-better, C-Captain,' said Fraser, and he too shook his head, regretfully. 'And what m-must ye think of me?'

'You were only trying to help. It's Reno I'm worried about. He's a bully.'

'Yer wondering if a leopard c-can change its spots? Ye m-must r-remember, C-Captain, he is only a child with no p-parents to guide him. He still has t-time to become a good p-person.'

Robert felt slightly relieved, but he knew it would take a lot of effort to trust Reno in the future. Fraser though, was alright!

'Some say there's life on the m-moon,' Fraser said, looking up at the large celestial body shining in the night sky. He was fascinated by astronomy.

'And what about you?' queried Robert. 'Do you think there's life on the moon?'

'No, I don't r-reckon there is, C-Captain.'

'Why not?' asked Robert, intrigued.

'Cos there's no g-green on it, C-Captain, and if there's no g-green, then there's no life.'

Robert was impressed. 'You're right. It's nothing but a desert.'

'I know all the p-planets in order, C-Captain,' said Fraser immediately. 'I read about them in my b-books. Next to the Sun is M-Mercury, then Venus, Earth, M-Mars, Jupiter, and farthest out is Saturn. All six of them.'

'Well you're going to have to add three more, because there's really nine.'

Fraser was enthralled. But Robert's mind was a blank and for the life of him he couldn't remember the other three. Fraser was on tenterhooks.

'Pluto,' said Robert suddenly. 'Although, they now say it's just a big rock and not a true planet.' And then it came to him. 'Uranus and Neptune!'

'So there's nine, C-Captain, b-but really only eight,' Fraser mused. 'Ye m-must write the names down for me so I shan't f-forget.'

'No problem. But what is a problem is what are we going to do. We can't just sail around the world for ever. We need a plan.'

Fraser faced Robert, his fair hair catching the moon's light. Should he propose something? Would they fall out again? Once bitten, twice shy, turned over in his mind.

Robert noticed his friend's discomfort. 'Please Fraser,' he said. 'I didn't listen before, but now I will. Along with Bennett, it's up to us to make the big decisions.'

Fraser was much relieved. 'Then we must f-find The B-Book of M-Maps, C-Captain. It's the only way you'll ever get back to R-Rum. The last c-captain couldn't have managed without it. And boy, how he tried. And the t-treasure we must use for schooling and a home for us all. As ye say yersel, we can't just sail around the world f-forever.'

'So where is this Book of Maps?' asked Robert, fed up hearing about the thing. 'I don't have it.'

'But you hid it, C-Captain.'

'Where?'

'On an island, C-Captain.'

'Which island?'

'Nobody knows, C-Captain. Only thee.'

'But that's just it. I don't know!' cried Robert. 'And there's no other way I can get home?'

'No C-Captain,' said Fraser, shaking his head. 'Only after f-finding it, did the last c-captain know what to do. B-But I'm certain the information we need is inside yer h-head. We just need to unlock it somehow.'

'Any ideas?' asked Robert gloomily.

'Of course, C-Captain,' said Fraser. 'But it's a shot in the d-dark.'

'Then fire away,' said Robert. 'I can't see that there's much to lose.'

'There's an old b-blind man in T-Tortuga, P-Peg's his name, who can see into the f-future. Well, maybe he can see into the p-past as well.'

'So where's this Tortuga?'

'North of Hispaniola, C-Captain. Not too f-far from here. Nearer with the f-fog.'

'And this old blind man is good and will help us?'

'P-Possibly, C-Captain. Ye went to him before and r-reckoned he helped ye. P-Pirates are a superstitious lot, the old man must be sitting on his own t-treasure. I think it's worth a shot. But it's a d-dangerous p-place and there are lots of eyes and ears around. If anybody were to g-get a whiff of what we're seeking, we'd b-be in b-big b-bother.'

Robert took a second to digest the information. Travelling on a ship, with the warm breeze and the bright stars, which you could nearly touch, made everything seem like a dream. He'd been lucky up until now. A little more luck and he'd be going home.

'Then Tortuga it is, Fraser!'

'Aye, aye, C-Captain. But that's for t-tomorrow. Now ye had b-better rest.'

'And you too, yes?'

'I'll k-keep lookout for a little longer, C-Captain. Don't f-fret, B-Bennett's due to relieve me soon, then R-Reno after that.'

Robert's eyes hardened at the very mention of Reno's name and Fraser noticed.

'He's a g-good sailor, C-Captain,' said Fraser. 'He can be t-trusted.'

'Then goodnight, Fraser,' said Robert, and returned to his cabin where he immediately fell fast asleep.

14. The Two Pegs

The island of Tortuga lay northwest of the much larger island of Hispaniola. Shaped like the shell of a turtle, most of it was covered by a dense carpet of towering trees, surprising for such a mountainous island. The port was situated on the southern coast.

Knock! Knock! Knock!

Robert awoke, someone was knocking on his cabin door. It was dark, darker than when he'd gone to bed.

'It's me,' came a familiar voice.

Robert recognized it as Reno's and he didn't want to open the door. A few hours ago someone had likely tried to kill him, and the culprit was now standing outside his room. But he recalled Fraser's reconciliatory words and reluctantly opened the cabin door.

'It'll soon be daybreak,' said Reno immediately. 'Bennett said we're heading for Tortuga. As ye see, the fog has come. Maybe we can use it before it clears.'

Robert observed the tall boy and the thick fog all around him. He simply had to let bygones be bygones.

'Yeah, good idea,' said Robert, stepping out into the surprisingly cool night.

Forthwith, Reno withdrew a map from inside of his jacket and unrolled it. 'That's where we are, and that's where we're heading.'

Robert could barely see the map, but he took it anyway. Now what was he to do? Was there a special procedure he had to follow in order to guide a ship? Then he recalled his previous ritual and hastily dropped his head and closed his eyes. The situation was fast becoming cringeworthy, as he felt Reno's eyes boring into him.

Robert couldn't do anymore and opened his eyes. Then, all of a sudden, the fog vanished, the sun was poking itself above the horizon, and everything became visible.

'So are we there?' asked Reno bluntly.

'Near enough,' said Robert. But he had no idea.

The very next moment, just as if someone had waved a magic wand, the ship began to come to life.

'Captain!' said Bennett, appearing from nowhere and striding towards Robert. 'There's nobody in the crow's nest. In the dark we take our chances, but we need a lookout when it's light, and especially in these waters.'

'Yes,' replied Robert. He'd just been told off and it didn't feel good.

'Cooper! Get up those ropes and keep an eye out!' yelled Bennett, and the boy who had scarcely poked his head out from down below, instantly obeyed.

'How many will g-go ashore, C-Captain?' asked a sleepy eyed Fraser, appearing on the scene.

'Eight should suffice,' said Bennett. He had been going over the logistics ever since Fraser had informed him of their destination the night before. 'Any more would be too conspicuous, any less would be too light if we were to get into a scuffle. Unless of course the Captain has something else planned?'

'No, no, your plan sounds good,' said Robert, pleased that he was not alone in shouldering all the responsibilities. 'We just have to decide who goes.'

'The bigger the better,' said Bennett. 'Me, Reno,' he nodded to Reno. 'Yersel, Captain, Barrell, Boxer's good with a cutlass, Leo, he can shoot a pistol better than any of us ... '

'We're coming too!' interrupted Mouse, as he and Titch belatedly joined the conversation.

'Ye can't fight!' snapped Reno. The old Reno was back.

'But we know the way, and nobody else does,' said Mouse.

'Is it true?' asked Robert, hopeful that it was, and ignoring the safety aspects. Some friendly faces would be much appreciated.

'I hadn't thought of that,' said Bennett.

'So we're in!' declared Mouse.

'I told ye we'd be going,' said Titch, and the two boys smacked hands together.

'Well now we know who's g-going,' said Fraser. 'We should g-go now, when three quarters of the island is still asleep.'

'Ye mean, before breakfast,' cried Mouse.

'Ye won't die,' returned Bennett. 'Fill yer pockets with some biscuits to scoff on the way.'

'Tortuga straight ahead!' shouted down Cooper from the crow's nest.

The island loomed up in front of them in no time, and after a brief stop not too far from the harbour, one of the ship's two small boats was swiftly lowered. A number of other vessels had also come into view and danger was now lurking.

'Every four hours, on the hour!' shouted a nervous Fraser, as the rowing boat with eight excited souls on board, headed for Tortuga's main harbour.

It was still early morning but it was fully light and a stifling atmosphere was again building. All eight boys rowed with aplomb. There was a job to be done and each one bore a face of determination.

The port, the island's main settlement, was a conglomeration of everything. There were wooden, stone and brick buildings, all different sizes and all tightly packed together. The ground was muddy and puddles lay everywhere, a result of the frequent downpours and the lack of a drainage system. A plethora of discarded items were strewn along the docking area, giving the place a grubby, neglected appearance.

A few vessels were already active when the boys rowed ashore, most though were like ghost ships, gently bobbing up and down in the gentle swell. Nobody paid the boys any attention.

'We tied up there last time,' said Mouse, pointing to a quieter area which already held some similarly sized boats, most of which were either run aground or overturned farther inland.

'Will I stay with the boat, Cap'n?' asked Leo. 'I've got ma pistol.'

Robert was undecided. Things were getting serious. He inhaled deliberately.

'It's always best, Captain,' said Bennett. 'But I shouldn't think our little skiff will interest anyone.'

'Alright,' said Robert. 'But don't try anything heroic. If somebody wants the boat so much, just abandon it.'

141

'Aye, aye, Cap'n,' said Leo, a cheerful boy with an ever present radiant smile.

Immediately, the seven boys disembarked and the small boat was tied up to a weathered wooden post. Leo remained, pistol on lap, but hidden by his oversized waistcoat which he had just taken off.

'We shan't be long,' said Mouse. 'It's not too far.'

'Alright,' said Leo, but his voice was unsure and Robert nearly had second thoughts.

'We should hurry, Captain,' said Bennett, eager to speed things up. The port was beginning to stir.

The party moved quickly under Mouse and Titch's guidance. The alleys were narrow and dirty, the buildings tired and decaying. Nasty smells were everywhere.

Soon, they were in the middle of a long, narrow enclosed street and Robert was feeling nervous. There was nobody about except for the boys. It was the perfect place for a trap.

Suddenly, a man stepped out from behind a concealed doorway and blocked their path. He wore a large brimmed hat with a protruding feather, a waistcoat, trousers ripped at the knees, and sandals. His face was brown, with a long moustache and hooped gold earrings.

'Now, what would you lads be doing so early a fine morning?' he asked foxily.

'Leave us be!' returned Bennett. 'We don't have anything to steal.'

Robert quickly stepped up to Bennett's side. 'Let us past, please. We don't have anything.'

In a flash, the man yanked out a pistol from nowhere, pulling back the hammer as he did so. 'I'll be the judge of that. Now answer my question and empty yer pockets, before my finger gets twitchy.'

'There's only one of you,' said Robert, more angry than frightened.

Bennett made a noise, and Robert looked ahead. A second man was standing at the end of the alley.

'And there's two more behind,' Boxer added.

'And that makes four,' grinned the robber, who had no front teeth. 'So I'll be taking that necklace for starters. I like necklaces me.' Indeed, around his sturdy neck he wore two necklaces, one with a gold coin attached and one with a pointed tooth. 'The necklace, lad! Before my finger twitches.'

Robert was about to lose the Captain's pendant. He didn't know exactly, but he was certain it was the key to something. 'It's made from real lion bone,' he said, holding the pendant in his left hand, but not removing the strap from around his neck. The man's eyes became curious. 'It has magical powers if you know how to use it.'

The man's eyes were now on stalks. He knew of black magic and white magic, particularly on these islands. He'd never touched a real lion bone before. And for a fleeting moment his mind wandered.

In the bat of an eye, Robert slid out his cutlass and with the hilt knocked the robber's pistol clean out of his hand. And in the same single motion pushed the tip of his sword into the man's belly. Everyone, including the robber, were open-mouthed.

'Tell them to back off!' shouted Robert. 'Or I swear I'll cut you open before you blink!'

'Back up!' ordered the robber to his advancing comrades. It was clear he held the authority.

Bennett hurriedly withdrew his cutlass in support of Robert, and the rest of the crew followed.

'Tell them to drop their weapons and take off their clothes and shoes!' Robert ordered. He'd seen something similar in a film once.

'Do as he bids! They won't get far.'

The three men reluctantly dropped their weapons and began to undress.

'Now tell that one there to go back to the other two,' said Robert, nodding in front of him. 'And no tricks.'

'Night Watch! Ye heard him. Get over there!' growled the robber.

'Aye, Cap'n.'

The partially disrobed robber walked briskly from where the boys were heading to where they had just been. As he passed, they pointed their cutlasses like a guard of honour. If he tried anything they'd be ready. But nothing happened.

'Now you take off your clothes,' said Robert.

'And no fancy stuff,' said Reno, having picked up the robber's dropped pistol. Amazingly, it hadn't discharged and was still primed.

'I'll cut out yer livers when I catch yous,' said the robber, as he undressed. 'Mark ma words! Every last one of yous. An I've got a good eye for faces. Yer own mothers will no recognize yous after I'm done with ye.'

143

'Start walking,' said Robert.

'And if ye try anything, I'll shoot ye in the back,' said Reno, holding the pistol aloft.

'What now, Cap'n?' asked Boxer.

'Run!' cried Robert. And on that command, the seven children spun round and took to their heels.

'Which way now, Mouse?' puffed Bennett, as they led the way.

'Here, I reckon,' replied Mouse rather unconvincingly, and they veered off to the right.

'And now?'

'Eh, here,' panted Mouse, but he wasn't really sure.

It was a dead end, with not a window nor door in sight, and before Bennett or Mouse could rectify the mistake, the others were bunched up behind them.

'It's the wrong way!' cried Titch. 'We should have gone straight on.'

Suddenly, footsteps smacked against the stoned ground nearby. 'This way!' shouted a gravelly voice.

'We can't climb that!' said Reno. 'It's like the blind leading the blind with you two!' And he glared at Mouse and Bennett.

Like everybody else, Robert looked upwards. The brickwork was even and time was fast disappearing. There was nothing else for it: they would have to fight.

'Cap'n! Over here,' said Titch. 'There's a hole and it goes right in.'

Everybody turned as one to see Titch stooping and peering into a tiny opening at the base of the wall.

'It's drainage,' said Bennett. 'If it's full we're done for.'

'We'll chance it. Everybody in!' ordered Robert.

It was like water draining down a pipe, so fast and fluid did they disappear into the hole at the base of the wall. Then it was Robert's turn and in he dived, head first. The drain was extremely tight but he scurried on.

'Over here!' shouted a voice, and feet pounded the ground. 'I heard something.'

'There's nobody here!' complained a second voice, louder now.

'Well, they're going nowhere, cos they'll no get off this island. We'll round up the crew and hunt them down. They'll be begging me to shoot 'em before I'm done with 'em.'

Robert crawled along on all fours. The ground was wet, slimy and bumpy, and he couldn't see a thing. 'Is anybody here?' he asked.

'Yeah,' replied Mouse instantly. 'We're right here, Cap'n,' and he outstretched a hand backwards.

'Ow, that hurt,' said Robert, as Mouse's finger prodded him straight in the eye.

'Oops. Sorry, Cap'n.'

It was then that Robert realized that Mouse was accident prone. It was now more than a hunch.

'Should we keep going, Captain, or sit it out?' asked Bennett, who was at least four bodies further up the drain.

'Keep going, I guess,' said Robert. 'Until there's a way out. I don't think I can turn around anyway.'

'There's light ahead,' said Titch, soon after.

'Ah, I was enjoying this,' said Mouse. But he was on his own.

'It's all clear, Cap'n!' said Titch. 'Do ye want me to try and get out?'

'Yeah, but double check it's all clear first,' answered Robert.

Titch peeked out of the small gap, and after seeing nothing of note, squirmed out into the daylight.

'What now?' asked Barrell, after everyone had squeezed out.

'We need to hurry,' said Reno. 'They'll be searching for us. And Titch leads this time!'

'Don't want to lead now anyway,' muttered Mouse.

'We'll take up the rear,' said Bennett, putting his arm around the small boy's shoulder.

'Then let's get moving,' said Robert.

As the procession trotted briskly along, Robert caught up with Titch at the front. 'Do you still know where we're going?'

'I reckon so, Cap'n.'

Robert was terrible at directions. He'd gotten lost loads of times, at the cinema, in a supermarket, at a football match, even when coming home from school once after he'd taken a shortcut.

Then, Titch halted abruptly. 'I reckon this is it, Cap'n. Peg's house.'

The half wooden, half brick house, was set back from the street, with an extremely overgrown garden in front. Like the majority of things on the island, what was visible was shabby and neglected. The chimney stack was leaning so much a solitary bird could have brought it tumbling down, if it happened on resting for a moment. A green rickety fence with a rusted gate separated the garden from the street.

'That's it for sure,' said Mouse. 'I remember the gate. See, it has a moon on the front.'

The shape of a crescent moon was barely, but nevertheless distinguishable, amidst the rusted metal.

'Yeah, ye remember everything,' sneered Reno. 'Only, after it's already happened!'

Gently, Robert pushed open the gate, fearful that it would disintegrate into a pile of dust if too much pressure was applied. One by one the seven boys entered.

'Is this safe?' asked Robert, having second thoughts. 'We've already been ambushed once today.'

'Maybe we should turn back,' said Boxer. 'It looks creepy. I hope there aren't any witches.'

Mouse was not so afraid and boldly pushed forwards and knocked on the blackened door. No answer. He tried again. Still no answer. The seven boys looked at one another.

'Oh well ... ' said Boxer. 'Nobody's at home.'

Suddenly, a window was thrown open right beside them, and an old woman with no teeth and a large hooked nose, eyed them. Robert felt it was everything a witch would look like.

'Be off with yous!' she cried. 'Or else I'll put a curse on ye for the rest of yer miserable lives. Waking the dead at this unholy hour!'

'That's it, I'm going,' cried Boxer, but Bennett blocked him.

'We've come to see Peg,' declared Mouse.

'I've never heard of him. Now be off with yous!'

'We've got gold,' said Bennett.

'Ah, I forgot about that,' said Mouse.

'Stay there!' ordered the old hag, closing the smeared window and disappearing.

'That's his wife,' said Titch. 'She's gotten even uglier since last time. Pegma's her name.'

'Peg and Pegma. What funny names,' said Robert.

The door opened sharply and they were beckoned inside. 'Come on! Come on! The wings of a bat and eyes of a toad are waiting,' she cackled.

'I'll stay outside and keep lookout,' said Boxer swiftly, and before anybody could stop him he had jumped behind a bush and totally disappeared.

The small entrance hall gave way to a larger room, which was as equally dark and dreary. The spartan conditions were only interrupted by a blackened old stove sat against one wall, a table with benches in the middle, and a set of crumbling stairs. The smell of old smoke was everywhere and filled the boys' nostrils.

'Gold!' said the greedy old woman.

Bennett immediately delved into his pocket and brought out a small leather pouch. Carefully he pulled out two small silver coins and placed them onto the table alongside the dirty plates, and a burnt-out candle.

'Aha!' cried the old woman. 'Ye try to cheat me! Ye think I'm as blind as my old man and as stupid as a donkey. Gold, my boy. Ye said gold.'

Bennett, with purse still in hand, placed another silver coin onto the table. 'That's all yer getting. Ye won't wheedle any more out of us.'

'Not enough! Now get out of my home.' And she hobbled towards the door.

'Pegma!' roared a voice from upstairs. 'Take the offering and send them up!'

The old woman's face could have turned milk sour. 'Well, ye heard the old fool. Follow me.' And after scooping up the money, she started to climb the rickety set of wooden stairs in the corner of the room. The boys looked at one another for a brief moment and then followed on.

'Here's yer miserly clients,' she announced, on entering a fair sized room with little light and no door. 'Everybody wants something for nothing these days,' she grumped. 'How are we supposed to feed ourselves? We might as well just roll over and die. And then they'd still pick our bones clean, one by one.'

'Oh, hold yer tongue, old woman,' said an old man who was sitting on a rocking chair by a covered window.

The six boys lined up, backs against the wall, and tried to decipher their host in the dim light. He was a stout man, bent over, with long straggly hair tied back into a ponytail. His face and hands looked brown and strangely lumpy. He made no effort to turn to them.

'Welcome to ma humble abode,' he said in a friendly manner, which emphasized the full mercurial nature of the fellow. 'Now what can I do for ye?'

'I was told you have magical psychic powers,' began Robert. 'If it's true, we need your help please.'

'Well then, seeing as yer so plainspoken, lad. Would ye be seeking particulars on The Book of Maps?'

Robert was surprised but didn't let on. 'Do you know where it is?'

'Come, shake ma hand, lad and sit down beside me. They call me Peg.'

There was a short, worn stool in front of him, which looked like it was used to rest his feet.

And then Mouse remembered something very important. 'Leprosy, Cap'n,' he whispered out of the side of his mouth. 'He's got leprosy.'

Robert walked over and shook the old man's outstretched hand.

'Everybody out!' cried Peg, straight out of the blue. 'You too, old woman! Only the lad stays.'

'You'll no be ordering me about ye old codger!' returned Pegma, but nevertheless she began her retreat. 'Ye heard the man. Shoo! Be off with yous, ye young scamps.'

Bennett immediately caught Robert's eye, who half nodded. And so the five boys departed with the irate and thoroughly offended Pegma.

Robert was now alone with Peg, and he stared at the old man's distorted face, unsure what was now going to happen. Suddenly, Peg looked back, his eyes no longer unfocused, but fixed directly onto Robert's eyes.

Disconcerted, Robert spoke. 'Can you see me?'

'Does it bother ye if I can?'

'No, I suppose not,' replied Robert, rather unconvincingly. 'How did you know I was looking for The Book of Maps?'

'Cos that's what ye asked about last time ye were here. Don't ye remember? Although, there's something different about ye that I canna put ma finger on.'

Robert said nothing and for a brief moment there was silence, then Peg cleared his throat and spat out of a small gap in the window which was behind the all but drawn curtains. 'Why did ye shake ma hand, lad? Yer pal warned ye, I heard so myself.'

'I trusted you,' said Robert. 'Why should you wish to harm another human being?'

'Ha ha. Ye trust too easily lad.'

'So, should I be worried?'

Peg hummed. 'No, but that's between me and thee.'

'Then I was right to trust you,' said Robert.

Peg huffed and then tugged at one half of the stained torn curtains. Light instantly entered the room and Robert could now see everything more clearly.

'Can you help me or not?' Robert asked impatiently.

'I believe so, ma lad. But first ye must make me a promise, Robert MacSpoon. Ye see, I gave ye a thought after yer last visit.'

Robert was taken aback. Not only did Peg remember Robert's name, but the old man was looking for something in return. 'If it's not something bad, and I can do it, then I will agree,' he said, sceptically.

Peg nodded. 'Over there,' he said, pointing to a large object on the floor with a rug thrown over it. 'Look inside.'

Robert got up, walked over, and pulled away the rug to reveal a large wooden chest similar to the one he'd hidden in at Rebecca's house.

'Open it,' said Peg.

Robert did as he was bade. 'There's nothing in it but a cloth.'

'Remove the cloth.'

Robert obeyed and there lay a small pile of gold coins.

'Gold Doubloons,' said Peg, grinning. 'Wonderful sight isn't it? And I've got more, lot's more.'

'I'm not sure,' replied Robert, viewing the meagre surroundings. He was no profligate this miserly old man.

'I expect yer wondering why I live like this when I have such riches, eh lad?'

'Yes,' said Robert, pausing. 'Why not spend some of it, or even better, give some of it to the poor.'

'Ha ha. I don't want less, lad, I want more. Why do the rich cast covetous eyes on their richer neighbours? No matter how much ye have, ye always want more. The love of money is the root of all evil, Robert MacSpoon. And it's smitten me for a long time.'

'Where did you get it all from. And why are you showing me?'

'Well, I never earnt it from this. Yer the first we've seen in months. Leprosy startles folks ye see. Which is understandable.' Peg hesitated. 'Yer promise. I'm a bad man, Robert MacSpoon. I've done a lot of bad things in my time. Pirating, murdering, torturing, cheating, that's where it came from. So long as I live, though, they'll keep their distance. But when I die they'll be circling like vultures round a carcass.'

'Who?' asked Robert. And what was it to do with him?

'My so-called brothers in arms.'

'What promise do you want?' asked Robert. He was becoming restless. His friends were waiting. Could this man help him or not?

'It's not for me ye understand. I want nothing for myself. I deserve nothing. But Pegma will need yer assistance. They will take it all from her, lad, and then murder her. I need ye to promise me, lad, to come back here when I'm passing.'

Robert was wide eyed. 'And what could I do?'

'Take her away from here, before they get to her, to someplace safe. Where you're from, let's say. And for yer troubles, you'll get a share of it all.'

Robert was flabbergasted. 'Does she know about the treasure?'

'She knows of it but not its full extent, nor its whereabouts. I'll only tell her when I'm passing. But the other thing, she knows nothing of. She is a good woman, kindhearted, good with children.'

Robert nearly choked. Were they speaking about the same person? She was like a witch.

'Yer promise stands, lad?' said Peg finally.

'Why me? There are plenty of people who would do as you ask for such a healthy reward.'

'I have no family, except for her, and no friends and trust no one.'

Robert considered. 'But you're trusting me, aren't you?'

'Yer different. Ye have different morals. Ye have goodness inside ye, lad. And yer strong, I can feel yer strength.'

Robert was somewhat sceptical at the last comment, but he'd made up his mind. 'I can promise you. I will do all I can.'

'Thank ye, lad. You'll know when I'm ailing. But now I shall fulfil my part of the bargain.' Peg closed his eyes and became motionless. Some minutes passed and Robert was about to prod the old man in case he'd fallen asleep.

'The necklace points the way,' Peg suddenly mumbled. 'Your cabin holds a secret.' He paused. 'Beware the crab!'

Robert pursed his lips. Was that it! He already knew the necklace was for something, the cabin had held his cutlass, and Mr and Mrs Crabb were old news. 'Ah,' he said. 'Is that all?'

Peg opened his eyes. 'I'm sorry to disappoint ye. Perhaps if ye had given gold instead of silver, I could have helped ye more. I jest, lad! I can offer ye nothing else. What ye do with it is up to you. But one more piece of advice Robert MacSpoon. Eat or be eaten! It's the law of the sea. Now ye should go, and hurry, I sense something bad is happening.'

Robert quickly departed. 'Necklace, cabin wall, crab,' he muttered to himself, as he skipped down the flimsy staircase. On reaching the bottom, he couldn't believe his eyes. His five friends were all sitting around Pegma's table scoffing and drinking. He immediately felt guilty, perhaps the old woman had a heart after all. 'Come on, we must go,' he said, somewhat jealous of his colleagues. 'Hurry!'

The boys jumped up, Mouse sticking another piece of bread into his already full mouth as he did so, and grabbing a second bit to take with him.

'Thank ye for the food,' said Bennett politely. It had been a surprise for him also.

'Eat yer thanks,' snapped Pegma. 'I want to know who's paying, the monkeys or the organ grinder?' And she peered at Robert with her wrinkled warty face.

'But I didn't reckon we had to pay,' said Bennett. 'And besides, we've already paid ye.'

'Ye paid him, no me!' cried Pegma. 'Cheating an old woman. You'll no live beyond today, any of yous. I'll put a curse on every last one of yous.'

'Can you give her something,' said Robert earnestly. 'Peg said we should hurry.'

'It's our last, Captain,' said Bennett, dipping into the leather pouch and reluctantly placing another small silver coin onto the table. The old woman eyed it with relish. Quickly, the boys filed out.

Eager to find out the success or otherwise of their mission, Mouse was the first to ask. 'So did he help us, Cap'n?' And at the same time he offered the chunk of bread which he had freshly procured.

Robert was pleasantly surprised. 'Thanks.' And he took a bite, not caring about either of their filthy hands. 'Not as much as I thought. He said my necklace is a sort of map and something's hidden in my cabin on The Lightning.' He decided to keep the crab warning to himself.

'Mm,' said Bennett. 'Fraser should be able to help out.'

'Boxer!' growled Reno. 'We're going!' No reply. 'Boxer! He's likely fallen asleep.' Still nothing.

Irritated, Reno disappeared behind the bushes. 'He's not there!'

Immediately, everyone started to scour the overgrown garden for Boxer. But he had completely vanished.

'That's his neck scarf,' said Mouse, pointing to a scruffy blue-grey piece of material hanging on a prickly tree branch.

Bennett picked it up. 'It's his for sure. No way would he have left it accidently. Something's happened!'

'We have to look for him,' said Robert uneasily. 'But we'll need to keep our eyes peeled for danger. If he's been grabbed then whoever did it, could still be around.'

The six boys tentatively left the garden.

'Try and stay hidden,' said Robert. 'A quick look round then straight back here. If anybody gets into trouble, shout!'

Thus, the nearby surroundings were hurriedly checked, but Boxer was nowhere to be found.

'It's bad, Captain,' said Bennett. 'But we really should get back to the skiff.'

'I agree,' said Reno. 'We've wasted enough time and we can't scour the whole island.'

'Then we should form a line with big spaces between us,' said Robert. 'That way we've less chance of being noticed.'

'I'll lead,' said Mouse immediately. 'I definitely know the way this time.'

'I'll take up the rear,' said Reno. And so a long line was formed and off they hastened.

The streets were busier now and Robert felt on edge. He was second in line, keeping behind Mouse, not too near, not too far. Third in line was Barrell, who kept much closer. The sun was high in the sky and the atmosphere was suffocating.

'Stop a second, Mouse,' said Robert, in the middle of a busy bit. 'We should check on the others.'

Barrell and then Bennett soon arrived. Titch was next, but there was no Reno.

'Where's Reno?' asked Robert.

'He was right behind me,' replied a surprised Titch. 'Just a moment ago. I'll go and get him.' And he about turned and was swallowed up by the stream of people.

'No!' cried Robert, but it was too late. Titch was gone and now there were only four.

'He wasn't far abaft me too, Captain,' said Bennett. 'They shouldn't be long.'

But five minutes passed and neither Reno nor Titch returned. The boys were also starting to receive inquisitive looks from the assortment of strange individuals who were hanging about. Bennett was getting nervous. 'I'll go and fetch them,' he said.

'No!' protested Robert. He didn't want to lose any more.

'But, Captain,' returned Bennett. 'Reno can take care of himself, of that I have no doubt, but Titch is no fighter. He could be in trouble. I'll only be a moment.'

Robert relented. 'Alright, but when you find them, go back to the boat. I don't feel safe standing here. We'll meet you there.'

'Aye, aye, Captain,' said Bennett, before heading swiftly off.

'Come on,' said Robert. 'Let's go.' And the three boys continued on their way back to the rowing boat and Leo.

'I'll be glad to see Leo,' said Mouse. 'We're dropping like flies in the wintertime. There'll be nobody left soon.'

Robert smiled, but the situation had actually become quite serious. Still, he hoped that all eight of them would be gathered together and ready to set off within the hour.

They arrived at the port, but it was a wholly different one now compared to the one at dawn. People were bustling around, stalls had been set up, goods were piled high, crews were dangling from riggings, shifty characters were lurking. And Robert had completely lost his bearings in the hubbub.

'Do you know where we are, Mouse?' he asked, tentatively.

'I reckon so,' said Mouse. 'The boat should be just beside that broken down jetty over there. Everything looks so different now though!'

Mouse's final remark did not inspire Robert with much confidence; nevertheless, the three of them hurried forth. They veered off to the right, rounded an old wooden shack and jumped down onto the sandy stony beach.

'Oh no!' exclaimed Mouse. 'It's not here!'

Robert studied the surroundings. It did look familiar. But their small boat was definitely gone, and so was Leo. The eight boys which had started out were now reduced to a mere three.

15. A Lucky Spider

Robert scanned the area again, but any lingering doubts were fully extinguished, this was the correct place, and Leo and the boat had definitely gone.

'What now, Captain?' asked Barrell grimly, his arrogance far removed from when Robert had first set eyes upon him.

'We'll wait for the others, but not out here in the open. Come on, let's find someplace safe to hole up and watch.'

'That shack sure looked deserted, Cap'n,' offered Mouse immediately. 'There was even moss on the lock. Maybe we could find a way in.'

'Alright, let's check it out,' said Robert. 'Anything's better than standing out here in the open.'

The shack was constructed mainly from slats of wood, with the odd sheet of tin interlinked. The wood was dark and appeared quite rotten in places, while the tin, though whole, was greatly rusted. It appeared to be abandoned, but appearances could be deceptive, as Robert recalled the tumbledown nature of Peg and Pegma's home.

'Let's see if there's a way in,' said Robert, touching the thickly mossed lock. Even the keyhole had been plugged, with only a small indentation remaining.

Thereupon, they each took a section and set about searching for a weak spot.

'Over here!' said Mouse. 'See, this bit moves,' he gasped, while tugging furiously. 'If only it would move a bit more.'

'Shift over,' said Barrell. 'This needs a man's hand.'

Mouse didn't budge, and so Robert joined in. With all their might the three boys pulled at the loose wooden slat. And eventually it turned, not much, but a sizeable gap appeared.

'I can get in,' said Mouse confidently. 'Watch this!' And sure enough, in he squeezed.

'What's it like?' asked Robert, even before Mouse had had the chance to wriggle his legs through.

'Kind of empty, Cap'n. And really smelly. But one or two little holes to keep an eye out.'

'Great, sounds perfect,' said Robert, and turned to Barrell. 'Maybe you should go next.'

'Couldn't I go after you, Cap'n?'

Having no objections, Robert followed Mouse inside. Then it was Barrell's turn, down he knelt and in he squeezed. But no matter how much he twisted and turned and pushed, he just couldn't get all the way through.

'Push more!' cried Mouse, relishing Barrell's predicament.

But nothing happened. Nothing changed. He was well and truly stuck!

'Help me!' pleaded Barrell. It was the last thing he wanted to say to these two, especially the pathetic Mouse.

'Let's each take a hand,' suggested Robert.

'Heave!' cried Mouse, unable to wipe the grin from his face, and they both pulled with all their might. And out the meaty boy popped! Like a cork from a bottle.

'Thanks,' said Barrell, straightening himself up and wiping himself down. 'I reckon I got snagged on something.'

Robert immediately expected a quip from Mouse, but none was forthcoming. How much better it would be if everybody just got on! There were so many other real enemies to face.

'Now we watch and wait,' said Robert. 'Boy, it sure is stinky in here.'

The three boys each took a side and settled down to observe the forthcoming events. There was nothing to sit on, and with the floor being somewhat soggy, they were left to squat on their haunches.

'This is fun,' said Mouse, after a short time.

But nobody answered. For Robert, it was a nightmare. What if nobody turned up? What then? Quietness returned as the boys watched intently.

'Help!' screeched Barrell suddenly.

Robert and Mouse turned sharply to see a gargantuan black hairy spider perched on Barrell's shoulder, and the poor boy with a terrified expression on his face.

'Get it off! Get it off!' he cried, but his hands remained fixedly by his sides. 'Whack it! Whack it!'

'Don't touch it!' cried Robert, remembering all the nature programmes he'd watched. 'Wait for it to go off itself. If you thump it, it'll definitely bite.'

Mouse was euphoric. Things couldn't get any better. Then, unflinching, the small boy walked over to Barrell and put his hands out.

'No!' yelled Robert.

But it was too late. Mouse picked up the big hairy beast and set it onto the palm of his hand. The thing was so large, and what with Mouse's small hands, its legs drooped over the sides. But there it sat, motionless and clearly contented.

'I like spiders,' declared Mouse calmly. 'They're so unlike us. Fraser says they've got as many eyes as legs. Is it true, Cap'n?'

'Some of them do, it's true,' replied Robert nervously. 'But can you put it down now? Some of their bites can kill you, and it doesn't take very long.'

'Yeah, stick it on the floor and I'll stand on it!' said Barrell, his confidence replenished. Unlike Mouse, he was wearing a pair of shoes and the sweet taste of revenge was coursing through his veins.

'It didn't bite you, so you can leave it alone,' said Robert. 'Put it over there in the corner please, Mouse.'

'Aye Cap'n.' And Mouse placed his hand with the hairy monster on it, onto the damp floor. But the thing didn't budge! 'I think it likes me. See, it doesn't want to leave. Can I keep it, Cap'n?'

'Better not, Mouse, animals don't really like being on boats.'

'Ah, I hadn't reckoned on that,' sighed Mouse.

Somehow sensing its time was up, the creature plopped onto the floor and crawled under a piece of crumbly wood.

Mouse sighed again. 'I've always wanted my very own ... '

'Sh!' mouthed Robert, placing his forefinger over his lips.

'They're no here!' growled a voice. The revolting individual then raked his throat and spat.

'Doubtless we got here before 'em,' said another milder voice.

'Possible,' added a third, familiar voice. 'But no likely. They're probably hiding out somewhere, hoping we lead them to that skiff of theirs.'

157

Robert stared at Mouse and Barrell, who were both staring back with a burgeoning fear. It was surely the pirates who had tried to rob them.

'What about that old shed there, Cap'n?' said the milder voice. 'They could be eyeing us this very instant.'

'My old mother's got more inside her head than thee, Night Watch,' retorted the Captain. 'If they're daft enough to be inside that there shack I'll lay ye ten pieces of eight.'

A number of different grunts of agreement instantly broke out, escalating the boys' concerns, for now they knew that there weren't merely three pirates standing outside, but possibly as many as a dozen.

Suddenly, the door was violently kicked, and a rusty nail with a sharp twisted end bounced onto the floor. The boys looked at one another. It wouldn't take much before the flimsy wooden door gave way.

Is this the moment my luck finally runs out, thought Robert. He would certainly fight, as would Mouse, of that he had no doubt. He wasn't so sure of Barrell though. He didn't really like Barrell. Barrell didn't exactly like him.

Again the door was kicked. This time a slice of black wood pinged onto the ground. Robert touched his cutlass. It felt cold. His legs were jellifying. Once more the door was struck with a powerful blow, and a second nail flew off. It wouldn't be long now!

'Cap'n! Cap'n!' suddenly cried a voice, panting with exertion. 'Blackjack's on the island!'

You could've heard a pin drop, and immediately the water lapping on the shoreline became audible.

'Ah,' said the Captain. The three boys were all ears. 'And it was definitely himself?'

'For sure, Cap'n. I saw him with these very eyes. Walking round like he owned the place. A proper peacock he was.'

'Well, he's fortunate we're on our way,' announced the Captain, after a short pause. 'Me and him have got some unfinished business. Round up the crew! We sail within the hour!'

'And what about the lad, Cap'n?'

Robert's eyes lit up. In a flash he was on the floor, his belly rubbing against the dirt as he wriggled into position.

'Kill him!' replied the Captain. 'And open up his innards. His mates will get a taster of what's coming.'

Only the pirates' feet were visible through a thin gap in the wood. Robert flipped himself onto his back. Mouse and Barrell were aghast. What was their captain up to?

'And the skiff, Cap'n?' came the voice from outside. 'What's to be done with it?'

'A drum's got more inside it than your head! Sink it, burn it, who cares, just make sure that lad dies. Now clear out! We're wasting time.'

Suddenly, the door shook again and a splintering sound echoed around the shed. Like a shot, Robert jumped up and beckoned Mouse and Barrell to quickly follow him. In a trice, the three boys were huddled together in the corner, right beside the hinges of the failing door.

'Night Watch!' yelled the robbers' Captain, from a noticeable distance. 'Will ye leave off kicking that damn door!'

'Aye Cap'n!' returned Night Watch, then released one last kick.

The door flew open! And the pirate looked inside. 'Blooming spiders!' he cried, as a big fat hairy spider scurried along the ground towards him. 'I'll be glad to get back out to sea.' And off he went at a canter to join his colleagues.

'Hurry!' said Robert. 'We need to save Leo!'

'But how, Cap'n?' asked a confused Mouse. 'We don't know where he is.'

'We don't. But he does!' said Robert, pointing into the distance.

'Who?' asked Mouse instantly, screwing up his eyes and following Robert's finger. For him the pirates had disappeared like rabbits down a hole.

'There!' said Robert. With his keen eyesight and the sun at his back, he had his quarry in sight. 'Hurry! Come on.'

The three boys moved at a fair lick, with Robert taking the lead.

'But how do ye know which one to follow, Cap'n?' puffed out Mouse, as they neared a busy bit.

'That's why I lay on my back. To see who was talking.'

'I reckoned so,' said Barrell. But Robert didn't believe him.

'You see that red scarf weaving in and out,' said Robert panting. 'That's our target. We mustn't lose sight of him.'

On the three children sped, rarely losing sight of the red scarfed pirate. Farther and farther they sank back into the town, until Mouse abruptly stopped. 'Isn't this the way back to Peg's!' he exclaimed.

Sure enough, they were in the same lengthy street where they had been ambushed a few hours ago. Robert gulped. Was this another trap? Had he been outsmarted?

'We've got no choice,' said Robert resolutely, and setting off again. 'Hurry. We can't abandon Leo.'

'I canna go on, Cap'n,' groaned Barrell, gasping for air. 'Leave me behind.'

'No!' insisted Robert. 'We all go together. Hurry, or we'll lose him!'

Barrell accepted the order and pushed himself onwards. But at the end of the street they again stopped. The red scarfed pirate was nowhere to be seen. Suddenly, someone coughed. Robert's heart skipped a beat. Again a cough. It was coming from above. He looked up, to see an old man precariously balanced on a roof, with a tool of some sort in his hand.

'Excuse me, sir!' said Robert, as politely as he could muster. 'My father passed a moment ago, did you see him. He wore a red scarf.'

'Right, and then straight on, he went,' replied the man, without raising his head.

'Thank you,' said Robert. What a stroke of luck!

They quickly followed the old man's directions, and soon passed Peg and Pegma's house. Then the street finished, and vegetation began.

'Where now?' asked Mouse, forlornly.

Straight ahead was a dirt track, to the left lay another smaller dirt track, and to the right an even narrower pathway.

Robert considered the options. 'This way! We need to go this way.'

'Why not left or straight on, Cap'n?' asked Barrell instantly. 'They look more worn.'

'Left takes us uphill,' Robert replied. 'Away from the shore. And there are no broken bits straight on. Look! See the broken stalk on the right, someone's passed here recently.' He held a juicy green leaf in his palm. The stalk had been snapped. 'Let's go!'

Robert led, Mouse followed directly, and a weary Barrell took up the rear. The undergrowth was becoming denser and the tree branches more convoluted. It was also getting decidedly soggy underfoot.

Suddenly, Robert stopped dead. Voices. There were voices not far ahead. 'Sh!' he whispered, finger on lips. 'We need to take cover.'

Forthwith, Robert sank into the undergrowth, followed closely by his two friends. Down they huddled and edged forwards. Then, in a small clearing right in front of them, was the red scarfed pirate, their stolen boat, and a troubled Leo.

Straightaway, Robert withdrew his cutlass and was ready to charge. Crack! One of them had stood on a twig. It was Barrell.

'I can see ye!' shouted the pirate. 'Come out or I'll cut his throat.' Immediately, he grabbed Leo by his top and held a knife to the terrified boy's throat.

'Go!' whispered Robert, pointing. 'You need to go.'

Barrell went as white as a sheet and remained stock still. Robert jabbed his finger unsympathetically. Grudgingly, the boy did as he was told, and raising himself up, moved into the clearing, hands held high.

'And the rest!' snarled the red scarfed pirate. 'I wasn't born yesterday.'

'Go,' said Robert reluctantly. Was he doing the right thing? Without complaint, Mouse weaved through the bushes and undergrowth, hands held high.

'And the other one!'

'There is nobody else,' said Mouse.

'Well, get over there with yer chubby mate. And keep those hands up high where I can see them. Both of yous! And drop those cutlasses and anything else yer carrying. I reckon I need ma pistol for this one.' And he hurriedly withdrew his gun and pushed Leo to the ground.

'We need to keep our hands up and drop our cutlasses?' asked Mouse confused. 'How do we do that?'

The pointy nosed pirate took a second to think. The tanned skin on his face wrinkling up in different directions. 'Lower them to drop the cutlasses, then raise them again afterwards. Ye cheeky mite!'

Robert looked on, racking his brains trying to come up with a plan.

Suddenly, a firm hand fell onto his shoulder and he physically jumped from shock. It was as if he'd been punched in the stomach.

'Cap'n, it's me, Boxer,' whispered a friendly voice.

Robert turned to see a jubilant Boxer grinning from ear to ear.

'I nearly died there,' said Robert.

'Sorry, Cap'n. I was so excited, I couldn't speak.'

'Where've you been all this time? We thought something bad had happened to you.'

'It's a bit of a yarn really. When I was in Peg's garden I heard voices talking about a skiff and a boy. I just knew straightaway it was our skiff and

Leo. So I followed them. But they never left him alone. So I went back to Peg's. But I got lost. And when I found it, ye were all gone. So I came back here.' He took a breath. 'What're we gonna do, Cap'n?'

'I'm thinking,' said Robert slowly. 'Do you have any ideas?' He looked at Boxer's pleasant face, and saw it changing from jolly to serious.

'Well, I'm good with a cutlass, Cap'n.'

'I know. Bennett said.'

Boxer nodded in appreciation of the compliment. 'But I'm even better with a knife. Throwing it like. I can hit an apple ten yards away. If we could only get him to turn sideways, I could knock the pistol from his hand and you could run in with yer cutlass before he has time to do anything.'

Robert considered. 'Well, if you really think you can do it, then that's what we'll do. I'll throw something to draw his attention.'

Boxer again nodded. 'May I have yer knife, Cap'n?'

'But I don't have one. I thought you had one.'

'Not me, I've only got ma cutlass.'

'Me too,' said Robert, dejectedly. 'I guess we need another plan. And fast!'

'I've never done in three young'uns before,' said the red scarfed robber, after Barrell and Mouse had finally dropped their weapons. 'Now turn out yer pockets. Yous must have something worthy lurking inside.'

Robert looked down and around. A short sturdy piece of branch jumped out at him. He picked it up. Not too heavy, not too light. 'How about this, Boxer? Could you throw this?'

Boxer felt the branch. 'You bet, Cap'n.'

'Then we're set,' said Robert, picking up a stone. He spotted a gap in the branches and foliage, and launched the missile sideways. Thump!

Instantly, the red scarfed robber turned, along with his pistol. Boxer seized his opportunity and launched the lump of wood through the air. Whack! Direct hit. The robber's pistol tumbled to the ground. Robert immediately leapt out and pointed his cutlass at the startled man.

But amazingly, the robber just ignored him and lashed out with a hand while attempting to retrieve the pistol with the other. Robert caught the full blow on the side of his mouth, but somehow managed to thrust his cutlass into the flailing arm, stopping the robber dead in his tracks. The robber's brief shock allowed Mouse to spring forward and grab the gun.

'Ah!' cried the robber, as blood started to pour into his shirt. 'You'll pay for that!'

'If you move one more inch, I'll stab you again,' said Robert. 'Boxer, watch him! Mouse, aim the pistol!'

Mouse duly obliged until Barrell, who knew his way around guns more, took over.

'Get on the ground!' shouted Barrell. 'Onto yer belly!'

'Mouse, untie Leo,' said Robert.

'Sorry, Cap'n,' sniffled Leo, as tears rolled down his dirty cheeks. 'There were too many of them.'

'It wasn't your fault,' said Robert. 'Mouse, use the rope and tie him up. Barrell, shoot him if he moves. Boxer, go to his feet, stab him in the legs if he tries something.'

'Lads, lads,' bantered the prostrate robber. 'There's no need for all of this. Just let me go and we'll call it quits.'

'Let ye go!' exclaimed Barrell. 'Ye were gonna kill us. Now it's you who's gonna die. I reckon I'll shoot ye between the eyes, for it's all ye deserve.'

'But ye can't shoot a man in cold blood,' said Leo. 'Are we really gonna kill him, Cap'n?'

'He was gonna slice yer throat open, ye fool!' cried Barrell, before Robert could respond. 'And me and Mouse were next.'

'Hold your horses, Barrell,' said Robert. 'Boxer, Mouse, what do you both say?'

'I've only ever seen a dead person once before,' said Mouse, thoughtfully. 'And I didn't like it. He can't do anything to us now anyway,' he added, while tugging at a piece of rope. Not only had the robber's hands and feet been bound, but Mouse had also joined the two lashings with a taut line, such that the man's feet were somewhat raised off the ground.

'I don't want to kill anybody,' said Boxer.

'You wouldn't have to,' roared Barrell. 'I've got the pistol. Cap'n, an eye for an eye!'

'No,' said Robert. 'Two wrongs don't make a right. We'll leave him. He'll eventually untie himself or somebody will find him. You can lower the pistol now, Barrell. Barrell, lower the pistol!'

The peeved boy grudgingly lowered the gun and instantly everyone's mood lightened. Even Barrell accepted the decision and began poking fun at Leo for getting kidnapped.

'It could've happened to anybody,' groaned Leo. 'Can I have my pistol back now?'

'What!' cried Barrell. 'Ye mean to say we were about to be shot by our very own pistol?'

Everybody chuckled and then boarded the rowing boat. It dropped under their weight, and Mouse cast off. The sea was blue, the sky was blue, and everything was becoming good again. Even the red scarfed robber decided against a final show of defiance, and ceased his obscenities.

The four boys rowed gently, as the slight current was in their favour, pulling them like a magnet to the port. Robert had wanted to row, but hadn't been quick enough, and uneven numbers on each side was unworkable. It gave him time to think.

'Do ye reckon Bennett and Titch will be waiting for us, Cap'n?' asked Mouse between strokes. He would never willingly say Reno's name.

'Possibly,' said Robert. 'But I doubt it. As soon as they see the boat and Leo gone, I think they'll hide somewhere like we did, and wait. I just hope those robbers are true to their word and have scarpered.'

They deliberately hugged the coastline for safety. Thankfully, the robbers hadn't taken the boat far, and the boys were soon alongside the harbour. There were more ships now and infinitely more smaller boats. At least they wouldn't stick out like a sore thumb. The noise levels had also been turned up a few notches, as orders, discussions and disagreements carried in the warm air. Robert was nervous, he knew the robbers could still be in port.

'Stop rowing!' said Robert. Nerves had gotten the better of him. 'We should pull in behind these branches.' An overhanging tangle of vegetation provided meagre but nevertheless welcome cover. 'We'll tie up here and go on foot.'

'All of us, Cap'n?' asked Leo immediately. There was a reluctance in his voice.

'No, we'll split up,' said Robert. His mind was working feverishly. Leo didn't want to go, he'd been through enough. Barrell couldn't go, he was too tired and too slow. Boxer looked shattered, he'd run more than anyone.

There was little other option, Robert would have to go with Mouse, who knew the port the most.

'I'll go with Mouse,' said Robert eventually, as everybody's eyes remained fastened on him. 'You three can watch the boat.'

Leo's relief was visible, as was Barrell's. However, Mouse wasn't in agreement. 'Can I no go alone, Cap'n? Yer mouth looks awful sore.'

Robert had completely forgotten about the blow to his face. He touched his jaw. It fairly hurt.

'Besides,' added Mouse. 'I'm smaller than you, and it's easier to hide if there's only me. And I can always climb on the roofs if I get into bother. I'm not sure yer used to climbing much, Cap'n.'

Robert suddenly felt queasy – pain or the sight of blood usually had that horrible effect on him. 'Alright, Mouse, you can go on your own. But watch out for those robbers.'

'Aye, aye, Cap'n,' said Mouse. 'I shan't be long.' Where had Robert heard that one before!

Forthwith, Mouse sprang over the gunwale and skipped off. Keeping close to the shoreline, he soon arrived at the port. It was very busy. Moving from hiding spot to hiding spot, he arrived at the shack where they had hidden earlier. There were plenty of people about, but no Bennett nor Titch nor Reno.

Turning over his options, Mouse jumped down to the shore. Immediately, an old man peered at him suspiciously. Then, another man sidled over, both staring in Mouse's direction.

'If yer thinking of thieving, I'll cut yer hands off!' called out the old man.

Mouse moved briskly away, then something caught his eye. A chalk hangman was drawn onto a large protruding stone, accompanied by a small arrow. 'Yes!' he exclaimed with joy. 'They're here.'

He followed the arrow and sure enough came across another hangman, on a wall this time. But no arrow. Hurriedly, he scrutinized the building, and found the accompanying arrow located right on the bottom of the grimy wall. This pattern continued, pulling Mouse deeper and deeper into the town centre. Until, the next arrow directed him into a narrow shady alleyway overflowing with clutter and junk. Things were becoming risky, but Mouse had the heart of a lion, and in he stepped.

Suddenly, there was a noise behind him. He tried to turn, but it was too late. A coarse smelly sack was forced down over his head and most of his body, and he was flipped onto the ground. Then, blows began raining down on top of him.

'Help!' cried poor Mouse, with all his might. 'Help me!'

'Stop it!' shouted a voice. 'Who's in the sack?' It sounded like Bennett!

'I didn't see!' It was surely Reno.

The sack was pulled from Mouse and the small boy looked up. There stood Bennett, Reno, and a sleepy-eyed Titch.

'Ye really are cruel,' said Bennett. 'How could ye? Ye knew fine it was Mouse.'

'I was only jesting,' said Reno. 'I hardly touched him. He should be more watchful in future.'

Mouse glared at the tall muscular boy, while plucking dusty fibres from his mouth. How he hated Reno, who was nothing less than a big bully.

'Ye found us then?' said Bennett, giving Mouse a hand up.

'I told ye the hangmen and arrows would work,' said Titch.

'We went to the skiff,' said Bennett. 'But it was gone. We figured you'd moved it for safe keeping and would come back later. So we hid out here and decided to catch some slumber. Reno was first watch.'

'So why did ye move the skiff?' asked Titch. 'Did something happen?'

'Sort of,' replied Mouse, understating events to the extreme. 'Leo got kidnapped and the skiff got stolen. The Cap'n stabbed one of the robbers and I tied him up. We need to get moving. The Cap'n said to make haste. Oh, we found Boxer!'

Mouse explained everything in greater detail on the way back to the boat. Bennett and Titch questioned him frequently, while Reno was completely indifferent.

When Robert saw the four boys emerging from the bushes, he could barely contain his excitement. All eight of them were together again, safe and well. But then his mood changed as Reno drew nearer, grinning from ear to ear.

'Where did you get to?' asked Robert, making a beeline for the tall boy. 'You can't just disappear when you feel like it!'

'I didn't,' replied Reno coolly. 'I was right behind Titch when I bent down to tie my shoelace. Whereupon, a pickpocket pinched my silver snuffbox.'

Robert glanced down at Reno's shoes. They were old and battered. One lace was done and the other undone.

'Of course, I gave chase,' continued Reno. 'Caught the rascal, he was about my size, and gave him a good thrashing.' Next, he removed from his pocket a small rectangular silver box with scalloped shaped edges, opened it, took out a pinch, stuck it on his hand, and sniffed it up.

'Is that tobacco?' asked Robert, horrified.

'The best quality there is.'

'Give it to me,' demanded Robert.

Reno reopened the box and proudly offered the contents.

'I want the box,' said Robert.

Reno tried to object, then reluctantly did as he was told, and handed over the pretty little box. Whereupon, Robert took it and turned it upside down, shaking out all of the dark powder onto the soggy ground.

'What did ye do that for?' snapped Reno, as the small cloud of tobacco disappeared. Everybody looked on with a mixture of horror and intrigue. 'I ought to thump ye.'

'Tobacco is now banned,' declared Robert. 'Whether it's sniffed or smoked. Not only does it stink, but it kills you.'

'Well am no dead,' retorted Reno sharply. 'And the last captain didn't bother. Why, he himself would often smoke a pipe!'

'I'm not the last captain!' declared Robert hotly. 'Tobacco kills. End of story. From now on, anybody caught using it, will be punished.' And he handed back the empty box to Reno. 'Come on, it's time we left.'

'Aye, Cap'n,' chorused everyone except for Reno, who was seriously annoyed.

'If we hurry, Captain, we might just catch The Lightning,' said Bennett, casting off. 'Otherwise, we'll have another four hours to kill.'

16. Looking For Clues

The whole ship showed up to greet the returnees, with everyone eager to discover if the mission had been a success or not. Fraser was positively hyperactive, even more so when he heard what had happened.

'We seem to be m-making enemies at every t-turn,' he bemoaned. 'It's not g-good, C-Captain. We need to leave here and f-fast!'

With those wise words, The Lightning headed out into deeper waters.

Dinner was served on the open sea, on the main deck. A long line of crude wooden tables, and accompanying benches, began on the stern side and stretched into the distance towards the bow, where the food was coming from. Children were squeezed in like sardines, each with their own wooden bowl and spoon. It reminded Robert of school dinners, without the teachers.

Robert sat with Bennett on one side and Mouse on the other. Titch was directly opposite, with a new face beside him. His name was Pudding and he was the cook. He didn't, however, serve the food – that was someone else's job.

'What do ye think of the soup, Cap'n?' asked Pudding expectantly, after Robert had taken a few mouthfuls.

Robert didn't like it. It was incredibly salty, fatty and lacking in vegetables other than peas, which it seemed to be swimming in. Robert didn't really like peas. Also, there were no herbs or spices to boost the flavour. In other words, the soup was disgusting and only edible because there was zero alternative. It seemed, however, he was in the minority, as everybody else appeared to be wolfing it down.

'It's ... ' began Robert slowly. To lie or not to lie? Avoid the question, that's what his mum always did. 'Did you add any salt to it?'

'Of course, Cap'n,' replied Pudding. 'I always add loads. I can add more if it's not enough for ye.'

'No, no,' shot out Robert. 'I think perhaps a little less salt might be better, so we can really taste how good everything ... blends together.' He was sounding like his mum.

Pudding looked straight at him. The last thing Robert wanted to do was to hurt anybody's feelings.

The cook wasn't the tallest member of the crew, but he was certainly the plumpest. His pink round chubby face even made his eyes appear smaller than they really were. He had dark blonde wavy hair, which was tied back into a tiny ponytail. His lips were big, as were his ears.

'Thank ye, Cap'n,' he said, after a little thought. 'I sometimes think this lot will eat anything. It's good to hear what somebody new thinks. I shall put a tad less salt in, in future.' He then excused himself and disappeared towards the ship's galley, which was sited in the forecastle, in order to give out some very important instructions.

'Mm,' considered Bennett, after Pudding had gone. 'Adding two and two together, Captain, am I right in saying that they will discover that salt is not good for a body?'

'You could say that,' replied Robert, nodding his head.

'And is it the heart, Captain, it is bad for?'

'I suppose, yeah,' said Robert. His nana had heart problems and she would never add salt to anything. Not even chips!

'By Jove, Fraser's forever saying as much. He's always preaching, how could salt be good for a body, when it's so bad for everything else.'

Robert again nodded. 'We'll just need to persuade Pudding his soup tastes better without it.'

'I've never liked salt, me,' said Mouse, thoughtfully. And nobody could think of anything to add after such a sweeping statement.

It was late afternoon when dinner came to an end. Robert headed back to his cabin accompanied by Bennett and Mouse. Titch was to collect Reno, and Fraser was passed on the way. Robert hadn't wanted to invite Reno, but Bennett had persuaded him otherwise. The council was arranged to discuss what Peg had said.

169

Robert immediately took position in the centre of the floor and prepared himself. However, it was Fraser who felt the desire to speak first. He was quite clearly in his element with a puzzle to solve.

'We have two p-parts to the p-puzzle,' Fraser began. Mouse had already filled him in.

'F-Firstly, there is the necklace,' continued Fraser. 'We must f-find out what it tells us. Secondly, we have to search the c-cabin, with the C-Captain's permission of course.' And he turned sheepishly to Robert, fearful that he had overstepped his authority.

Robert swiftly removed the pendant and held it in the palm of his hand. Bennett, Fraser and Mouse crowded round.

'I think it's a drawing of a group of islands somewhere, but where I don't know,' said Robert. 'Maybe this line is the equator.'

'No, I don't think so, C-Captain,' said Fraser instantly. 'The equator doesn't have islands around it on this side of the Americas. And I suspect it is this side of the Americas. I think it's simply a line of latitude. I can check it against some m-maps of the area, assuming R-Reno hasn't b-burnt them, that is. I can do that, C-Captain, while everybody else searches the c-cabin.'

'Alright,' said Robert, and handed the pendant over. Then, he turned to Mouse and Bennett. 'That leaves us to search the cabin. I suppose if there's something hidden, it must be in the walls somewhere.'

'Well, let's get started,' said Bennett enthusiastically. 'I thought Titch was supposed to be coming with Reno!'

Just then, Titch arrived, accompanied by Reno and Barrell.

Super, thought Robert. Both of them!

'Something's probably hidden in the walls,' said Reno immediately. But nobody replied. The search had already begun.

'We've already searched a few places,' said Barrell, absentmindedly. Reno instantly shot him a look that could have killed. 'For things to eat,' he added, rather unconvincingly.

So, thought Robert. They've been digging around. Fraser, meanwhile, was lost in a world of maps.

Time passed, as the children searched the cabin and its contents. The walls, floor and roof were tapped, prodded and pulled. Drawers were removed, tables turned upsides down, chairs literally ripped apart, maps fingered through, much to Fraser's annoyance, everything possible was done. But nothing turned up. Eventually, darkness started to creep into the room and everyone's enthusiasm drained away.

'I r-reckon I've f-found the p-place,' announced Fraser excitedly. 'Look here, C-Captain!'

Everyone immediately encircled Fraser, who had his finger placed on an old brown raggedy map, which had been pinned down by a wooden plate and two wooden spoons. A lighted candle flickered on the table. The pendant lay below it. The similarities between the two were clear, as was the one big difference. The pendant was clearly lacking islands.

'I know it's not a p-perfect m-match,' said Fraser, apologetically. 'But the orientation and distances seem to f-fit for what's there.'

'Finding the island means nothing,' said a decidedly unimpressed Reno, '... if we don't know where to look when we're on it. We've as much chance hunting a fish in an ocean. I'm off!'

'Me too,' said Barrell, and the two late arrivals left first.

'I need to go too,' said Titch, suddenly remembering. 'It's my turn on watch! Do ye want me to get some replacements, Cap'n?'

'Nah,' replied Robert. 'It'll soon be dark. There's not much point now.'

'I'm p-pretty certain it's the right p-place,' said Fraser, peering at the map in the twitching candlelight.

'Reno's right, though,' said Bennett, dejectedly. 'Even if we guess the right island, where do we look? We've got to search this place again tomorrow and find whatever's hidden.'

'And if we again find nothing?' asked Mouse.

'Then Peg's been leading us up the garden path,' said Bennett.

Robert turned away and carefully scanned the room. He didn't believe Peg was lying. Something was hidden in this cabin, but where?

'Why is the wood in the centre of the floor cleaner?' Robert eventually asked, with slight curiosity.

'There was a t-table there, C-Captain,' said Fraser. 'Until R-Reno r-removed it.'

'It's in the forecastle now,' added Mouse. 'For Reno's dice games.'

'Do ye think it could be hiding something, Captain?' asked Bennett, his face brightening up.

'Well, there's only one way to find out, I suppose,' said Robert. 'We need to fetch it.'

The four boys headed towards the forecastle in the bow of the ship. They moved with a vigour as dusk was rapidly turning into darkness. Inside the cabin were a number of boys, some were dozing, some were tidying up around a clay brick stove, but the majority were crowded around a sizeable wooden table, playing a game with dice. Unsurprisingly, Reno and Barrell were present.

'Sorry, everyone,' said Robert. 'I'm returning it to my cabin.'

'What?' asked a baffled Reno.

'The table! Bennett, Fraser, get the back. Mouse, we'll take the front.'

'Aye, aye, Cap'n,' they replied simultaneously.

'It needs to go on its side,' offered Pudding, helpfully. 'Otherwise it won't get through the door.'

'Are we getting it back?' asked Reno, his arms folded across his chest in his typically defiant fashion.

'Nope,' answered Robert. And the four boys hoisted up the weighty table and set forth.

After some toing and froing, the table was back where it belonged, in the captain's cabin. And they placed it exactly where it had been before.

'It's too d-dark to see anything,' said Fraser. 'I'll go get a lamp.'

'He's always fussing,' said Mouse, after Fraser was out of earshot. 'There's enough light from that there candle.' And he grabbed the shrinking candle and ducked down underneath the table with it.

Robert and Bennett looked at one another and immediately started to examine the surface and legs of the table in the semi darkness.

'Got something!' cried Mouse.

Robert's heart was a flutter. Now things were really going to move forwards.

'Only jesting!' shot out Mouse. 'The candle burns the table if ye get too close. I reckon we need a lamp.'

'Yer not funny, Mouse,' complained Bennett. Thereupon, Fraser arrived with the lamp.

'Hurry up, Fraser,' said Mouse impatiently. 'My nana moves quicker than you!'

'But ye don't know yer n-nana!' retorted Fraser, placing the lamp directly underneath the table.

'Well, if I did,' quipped Mouse again. 'She'd certainly be quicker.'

It was at that exact moment Robert concluded Mouse was the most argumentative, impatient, cheeky child, he'd ever come across. Mouse could start a squabble in an empty room. Nevertheless, Robert couldn't stop himself from liking this small irrepressible boy.

'If we each take a corner, then we shouldn't miss anything,' said Bennett.

Forthwith, they all ducked down to begin checking their individual corners. And there were plenty of cracks and holes present to hold a small secret.

'Got something!' cried Mouse immediately. The silence was deafening. 'No really!' he added, and spun round and held out a tiny rolled up piece of paper.

The four boys looked at one another with escalating excitement. Was there really a message inside?

'Here, Cap'n,' said Mouse, handing over the miniature scroll.

Underneath the table and in the twinkling light of the lamp, the whole situation had a magical feel to it. Robert delicately unfolded the tiny piece of paper.

'What's it say, Cap'n?' asked Mouse eagerly. 'Is there a message inside?'

The piece of paper had four tiny, barely readable sentences on it. 'Everything's so small,' said Robert, squeezing his eyes together. 'But here goes. Follow the thing against your chest. The farthest one to the west. The tallest object with a nest. Underneath ends the quest.'

'What a load of twaddle!' cried Mouse.

'First, let's get out from underneath this blooming table,' said Bennett.

Robert placed the small scrap of paper onto the table, and they all gathered round and stared at it.

'It's from the last c-captain,' said Fraser. 'He m-must have written it j-just before he left us. It seems he liked a p-puzzle.'

'Peg was right then,' said Robert, not paying any attention.

'It appears so,' mumbled Fraser, while reading over the sentences to himself. 'The first p-part is easy. Follow the thing against your chest. Well, it's referring to your chest C-Captain. Which means the p-pendant. We must follow the p-pendant.'

Robert quickly removed the pendant and placed it beside the miniature letter.

'The farthest one to the west, must mean the island most to the west,' added Bennett, picking up the mantle. 'That one I presume,' and he pointed. 'Fraser, get the map.'

Fraser went over to one of the side tables, shuffled around with the umpteen maps there, and returned with the desired one. A crude specimen of a thing if ever there was one.

'As I said before, it's not an exact m-match but it's p-pretty c-close,' said Fraser. 'P-Perhaps the old c-captain decided against making an exact c-copy, for safety reasons.'

'It's possible,' said Robert, but he was sceptical. What would be the point?

'So that one,' offered Bennett, laying his big finger on the likely candidate.

'Agreed,' said Robert. But he wasn't wholly convinced.

The island in question was smallish, fairly circular, and appeared to have a significant mountain smack bang right in the middle of it. A number of thin rivers snaked to the sea.

'The m-mountain makes sense now,' said Fraser, thoughtfully. 'The t-tallest object with a nest is surely a t-tree. But how can ye work out which is the t-tallest t-tree on an island? Ye can't! But if it's on t-top of a m-mountain, then it must be the t-tallest. And the last b-bit is easy. Underneath ends the quest. We d-dig!' He was beside himself with joy.

'Then we have everything,' said Bennett. 'The Book of Maps is within our grasp, again.'

While Robert agreed with Fraser's deductions, he was not so willing to count his chickens as Bennett so clearly was. 'And these islands are safe to explore?' he said. 'I mean, there won't be any savages trying to chop our heads off, will there?'

'Not according to this map, Captain,' answered Bennett. 'Look, Blackjack's drawn skulls on the dangerous islands. Our island has no such skull. The natives must surely be friendly.'

'Or the island is uninhabited,' said Fraser. 'A lot of p-places in the C-Caribbean have been totally c-cleared of n-natives. It's very sad r-really. Their ways of life gone f-forever.'

'Or Blackjack just hasn't visited it yet,' offered Mouse, innocently.

Everyone immediately turned and looked at the small boy, his impish grin slightly turned up at one corner. This suggestion was undoubtedly the least appealing of the three possibilities.

'So, are we going Cap'n?' asked Mouse, excitedly.

'Of course we're going,' replied Robert. If The Book of Maps truly held untold riches, then his crew, a bunch of homeless children, deserved the spoils more than anyone else in the whole wide world. And a deserted island held no fears after what he'd been through. 'But tonight we must sleep. And tomorrow we'll make plans.'

Mouse immediately threw his small hand onto the table. Fraser instantly followed. Bennett was next. Robert topped them all. This was getting exciting!

17. Cannibal Island

The next morning everyone was buzzing, even Reno. Things had been discussed and it was decided that they would travel to the chosen island early afternoon. They would view the island from afar and then formulate a final plan of action. The mood was positively boisterous and laughter abounded.

Robert leaned against the bulwarks and marvelled at the blueness of the sea and sky. There was hardly a breath of wind and the sails above him were limp. It didn't matter, though, as they wouldn't be using the elements to undertake their journey. He'd called the fog twice already, how, he didn't exactly know, but it didn't matter. He somehow knew he could do it again.

'C-Captain?' came a voice from behind him. Robert turned to see Fraser smiling.

'May I ask ye a question p-please?' asked the fair haired boy.

'Sure,' replied Robert. 'I hope I can answer it.'

'How do ye c-call the f-fog, C-Captain?'

'Ah! I think you might've picked the wrong question, because I'm not really sure. I close my eyes and imagine what fog looks like in my head. Then I'm right in the middle of a blanket of fog.'

'And how do we arrive at the exact location, C-Captain?'

'Well, I also try and imagine what the place would look like, and then when the fog clears, the place is standing right before me.'

'Mm,' pondered Fraser, and then he asked. 'Do ye think it's the r-right island, C-Captain?'

Robert wanted to tell the truth but he couldn't bring himself to. He was the captain, and all captains were brave, enthusiastic, and above all optimistic. 'Yeah, I do,' he answered, as positively as he could muster.

'And ten m-men will be enough, C-Captain? Ye could have done with m-more on T-Tortuga.'

'We'll have an extra two. It should be enough.'

'Aye, aye, C-Captain.' And Fraser returned to the wheel in a more peaceful frame of mind.

All hands appeared on deck early afternoon, eager to see how their captain carried out his magic. Even those swabbing the deck all seemed to suddenly become engaged in and around the mizzen mast, the place where Robert was now standing. Now, though, he no longer felt like the new boy in class, but rather part of one big homogenous group, all pulling the same way.

'Remember, Captain, not too close,' said Bennett. 'A few miles back should give us a good look.'

'I'll try my best,' said Robert, but he knew the exact location was sort of out of his hands. Still, it felt good that so much trust and hope was being placed in him.

Robert lowered his head, closed his eyes, and imagined fog all around him. And then how an island, with a giant mountain on it, would appear in the distance as the fog began to lift. He stood like this for at least a minute and then opened his eyes expectantly.

He couldn't see a thing. A dense fog had engulfed the whole ship, and the temperature had plummeted. 'Is everybody alright?' he asked immediately.

'Aye, Cap'n!' came a resounding reply from all around him. But then a deathly hush returned, as each and every crew member on board held their breath. Even the creaking timbers and flapping canvas seemed to abate.

'It's gotten very c-cold,' said Fraser, breaking the eerie quiet. Nobody responded.

Splash! An almighty splash cut through the silence like a hot knife through butter.

'Man overboard!' shrieked a voice which seemed to hang in the air for ever. 'Starboard side!'

'Are ye sure?' shouted Bennett, into the emptiness.

'I reckon so,' replied the voice.

'We need to stop the ship!' cried Robert. 'Lower the anchor!'

'We can't!' countered Reno sharply. 'The ship'll break up. We don't know what rate we're going.'

'Heave to! Captain's orders! Unfasten the anchor! Man the capstan-bars!' yelled Bennett. 'We're stopping this ship!'

Robert couldn't see a thing, but could plainly hear a multitude of hands and feet, fumbling and stumbling towards the bow of the ship, where the drum-like capstan was positioned to raise and lower the anchor.

'Do we know who's gone over?' asked Pudding concernedly.

'Somebody said Mouse,' replied Cooper, and Robert's blood froze.

'Mouse!' shouted Robert, as he clumsily followed the receding crowd. 'Mouse!'

'Mouse!' shouted everyone. But no reply was forthcoming.

'Can he swim?' asked Pudding.

'No, last time he nearly drowned,' said Titch. 'Bennett had to jump in and save him.'

'Fish food,' said Reno. 'We're just wasting time. It's no like we'll be able to see anything in this fog.'

When Robert reached the capstan, the anchor was already in the sea on its journey downwards, and there was no space on the bars to lend a hand. Suddenly, what Reno had said struck a chord. Robert immediately closed his eyes and began to wish the fog away. One second, two seconds, three seconds.

'Heave-Ho!' resounded over the ship. 'Heave-Ho!'

Robert opened his eyes, and almost straight away the fog started to lift, and the crew reappeared.

'What now, C-Captain?' asked Fraser, whose face was pale with shock. The fog was virtually gone.

'Who's in the crow's nest?' shouted Robert.

'Jelly!' hollered a voice high up on the mast, before anyone else answered.

'Can you see anything?' shouted Robert.

Jelly held the brass telescope to his eye and scanned the water. Everyone waited with bated breath. 'Nothing, Cap'n! Just empty blue sea!'

'The sharks will have swallowed him whole, he's so small,' joked Barrell.

'That's not funny!' snapped Robert. 'I'm going up. Who else has got good eyesight?' Not waiting for a reply, he immediately started to scale the rigging.

'Pudding,' said Bennett. 'You've got eyes like a hawk. Get up there!'

The plump boy needed no further prompting and swiftly began his ascent.

Instantly, a competitive edge appeared in Robert's climbing. Yes, he wanted to save Mouse more than anything, but he also wanted to beat Pudding to the summit. And he couldn't have selected a better opponent if he had done so himself. Pudding was hardly an Olympic athlete.

As Robert moved confidently upwards, a satisfaction swept over him. Then, when the crow's nest was within touching distance, he made a fatal mistake. He looked down! A long, long, way down. Suddenly, his hands gripped the ropes with a vengeance and his knuckles whitened. He could now feel the swaying of the mast. With the centre of gravity far below, the fluctuations high up were being greatly exaggerated.

Noticing the blockage up ahead, Pudding simply moved to the side, overtook, and entered the crow's nest alongside Jelly. Within seconds, the cook had the brass telescope to his eye and was scanning the water.

'Man ahoy!' he shouted, almost at once. 'Or should I say, Mouse ahoy! Something's definitely there! Astern, three miles!'

'Weigh anchor! Change course!' ordered Bennett.

In double quick time, the anchor was raised, the sails unfurled and adjusted, and the ship turned. Everyone's speed and skill was supreme. Meantime, Robert gingerly made his descent, making sure not to look down. For the first time since the ferry, he was feeling somewhat queasy.

'It's surely him!' hollered Pudding shortly, with the telescope still pressed to his eye.

'Is he alive?' shouted up Bennett.

'Can't tell! But his head's definitely above water!'

'It'll be a m-miracle if he is,' said Fraser, as Robert's feet finally touched the deck.

The Lightning quickly ate up the distance between it and Mouse, until Pudding could make a more definite judgement. 'He's alive!' he cried. 'I think he's waving!'

A cheer spontaneously erupted at the news, and Robert felt as if a stone had been lifted from his heart.

When a saturated Mouse was eventually fished out from his watery prison, he was surprisingly unperturbed about the whole incident. 'I knew it was only a matter of time before ye came back for me,' he calmly said. 'A little faith is all ye need.'

'But ye can't swim,' said a puzzled Titch.

'True enough,' returned Mouse, as everyone continued to squeeze around him. 'But I minded what Bennett told me. First, don't panic. I didn't. Second, don't breathe in when ye go under. I didn't. And third, kick and wave yer arms, and you'll float to the surface. I did. And then of course, I had this.' And he opened up his sodden clothes and pulled out a fully inflated water bag. 'I always get thirsty ye see, after Pudding's salty fare. So, instead of going back and forth to the water barrel the whole time, I fill up a bag and stuff it into ma clothes. Then, when I was in the water, I only blew into it and it floated like a cork.'

'Luck of the devil, I say,' said Reno, pushing forwards.

'But how did ye fall in?' asked Bennett.

'Oh that,' said Mouse. 'I was leaning over the bulwarks to try and see how fast we were moving. And I lost my grip.'

'Well, it's good to have ye back,' said Pudding, planting his feet back on deck. 'The place wouldn't be the same without ye.' .

After such an eventful afternoon, it was good to get back on track. The ship was again turned around, and the water simply slipped by beneath them.

'Land ho!' shouted Jelly, soon after. 'Straight ahead! Port side!'

All hands immediately congregated at the bow and waited for their destination to appear. Promptly, a big green mass with a greyish peaked mountain on top broke the continuity of the sea.

'It's a lot bigger than I thought,' said Robert.

'Isn't it,' added Bennett. 'But we shouldn't get too close, Captain, just in case somebody's watching us. Shall I give the order?'

Robert nodded.

'Heave to!' hollered Bennett, and the ship gradually came to a halt.

After double-checking the lashing on the wheel, Fraser joined the discussion on what to do next. 'We should go t-tomorrow before d-dawn,' he said, when a momentary lull in the conversation came. 'Undercover of d-darkness. To be on the safe side.'

'I say we go now!' returned Reno. 'Strike while the iron is hot.'

'Mm,' said Robert. 'I agree with Fraser. It'll be safer to go when it's still darkish.'

Reno immediately humphed and walked off.

'We'll move a bit closer tonight, if there's no moon,' continued Robert. 'Then, before dawn we'll take the rowing boat.'

Everyone nodded in agreement and Robert was pleased.

'And The Lightning, C-Captain?' asked Fraser. 'What's to be done with her?'

Robert considered. 'Sail her in a straight line out to sea, so we know where you are, and then turn around and come straight back again. Pick us up at dawn the following day. And if we're not there, then the next dawn.'

'We're gonna stay the night, Cap'n?' asked Titch.

'We've no choice,' answered Bennett. 'The place is a lot bigger than we reckoned.'

That evening, as darkness fell, clouds began to fill the sky. There would be no moonlight or starlight to reveal their presence. And so, with sails drawing, The Lightning moved in closer and waited for predawn.

The next morning, a little before the crack of dawn, a small rowing boat laden with provisions and ten excited boys, headed towards the deserted island. They aimed for an area well to the left of the map's marked anchorage. The going was easy with the direction of the water, but someplace was taking a battering, as the surf roared increasingly the closer they got to shore. The anchorage itself was nothing more than the mouth of a river, with marshy patches packed with trees at its edges.

They touched land in a secluded bit, which was relatively firm underfoot and tied up the craft. It was now getting light.

'Who's carrying the spade?' asked Jelly, as only the cumbersome implement remained in the bottom of the boat.

'I'll take it,' said Robert, pulling out the heavy shovel.

Next, Bennett withdrew his pocket compass and took a bearing of the mountain. 'Northeast, pretty much on the nose,' he concluded, as some of the group looked at him questioningly. 'Just in case we get a bit disorientated in the trees,' he explained. 'And I reckon we should do a few hangmen.'

After a brief exchange they decided against leaving a guard and set forth into the jungle. It was hard going; strange twisted trees and dense tangled plants blocked their path and grabbed at their bodies. The atmosphere was hot and sticky, and altogether unhealthy. Decaying plants squelched underfoot. Only the warbling birds brought a semblance of life to the place. Not surprisingly, they lost sight of the mountain on numerous occasions and were glad of Bennett's foresight.

'And we're definitely on our own here?' asked Leo, nervously.

'Only us and the birds,' replied Jelly from behind, and instantly broke out into a perfect imitation of one, then another. It was simply mesmerizing and everyone stopped for a second to listen, and of course to catch their breaths.

Robert's eyes wandered and he caught sight of some beautiful purple flowers hanging in a gigantic shower. How could something so wonderful be in someplace so yucky?

Onwards they pressed, through the sometimes-impenetrable jungle, and forever going upwards. How they longed to catch a lasting glimpse of the sun. It was surely there, valiantly fighting its way through the leaves and branches. Steeper and steeper they climbed, as the pace invariably slowed.

'Give us a song, Mouse,' entreated Bennett, eager to break the monotony.

Mouse immediately cleared his throat in preparation, and then starting softly, began to sing.

'Over the seas a pirate sails,
Working a breeze or a howling gale,
Searching for gold on the deep blue sea,
He could be anyone, me or thee,
But a pirate's life is hard and fast,
And some'll do anything to make it last,
So watch yer front and watch yer back,
Or be buried at sea in an old brown sack,
But worst of all,
To end all hope,
Is to swing up high,
On the end of a rope.'

'I'd give my eye teeth to mind all that,' said Jelly, from the back of the line.

Unconsciously, they had separated into three distinct groups, with Bennett and Reno striking out alone up front, and Jelly, Cooper and Boxer at the back. Barrell was the only one to change positions. He had started out in the lead group but fatigue had forced him into the tail one.

'It's not so difficult,' grumped Barrell, and he spat against a low lying leaf which was the size of a saucer.

Jelly discontinued the discussion. Like the majority of the crew, he was fearful of Barrell.

Suddenly, Mouse rushed forwards. 'Stop!' he cried. 'Can ye hear it?'

Reno swivelled on a coin. 'Shut up! Ye fool!' he snarled. 'It's not dark yet. The goblins are still asleep.' And he laughed, while resting a hand on one of a brace of pistols which were stuffed into his leather belt. A powder-horn dangled at his side.

Mouse ignored the rebuff. 'Sh! Listen.'

'What can you hear?' asked Robert, straining his ears. The sounds of insects obliterated everything.

'I canna hear anything,' said Bennett, shaking his head.

'Maybe it's the birds,' added Jelly, rather unhelpfully.

'No, it's like a low rumbling,' said Mouse, ears cocked. 'Moving water! That's what it is.'

'There must be a river up ahead,' said Robert. 'We'll need to watch we don't fall in.'

'Shouldn't Mouse lead, then,' said Reno instantly. 'It's no as if we'll lose anything if he goes over.'

'I don't mind,' said Mouse calmly, before Robert could respond to Reno's jibe.

'Get moving then!' ordered a grinning Reno, while flicking his thumb.

'We could tie you to one of the ropes,' said Robert.

'No, Cap'n, I'll be fine,' said Mouse. 'My ears will keep me safe.' And off he weaved to the front of the party.

The trek quickly resumed, except now there were four groups, with Mouse being one group all by himself. He stayed a good distance in front, keen to give his comrades ample warning of any impending danger. But no sooner had things thus settled down, than he again abruptly stopped.

'Come and see this, lads!' he cried excitedly. 'Just watch yer step!'

Everyone hurriedly, yet cautiously, moved forwards. Whereupon, as if from nowhere, the rushing of water hit their ears, escalating exponentially the closer they got to an exhilarated Mouse.

'Wow!' said Titch.

'Wow!' said Leo.

They were standing at the overgrown edge of a vertical cliff and straight out in front of them was an almighty chasm, at the bottom of which raced a stony river. The other side, which too was overflowing with vegetation, seemed an awful long way away.

'How are we gonna get over that?' asked Leo.

'Try over there,' said Mouse, pointing to the side.

Everyone gingerly eased forwards, craning their necks. What they saw was a rope bridge, about a stone's throw away. It consisted of three lengths of rope spanning the deep gorge, two were above and were clearly for hands, and one was below, for feet. The whole structure was stabilized with further ropes interlacing the main three lines.

'Wild horses wouldn't get me on that,' said Barrell, after nosing through.

'Let's have a peek,' said Jelly, and Bennett moved over.

'Does that mean we're not alone?' asked Leo, for a second time.

'Not necessarily,' pondered Bennett. 'Fraser said a lot of these islands used to be inhabited but are now empty. We need to take a closer look at that bridge and see how old it is.'

'Can we go on it, Cap'n?' asked Mouse.

'First we should check it out,' replied Robert. 'It could be rotten.'

The ten boys doubled back a little, and veered off to the left side. Nobody spoke, most were tensed up about the prospect of having to cross the bridge. Only Mouse was truly untroubled. He simply loved to climb, and just knew he could get across.

They soon emerged into a relative clearing, where dead tree stumps poked through an abundance of ferns. At first glance, the place appeared abandoned. The bridge itself was not in good condition, being lopsided and its ropes greatly frayed. It was, however, fundamentally intact.

'What do ye reckon, Captain?' asked Bennett, while holding one of the main lines in his hand. 'I, myself, don't think it's safe.'

'I agree,' said Robert. 'We need to find another way to cross.'

'But, Cap'n,' pleaded Mouse. 'We can cross here, I know it. Let me try.'

'We should let him, he's by far our best climber,' said Reno. 'Anyways, we don't even know if there is another way over.'

'Yeah, somebody should try it out,' said Barrell. 'And Mouse is the best climber by a long shot.'

Robert pinged one of the main ropes. Pieces of it flaked and floated to the ground. 'No! It's too dangerous. We'll go downstream and see if there's an easier way over.'

'But what if there isn't?' insisted Reno. 'We'll just have to traipse all the way back here.'

'There will be!' said Robert. 'Rivers always spread out downstream.' 'We can tie ourselves together and wade across.'

Henceforth, Bennett pulled out his silver pocket compass and took a bearing. 'Southeast-ish!' Nobody said a word. The previous readings had more than come in useful. 'I'll take the lead Captain.'

Off they trooped again, keeping a reasonable distance between themselves and the cliff's precarious edge. They were all a tad downhearted at the detour, but nevertheless relieved at having avoided the bridge.

All of a sudden, a thought flooded through Robert's head. 'Stop a second! Are we all here?'

'I'm here!'

'Me too!'

'Am here, Cap'n!' Everybody called at once.

'That doesn't help,' groaned Robert, getting more than annoyed. 'Can everybody bunch up together.'

But, before everyone had had the chance to meet in the middle, somebody said, 'Mouse! Mouse isn't here!' It was Jelly.

'That guy's no better than a weevil in a biscuit!' growled Reno. 'We should leave him behind as a punishment.'

'Yeah, maroon him on the island,' said Barrell. 'That's what real pirates do.'

Robert was getting sick and tired of Reno and Barrell's sniping, but he held his tongue. 'Come on, we're going back,' he said. 'Something might have happened to him.'

After a few moans and groans, they began to thread their way back over the path they had just trodden, Robert in the lead, Reno and Barrell reluctantly bringing up the rear. But Mouse was nowhere to be seen. Again, the noise of rushing water hit them as they emerged into the clearing at the start of the bridge. However, it wasn't the only sound which grabbed their attention.

'Captain! Captain! Over here!' cried a voice. It was Mouse, and he was on the other side of the deep chasm.

'Ye fool!' shouted Bennett, moving level alongside Robert.

'It's safe!' cried Mouse, bouncing about enthusiastically. 'Think of the time it'll save us!'

Although this was an undisputable fact, what was much more relevant was that not everyone wanted to go. Barrell was defiant. Leo was troubled. Cooper was complaining. While Reno was desperately trying to appear indifferent. The result was, an almighty squabble erupted.

'Me or Jelly don't bother,' said Titch. 'We're the lightest.'

'No! I'll go,' declared Robert.

'Ye mustn't, Captain,' voiced Bennett. 'Titch is right, he's the smallest.'

'Exactly! And what will it tell us? Nothing! We need somebody in the middle. If it takes me, then it should take any of us.'

Robert wasted no time and prepared himself at the start of the bridge. Gripping the coarse rope in his damp hands, he didn't want to let go. Eventually, though, with thumping heart, he put a foot onto the bottom rope. 'Don't look down,' he whispered to himself. But he had to, in order to locate the swaying foot rope. His mouth was dry, his hands soaking, yet onwards he edged. Everybody held their breath.

The further Robert advanced the more difficult it became. And before long, he was going significantly downhill and swaying from side to side, as the movements of the bridge dramatically increased. But his focus was so intense that only the rope in front of his big toe mattered. The pellucid currents rushing far below could have been a million miles away.

'Yer half way across, Cap'n!' shouted Mouse.

Suddenly, Robert's concentration was broken. He leaned too much to one side. The ropes swung violently. Panic set in. He was still a fair distance from the end. Then, his worst nightmare came true.

'It's breaking, Captain!' yelled Bennett and Boxer together.

'Hold on!' screamed Jelly. 'Hold on!'

Robert didn't have time to think. Instinctively, he hooked his arm into a bunch of zigzag ropes, as his feet gave way. He was dangling, but he was alive. For a brief second, he breathed. Then, the whole thing collapsed and parts of the structure cascaded to the ground. Like a pendulum, he careered towards Mouse, as the anchorage on that side stood firm. Whack! He struck the cliff face, but somehow managed to hang on. Then, everything stopped and only the moving water could be heard.

'Climb, Cap'n!' cried Mouse, forcefully. 'Climb!'

Robert's shock passed, and in fear for his life, like a madman he hoisted himself up the battered, creaking, now vertical bridge. It was like climbing an over complicated rope ladder.

'Nearly there, Cap'n,' said Mouse, holding out a hand.

Robert ignored it. He might have pulled his small friend over too. Anyway, the worst was over, and with a final push he rolled onto the ground beside a jubilant Mouse. Safe! They had both been foolhardy, and Robert knew it.

'I thought you'd kicked the bucket there for sure, Cap'n,' said Mouse, grinning. Then, in typical fashion he asked, 'What are we gonna do now, Cap'n?'

'Are ye alright, Captain?' shouted Bennett, from across the deep divide.

'I'm alright!' shouted Robert, in the middle of inhaling large deep breaths. 'No bones broken!'

'We'll head downstream, and see if there's another way across! Will we double back and meet ye here, or see ye up on the mountain?'

Robert quickly thought. For the others to double back would be a complete waste of time. 'We'll wait for you on the mountain top!'

'You'll need this then! Best take cover!' And Bennett picked up the spade which Robert had been recently carrying, and launched it into the air. It came down within a whisker of where they had just been standing.

'Throw over some biscuits!' shouted Mouse. 'I could eat a horse.'

A bag of biscuits duly landed beside them, along with two circular wooden water bottles with long leather straps.

'Wow, this is exciting,' said Mouse. 'Just us, Cap'n! Hope we don't meet any wild animals. Would be fun though.'

'Do ye want the compass?' shouted Bennett.

'No!' shouted Robert. 'You'll need it more than us!'

'Good luck!' shouted Bennett, but his mood was sombre. Something bad was going to happen. He could feel it in his bones.

As the others began to melt away into the green background, Robert too was fast approaching melancholy, but it didn't arrive. It was impossible with a companion of Mouse's disposition.

'I'm gonna pig out on all those biscuits,' said Mouse, as they turned to start their journey. Alone!

They hadn't been walking long before the makeup of their surroundings began to change. The leathery leaved trees and plants started to disappear, and pine trees and bushes took their place. Some bushes were thick with brightly coloured berries, but they let them be, unsure whether they were edible or poisonous. It was also becoming much nicer to breathe as the air filled with the resinous odour of pine trees.

'Wouldn't it be good to live here forever, Cap'n,' said Mouse, as he guzzled some water. 'We could fish and hunt, and even grow our own food.'

'Mm,' replied Robert. But he was really missing his mum and dad, and of course Sparky. And now being only the two of them, merely served to exacerbate the hollow feeling inside of him.

Gradually, the pine trees thinned out too, with brush and grasses taking over, and the birds dropped their singing, supplanted by the monotony of invisible chirping insects. It was also getting much steeper and gravelly underfoot, while the spade was becoming a weighty problem.

'Do ye reckon there's gonna be treasure under the tree, Cap'n?' asked Mouse. 'Imagine, bucketfuls of gold coins and diamond necklaces.'

Robert often didn't have time to answer, before chatterbox Mouse had jumped onto a completely different subject.

'I can take the spade, Cap'n,' said Mouse. 'It's not overly fair if you always have to carry it.'

'I'm alright,' said Robert. 'Besides, you've got the biscuits and water to carry. A little bit farther and we'll have a rest and something to eat.'

Shortly, they came across a couple of big boulders and using them as seats, rested their weary legs. Robert propped up the spade as Mouse handed over the water and biscuits.

'They didn't give us many,' said Robert, peering into the bag.

'Ah,' said Mouse, a guilty look appearing on his face. 'I've only eaten half, I swear on my life. Mind you, I've never been very good at counting. Sorry, Cap'n. I can't even remember eating them. Ever so crunchy they were. The problem is when I start, I can't stop.'

'Well, don't eat any more. Otherwise we'll have nothing for supper or breakfast.'

'On my life, Cap'n,' declared Mouse, immediately. 'Ye can put me to the gallows if another biccy passes these lips.'

The two boys paused to gaze out and down on the sharp treetops far below. Meaningful trees were now few and far between, replaced by thickets on the increasingly grassy slope. The land had seemed expressionless on their ascent but from their current position they could clearly see that it was full of varying contours. The sea appeared an awful long way away.

Robert screwed up his eyes. A white sail was fairly visible on the eastern side of the island. 'Look!' he said, pointing.

Mouse broke off from biting his fingernails and shielded his eyes with both hands. 'It's The Lightning, Cap'n.'

Robert was perplexed. 'It must be The Lightning! But it's a bit strange, I told Fraser to head straight out. He's gone off to the side!'

'There's always a reason with Fraser, Cap'n. He'd never disobey an order for nothing.'

'Shouldn't they be long gone by now,' continued Robert, becoming more and more puzzled.

'Aye, Cap'n. But ye mustn't fret over Fraser. He's more than worth his salt, he is.'

They didn't spend long in reflection and soon restarted their journey. It would be dusk in a few hours and there was still a good chunk of mountain to climb.

The ground was becoming hard and stony, with tufts of grass sprouting up between endless rocks. The mountain itself was no longer a faraway point, but a plateau atop a progressively desolate landscape. The boys were tiring. Robert's head was more and more falling downwards, and the spade increasingly digging into his now throbbing shoulder.

'It's a tree, Cap'n!' cried Mouse, jerking Robert out of his exhaustion.

A single pine stood pointing to the sky, less than brim-full, but there it was. With nothing remotely worth comparison, they knew this was their intended target. Immediately, their weariness disappeared and an enthusiasm flowed through them. The last few steps eased by.

Up close, the two boys viewed the tree with disappointment. It was quite bare, with no nooks or crannies on its trunk or in and around its roots, and although alive it was hardly flourishing. A slab of flat rock was inhibiting it on two sides, causing it to lean over. This also meant there was little viable soil around it. Good news for the boys!

'Well, this shouldn't take long,' said Mouse. 'There's more dirt between ma toes. Can I dig first, Cap'n? Ye look dead on yer feet.'

Robert willingly handed over the spade, and Mouse began to dig in earnest. In the soft golden light of late evening, the sound of metal striking stones seemed to echo everywhere.

Robert shivered; there was a chill in the evening breeze, and it was drying off his sweat. He knew he had to help Mouse, but his legs were leaden and his breathing laboured. He sank down onto the warm rock and wanted to sleep.

'Those shirkers are probably lying with their feet up, Cap'n,' said Mouse panting. 'While we're left with the hard graft.' And the small boy wiped his dirty wet brow.

Robert raised his exhausted body, his conscience had been pricked.

'Got something!' cried Mouse immediately. 'And it's not another stone, it's softer. If I can just jiggle it about a bit.'

Robert peered into the hole which had materialized at the base of the tree, and was amazed. A full scale excavation had taken place. There was little if any soil left to shift.

'It's moving, Cap'n,' said Mouse excitedly.

'It kinda looks like a tree root,' said Robert, on moving closer.

'No, no, Cap'n. It's a wooden box for sure.'

Mouse kept on digging, eventually managing to wiggle the spade underneath the box. Then he levered it up expectantly. 'It's a root!' he groaned, and slumped dejectedly onto his bottom. 'I'm dog-tired I am.'

'You need a drink,' said Robert, offering a water bottle with not much swishing around inside. The other one was empty.

'Maybe I've missed it, Cap'n,' said Mouse.

"I don't think so. You've dug away all of the earth and this rock is solid.' Robert emphasized the point by kicking patches of the dark rock which partially encircled the lopsided tree. It was steadfast.

'Are ye saying this is the wrong tree, Cap'n?'

'It might even be the wrong island. It seems strange to hide something so far away. It's kinda silly.'

'Mm,' considered Mouse. 'May I see the pendant please, Cap'n?'

'Sure,' said Robert, and after removing the pendant, he sat down beside his friend.

'Mm,' said Mouse again. Then he gently rubbed the face of it with his small flexible thumb.

'Do you see something?' asked Robert hopefully.

'Not really, Cap'n.' And Mouse adjusted himself. 'What are we gonna do now?'

Robert considered. 'Sleep. It'll be too dark to do anything soon. Tomorrow we'll try and find the others, and then head back to the ship.'

'Sleep! But where? In this hole?'

'It's big enough,' said Robert. He had noticed how his legs no longer felt the icy chill of the wind. The hole would be the perfect shelter for the night.

Darkness descended rapidly, and as they polished off the last biscuit it was pitch black. The booming of distant breakers striking the island seemed to get even louder.

'I wish we had a lantern or a torch or a candle,' said Mouse. 'I don't like the dark. Do ye reckon there'll be a moon tonight, Cap'n?'

'I'm not sure. Anyway, I quite like the night-time. Everything's different when you can't see, you need to use your other senses more.'

'But what about the monsters, Cap'n? Ye must be fearful of them?'

'There aren't any monsters, Mouse. It's just in people's imagination.'

'Nope. They're definitely there, Cap'n. And they come out at night.'

Robert was bemused. Mouse was scared of absolutely nothing, except for imaginary creatures. 'So what do they do during the day?'

'They hide of course, Cap'n. That's plain.'

'Well, I didn't see any on our way up here. And there's only small bushes for cover now.'

'That's where they must be hiding then.' ·

'So, how small are they?' asked Robert, teasingly.

Mouse fell silent and considered. Then, all of a sudden, the moon appeared, a big circular silvery moon, and with it a number of stars. It was like someone had just switched on their Christmas tree lights. Mouse's mood instantly lifted.

'See that star there, Cap'n,' he said, pointing. 'It's the North Star. Fraser says it points straight to north. Truer than any compass, so Fraser says. Or is it that one!' And he shifted his finger sideways. 'It's that one or that one, but definitely not that one!'

'Can I ask you something, Mouse?' said Robert, as Mouse debated with himself which was the correct star.

'Sure Cap'n. Fire away!'

'Where did all the crew on The Lightning come from?'

'Ah, I know yer the captain, Cap'n, but I can't say. None of us can. We all took oaths, ye see. To bury the past.'

191

'Who made you take the oaths?' queried Robert further, but he was tiring rapidly.

'Reno and the last captain. They said we should forget the past and everyone agreed. So we're not permitted to speak of it, ever.'

'Speak of what?'

'The orphanage, Cap'n. Oops. I didn't say that.'

Robert didn't have the energy to continue. 'I think we should sleep now. It's gonna be another long day tomorrow.' But he'd found out something, eventually.

The two boys were not quite as snug as a couple of bugs in a rug, but they were fairly comfortable, happy to be out of the biting wind. The hole was tight and they leaned against one another. Robert soon started to drift into sleep. And how pleasant it was.

'Captain?' said Mouse, out of the blue.

Robert started. 'Eh, what?'

'I need to tell you something.'

'Can't it wait till tomorrow?'

'Not really, Cap'n.'

'Well, what is it then?'

'Ah, sorry Cap'n. First ye must promise not to do anything.'

'But that depends on what you've got to say.'

'I can't tell ye then, Cap'n.'

Robert was impatient to sleep and didn't have the will nor inclination to argue. It was probably irrelevant anyway. 'Fine, I promise,' he barely mumbled.

'Remember when I fell overboard, Cap'n?'

Robert grunted sleepily. Who could forget?

Mouse took a deep breath. 'I didn't fall. I got pushed.'

Robert was thunderstruck!

18. Robert And Mouse To The Rescue

Robert opened his eyes. It was as dark as coal. The moon and stars had completely vanished. He could feel Mouse's warm head lying on his lap, and hear him too. The small boy was snoring like a tractor.

Robert closed his eyes and yawned sleepily. Then, immediately, he reopened them. Something had caught his attention. A flickering light stood out in the darkness like a beacon. A yellowish red light, way off in the distance. It was surely a fire.

'Mouse, wake up!' said Robert sharply.

'I don't think I want to, Cap'n,' groaned Mouse, stirring not one iota. 'Am not really a morning person.'

'Well, you're already awake now, so sit up and look over there.'

Mouse raised his head and did as he was told. 'I was sleeping like a log there ... It's a fire, Cap'n!'

'That's what I think. The others must have started one. Maybe to dry their clothes.'

'Boy, they must've gotten up awful early. It looks fair stoked. Unless of course it's still night-time, and I've only been asleep for five minutes. But ma belly's growling like a bear so it must be morning, well kind of, seeing as it's still dark.'

Robert got up. 'Come on, we're gonna follow that fire when we can still see it.'

'It's awful dark, Cap'n,' said Mouse nervously, fumbling for the spade. 'The spade, Cap'n. It's gone! The monsters have taken it.'

'I've already got it,' said Robert, and he kicked the spade's metal head to reassure Mouse. 'There are no monsters, remember.'

Just then, to the east, a thin peachy coloured line appeared on the horizon. A new day was beginning. Now the boys would really have to hurry.

'Won't we lose sight of the fire when we get off the mountain, Cap'n?' asked Mouse, as they blindly began their descent. 'And it's getting lighter, the fire will shortly disappear.'

'I'm working on that,' said Robert, as he stubbed his toe on a rocky outcrop. 'I've got it! We'll use those pointed rocks in the water as our guide.' A cluster of sharp rocks projected from the peachy sea a short distance from the island's mainland, and they were directly in the background of the fire. 'As long as we keep the mountain top behind us and those rocks in front, then the fire has got to be directly in our path.'

'And when it's light enough we can maybe follow the smoke, Cap'n,' added Mouse. 'I can't wait to see the others. I wonder if they've got any biscuits left!'

The two bleary-eyed boys moved surprisingly quickly down the mountain. Gravity now aiding their progress, rather than stalling it like the day before. The pointy tree-tops of the pines were now no longer so far away.

With their current situation sorted, Robert turned his attention to the previous night's revelation. And he just couldn't fathom out why anyone would do such a thing. 'About what you said last night, Mouse. You definitely felt hands on your back?'

'No, Cap'n.'

Phew! thought Robert. It was merely a misunderstanding because of tiredness.

'They hoisted up ma legs, Cap'n,' continued Mouse. 'But as ye said yersel last night, there might be some sort of explanation. Best we forget about it. It'll only stir up bad feelings amongst the crew.'

Robert was not a very forgiving person by nature. But he would hold fire. For now!

It didn't take long for the boys to leave the mountain behind and find themselves back in the middle of greenery. The ground was much more undulating on this side of the island, and having had nothing to eat or drink since yesterday, the friends were wearying fast.

'Let's stop for a rest,' said Robert, and he immediately flopped to the ground exactly where he had been standing. Mouse promptly followed suit.

They were in an area surrounded by angular rocky faces. It was surprisingly quiet and peaceful, no birds, no insects. Even the sea was hardly audible.

Mouse suddenly cocked his ear. 'Do ye hear it, Cap'n?'

Robert listened. 'What?'

Mouse sprang up like a baby lamb. 'Back in a tick, Cap'n.' And he promptly dashed off sideways, disappearing behind some tall prickly bushes.

Robert didn't move. He was becoming accustomed to Mouse's boisterous behaviour.

Five minutes passed. Robert lay back on the ground. It was sloping and remarkably comfortable. He examined his filthy clothes. How his mum would have shouted at him, and they weren't even his. He hadn't washed his hands or face in ages and his fingernails were black.

Ten minutes passed. It was like he had the whole island to himself.

Fifteen minutes passed. Now he was getting worried. He sat up. Please nothing bad, passed through his mind.

Suddenly, the bushes shook and then parted. 'Woo Hoo!' cried Mouse, popping out. 'Look what I've found, Cap'n.' He was holding a massive pineapple in each hand. 'Grub's up!'

Robert jumped up, not believing his eyes. Now he was going to pig out.

'And I found water, Cap'n. It took ever so long to fill up both bottles.' He slipped off the two wooden water bottles and handed one to Robert, before holding the other one to his lips. 'I haven't even had a proper swig myself. I reckoned ye might have been fretting over me.' And a driblet of water escaped from the corner of his mouth.

Robert nodded. He couldn't speak, he was too busy guzzling.

Then, using the cutlass, they chopped off the tops, bottoms and sides of the pineapples, and started to eat. They were delicious, mouthwatering, truly scrumptious and ever ever so sweet.

After quenching their thirst and satisfying their hunger, Mouse led Robert to the water source. It wasn't much, a miniscule stream trickling out from one rock and dripping behind another, before disappearing for good.

195

The sound it made was next to nothing. Mouse's hearing was beyond human. They topped up their bottles, and with full bellies, continued their journey, passing through the patch of pineapple plants. Robert was surprised at how orderly it was. A thought flicked through his mind but he tried to ignore it.

Soon, they were in the heart of the woods again. With the sun now high in the sky, it felt good to be in the cool shadow of the trees, and what with going downhill, their walk had become a pleasure. Though, quite a few times Mouse had to climb a tree to check if they were still heading in the right direction.

Eventually, though, their path was blocked by a river. A slow moving, wide expanse of water.

'Do ye reckon it's the same river, Cap'n?' asked Mouse, while skimming a stone over its surface.

'It's possible, I suppose. We've travelled a fair bit.'

'It doesn't look very deep. Do ye reckon we can just walk across it, Cap'n?'

'Maybe,' said Robert, studying upstream and then downstream for a better place to cross. There was a swirl in the middle of the river right in front of them. It was probably nothing, but he knew of eddy currents and how dangerous they can be. His dad had often spoken of them while out walking together alongside rivers and lakes.

Then, a little upstream, Robert noticed a couple of smooth stones poking their heads up just above the gently lapping water. 'Let's try over there. It looks shallower.'

On closer inspection, Robert's first impression proved correct. Even more stones were visible just below the surface, extending out into the water, where they seemed to be atop a raised stony bed.

'They kinda look like stepping stones,' said Mouse.

'They do, don't they,' said Robert. 'Must be from years ago when the island was lived on. I'll go first, seeing as I can swim. But wait till I'm completely across, before you start.'

'Aye, aye, Cap'n.'

Robert quickly removed his trainers and socks, and stuffed them into his shirt. Then, holding the spade like a balancing pole, dipped his feet into the crystal-clear water. It was cold, but the feeling soon passed.

The further Robert ventured forwards, the deeper the water became. Fortunately, the stepping stones did not disappear, they simply got lower and lower, although this meant he had to increasingly concentrate on locating the best spot for his foot. Then Mouse said something, but Robert didn't catch it.

Getting no response, Mouse shouted louder. 'Crocodiles, Cap'n!'

'What!' screamed Robert, nearly having a heart attack. 'Where? What side?' His balance was wavering. He had to run.

'No, no, Cap'n!' cried Mouse hastily. 'I only said, I hope there aren't any crocodiles, Cap'n!'

Robert released the largest sigh of relief he'd ever made in his life. But now he was acutely aware of possible dangers, and he hurried on fearing the worst. Only when his feet touched dry land did he compose himself, even then, Mouse still had to run the gauntlet.

'Alright, Mouse. Now it's your turn!' Robert shouted over. 'I'll watch for any crocodiles! Just keep moving! If I see one, I'll come and thump it with the spade!'

'Aye, aye, Cap'n!' returned Mouse, and after securing his baggage, he launched himself into the water.

As Robert stood guard, waiting to strike, Mouse literally danced over the stones. The small boy was like a ballerina in full flight.

'Made it,' said Mouse on arrival. Thence he became apologetic. 'Sorry, Cap'n. Sometimes I should keep ma trap shut.'

'Forget it. It's probably too shallow for crocodiles anyway.'

'No, no, Cap'n. Fraser says they can hide in just a few inches of water. And run and swim faster than any man.' He paused. 'Ah, best I keep ma trap shut.'

'Mm,' said Robert. Mouse definitely had foot in mouth disease!

After heading off, they soon discovered that the forest on this side of the river was much denser, and Robert worried about losing sight of where they were going. Sure enough, it wasn't long before they felt they were walking in circles.

'I reckon we're lost, Cap'n,' said Mouse. 'Do ye want me to climb another tree?'

'I don't know if it'll help, Mouse. The trees are so close together now, and look how tall they are.'

'Ye fret too much, Cap'n. We've surely got nothing to lose. If I canna see anything, then it's the exact same as me not climbing up in the first place.'

Robert nodded. Mouse's wisdom was sound.

In the blink of an eye, the small boy zipped up one of the trees surrounding them. It was impossible to select the tallest one, as they couldn't see any of the tops. The initial creaking of branches and rustling of leaves quickly subsided, as Mouse vanished from view. Then there was a hush.

Something cracked behind him and Robert jumped. Being alone in the jungle was spooky. He wished Mouse would hurry up.

'Mouse!' shouted Robert. No reply. 'Mouse!' Again no reply.

Suddenly, a twig snapped and a hand dropped onto Robert's shoulder. He turned in alarm.

'Boo!' said Mouse, grinning.

'Mouse!' cried Robert. 'You can't do something like that.'

'Sorry, Cap'n. I was only trying to cheer ye up.'

'Didn't you hear me calling?'

'No, Cap'n. It was so thick up top, I even ended up coming down a different tree.'

'So did you see anything?'

'I couldn't see those rocks in the water, Cap'n, but the smoke was as clear as a bell. No more than half a mile I'd say. I reckon they've caught some wild animal, and it's cooking over a big fire, right this very minute. The juices dripping onto the flames. Ah, ma mouth's running just thinking about it.'

'So which way are we heading?' asked Robert, as Mouse took a breath.

'That way, Cap'n,' answered Mouse, with a nod of the head.

No sooner were they on their way again than Robert stopped and sniffed sharply. 'I can smell the smoke now. We can't be far away.'

A little farther and it was Mouse's turn to come to a complete standstill. 'Cap'n, I reckon I can hear singing.' And untypically, a slight anxiety was present in his voice.

'Is that so bad?' asked Robert.

'It is, Cap'n, cos I don't recognize the tune, nor the tongue.'

Robert gulped. Mouse's hearing was clearly unquestionable. So who had they been following all this time?

'Are we going on, Cap'n?' asked Mouse.

Half of Robert wanted to continue while the other half wanted to flee. But curiosity was getting the better of him. 'Maybe a wee look. But we'll have to keep undercover, we don't know if they're friendly or not.'

Mouse was grinning from ear to ear. 'I reckon they're friendly, Cap'n. Why, they might even share their roast with us.'

'If you want, you can go first,' said Robert. 'You're quieter than me.'

'Sure, Cap'n,' said Mouse, chuffed to bits.

The two boys immediately began to sneak closer, with Mouse taking the lead. The small boy tiptoed with such a delicacy that not a sound came from him. Conversely, Robert cracked twig after twig, even clunking the head of the spade against a protruding branch.

'Slowly, Cap'n,' whispered Mouse, shortly. 'We're there.'

The boys nervously peeped out. Directly in front of them was a large clearing, and roughly in the middle of it a great open fire, around which dark skinned natives were dancing and singing. The men, who there seemed to be more of, displayed more decorations on their bodies than actual clothes. Many had feathers in their hair, one even wore a feather headdress. All were heavily painted and not one showed any sign of a beard. Menacingly, each carried some sort of weapon, mostly a thick wooden club. The women, on the other hand, were less decorated and not so involved in the singing and chanting. The majority of them merely idled around stony-faced, tending to tasks and their strangely placid children.

In the background, thatched structures sat untroubled, behind which a steep gradient led onto a grassy hilltop. The foreground was bald and had evidently been cleared by scorching, the odd blackened tree stump bearing testament.

'There must be three score of the fellows, Cap'n,' said Mouse, in a hushed voice. 'I'm not sure they're awful friendly, though, those clubs look mighty fierce.'

'I think we should go before they see us,' said Robert, uneasily.

And then he noticed something which sent a shudder down his back. Way off, next to one of the thatched huts, a post was driven into the ground, and sitting on top of it was a human head, with all its hair still attached. Then, even worse, he noticed a second and third post similarly festooned with human heads.

199

Seeing Robert's shocked expression, Mouse had followed his captain's gaze.

'They're savages, Cap'n,' said he, rather too loudly. 'Cannibals even. I reckon we've stumbled across a real wasp's nest here.'

'Come on,' said Robert, quietly. 'We'll need to find the others and get off this island fast.'

Just then, the smoke from the fire, which had up until now been rising straight up, changed direction, and billowed right into the faces of a huddle of natives. They soon started to move, while all the time the chanting and singing never ceased.

Then, as soon as the smoke was blowing in this new direction, it changed back again, heading directly upwards once more. Now, what was once hidden from the boys by the huddle of natives and then latterly by the smoke, appeared before them. A wooden structure, bound together by numerous ropes, not very high and not especially wide.

The boys halted momentarily. 'It's like a cage, Cap'n,' said Mouse. 'I pity the poor beast they've got trapped in there. They'll probably roast the thing alive.'

Suddenly, a hand shot out from the top of the cage. A white hand. Robert and Mouse couldn't believe their eyes. Straightaway, the truth dawned on them.

'They've got the crew, Cap'n!' cried Mouse.

'We don't know for sure,' said Robert.

'Then I shall find out, Cap'n.' And before Robert could argue, Mouse had dissolved into the undergrowth.

Robert crouched alone and considered. What difference did it make if it was the crew or not? They had to try and help. But what could two boys do against a small army of savages? He could hear himself panting with anxiety; it was as if breathing through his nostrils wasn't an option. 'Hurry up, Mouse,' he mouthed.

Thankfully, it wasn't long before a puffing Mouse returned.

'It's the crew, Cap'n, for sure. But I could only make out five of them. There's no Titch or Jelly or him, Reno. Ye don't reckon they've already cooked them. Do ye, Cap'n?'

'No, no way,' said Robert. 'They must be in another cage somewhere.' He hoped Mouse had been calmed, but he himself was not. It was glaringly obvious they had to do something, and fast. But what?

'What are we gonna do, Cap'n? I don't reckon they'll turn tail from just the two of us.'

'I know. But if we had some sort of diversion, a noise, or a shout, or something happening, we might have a chance of sneaking in.'

'What about a fire, Cap'n?' said Mouse instantly. 'Let's start a fire. And when they go to investigate, we'll run in and free the crew.'

'But we don't have anything to start a fire with.'

'Course we do, Cap'n. Flint!'

Robert had heard of Flint before, a type of hard stone which sparks when you strike it with steel. But he'd never actually used it. 'And you've got some of this flint?'

'I've always got a bit of flint, Cap'n.' And Mouse delved into his trouser pocket. For a second he burrowed about inside. Then, two fingers poked out through the material. 'Ah, I seem to have gained a hole, Cap'n. We could rub two sticks together. Fraser did it once. Took some time if I recollect rightly.'

'We need to think of something else and quickly.'

'We could wait till nightfall, Cap'n. And then sneak in and cut everybody loose. Or better, I could wave to the critters and run off, and when they give chase you can slip in unnoticed.'

Robert turned over this last option in his head: doable or suicide, he couldn't make up his mind.

Suddenly, a gunshot ripped through the forest. The boys jumped in unison as skittish birds flocked to the sky. Then, a blood curdling scream cut through the air.

'What was that, Cap'n?' asked Mouse, eyes wide in astonishment. 'Something's afoot.'

'Do you think it's Fraser with the rest of the crew?' said Robert.

But before Mouse could respond, a volley of pistol shots erupted from the jungle, followed by a wild roar and shouting.

'Well it can't be our lads, Cap'n,' said Mouse. 'We don't have that many pistols.'

The boys were now spellbound at what was unfolding before them. The natives themselves had already abandoned their festivities and were moving rapidly towards the trees, brandishing their weapons. However, they were stopped dead in their tracks when one of their own fellows burst through the jungle wall. The man stumbled wildly, then collapsed to his knees frothing at the mouth. For a brief moment, he knelt unmoving, until finally falling face forwards. Dead!

Robert had never seen a dead person before, but he couldn't ponder long, as with another volley of gunfire, a line of pirates charged out from the undergrowth.

'It's Blackjack's lot,' said Robert. 'What are they doing here?'

'Don't matter, Cap'n. They might just have saved our skins.'

'That's if they don't kill us too.'

After the initial shock, the native men raced to confront the pirates head on, as the women and children frantically began to retreat up the hill.

'Ah, the yellow-bellied scoundrels are running for it!' roared Blackjack, with a pistol in each hand.

The buccaneers' attack was devastating, with muskets and pistols flashing, they dropped the natives like flies in the wintertime. The natives attacked fiercely with their wooden clubs and spears, but it was an unfair fight. Even when the pirates resorted to cutlasses, wood against hard steel was never a match.

Robert and Mouse observed the ensuing battle with growing interest. The fighting was taking place on the opposite side of the clearing. The great fire too was doing its bit to help them, by belching out thick grey smoke like a stack of chimneys on a frosty morning. The native women had deliberately thrown on green foliage before their hasty withdrawal.

'We should go now, Cap'n,' said Mouse. 'Before the savages are routed.'

Robert didn't reply, he was transfixed by the gory events taking place before him. Blackjack's crew, with their glistening cutlasses and shouting of oaths, were cutting down the natives mercilessly. Corpses lay everywhere while the soil was stained with blood.

'Captain!' said Mouse. 'Should we not be going?'

'Yes,' replied Robert, jumping back into reality. 'Let's go.'

The two boys hugged the edge of the forest, staying undercover as much as possible. Mouse led, as Robert followed closely behind. It didn't matter how noisy they were now, as their sounds were easily drowned out by the battle taking place but a short distance away.

'It's here, Cap'n,' said Mouse, pulling up.

Robert hurriedly withdrew his cutlass and jabbed it a couple of times. His heart was thumping. Would there be a guard to overcome? Would they be spotted? Could he strike someone again? Boy, his eyes were stinging with the smoke!

'Ready, Cap'n?' asked Mouse.

'Ready!' declared Robert. And out they both leapt.

'It's the Cap'n!' cried Boxer immediately.

'We're saved,' said Cooper, a toothy grin instantly lighting up his blackened face.

'Hurry, Captain,' said Bennett, but his head didn't turn.

Robert could see why. Bennett, Barrell and Leo all had their hands bound behind their backs, and a long pole pushed through their arms, joining the three of them together. The pole was then fixed at either end to the frame of the cage. They were completely immobilized. And opposite, it was the exact same with Boxer and Cooper, except that Boxer had somehow managed to wriggle a hand free.

Suddenly, a lead ball whistled through the air and cracked into one of the posts. Everyone ducked.

'Is everybody alright?' asked Robert, as he began to slice the bindings with his cutlass.

'We're all well, Captain,' answered Bennett swiftly. 'But they're holding Reno and the others someplace else.'

'Whereabouts?'

'Towards the hill, Captain. It can't be far off cos Jelly's been whistling to us.'

'I can go, Cap'n,' said Mouse.

'No, I'll go,' said Robert. 'Here, take my cutlass. It'll be quicker than that knife you're using.'

Mouse took the sword and again set to work.

'Should we wait for ye, Captain?' asked Bennett, stopping Robert dead in his tracks.

'Eh, yeah. But only for a few minutes. Then go. Do you know where you're going?'

'Aye, Captain. I know exactly where to go. And if we don't see ye, we'll mark the trees with chalk.'

'Good luck, men,' said Robert, darting away. He immediately checked himself. He was sounding like a bona fide captain!

'Good luck, Cap'n,' returned six voices behind him.

Robert moved with mounting haste. He was hopeless with directions. He had to find the others and get back to Bennett before they left. Finding chalk marks on trees would be a nightmare.

There was nobody about but he tried not to make a sound, consciously tiptoeing on the sandy ground between the natives' homes. He was in the open and vulnerable, but he had little option. Reno and the rest were definitely here, but where?

'Psst!' he called out quietly, as he scurried along. 'Psst!' a touch louder. 'Reno ... Titch ... Jelly.'

'In here, Cap'n!' said someone.

Robert recognized the voice. It was Jelly.

'Where? In the house?' asked Robert.

'Yeah! We're trussed up like chickens in here.' It was Reno.

Robert rushed around the thatched dwelling and found a small interwoven door. Bereft of hinges he simply yanked it aside.

'Cap'n!' cried Jelly.

'We thought we were goners for sure, Cap'n,' said Titch.

'Untie me,' bade Reno. 'Who's attacking? Pirates? Do we know them?'

'It's Blackjack and his men,' answered Robert, as he viewed the three captives.

They sat facing him, hands tied behind their backs, with a long horizontal pole to their rear, which was anchored at either end. It was a mirror image of the others. Robert pulled out his knife and went over to Jelly who was at one end.

Reno was instantly angered. 'Why cut him loose first? If those savages come back now, what's he gonna do? Whistle a tune!'

Robert didn't respond. He was too busy trying to slice through the ropes around Jelly's wrists. The bone handled dagger which Fraser had given him on departure was anything but sharp. Perhaps Reno's comment was sensible after all.

Finally, the last few threads encircling Jelly's wrists separated.

'Try and untie Reno,' said Robert immediately. 'I'll do Titch.'

'Did ye no hear me or something,' snapped Reno. 'Ye should have done me first. Those two would fight like a couple of lassies.'

'But you're faster than them at running,' said Robert. The truth was, he didn't trust Reno to stay and help.

'Nothing's budging,' said Jelly, panting. 'I'd have more chance if he'd been clapped in irons.'

After a final cut, Titch's bindings dropped to the ground.

'Do ye want us to do anything, Cap'n?' asked Titch, raising himself and quickly stretching his limbs.

Robert thought. Titch and Jelly should really go now to have a chance of catching Bennett and the rest of the crew, but he was loath to be left alone with Reno.

'Shouldn't they be scarpering, seeing as they're so much slower than me?' said Reno, as if he'd just read Robert's mind.

'Yeah,' said Robert, as he tackled Reno's bindings. 'Reno's right, you two should go now. I told Bennett not to wait long.'

'Isn't it better if we all go together, Cap'n?' said Jelly.

'You heard!' snapped Reno. 'Scarper, the both of ye. We'll be right behind ye.'

'Come on, Jelly,' said Titch, and the two small boys took their leave.

'That way,' said Robert, briefly pointing with his thumb. 'Around the edge and hurry.'

'Aye, Cap'n,' were Jelly's final words.

Reno's ties were made with a thicker, coarser rope, and Robert struggled to make any headway. His blade, too, was now no longer shiny and smooth but had gummed up and blackened somewhat.

'Give it to me!' said Reno impatiently.

'What?' questioned Robert.

'The knife, of course. I'm stronger than you. Put it into ma hand.'

Robert had no choice. He was struggling and he knew it. Grudgingly, he placed the dagger into Reno's right hand.

Robert looked around the marginally see-through hut. There wasn't much to speak of, a few tatty animal skins on the ground and a flat slab of stone at the back wall. There weren't even any windows.

'Are ye gonna stand there all day?' said Reno, straight out of the blue.

Robert turned sharply to see the tall boy standing in the doorway, dagger in hand. The two boys stared at each other. Neither said a word. Then, Robert's heart started to quicken as Reno's hand twitched with nervous tension.

In a flash, Reno raised his right hand and launched the dagger through the air. It happened so fast, Robert didn't have time to move. The knife sailed towards him like an arrow, then embedded itself in one of the supporting pillars.

'Yer knife, Captain,' said Reno, grinning. 'I'm off!'

'Wait up. We're going together,' said Robert.

'No can do. Those savages have got ma pistols, and I aim to get them back.'

Reno immediately about turned and ran off.

Yet again, Robert found himself alone. He grabbed at the knife. It didn't budge. He gripped it with both hands and pulled. Nothing. He thumped it with the palm of his hand. No movement.

Breathing! Suddenly, someone's laboured breathing sounded behind him. Surely Reno had changed his mind and come back. But when Robert turned around, he got the biggest fright of his life. A native, wielding a huge wooden club, was standing in the doorway, staring at him and grinning.

Robert groped for the knife behind his back. He couldn't locate it. The native moved closer. Robert moved sideways. Then, with a low roar, the native attacked. Instinctively, Robert twisted his body, but the blow glanced him and he crumpled to the ground exactly where he had been standing.

Robert was now lying on his back with the stockily built native leaning over him. But the moment was brief as the man raised his club to finish the job. Shouldn't Reno be back, flitted through Robert's mind, as his hands scrambled in the dry dusty ground around him. Then, like a blacksmith's hammer the club fell, but at the exact same moment Robert hurled a cloud of dry dirt into the air.

Momentarily, the native was blinded. Seizing his opportunity, Robert rolled to the side, righted himself, and bolted out of the door. But the sight that greeted him was terrifying. Literally hundreds of savages were careering down the grassy slope towards him, each one armed to the teeth. Reinforcements had arrived. Wasting no time, he charged into the sanctuary of the jungle.

Robert ran with all his strength along the forest edge. He could hear Blackjack's men crashing through the trees and bushes as they ran helter-skelter in their retreat. Bennett would be long gone, and surprisingly Robert found himself hoping to come across Reno.

Alas, as Robert had suspected, on drawing level with the empty cage, nobody was waiting. And so, with a deep foreboding, he entered into the jungle proper in search of chalk marks. Fortunately, the first one was easy, a white arrow the height of his waist. The second one too was clearly visible. He paused. He'd heard something.

'Hey!' came a voice. 'Hey there!'

'Who's there?' asked a surprised Robert.

'Over here.'

Robert backtracked a little. It certainly wasn't one of his crew. It was a man's voice. 'Where are you?'

'In the hole,' answered the voice.

Robert feared it was one of the pirates, yet he was attracted to the voice like a moth to a light bulb. His curiosity had completely gotten the better of him. 'Who are you?' he asked, just as he found the hole. Amazingly, he had run straight past it.

'Help me, laddie. Ah, it's you, MacSpoon,' said none other than Giant.

Robert gingerly peered into the hole, slightly fearful it could be a trap of some kind. It was deep and the walls were of damp mud and sheer-sided, while overlain branches obscured the opening. It was easy to see how Giant had dropped in and couldn't get back out.

'Why should I help you?' demanded Robert.

The tall muscular man instantly grinned as if butter wouldn't melt in his mouth and then he held up his hands. 'I'm at yer mercy, MacSpoon lad. Ye know what they'll do to me, they'll roast me alive. Ye want that on yer good conscience? Yer like me, MacSpoon, we're two peas from the same pod. Help me and I'll be indebted to ye lad, pirate's honour. I'll repay ye ten score over.'

Robert didn't believe one word from the pirate's mouth. However, he would help. But he had to hurry.

'Where ye going?' snapped Giant, as Robert turned away.

'To find something to help you,' said Robert. There were no vines conveniently lying around like in the films and he wondered what to do.

'Are ye still there?' growled Giant, impatiently.

Robert didn't reply. He wanted to leave. The man was horrible. But a lengthy log gave Robert an idea. Gripping one end, he pulled it towards the hole. Then, going to the opposite end, he pushed with all his might.

'Ah, yer a good one MacSpoon. Two peas in a pod we are,' said the pirate, as one end of the log hung in midair over the hole.

Suddenly, Giant grabbed it and up it flicked, nearly taking Robert's head off. Instantly, the log slid down and nestled into a position for

207

climbing. In two shakes, the pirate was halfway up the hole, before stopping and stretching out his considerable hand. 'Help me, lad,' he begged. 'I'm slipping.'

Unthinking, Robert grasped the pirate's hand. And it was too late to change his mind. In a flash he was propelled headfirst into the hole and Giant was free.

'You're nothing but a cheat,' cried Robert, painfully pulling himself to his knees. The log was gone.

'Where's The Book of Maps? And I'll let ye out,' growled Giant.

'I don't know. Now let me out.'

'Last chance, ye little whippersnapper. The Book of Maps!'

'I told you, I don't have it. Let me out!'

'Farewell, MacSpoon,' grinned the pirate. Then, spitefully, he picked up a small branch and lobbed it into the hole. 'Now we're square.'

'I helped you,' exclaimed Robert. But his pleas were falling on deaf ears as the big buccaneer was already gone.

Frantically, Robert tried to clamber up the muddy sides, but the damp earth just crumbled to the ground. He could see the marks Giant had made earlier in his unsuccessful attempts. The situation was bleak, there wasn't a grain of hope of getting out without assistance.

Robert sank to the ground and looked up at the canopy above. His head and neck immediately ached from the fall. He lowered his head slowly. There were plenty of leaves and small branches surrounding him, but nothing of any use. Life was kicking him at every turn, and he'd had enough. Things couldn't get any worse.

All of a sudden, voices penetrated the sounds of the insects and birds. Robert held his breath as they got closer and closer, until ultimately he could hear the very words, none of which he understood. In a frenzy he grabbed at the branches and foliage and started to cover himself.

His pursuers were nearby now, he could hear them softly panting with exertion and gabbling under their breath. Then, a twig snapped right above him and his heart jumped against his chest. Someone was standing there and a little earth dribbled into the hole. Not a muscle did he move as he waited to be discovered or for the sharp point of a spear to be driven into him.

It was a long time before Robert had the courage to poke his head out from his hiding spot. It was slightly cooler and darker now: evening had arrived. After making sure he was definitely alone, he again tried to climb out. Further fruitless attempts passed until he eventually gave up. Exhausted, he lay down on the carpet of leaves and drifted into sleep.

Robert awoke with a start. It was completely black in the hole. He'd been dreaming of birds singing and dancing before him, as he sat on top of a giant haystack. It was ever so pleasant. He smiled to himself and promptly fell back into sleep.

19. Sabotage

Robert's eyes were wide open, but he wasn't wholly convinced he wasn't still dreaming. He couldn't see a thing as it was still pitch black and the birds hadn't stopped singing. Well, one bird in particular. What a beautiful song it sang, over and over. Oddly, it even sounded familiar.

Suddenly it clicked. 'Jelly,' he mouthed. 'It's Jelly.' But would he stake his life on it? Did he have a choice? At least now he knew he wasn't dreaming. Didn't he?

Robert immediately tried to imitate the whistling. It was rubbish. His mouth and lips were too dry. He collected some saliva on his tongue and moistened his lips, then tried again. His second attempt was better, though nowhere near as good as Jelly's offering. If indeed it was Jelly.

Robert stopped and listened nervously. Was he tempting fate?

Not far off, something shuffled through the vegetation. Then there was silence. In for a penny, in for a pound, thought Robert, and he emitted another brief whistle. At once, the trilling of the bird resumed, increasing in volume right up until it seemed to be directly overhead.

'Captain?' said a voice tentatively.

'Jelly?' replied Robert.

'Yeah, it's me,' said Jelly. 'Are we glad we found you. We've been searching all night.'

'I'm here too, Cap'n,' added Boxer, eagerly.

Robert was over the moon. Although, he couldn't see either of them.

'Is it deep, Cap'n?' asked Boxer.

'Yeah, I can't touch the top. Aren't there any savages about, though?'

'All gone, Cap'n. Chased after Blackjack's lot then never came back. Might still be the odd one, though, so we're keeping our eyes peeled, well mainly ears in this darkness. We've got some rope. Here Jelly, tie this end onto a tree.'

'Did everybody make it back to the boat?' asked Robert, concernedly.

'All except Reno, but he passed us a short time ago heading in that direction. He must have gotten lost. Watch yer noggin, Cap'n, here comes the rope.'

'Mm,' mumbled Robert. 'He must have done.'

'What did ye say, Cap'n?' asked Boxer.

'Eh, nothing. I'm glad you're here.'

'Hold on tight, Cap'n,' said Boxer. 'We'll pull. It'll be easier.'

Robert gripped tightly and started to climb as Boxer and Jelly pulled. And in the twinkling of an eye, the three of them were side by side.

'How did you find me in this darkness?' asked Robert, totally puzzled.

'Compass,' said Boxer. 'Bennett worked it all out. You'll be seeing in two ticks.'

Robert knew there were no torches with batteries, and with no moon or stars the sky was jet black. So how could they see the compass?

Click! Click! A small flash of light appeared and for a split second Robert saw Jelly with a knife and flint in his hands, and Boxer with Bennett's compass.

'Mouse borrowed me his flint last week,' said Jelly.

'Lent,' said Robert. 'He lent you it last week.'

'How did ye know that, Cap'n? I guess that's why yer the Cap'n.'

Robert gave up. 'So which way are we going?'

'Thataway Cap'n,' said Boxer, holding up Robert's hand. 'And I reckon we should make haste, otherwise we'll be stuck on this island for another night.'

Every few minutes, like clockwork, Jelly and Boxer repeated the same procedure. Thus, the boys steered themselves through the jungle.

'It was supposed to be me and Mouse, Cap'n,' said Jelly, through the darkness. 'But he fell asleep and Bennett said not to stir him. He'll be ever so vexed at Boxer taking his place. Anyhow, can't believe the whole thing's been one big wild goose chase.'

'Mouse told you everything?' asked Robert, already knowing the answer.

'Sure did, Cap'n,' replied Boxer. 'How ye dug the whole night and found nothing except an old tree root and some juicy pineapples.'

'Ye can keep yer juicy pineapples,' said Jelly swiftly. 'I'll be glad to see the back of this place. It's scary. I don't mind dinner so long as I'm not the thing being eaten.'

'How did you get captured?' asked Robert, realizing that he had a hundred different questions.

'When we were sleeping, Cap'n,' replied Boxer. 'We were tied up before we knew it.'

'Didn't you have somebody keeping watch?' asked Robert, surprised at both Bennett and Reno's oversight.

'Aye,' groaned Jelly. 'Me, Cap'n. But I fell asleep.'

'Ah, well we all make mistakes once in a while,' said Robert.

'Thanks, Cap'n. I just hope everybody sees it like that.'

Soon, they came to a thin path in the vegetation. It wasn't much but it made the going a lot easier, even though the surface was uneven and nearly disappearing in places.

'It's an animal track,' said Boxer. 'And it goes our way.'

'Bennett says the risks outweigh the benefits,' said Jelly, itching to join in.

'The benefits outweigh the risks!' said Boxer promptly.

'That's what I said,' complained Jelly. 'You can't hear properly in this darkness.'

'Halt! Who goes there? Friend or foe?' said a voice from nowhere.

'It's us, Cooper,' said Boxer, into the sultry night.

'I know, I heard ye gabbing a mile off. Did ye find the Cap'n?'

'Yeah, they found me,' said Robert, feeling somewhat embarrassed. Some captain!

'Where's Leo?' asked Boxer.

'Up a tree,' said Cooper. 'He reckons it's easier to hear the higher up off the ground ye are. He's likely fallen asleep. Leo!'

'I'm right beside ye,' said Leo in a deep voice, and everybody jumped.

'I hate this place,' said Cooper. 'It gives me the creeps. I'm gonna have nightmares about this.'

Then, a small flash of light lit up the night, and the five boys glimpsed each other for a fleeting moment. It was heartwarming for them all.

'Shall I do it again, Cap'n?' asked Jelly, flint and knife at the ready.

'We should keep moving,' said Robert. 'We need to get back to the boat when it's still dark, otherwise Fraser will just turn round again. How much farther is it?'

'About half a mile, Cap'n,' answered Leo. 'But it's easy going.'

'Is everybody feeling strong enough to hurry?'

'Aye, Cap'n,' declared all, and off they trotted.

'Did you see Reno?' asked Robert.

'Aye,' answered Cooper. 'Not long before you came. He got his pistols back. He was mighty chuffed.'

Just as the first sliver of light appeared in the east, they reached the rowing boat. Bennett had somehow managed to move it to a more convenient location. Robert was impressed.

'Glad ye could make it, Captain,' said Bennett, cheerfully.

Robert sighed with exhaustion as the cool sea breeze struck his face. But, for the first time in what seemed ages, he was starting to see again. 'Glad to be back. Now let's find Fraser.'

Bennett turned his back and busied himself with something. Suddenly a flame licked up the head of a torch. 'That should help Fraser see us. But we'll have to make haste. Reno, Barrell, grab an oar. I'll ... '

'You'll no be ordering me about,' snapped Reno. 'And you!' he snarled, jabbing Jelly fiercely in the ribs. 'Remember what's coming to ye.'

'Keep your fingers to yourself, Reno,' said Robert. 'We need the strongest on the oars. Whoever's not tired.'

Everybody jumped into the boat, and predictably Reno took a place at the oars. Bennett joined him, handing the flickering torch to Titch, who held it aloft. A groggy Mouse was left to cast off.

'Keep it up high,' said Bennett. 'It'll be plainer to see against the dark trees.'

In the advancing dawn, the boys moved swiftly to where they hoped Fraser would be. Each and every one was hungry, thirsty and exhausted, and more than anything they longed to see The Lightning's outline heading towards them.

'Wave the torch from side to side,' said Robert. 'It'll be more visible.'

Those not rowing strained their eyes at the horizon. None wished to return to the island.

'Remember, they'll see us before we see them,' said Bennett. 'The higher ye are on the water, the farther ye see.'

'We're no two year olds,' snapped Reno. 'Next you'll be telling us how to wipe our bums.'

Robert ignored the squabbling and peered into the blackness. It might have been getting light in the east, but on the other points of the compass it was still darkish. Then he smiled to himself. 'I see something.' He paused. 'It's a ship for sure.'

'I see it too,' said Cooper, after a few seconds.

'I reckon a blind man with a stick could see it now,' said Reno, viewing the dark silhouette with his turned head.

'I was just saying,' said Cooper quietly.

By the time they had boarded The Lightning and winched up the rowing boat, it was quite light. Fraser and the crew were thoroughly bubbling with excitement, even saluting the returnees at one point. But their moods quickly changed on hearing the adventures which had taken place on the perilous island.

'So it was the wr-wrong island, and you all nearly lost yer lives,' said Fraser, wringing his hands. 'It's been a total d-disaster.'

'Yeah, ye stuttering idiot,' barked Reno. 'We all could've gotten killed cos of you. I said it was the wrong bleeding place.'

'No ye didn't, ye liar,' said Mouse immediately.

'What did ye call me?' roared Reno, squaring up to the small boy.

'A liar. You wanted to go sooner.'

Suddenly, Reno shot out a hand and gripped poor Mouse by the throat. 'I've had ma fill of you and yer mouth.'

'Get off him!' shouted Robert, and he grabbed Reno's arm.

'Or what?' said Reno.

'Just get off him. Fighting amongst ourselves is stupid. There are bigger battles to fight.'

Reno released his grip and immediately selected another victim. 'He's gotta be punished!' And he pointed a finger at Jelly. 'Eight lashes with the cat-o'-nine it is.'

'What are you talking about?' asked Robert.

'Falling asleep on yer watch earns eight lashes,' said Reno. 'Them's the rules.'

'Is that right?' asked Robert, turning to Bennett.

Bennett nodded his head deliberately. 'Last captain said discipline was the most important thing on a ship. We all voted for it.'

'See!' crowed Reno. 'Barrell, get the cat.'

'I don't agree,' said Robert. 'It's not as if he deliberately fell asleep.'

'Now's too late,' said Reno. 'We can change the rules for the future but not for the present.'

'But ye can change the number of lashes, Captain,' said Bennett. 'Captain's privilege.'

'So I can change the number of lashes to anything?' asked Robert.

'Aye, Captain,' answered Bennett. 'Ye can alter the number to whatever ye like. Eight is only a recommendation.'

'Then I say one lash.'

'What?' cried Reno. 'One lash is for a girl.'

'Captain says one, so one it is,' said Bennett.

Barrell promptly returned with the cat-o'-nine tails and handed it to Reno. The whip, with its nine knotted strings, looked barbaric. Reno flicked it expertly and it cracked.

'Up against the mast, Jelly boy,' ordered Reno. 'I intend making the one count. No point in brooding now. What's done is done.'

'Hold on,' said Robert. 'Who carries out the punishment?'

'Again, Captain's prerogative,' said Bennett.

'Then I pick Cooper,' said Robert. 'Give the cat to Cooper please, Reno.'

'Are ye jesting?' returned Reno, flicking the whip irritably.

'Them's the rules,' said Robert sternly. 'Give Cooper the cat, please.'

Reno hesitated and then reluctantly threw the whip at Cooper, who barely caught it.

'One lash, Cooper,' said Robert. 'On the back. Jelly, are you ready?'

'Aye, Cap'n.'

Cooper reluctantly stepped forwards, holding the whip awkwardly in the middle.

'Blimey, he canna even hold the thing properly,' howled Reno.

Timidly, Cooper raised the whip and brought it down onto Jelly's bare back. A relieved Jelly turned to go.

'Looks like it's yer lucky day, Jelly boy,' said Reno, spitefully. Then he addressed the crowd. 'But it's an open invitation to anarchy and mutiny, is what I say. Though I'll hold ma tongue.'

'Now we should eat,' said Pudding, arriving. 'I've got a tasty pea soup bubbling away.'

Everyone smacked their lips. Robert groaned.

Mealtimes below deck on The Lightning were invariably congested, and today was no different. Even though, as Pudding explained, half of the crew had already eaten, himself included. Predictably, the soup was over salted and Robert had to repeatedly lick his lips.

'I take it ye must be finding it overly tasty, Cap'n. Yer licking yer lips,' said Pudding, as he tucked in with his wooden spoon. 'Not too salty today then?'

'Delicious,' replied a ravenous Robert. He would find the store of salt and chuck it overboard. He promised himself.

Reno was impatient to open discussions on what they should do next, and as soon as he had finished licking his wooden bowl, he began. 'That island was plain wrong, so the question is ... Where is the right one?'

'I'll give ye another question,' said Bennett promptly. 'How did Blackjack and his crew end up on the selfsame island as us?'

'They likely followed us,' offered Barrell.

'Or coincidence,' said Reno.

'A fair coincidence,' mumbled Mouse, who was sitting on a stool away from the main table.

'And who rattled your cage?' snapped Reno. 'Ye couldn't even read the word if it was written on yer hand.'

'So I can't read,' returned Mouse. 'Can't be that hard, you managed.'

Reno raised himself, but Mouse sprang away.

'Fighting amongst ourselves gives us nothing,' declared Robert. He removed the pendant from around his neck. 'Anybody got any ideas? Otherwise, we'll have to start comparing it to maps again.'

A huddle quickly formed around Robert, but alas, ideas were few and far between. Gradually, the flummoxed crew returned to their tasks and only a handful of boys remained.

'Shall we r-reconvene in yer c-cabin, C-Captain?' said Fraser, getting up. 'I m-must check the wheel.'

'I must be off too,' said Bennett.

'My cabin, in an hour?' suggested Robert. He was tired and didn't feel like getting up. The hard wooden bench had eventually become quite comfortable.

'Aye, aye, Captain,' answered the departees.

Reno and Barrell also left, and other than a few stragglers mopping up their soup, only Robert and Mouse remained.

Immediately, Mouse placed his hands onto the raw wooden table and looked around the room suspiciously. 'Are ye no licking that bowl, Cap'n? Seems an awful waste of good food.'

'Ah, yes,' said a chastised Robert, and lifted the bowl to his mouth.

'I've got a hunch, Cap'n,' whispered Mouse. 'There's something tricksy about that there pendant.'

'What?'

'Follow me, Cap'n.' And Mouse shot off towards the stern of the ship, bowl in hand. Robert quickly followed, past the tables and benches and messed up hammocks, and straight into a side cabin with lots of stuff inside. Mouse gently closed the door. It was half light inside.

'I spoke to Fraser, Cap'n. It was his idea to see ye in secret. He reckons Reno might have a laugh at me, or something like that.'

'Mm,' said Robert. 'So you did see something up on the mountain. What did you see?' The cloak-and-dagger nature of it all was intriguing.

'Can ye give me the pendant, Cap'n?'

Robert handed it over.

'I reckon stuff's been added, Cap'n,' said Mouse, running his thumb over the pendant's face. 'Here, see how these bits are bumpy while the other bits are smooth.'

Robert checked the pendant and felt the tiny bumps.

Meanwhile, Mouse had pulled the lid off a barrel, dipped in a ladle, and filled up his bowl with water. 'Now Cap'n, if we were to wash the thing, I reckon it'd show up what's old and what's new even better.'

'Go for it,' said Robert, returning the pendant.

Mouse dipped the necklace into the bowl, and with the corner of his shirt, started to wipe away the dirt. Then, going to the open porthole, he observed the result. 'Yes!' he exclaimed. 'The new etchings are as plain as the nose on yer face, Cap'n.'

Suddenly, Mouse cocked his ear. 'Somebody's observing us.'

Instantly, Robert raced to the door and flung it open, while hurried footsteps disappeared along the deck towards the bow.

'Get 'em, Cap'n!' cried Mouse.

Robert threw himself around the corner and immediately tripped over a wriggling bundle on the floor. Headfirst he tumbled onto the rough wooden deck.

'Titch?' said Mouse. 'What are you doing under that hammock?'

'Somebody shoved me over,' groaned the small boy, tugging away the heavy cloth and cords which were encircling his body. 'Pudding sent me down to collect any dirty bowls. Next thing, I'm hitting the deck.'

'Did ye see who it was?' asked Mouse.

'Somebody big for sure. I only saw their feet, mind. But it kinda looked like Barrell. Mind you, Reno has the same shoes and same size feet.'

'Are we running, Cap'n?' asked Mouse, excitedly. 'We can still nab them.'

'It's too late now,' said Robert. 'Anyway, what's the point, there's no big secret, we're gonna tell everybody in a few minutes.'

'Nab who?' asked Titch, puzzled with the discussion. 'And how come I got knocked over?'

'Ah, somebody was fooling about,' said Robert. 'We wanted to catch them, but they ran off. Come on, the others will be waiting. Why not leave the bowls till later, Titch?'

'It's best I get them now, Cap'n. Pudding gets awful crabby if he can't get the washing done. That's why he wasn't best pleased when Reno was captain.'

'Alright. We'll see you in my cabin when you're finished.'

'Aye, aye, Cap'n,' said Titch, picking up a bowl.

Robert and Mouse made their way to the captain's cabin, which was sited in the stern of the ship on the upper weather deck. The crew were already there, but none had ventured inside, even though Robert never locked the door.

'We found something,' said Mouse, excitedly. Then, he looked around the faces for Reno, but he wasn't there, neither was Barrell.

'What?' asked everybody together.

'The pendant has been changed possibly,' said Robert, entering the cabin first. 'Bits have maybe been added. Mouse noticed it.'

'That would m-make sense,' said Fraser.

'Stop blabbing, man and get those maps out,' said Mouse, impatiently. 'I reckon we could be on the right island today. I can feel it in my bones.'

'As long as ye p-promise not to p-put yer grubby f-fingers all over them,' returned Fraser.

'Hey, I'll have ye know I washed these hands last week.'

Robert placed the pendant on the main table and Fraser went to fetch the maps.

'Only two?' queried Bennett.

'Actually, only one,' said Fraser. 'They're the same m-maps, only d-different scales. I already know which island it is now.'

'Go for it, Fraser,' said an enthusiastic Boxer.

'Go for what?' asked Reno, entering the cabin with Barrell.

'We've found the correct island,' said Bennett. 'Will we be going today, Captain?'

'I think best tomorrow, when there's the whole day in front of us.'

'Why, it's barely past noon,' said Barrell. 'No point in kicking our heels till tomorrow.'

Just then, Pudding rushed in, face crimson. 'Our drinking water's all gone Cap'n. I went down with Rabbit to fetch a keg of pork and found the whole place flooded, and most of the water barrels empty. The rats must have been gnawing away at them. Strange though, cos the kegs of pork seem to be untouched. But that's rats for ye. Not the brightest critters.'

'Actually, r-rats are very intelligent c-creatures,' said Fraser. But nobody was listening.

'How much water do we have left?' asked Robert.

'Enough for today, but little more Cap'n,' answered Pudding. 'I reckon we'll need to fill up presently, otherwise tomorrow's breakfast porridge is gonna be awful thick and the crew hate thick lumpy porridge.'

'We've got no choice then,' said Robert. 'We'll have to land somewhere and refill the barrels. Do we have extra barrels?'

'Aye, Cap'n. And I'll manage to repair some of them,' said Pudding.

'Any propositions, Fraser, for water?' asked Bennett.

'Well, B-Blackjack's m-marked a watering hole about thirty m-miles away. The wind's m-more than f-favourable. C-could be there in less than three hours.'

'That's where we're going today then,' said Robert. 'And tomorrow we'll go to our treasure island.'

'I'd better start pumping out the spilled water, then,' said Pudding, dejectedly. 'Anybody here wanting to help?'

Nobody answered. Removing dead water from a ship was a smelly and highly unpleasant task.

As ever, Fraser's calculations proved correct. In less than three hours The Lightning reached the island which Blackjack had marked as a good place to find fresh water. It had also been marked uninhabited.

On approaching, the island was curved, with the anchorage bang in the middle. To the rear was rocky and steep, but the front was one gigantic white beach, with luxurious greenery situated in between. The island was simply beautiful.

'Wow!' said each and every crew member.

'It's amazing,' said Fraser. 'It's a t-tropical p-paradise.'

Predictably, everybody wanted to go ashore and collect water, none wished to stay on board The Lightning. But Bennett and Fraser insisted that around half should remain in case of an emergency and to store the replenished water barrels. In the end, lots were drawn, and the lucky ones started to disembark. With one of the two rowing boats having developed a hole, it took a good few journeys to transport everyone ashore. But soon, all were standing on the baking white sand with a load of empty barrels. Robert also went ashore, but he desperately wanted to speak with Fraser, who as ever stayed behind.

With so many boys, a wonderful beach, and endless warm clear water, it didn't take long for hilarity to erupt. First, someone splashed someone, then somebody else splashed somebody else. Next thing, everyone was stripping off and abandoning their clothes on the beach. Although few could swim, everybody took to the water, except for Reno, who was in a mood. It was the first time Robert had seen the crew so happy and carefree. He just wished they wouldn't go so far out!

'Shark!' suddenly someone shouted. 'Sharks!'

Terror immediately raced through the bathers as everybody scrambled to get out of the sea. Arms and legs went flying along with cascades of water. Everyone was shrieking. Then, someone tripped and disappeared under the foaming frenzy. It was Jelly, and his plight went unnoticed in the fleeing mass.

'Jelly!' shouted Bennett. He had fleetingly glimpsed the boy's head disappearing below the water and not resurfacing. Like a shot, he launched himself into the water and raced towards the struggling boy. In no time, the tall boy had his long arms around his struggling friend, dragging him back to shore.

Lying on the white sand, Jelly coughed and spluttered like an old man. But he was alive. 'Thanks Bennett,' he said, when his breath returned. 'It's not easy running in water, ye lose yer balance.'

'Sometime, I don't know when, but everybody has got to learn to swim,' declared Bennett.

'So where's the sharks?' said Robert, scanning the crystal clear water. 'There's nothing there, as far as I can see. Who shouted?'

'Reno called out,' said Mouse straightaway.

All turned to look at Reno. 'I was only jesting,' said he. 'It got everybody out of the water. Didn't it? We've got work to do, water to collect.'

'Hmm,' said everyone, but sharks or no sharks, nobody felt like going back into the water. The fun was well and truly over.

Conveniently, Blackjack's map had a big cross at the source of the fresh water. He'd also written down 'waterfal' beside it, an attraction everyone was now looking forward to.

Behind a clump of trees, a track went in the right direction, and after following it, the crew arrived at their destination. Alas, the waterfall was a total disappointment. A thin stream dribbled over a small cliff, forming a small pond at the bottom.

'Aw,' said everyone.

'It's not much, is it?' said Barrell.

'Don't matter,' said Reno, cupping his hand and tasting the tumbling water. 'If it's drinkable, it's sufficient.'

The crew immediately set about filling the empty barrels. First, a barrel was taken to the waterfall on a small thin hand barrow with handles on both sides and disproportionately large wheels. Thence, it was filled up by many hands and wheeled back to the rowing boat. The shifting sand on the beach proved a formidable obstacle, but nothing would stop the industrious crew. Robert eagerly joined in the transportation of the full barrels and the difficult task of placing them into the rowing boat.

Soon, the first boatful was ready to return to The Lightning. Robert seized his chance and jumped into the rowing boat.

'Are ye going back already, Cap'n?' asked Titch, standing on the shoreline with the wet sand squeezing between his toes.

'Yeah, why?' immediately asked Barrell.

'Cap'ns don't have to explain what they're doing,' said Mouse swiftly.

'It's alright,' said Robert. 'I only wanted to see how the crew hoist up the barrels onto the ship. They're pretty heavy things to lift.'

'It's easy, Cap'n,' said Mouse, as he helped shove out the rowing boat with a handful of other crew members. 'It's way tedious. You'll be back in no time.'

Robert breathed a sigh of relief as they dipped the oars and the boat lurched forwards. No Barrell, no Reno. Super!

The Lightning was quite deserted when the fully laden rowing boat eased beside it.

'Where is everybody?' asked Robert, on climbing up the rope ladder and flipping over the gunwale.

'Hide and seek, C-Captain,' said Fraser, who was standing waiting on deck like a mother hen. 'I don't know why they b-bother p-playing, Leo always wins. He's got a special hiding spot nobody c-can f-find. It's like he just d-disappears into thin air.'

The crew soon noticed the rowing boat's return, and abandoning their game, began to organize the raising of the barrels. Robert, however, wasn't interested.

'Fraser, I need to speak with you,' he whispered, with mouth barely open. 'Can you come to my cabin?'

Fraser nodded discreetly and after delivering a few instructions, slipped away after Robert.

Inside the cabin, Robert hurriedly closed the door and gulped. 'Fraser, I think we have a spy onboard The Lightning.'

'I agree, C-Captain,' said Fraser, shifting his feet nervously.

'You do?'

'I'm afraid so, C-Captain.'

'Do you know who it is?' asked Robert keenly.

'P-Probably, but not d-definitely.'

'Ah,' said Robert. He was hoping for a much more assured reply.

'B-But I think it's b-best, C-Captain, if I don't offer my opinion until I am certain. I would hate to b-be wrong. A little more t-time is all I need.'

Robert understood and nodded. He would have to make his decision alone. After a brief pause, he asked, 'Why did the last captain go on his own to hide The Book of Maps?'

'I can't say for sure, C-Captain,' answered Fraser, shaking his fair head. 'B-But I guess it had something to d-do with our spy. He m-must have suspected something too.'

'Yes, but what? And who?' said Robert, as much to himself as to Fraser.

'Ye will only know the answer to that, C-Captain, when you see him.'

'Yes, I know,' mumbled Robert. 'But that's for another day.'

'What are we going to do, C-Captain?' asked Fraser, anxiously. 'If we f-find The B-Book of M-Maps t-tomorrow, it m-might be too late to do anything.'

'Unless, we find it sooner,' said Robert, thoughtfully.

'What do ye m-mean, C-Captain?'

'Eh, nothing, I need to think.' Suddenly, Robert gave a start. 'We should go, otherwise we'll be missed. We'll speak again after everybody's gone to sleep. Wait for a bit before you follow me out. Bye Fraser.'

'Aye, aye, C-Captain,' said Fraser.

Robert opened the cabin door and just about jumped out of his skin. 'Reno! What are you doing here?'

The tall boy was standing, hand poised to rap on the door.

'I heard ye had returned to the ship,' he said, eyeing everything in front of him.

'But how did you get back?' asked Robert instantly.

'I swam.'

'What about the sharks?'

'That was a jest, remember.'

'Did you want something?' asked Robert, tugging the door behind him.

'How many barrels should we fill up? If we fill up all of them there mayn't be time to bring them back before nightfall.'

Robert closed the cabin door. 'I'm going back to the island now, so I can see for myself. Are you coming in the boat or swimming?'

'Swimming, I reckon. I need to see Fraser. Do ye know where he is?'

Robert shook his head and moved away.

'Ach, I'll catch him later,' said Reno, accompanying Robert to the gunwale, directly above where the rowing boat was gently bobbing up and down in the see-through turquoise water.

The remaining hours of daylight were spent ferrying filled-up water barrels back to The Lightning. Having completed their part of the task first, it was the turn of the crew on the island to partake in a game of hide and seek. And what good fun it was. Although Robert couldn't get it out of his head that they may not be the only ones on the island.

As the light dimmed, the last boatful of barrels was rowed over and hoisted up onto the deck. The crew too had all left, and the island was once more deserted. But for a bunch of footprints, it was as if nobody had ever been there.

'Hoist up the rowboat!' ordered Bennett, wasting no time.

'No!' said Robert. 'I'd like it to be left out.'

'Why?' asked Reno, irritated. 'We'll only have to do it tomorrow morn before we set sail. Hoist it up, men!'

'No,' repeated Robert. 'The crew are tired. Besides, I might visit the island tomorrow morning before we leave.'

'Waste of good daylight, I say,' said Barrell. 'The island's got nothing more for us. A shark would be happy with the amount of water we've collected.'

'Make it fast, men!' ordered Bennett. 'The boat stays out, Captain's orders.'

'And, I'd like the anchor raised too,' said Robert, turning to face Bennett.

The tall boy looked surprised, wrinkling up the small freckles on his nose.

'This is getting plain daft,' groaned Reno, flapping his arms. 'And what might be yer reason now?'

'You're not the captain,' declared Mouse. 'We take the orders. The Cap'n hands them out.'

'Shut it!' snapped Reno. 'Or I'll shove yer teeth down yer throat.'

'No you won't!' returned Robert. 'Stop pushing people about.'

'It was m-me,' cried Fraser. 'I p-proposed weighing anchor. I wanted to see how m-much lateral d-drift there is with the waxing of the m-moon. This is the p-perfect spot to m-measure it.'

'What?' said Reno. Like the entire crew, he was thoroughly bamboozled at what Fraser had just expounded.

'He's been on the g-grog,' mimicked Barrell, cruelly.

'No he's not,' said Mouse. 'He reads stuff, unlike you.'

'Pot calling the kettle,' fired back Barrell, promptly squaring up to the small boy.

'You started it,' returned Mouse.

'We're fighting again,' groaned Robert. 'The anchor is coming up. Does anybody have anything else to moan about?'

'I p-prefer the Snake and the C-Crab myself,' mumbled Fraser, but nobody acknowledged him. They were all training their eyes on Reno's displeasure.

'I do,' said he. 'If we run aground on the whim of that stuttering fool, then dereliction of duty is what I'll cry. And nothing in this world will stop me from thrashing him till he drops.' Then he stormed off, barging into some of the crew as he did so.

Fraser's jaw dropped, and he looked at Robert searchingly.

'Dinner's ready, Cap'n,' said Pudding, appearing from nowhere. 'A nice pea soup with just a tad of salt. Just the way ye like it, Cap'n.'

'Weigh anchor!' yelled Bennett. 'Captain's orders.'

Food was served and eaten in near total darkness. There were few lanterns on the ship and little whale oil left to refill them. The number of tallow candles, the smelly alternative, was also dwindling. Supplies were running low aboard The Lightning.

Soon, everyone retired to bed and their respective hammocks. It had been a busy, yet most enjoyable day.

Robert lay awake in his wooden bed, tossing and turning. It wasn't because he couldn't sleep. He didn't want to. Instead, he was impatiently waiting for midnight when everyone else would likely be asleep.

He looked at his watch underneath his cuff. The fluorescent hands hadn't budged. Still broken! Now, he'd had enough. He stuck his legs out of bed, slipped on his trainers, and tiptoed forwards. The floorboards creaked as did the cabin door. He held his breath. Nothing. If he bumped into somebody, he would simply say that he was heading to the beakhead, for the toilet. Gently, he eased the door shut behind him.

The night was dark, there was no moon or stars. Electricity hung in the air. A storm was surely brewing.

Robert touched the ship's wheel. It was lashed tightly. Fraser was someplace else. Nobody was about, the silence was unnerving. He climbed the steps to the poop deck. There wasn't a breath of wind on his skin. He could have been anywhere in this darkness.

'C-Captain?' said Fraser, out of the blue.

Robert jumped even though he knew Fraser would be there.

'It's me,' whispered Robert, walking delicately towards the voice. 'Are we alone?'

'Aye, C-Captain. I've had a look round and there's not a soul. I p-passed P-Pudding about a half hour ago. He had a sore b-belly. B-But he's gone b-back to b-bed now.' He paused. 'Yer going alone, C-Captain, aren't ye?'

'Yes, I need to. I don't trust anyone except for you and Mouse. Oh, and thanks for covering for me with Reno and Barrell.'

'Yer welcome, C-Captain, I suspected ye were p-planning something. B-But surely you can trust B-Bennett and T-Titch and B-Boxer.'

'I'm only certain of you and Mouse,' repeated Robert quietly.

'Then what's yer p-plan, C-Captain? And how may I help?'

'I'm going to call the fog just before dawn and move The Lightning to the new island. Then I'll go alone in the rowing boat and get The Book of Maps myself.'

'And what shall I say to the c-crew, C-Captain in the m-morning? They'll know I saw you.'

'Tell them a storm was coming and the ship had to be moved. Then, I decided to go on my own because, because ... another storm was coming.'

'B-But a hurricane is c-coming, C-Captain,' said Fraser softly. 'It's m-moving northwards towards us as we speak. We're c-currently in the c-calm before the storm.'

'You think I should move The Lightning now, don't you?'

'Aye, C-Captain.'

Robert considered. He didn't want to waken any of the crew, and they would undoubtedly be more asleep later on. 'No, I'll stick to my plan. But if it starts to get windy, wake me up. Otherwise, can you come to me one hour before dawn.'

'Aye, C-Captain.'

'When do you sleep, Fraser?' asked Robert. It had begun to intrigue him.

'I c-catnap, C-Captain. I suppose I'll only ever have a truly sound sleep the d-day every m-member of this c-crew has a p-proper home on dry land, and these adventures of ours are b-behind us. M-Mine is a labour of love, C-Captain, as is yours becoming.'

'You need to cheer up, Fraser ... '

'Shh!' whispered Fraser.

'Who's there? Is that you, Fraser?' It was Mouse's squeaky voice through the darkness.

'Go b-back to b-bed,' said Fraser directly.

'I reckoned I heard voices.'

'Yer ears are too b-big. Go b-back to b-bed.'

'I was gonna have a blether with ye, but yer right grumpy. I'm going. You need to get some slumber yersel. Goodnight! Grump!'

'Goodnight to you too,' said Fraser.

Silence returned to the ship. Robert and Fraser waited.

After a few minutes, Robert said, 'I'll see you one hour before dawn.'

'Aye, aye, C-Captain.' Fraser paused. 'C-Captain, The Lightning won't run aground during the night, will she? I f-fear R-Reno would k-kill me.'

'I won't let her, don't worry. And remember, he needs us more than we need him. Night, Fraser.'

'Goodnight, C-Captain.'

Robert went back to his cabin, closed the door, and slipped into bed. In ten seconds flat he was sleeping like a baby.

20. The Book Of Maps

'*I*'m so sorry, C-Captain. I don't know what happened, I m-must have f-fallen asleep.'

'Eh, what?' said Robert, half awake. Surely he had just closed his eyes.

'I've scuppered everything, C-Captain. It's all my f-fault.'

'What time is it?' asked Robert, regaining his senses.

'It's not g-good, C-Captain.'

'Fraser!' declared Robert, grabbing his cutlass which he had unconsciously slept alongside.

'Less than one hour before d-dawn, C-Captain.'

'Then I can still make it, but we must hurry. Just no more apologies.'

'Aye, aye, C-Captain. B-But f-first I must t-tell you about the island yer going to. And it's b-best I do so in here.'

'There aren't any savages, are there?' exclaimed Robert.

'I'll be b-brisk, C-Captain. There are no savages. It's much too small. The island is shaped like a number six with the anchorage and a b-beach in the m-middle. B-Blackjack left a few p-particulars. The b-beach is shallow and sandy so you can easily b-beach the r-rowing b-boat. And the m-mountain is low, so c-climbing it should be straightforward. Our greatest p-problem, however, is d-darkness. There is no m-moon or stars tonight and I r-reckon it will be the same where we are heading.'

'Ah,' said Robert. 'Then we have a bit of a problem.'

'Not if I hold up a lantern, C-Captain. I've been c-cogitating a solution. P-Providing ye k-keep the light in front of you while yer r-rowing, then you'll be heading away f-from The Lightning and towards the b-beach.'

'As long as we know which way The Lightning is pointing and where the beach is.'

'That's child's p-play, C-Captain,' said Fraser.

'Then we're ready. Let's go!'

The two boys sneaked out and into the night, and Robert was immediately taken by surprise at the strength of the wind. The sails and rigging around him were flapping and groaning under the stresses and strains. He instantly felt sorry for Fraser, who had probably wanted to rouse him many hours ago, before inadvertently falling asleep.

'It's very windy,' said Robert. 'You should have woken me.'

'It's just a strong b-breeze, C-Captain,' said Fraser, but there was a palpable relief in his voice that now he wasn't alone. A problem shared was a problem halved.

Despite the total absence of light, Robert was amazed at how much he could decipher of his surroundings. He was standing beside the ship's wheel and could quite clearly make out the lashing around it. Fraser was standing abreast of him and picked something up.

'A water b-bottle, C-Captain,' said Fraser. 'A m-man can b-barely go a d-day in this heat without water, f-food yes, b-but water no. Although P-Pudding might b-beg to d-differ on that one.'

'Thanks,' said Robert. Had Fraser really attempted a joke! 'But now I must call the fog.'

Robert closed his eyes and started to imagine fog. and an island shaped like a number six with a white sandy beach in the middle, while all he could hear was the wind whistling around him. Then, all of a sudden, like someone had just switched off an electric fan, the wind ceased. He opened his eyes.

'Are we there, C-Captain?' asked Fraser. 'I can't see my own n-nose. This f-fog's thicker than one of P-Pudding's p-pea soups.'

'I guess so,' said Robert. 'The wind's stopped, so we must have gone somewhere.'

'And what if we've landed in the m-middle of the Atlantic Ocean, C-Captain? Surely we m-must wait until this f-fog c-clears and it lightens a little. Otherwise, I c-could be sending ye to a watery grave.'

'You're not sending me anywhere, Fraser, I'm volunteering, remember. Anyway, the fog will soon clear. And if I get lost, I'll just keep recalling it until I get back to The Lightning.'

'B-But a hurricane is heading our way, C-Captain, with waves as b-big as t-trees.'

'I'm going, Fraser. Now which way is the beach?'

'Well, there's no wind, C-Captain, so the ship will lie with the c-current. Although, b-being the C-Caribbean there are no t-tides, but the m-moon and sun are lined up, so there will be a slight t-tide. And using B-Blackjack's charts ... '

'Fraser!' said Robert impatiently. 'We don't have the time.'

'The b-bow will be p-pointing towards the b-beach, C-Captain. Guide the r-rowing b-boat to the b-bow of The Lightning and then aim straight ahead, k-keeping the lantern directly in f-front of ye. How far ye will have to t-travel though, I can't say.'

Robert hung the water bottle around his neck, felt his cutlass, and then touched Fraser's arm. 'Let's go.'

The rowing boat was tied up on the starboard side of the ship, and but for Fraser's help, Robert would never have located its lines amongst the profusion of ropes. Fraser knew The Lightning like the palm of his hand.

And so, as one boy eased himself over the gunwale, the other busied himself with untying knots.

'One slip here,' said Robert to himself, as he descended the springy rope ladder. 'And I'd be lost to this world forever.'

'The knots aren't b-budging, C-Captain,' said Fraser, anxiously.

'Just cut them!' said Robert, as he stumbled into the jiggling boat.

'B-But I d-don't have a knife, C-Captain. I never have one.'

'Then I'll do it,' said Robert, unsheathing his cutlass. In a jiffy, the three ropes were severed and he was on his way.

'Good luck, C-Captain,' said Fraser. 'R-Remember, k-keep the lantern directly in f-front of ye.'

Robert fleetingly touched The Lightning's hull with its encrusted barnacles, and then immediately lost all contact with the ship. He tried his hardest to head towards the bow with one of the paddles but he could see absolutely nothing. Then briefly, he glimpsed a light, but it was instantly swallowed up by the unwavering fog. Now, he was thoroughly alone, and the fog seemed to close in and around him.

Gently, Robert positioned the oars in the rowlocks and pulled on them lightly. How far away was he from The Lightning? He didn't know. Too bad, he had to get moving. Wherefore, he began to drive in the oars.

Rowing single-handedly was not at all easy. Dipping the blades simultaneously was anything but plain sailing. However, gradually he started to get the hang of it and make some headway.

Onwards Robert rowed, all the time hoping to strike land. But nothing happened. Had The Lightning been so far out? Or maybe he was indeed rowing out to sea? 'Blast this fog!' he groaned. 'Why doesn't it lift?' He might still be able to see Fraser's lantern. Maybe he was going around in circles. He knew from one of his favourite television programmes that with no reference points, a person will simply go round and round in circles.

'Ow!' he cried. Cramp! He had cramp in his right thigh. He stopped rowing and tried to stretch his tightened muscle. Then, he half stood, wincing in pain. But, immediately, the boat started to wobble.

Thud! The boat came to an abrupt halt. Robert scrambled out and extended his throbbing leg. The pain gradually began to fade, but his trainers were now sodden. At least he'd reached his destination. Would this fog ever go away? Right then, it evaporated, and dawn was breaking.

Everything that Fraser had told Robert, at this moment in time, proved to be correct. He was in a bay with a sandy beach below his feet. To his right was a towering spit, like the top of a number six. To his left was a bulbous mountain, not very high, and resembling the bottom of a number six. But what amazed him more than anything was how far out The Lightning was. It was way over near the mouth of the bay. No wonder he'd gotten cramp!

There was no time to waste and after dragging the boat in as far as he could, Robert set forth up the side of the mountain. A thick jungly start soon petered out with the increasing elevation, and bushes and grasses took over. Only a smattering of trees had set up home on the rocky ground of the mountain, which was really just an oversized hill.

Robert was grateful for the easy journey as it gave him time to think things over. Was it the right island this time? If it was, it would certainly make sense. An hour there, less on the return. Was Fraser getting a hard time? The crew were definitely up by now. Reno would likely be confrontational. Poor Fraser. And who was the spy? He had a fair idea, but would he stake his life on it? And what was The Book of Maps? And was it really to be found under a tree on this little island? And why hadn't he taken the spade? And what was Sparky doing right now?

Back on The Lightning, Fraser was indeed getting a rough time.

'I just can't believe it,' protested Reno. 'He left on his own. I thought we were a team. Yer a snake in the grass, Fraser boy. When did ye know? Speak!'

'I t-told ye. A storm got up and the C-Captain had to m-move the ship, and then he d-decided to go it alone before it c-caught up with us again.'

'Leave him be,' said Bennett. 'The Captain knows what he's doing.'

'I say we swim on over,' said Reno. 'The two of us can easily do it. It's not that far. He could be in trouble.'

'No chance. The sharks will eat us whole,' returned Bennett.

'Bah, sharks!' cried Reno. 'What sharks? We'll be on the beach before any sharks turn up.'

'Ye haven't seen what Pudding's been doing then, for the last half hour.'

Reno turned to observe Pudding standing at the gunwale, bucket in hand.

'What're ye doing there?' asked Reno.

'Why I'm chucking the scraps and bones over the side,' answered Pudding, much aggrieved at the cheek of the question. 'What's it to you?'

Reno wasn't a stupid boy, and the cook's actions instantly clicked in his head. He went over and looked down into the bright blue water, where the dorsal fins of half a dozen tiger sharks were circling above the surface.

'Big, aren't they?' said Barrell. 'Wonder what they're hanging around us for?'

'For the scraps, ye blockhead,' snapped Reno. 'The scraps which that idiot's been flinging into the water.'

'And what do ye expect me to do with the leftovers?' asked Pudding.

'Eat them!' cried Reno. 'Ye eat everything else.'

Pudding stormed off, locking horns with Reno was always best avoided.

Reno looked around for someone else to attack but couldn't settle on any one in particular. 'I'll load ma pistols then and shoot the beasts.'

'You'll only attract more of them with the blood,' said Bennett, moving off. 'Put yer trust in the Captain, like the rest of us.'

'Hmm,' said Reno. 'As long as he doesn't choose to go swimming.'

Meantime, on the island, Robert was nearly there. Surprisingly, a small copse had appeared up ahead and past that was the hilltop. He stopped to take a swig of water. It was getting hotter.

Snap! Something moved in the copse. Crack! Somebody or something was watching him.

'Who's there?' shouted Robert, stepping backwards. 'I've got a cutlass!' And he drew his sword. 'Come out! I know you're there!' Spooks didn't exist, but his heart was telling him something else.

Yet nothing happened. Not a peep. He now had two options, continue his journey and face being attacked from the rear, or enter the copse and confront the threat head on. So, pointing his cutlass and feeling brave, he entered the copse.

Suddenly, something galloped towards him. He braced himself. The bushes parted. And a goat sprang out, and got as big a fright as Robert did.

'Phew!' he sighed. 'Don't worry, boy, I'm not going to hurt you.'

Forthwith, with an elegant flick of its tail, the skittish animal skipped off.

After a further few minutes walking, Robert reached the summit. There were a few bushes and trees to consider, but first he wanted to view the island from his lofty vantage point. It was as he expected, fairly small, and he could easily see The Lightning sitting proudly in the bay, but the rowing boat was out of his field of vision.

'Now to work,' he said excitedly. 'Which tree is the tallest?' He paused to inspect them. Thankfully, there weren't many and one definitely stood out. His pulse quickened with anticipation. This was it!

He'd already decided that he would dig with his hands or a stick if he could find one. Using his cutlass would be a last resort. Slowly, he circled the tree's thickish brown trunk. To the rear at the bottom, a thin hole caught his attention. Surely too obvious. Probably a wasp's nest. But no wasps or bees emerged, and neither did any arrive. So he stuck his hand in and wiggled it about. But there was nothing inside and his heart sank. Then he had an idea, contorting his body and twisting his arm, he stuck his hand in a second time, just to make sure. Cold! Something cold and smooth was wedged in between the roots at the top. Excitedly, he yanked the thing out, and then immediately looked round his shoulder in case someone was watching him. He was still alone.

The item was a silver case, about the size of a small thin book. The front was ornamental, while the bottom was flat and featureless. A small lock was sited on the side, but it had been filled in with a red wax, along with the joins between the lid and the base.

'I've found The Book of Maps,' cried Robert. For there was no doubt in his mind, that that was what he was holding.

Then he noticed a set of initials in the corner, PMG. The owner of the case or the owner of the contents? Or both? He was itching to open it, but he stopped himself. It was sealed. Best wait till he was back aboard The Lightning. Could he really wait that long?

Robert stuffed the silver case into his clothes, secured the water bottle around his neck, and set forth back down the mountain at a fair lick. He was buzzing with excitement, The Book of Maps was his. He'd find the treasure, share it amongst the crew, with a share for himself obviously, and then get back to Rum. Boy, he'd miss the crew, though, unless they came with him. But not Reno or Barrell.

Robert emerged from the luxuriant vegetation at the base of the mountain, and got an unpleasant surprise. The sea had advanced marginally up the white sandy beach and taken away the rowing boat. It was now bobbing up and down about one third of the way to The Lightning. The wind was also up but the water surface remained curiously placid.

'So much for no tide,' groaned Robert. Now, he would have to wade out and then swim.

The crew had noticed him and immediately started to wave enthusiastically. They were shouting too but the wind sucked away their merry words. They were clearly as excited as him, and Robert waved back with pleasure. Soon, everyone would share his joy.

Robert's trainers were still squelchy but he had no desire to soak them a second time, so he removed them, tied them together, and hung them around his neck. The baking sand immediately singed the soles of his feet and he stepped into the water. Then, he checked his cutlass, and finally stuck the silver case into his mouth. Where else could he put it? It had to be kept dry. He would swim the breast stroke, his favourite stroke and one which would hopefully keep the case and his trainers out of the water.

Robert was set, and he started to wade out towards the drifting boat. And when the water came up to his waist he began to swim. All the time his eyes were fixed on The Lightning in the background, and the demonstrative crew, a number of whom had hoisted themselves into the rigging and were cheering and waving him onwards.

'We need to do something!' declared Mouse. 'There's more than two dozen sharks now.'

'And the Cap'n's splashing an awful lot. That's sure to attract them,' said Boxer.

'The sharks have spotted him!' hollered Titch from the crow's nest. 'They're already heading his way!'

'F-Fire a p-pistol,' said Fraser. 'The C-Captain will see something's up and turn b-back.'

'That's an idea,' said Bennett swiftly. 'Reno, make haste and fire a pistol into the air.'

Robert was enjoying his swim. It's true his clothes and the cutlass were dragging on him, but he was making steady progress. His only worry was getting into the rowing boat from water level and whether it would capsize.

Crack! A gun shot echoed around the bay. Robert had momentarily taken his eyes off The Lightning, but now he looked up to see a puff of smoke directly above the head of Reno. It was definitely him, there was no mistaking his tall, athletic body. Typical Reno, wasting what little resources they had by firing into the sky. He was probably shooting at some poor bird. Robert had never come across such a beastly person, and if he hadn't've had the case in his mouth, he would certainly have shouted something.

Then, something cold and slippery touched Robert's leg. A fish had inadvertently bumped into him, quite a big fish, he surmised. Well, he certainly wasn't bothered about a fish, maybe if it were a fish with teeth like a piranha.

The rowing boat was now nearly within touching distance and he felt a sizeable relief flowing over him – swimming with all these attachments was hard work. He could also feel the after effects of the cramp in his leg from earlier.

Suddenly, something big and powerful darted past him from behind. Then, out of the corner of his eye he noticed a grey shiny triangle. And then another one. Sharks! He was surrounded by sharks. Terror-stricken, Robert lunged forwards and grabbed hold of the side of the boat. Instantly, it pitched towards him. Immediately, he spat the silver case into the bottom and gulped some air. But his trailing legs were like a red rag to a bull, or a school of bulls. Think! In a flash he grabbed the paddle and hurled it into the air. Splash! A frenzy of sharks rushed to investigate the commotion. He tried to hoist himself into the boat. But he couldn't. It just tilted towards him. Concentrating everything he knew, he dropped his head and shoulders downwards into the vessel, and somehow rolled himself inside. He'd made it. How close was that!

'Am coming up, Titch!' hollered Jelly, whose turn it was in the crow's nest.

Robert righted himself and looked out. Every man on The Lightning bar one, was staring back at him, motionless and silent. He lifted a hand and they cheered as one. The sharks had already abandoned the floating paddle and were now cruising around his little craft, but their chance had passed.

'Pirates!' screamed Jelly. 'Pirates!'

The whole crew turned in unison, from their captain's escapades to the starboard side of the ship. There, they were met with the sight of three rowing boats jam-packed with pirates rapidly heading their way.

'It's Blackjack's mob!' cried Bennett.

'But how did they get so close?' exclaimed Boxer.

'Plainly we were too busy observing the Captain,' answered Bennett.

'Who's on lookout?' yelled Reno. And then looking skywards he got his answer. 'Jelly! Don't come down, Jelly boy, cos this time I will kill ye!'

Jelly opened his mouth but the words wouldn't come out.

'The Cap'n needs to call the fog,' said Barrell.

'He ain't here, ye blockhead!' snapped Reno.

Bennett raced back to the port side, where Robert, with his back to the fore, was busy rowing.

'Captain!' yelled Bennett. 'Don't stop rowing. Can ye hear me?'

'Yeah!' answered Robert.

'Can he hear ye?' asked Boxer.

'Can ye hear me?' yelled Bennett again.

'Yeah!'

'He said yeah,' said Mouse.

'Keep rowing, Captain! Don't stop! Blackjack is nearly upon us but you're nearer! You can beat him!'

Robert bobbed his head up and down exaggeratedly.

'He's nodding,' said Mouse.

'Prepare to be boarded, men!' yelled Bennett. 'Close all port holes! Remove all ropes or anything they can hang onto! Only one net stays down for the Captain!'

'Everybody grab a weapon!' cried Reno. 'Hurry, men! Leo, get yer pistol ready. Bony, get the busted pistols. They won't tell the difference. Barrell, get the musket. Get it loaded. And don't mess it up!'

Robert pulled on the oars as strongly as he could manage but his mind was equally engaged. The evidence was now overwhelming, there was most definitely a spy. And who did the finger point to? The same person who had tried to kill him the first time they met. The person who disappeared on Tortuga. The person who ran off on Cannibal Island. The person who pushed Mouse over the side. And now, the person who again guided Blackjack to them. Robert was settled, he would maroon him on the nearest island if they ever survived Blackjack's assault.

'Ready the lines!' shouted Mouse, from the shrouds just below the crosstrees. 'The Cap'n's about to board!'

Rabbit, a brown haired boy with large front teeth, immediately went to the gunwale where Cooper joined him.

Robert continued pulling on the oars right up to the point when the bow of the rowing boat bumped the port side of The Lightning. Cooper hurriedly threw out a line as Rabbit, who had been dangling from the climbing net, jumped inside.

'Hurry, Captain,' said Bennett. 'They're nearly upon us. There's at least a score of the rascals.'

Robert shot up the climbing net and over the gunwale. 'I know what to do!' And he dashed to the other side of the ship. Thereupon, he withdrew the silver case containing The Book of Maps. 'I need a knife! Somebody give me a knife!'

Pudding immediately pulled out a thin knife. 'Here, Cap'n. It'll cut bone, it will.'

Robert jammed the knife into the silver case and twisted it open. Then, after removing the contents, he flung the case on the deck and clambered up the rigging.

'Ah, MacSpoon!' hollered Blackjack. 'I thought ye were dead, lad. You've got more lives than a cat ye have. Anyways, am coming aboard to talk business.'

'Stop!' shouted Robert. 'Or else I'll drop it. I swear on my life. I will drop it.'

Thereupon, there was a gentle bump against The Lightning's hull from Blackjack's rowing boat. 'Come on! Who's dropping a line?' he shouted, impatiently.

'You're not coming aboard!' declared Robert.

'That I am, laddie. We'll be taking the ship and the article yer so dearly bearing.'

Blackjack's men, of whom there were at least twenty, prepared their grappling hooks, a frightening piece of equipment with a central shaft and three equally spaced hooks or claws at the end. Weasel was there, Giant too, and One-Eye with his long greasy pigtail.

'Then be prepared for a fight!' cried Mouse.

Blackjack looked upwards. 'Yer mighty opined for one afore the mast, laddie. So I'll tell ye, keep it shut! Or I'll climb up there and stick a knife in ye.'

'I'll give you it. But you're not boarding us,' said Robert.

'There's nothing ye can do to stop us. Am only taking back what's rightfully mine,' returned Blackjack.

'If you board us, I'll call the fog and you'll all come with me to the bottom of the world. I swear it!'

Blackjack's crew visibly jolted at this possible outcome and their murmurings were audible.

'I ain't going to no end of the world,' said One-Eye, who was on Blackjack's shoulder.

'Cast it to me, laddie,' barked Blackjack, after a moment's pause.

'Tell your men to turn around and I'll give it to you,' said Robert. 'I swear.'

'No! They stay.'

Robert had nothing else to bargain with and reluctantly tossed the thin book into Blackjack's eager hands.

The pirate pawed it affectionately. 'Ye haven't been a tampering with it have ye? I wouldn't take kindly if there's been any chicanery.' And he opened it and started to scan the pages. There weren't many.

'It's all there,' said Robert.

'I'll give ye that one,' said Blackjack, with a wink and a barely perceptible nod of the head.

'Then we're even!' said Robert.

'Ye see, laddie. I still fancy taking ma ship.'

'You can buy a hundred ships.'

Blackjack stroked his dark bushy beard, and shook his head deliberately.

'Then we'll go to the bottom of the world together,' stated Robert.

'Hold yersel, laddie. We're heading back, men! Our business is finished, for now.'

Robert, needing no invitation, instantly closed his eyes and prayed for fog. He was somewhat de-stressed, but not entirely. A small uninhabited island was what he needed next.

'Where are we g-going, C-Captain?' asked Fraser, the moment the fog appeared.

'Who cares,' said Barrell. 'Any place away from here.'

'Where are we heading, Captain?' asked Bennett, from somewhere close.

'To an island, not far,' answered Robert.

'I'm cold,' said Leo.

'It won't take long,' said Robert.

21. The Mole

*I*n the fog, Robert was feeling troubled. He would soon have to speak to the whole crew, and he hated addressing so many faces. He also had to accuse someone and that would be unpleasant, no matter how righteous his intentions were. And so it was with great reluctance that he wished the fog away.

Thereupon, bright sunshine appeared, along with a small perfectly proportioned desert island. But the whole situation was somewhat surreal as nobody had moved one inch in the meantime. It was like everyone had been frozen in time.

'Ah warmth,' cried Leo. 'I've never liked the cold. They never wanted to put the fires on.'

But his words were lost as Robert mounted the poop deck above his cabin and all eyes turned his way. He stared at the expectant faces; Bennett was there, Fraser, Mouse, who was unusually quiet, of course Reno, Rabbit and Cooper who had both come particularly close, Boxer, everybody. But none were prepared for Robert's topic of discussion. The loss of The Book of Maps was still foremost in everybody's minds.

'Men!' he started, and everybody hushed. 'Em, we, em, keep getting followed by Blackjack, and because of it, em, we lost The Book of Maps. Eh, the question is, how does he always find us? Well, I think I have the answer. Em, well, eh, we have a spy aboard the ship.' This was torture!

For a brief moment you could have heard a pin drop as the revelation sunk in. Surprised faces then swiftly changed to chattering ones. Robert quickly scanned the expressions, but he was really only interested in one.

And for someone who must have known it was he who was being addressed, Reno was appearing remarkably relaxed.

Thereupon, Cooper edged forwards. 'Captain,' he said. 'I have to tell ye something.'

Robert shook his head and continued to speak. 'And I've eh, decided that the traitor will be marooned on this island.' Everybody systematically turned to view the small picturesque island. 'What do you say, Reno? Do you agree with the punishment?'

'Why ask me?' said Reno. 'I have no objections to marooning.'

'Then you agree to go on the island?'

'What?' cried Reno. 'Are ye off yer head?'

'Don't pretend,' said Robert, moving to the top of the stairs. 'We all know you're the spy, and we're marooning you on this island.'

'Ye are off yer head. I'm no spy. You've always been against me.'

'Against you!' howled Robert. 'You tried to kill me the first time you saw me.'

'I challenged ye. That's how it works, if ye knew anything.'

'You disappeared on Tortuga and again on Cannibal Island. Why? Cos you were meeting up with Blackjack. That's why.'

'I already said what happened. On Tortuga I got robbed. And then on Cannibal Island I went to get ma pistols back.'

'You think you have it all worked out,' declared Robert. 'Well you don't. You pushed Mouse over the side. Explain that one?'

'What are ye talking about? I didn't touch Mouse. The fool fell in himself. He even said so. Anyways, I wasn't even near the idiot at the time.'

'Yes you were!' cried Robert. 'I saw you.' A small lie, who cared. Reno was guilty. 'Mouse got pushed and you pushed him.'

Reno sniggered to himself. 'Yer madder than a March hare. I pushed nobody. I spoke to nobody. Now ping off!'

'You ping off!' shouted Robert. 'You're getting off this ship.'

'Yeah! So make me.'

'Captain,' implored Cooper. 'I really need to tell ye something.'

'Titch was the spy!' cried Rabbit. 'And he's gone.'

'What?' said Robert, who had descended the small flight of steps to confront Reno.

'No way!' said Mouse.

'It's true,' said Rabbit. 'Me and Cooper watched him go. After we lashed the skiff, we went to the gunwale aside the stern. Then, a porthole opened and the very moment the fog showed its face, out he leapt, like a monkey, right into one of Blackjack's boats.'

'I saw him too,' said Dougal, a thin boy with a large head that made him look like a lollipop.

'I c-can't b-believe it,' said Fraser. 'He m-must have turned when he got c-captured. B-But why?'

'Then it was him who pushed me,' mumbled Mouse, still hanging from the rigging.

Everybody fell quiet and reflected on the bombshell. It was of course more than a revelation to Robert. It was a game changer.

'And it wasn't me who let Blackjack get close!' shouted down Jelly from the crow's nest. 'Titch was on lookout.'

'We all got duped,' said Bennett. 'Every last one of us.'

Robert felt rotten and he truly wished the ground would swallow him up. He absolutely hated apologizing. Then he took an uneasy breath. 'Sorry, Reno, that I accused you.'

'Let's forget it. Ye made a mistake,' said Reno. 'But I never liked that Titch. There was always something slippery about him.'

Robert didn't say anything. It would be difficult to say much against Reno now.

Thereupon, Pudding let out a welcoming cry. 'Dinner's ready!' And then he added in a quieter tone, 'A nice pea soup to fill everybody's belly.'

But it was a melancholy crew that gathered in the main deck. They'd been cheated by one of their own and each and every one of them was crestfallen, Mouse especially. They had been best friends, brothers even. They'd shared a bunk in the orphanage, then shared a hammock on The Lightning. Not even Pudding's hale and hearty pea soup could rouse his spirits or that of the crew's.

'Captain,' said Pudding, after Robert had barely dipped his wooden spoon into his wooden bowl. 'I must broach a subject. Provisions are running desperately low. The last keg of salted pork finished today. Our dried peas will finish in maybe a week. The green ones may last longer but the yellow ones will hardly see the end of the week. The beef finished weeks ago but was truly ghastly so nothing much was lost there. We'll shortly have only oatmeal and biscuits remaining. And the crew will find it tough.'

'Ye mean, you'll find it tough,' said Reno. 'Half of it likely went down yer own throat.'

Pudding didn't even acknowledge him. He rarely if ever spoke to Reno.

'It's a predicament, for sure,' said Bennett. 'We've no money to buy fresh supplies and nothing on the ship's worth bartering with.'

'Then we should become real pirates,' said Reno. 'And attack something.'

This immediately drew the crew's attention and Reno was delighted. Robert was much less enthusiastic. It sounded dangerous.

Dinner took considerably longer than usual, what with Reno's ideas on how they should go about attacking another ship. Thus, it was nearly dark before everything had been finished off, tidied up and the hammocks extended. When darkness did ultimately envelop the ship, Robert made his way back to the poop deck. Most of the crew were already in bed, and only a few stragglers crisscrossed the deck.

'C-Captain?' said Fraser, on hearing footsteps.

Robert took his place beside his friend and contemplated what to say.

'Yer leaving us, C-Captain. Aren't ye?' said Fraser. 'I know ye took the m-map of R-Rum.'

'You know?' said Robert, somewhat surprised.

'I saw B-Blackjack's f-feeble hints. And what will b-become of us, with no C-Captain. B-But ye m-must do what is r-right for yersel, C-Captain. It's not f-fair on ye, so much r-responsibility.'

'I'm not leaving,' said Robert. 'But you're right. I did take the map. It's in my shirt collar right now.'

'Yer staying, C-Captain?' cried Fraser.

Robert exhaled. 'I am.'

'Then this is the b-best d-day of my short life, C-Captain.' And he grabbed Robert and gave him a hug that would have done a bear proud.

'I'm pleased,' said Robert, as he clapped Fraser on the back. He wasn't really used to hugging anybody. It wasn't so bad.

'Bear hug!' cried Mouse, and ran up the steps to the poop deck. But Robert and Fraser quickly separated. 'So what ye hugging for?'

'The C-Captain's staying,' said Fraser.

'Tell me something I don't know,' complained Mouse. 'It's as plain as the nose on yer face, Fraser. We've gotten under his skin. Ain't that right, Cap'n?'

'I suppose it is, Mouse,' said Robert. If only he knew then, how many more adventures he was destined for before seeing his parents and Sparky again.